Lacy gazed through the arch of the Grecian-style gazebo at the beautiful blue lake. The water shimmered like a pool of liquid diamonds. Swans glided across its glassy surface.

Suddenly she heard a splash. Slowly, cautiously, she stepped closer to the lake and peered through the trees. She gasped. Standing in knee-deep water was a naked Indian. She was mesmerized by the beauty of his body—and there was so much of it! Guilty, she dropped her head into her hands and closed her eyes.

"Ah, come on now. Don't you like what you saw?" He raised an ebony brow and strode toward her.

Lacy tilted her chin, striving for a look of innocence. "I'm sure I don't know what you mean."

He drew closer—so close that the heat from his bare body warmed her. His bare legs brushed the folds of her gown. Looking down into her upturned face, he purred, "Sweet Peach, you don't have to put on airs with me." Hooking a finger under her chin, he tilted her head back. Her scent, like sun-warmed roses, filled his nostrils. Suddenly, roughly, he pulled Lacy against his bare chest and hungrily plundered her mouth. He felt her body melt against him, her lips like satin. He kissed her softly and gently then, over and over, tasting her sweetness. He stole her warm breath, and returned it to her, mingled with his own . . .

TERESA HOWARD
CHEROKEE
EMBRACE

ZEBRA BOOKS
KENSINGTON PUBLISHING CORP.

To Col. and Mrs. William L. Kinney—
my beloved aunt and uncle
who made Cherokee Embrace *possible.*
AND
My husband, George E.—
the handsome professor
who teaches me more about life and love every day.

Translations of Greek and Hebrew scriptures by Dr. George E. Howard.

ZEBRA BOOKS

are published by

Kensington Publishing Corp.
475 Park Avenue South
New York, NY 10016

First printing: January, 1992

Printed in the United States of America

Prologue

December 30, 1838
Camp of the 4th Detachment
of Emigrating Cherokees
Little Prairie, Mo.

The sight that met Lieutenant Evan Tarleton's eyes rendered him weak with shame. As a soldier, a white man, and a Georgian, he felt somehow responsible for the absolute devastation in evidence before him. Yet he had had no part in it.

He had not been party to herding human beings—human beings who were guilty of nothing, save the accident of their birth—and confining them in pens like the lowest of animals, then driving them at gunpoint over 529 miles of life-draining territory.

He could never be a part of such as that. His reasons were many, not the least of which was Nelda—Nelda Cruce, the lovely Cherokee girl that he yearned for with every beat of his heart. The Cherokee maiden that he vowed to find in this sea of misery, to find and protect for the final three hundred miles of this insane exodus.

Evan was brought up short by the shrill wolf-whistle that pierced the frigid air.

"Bless my soul, ain't he fancy?" the whistling soldier chortled, elbowing a slothful comrade at his side.

Evan stiffened in his saddle.

"Fresh from the Point, ain't ya, General?" another soldier taunted.

Evan knew full well that many men like himself, new graduates of the military academy who were sent to escort the Cherokees to Indian Territory as their first assignment, were easily identified by the seasoned soldiers. Starched uniforms and polished brass made them fair game for the unruly men they were called upon to command.

"Them shiny gold buttons've struck me plumb blind," a third man said as he staggered about the campfire, his filthy hands flailing the night air.

The word *insubordination* flashed through Evan's mind. He scowled, noting the small pools of displaced Cherokees huddled together for warmth, some starving, many visibly ill. The soldiers who were forcing them on this march were guilty of a hell of a lot more than insubordination!

And he was to be one of them. But he wouldn't think of that just now. First, he would find Nelda.

He plodded along, his hat low over his forehead to shield his eyes from the frigid drizzle. Squinting against the glare of the campfires, he scrutinized every Indian woman he came upon, hoping to see Nelda's face peeking up at him from among the folds of threadbare blankets that covered their heads.

Nelda might have succumbed to starvation, the freezing weather, or the abuse meted out by the soldiers. He dismissed the thought immediately. God would not do that to him; God would never give him more than he could bear, and he could never bear the loss of Nelda.

Purposefully, Evan wound his way through the enormous camp. All around him, soldiers laughed and cursed, ignoring the suffering Indians as if they were less than human. More than once Evan was forced to grip the pommel of his saddle

6

lest he dismount from his horse and physically vent his disgust on his fellow soldiers.

Just when he thought he could stand no more, a sound as sweet as God's court of angels reached his ears. It was a woman's voice raised in a familiar lullaby. Evan recognized the husky tones at once. Instantly, he was out of the saddle, running in the direction of Nelda's sweet voice.

Wearily, Nelda laid her sleeping son, Stalker, on the blanket-covered ground, and pulling the blanket from her own shoulders, she covered him as best she could. A tear trickled down Nelda's dusky cheek as she straightened, her soft voice trailing off.

When the big officer spun her around and enfolded her in his embrace, she fought with all the strength she could muster. This wasn't the first soldier who had made advances to her on the trail, but even in her terror she realized he was the largest.

"Sweetheart, it's me, Evan," Evan rasped, trapping Nelda's arms at her sides.

Disbelieving, she raised her ebony eyes and beheld the sight she had longed for for almost four years.

Nelda threw her arms about Evan's neck as he lifted her off the ground. Oblivious to the shocked faces around them, the couple kissed deeply, communicating the loneliness and longing they had experienced for so long.

Murmuring endearments, tears mingling, they communicated their mutual need. Neither knew quite how it occurred, but sometime later they found themselves away from prying eyes, sheltered beneath an outcropping of rock, wrapped in a cocoon of scratchy blankets and smoldering desire. Once they had loved long and well, Nelda lay cradled in Evan's arms, her head resting over his heart.

"I've missed you so," Evan whispered. "When I got back to Athens and found out what had been done to your people—that you had been taken—I thought I'd die."

Nelda tightened her hold on Evan. "I know," was all she

7

could force past her lips, so affected was she.

Then all too soon reality penetrated Nelda's consciousness; the time had come for her to tell Evan the truth about Stalker. Her heart rate accelerated. She couldn't escape the feeling that she had betrayed this man she loved. And she feared that her disclosure would cause her to lose him.

She prayed soundlessly, *Please don't let it drive him away—not now, when I've just gotten him back.*

Evan sensed the tension in Nelda's body and knew that she was troubled. But considering the plight of her people, was it any wonder? He just hoped she didn't blame him for what the white man was doing to the Indian. He would make it up to her, he vowed silently.

"Evan," Nelda's soft whisper sounded loud in the dark of night. "There's something I need to tell you." She angled upward, gazing down into Evan's face. She smiled weakly. "It's a deep, dark secret," was her pitiful try at levity.

Unbidden, Evan remembered how violently Nelda had fought him when he had first embraced her. An ugly thought formed in his mind. Had she been molested by a soldier? Was that her *deep, dark secret?*

"You don't have to tell me anything." Evan stroked Nelda's cheek tenderly with the back of his fingers. "Whatever happened while we were apart isn't important. We love each other; that's all that matters."

Nelda dropped a soft kiss to Evan's lips. "What I have to tell you is very important."

Evan started to object, but Nelda silenced him by placing her fingers over his mouth.

"You have a son," she said gently.

"What? When? How?" Evan grinned and sputtered once he found his voice.

How? Nelda chuckled, raised the blanket off Evan's torso, and looked downward.

Evan's chest swelled as if he'd accomplished a great deed. Laughing for the sheer pleasure of it, he threw his arms about Nelda and pulled her small body against him. His spirit felt as light as a snowflake. "Does this son of ours have a name?"

"Stalker," Nelda answered.

"And he is how old? No, wait, I can figure that out. I was in Europe for little less than a year, then away at the academy for three years, so that would make Stalker—three."

"Three, going on thirty," Nelda said, with more than a little pride shading her voice.

"Why didn't you tell me?" Evan asked the question Nelda had been dreading. "All those years . . . all your letters . . . you never said a word."

For what seemed like an eternity, Nelda didn't speak. She lowered herself back to Evan's side, unable to look into his eyes. She rested her head on his chest, her silky blue-black hair fanning across the muscular arm that clutched her possessively to him. When she finally spoke, Evan could hear the tears in her voice.

"I couldn't tell you. I knew your father had sent you to Europe and then to West Point to get you away from me. And whenever you would try to come home for a visit, he would find some excuse to keep you away. After all, he couldn't have his son—his only heir—married to the little Indian girl down the road."

Nelda's words pierced Evan's heart, for they were true. He just hadn't known that she was aware of the awful truth.

"You said you'd come back for me . . . that you would give your father four years of your life and then it would be our turn.

"I loved you so. A part of me hoped you would meet someone you could love, someone your parents could be proud of." When Nelda's voice broke, Evan squeezed her so tightly that it was a chore for her to breathe.

"I knew if I told you about Stalker, you would come home right away. Then what would you have had?"

"A wife and a child for one thing." With deadly calm Evan

9

betrayed the depth of his emotion. At this moment he hated all white men in general, and his father, Eli Tarleton, in particular.

Sensing this, Nelda implored, "Don't hate your father, Evan. He's a good man, and he loves you. The only thing he's guilty of is wanting the best for his son. Having Stalker—I can understand your father's actions."

Suddenly not wanting to discuss his father, the past, or anything else except Stalker, Evan declared, "I may be three years late, but do you think I could see my son?"

Nelda was half-dressed before Evan could unfold his long length from the ground. At long last the two people she loved more than anything else in the world were going to meet.

Hand-in-hand the young couple ran back to the spot where their sleeping child lay under the watchful eye of Nelda's parents. Together, Stalker's parents knelt on the blanket at his side.

Reverently, Evan stretched forth his big hand and touched an unruly lock of his son's black hair. His sharp intake of breath aroused the slumbering child, and in a moment long overdue, sky-blue eyes locked with sky-blue eyes.

In his son's eyes Evan detected no sign of fear, rather innocent curiosity. The two smiled shyly at one another.

Through her tears, Nelda couldn't help but notice that her son was a miniature reflection of the man she loved. "Stalker, this is your daddy," she whispered in Cherokee.

The little boy's eyes widened, and he popped into a sitting position. He shifted his gaze away from the kind stranger who bore his face—only bigger—and asked his mother in awe, "I have a daddy?"

When Nelda nodded, tears streamed down her face, falling unheeded on the blanket below. "A good daddy who loves us very much," was her fervent reply.

Evan couldn't understand a word they were saying, but that didn't keep him from hanging on to every syllable.

Stalker's ebony hair brushed his frail shoulders as he

turned his head and scrutinized the big man who was his daddy. Surprising the adults, he rose to his feet. Eye level with his kneeling father, he said in slightly accented English, "The People say 'I am come' when they greet someone."

Evan wiped the smile from his face. "I am come," he said.

Stalker nodded his head and replied quite properly, "It is good."

Then, to his enchanted parents' further surprise, he launched himself at his father, circling Evan's neck with his arms and holding on to him with all his strength.

In an instinct as old as time itself, Evan enfolded his child into his arms and held him close to his heart. He whispered to Nelda, "I expect he leads you a merry chase."

"Hmmm. Chase . . ." Nelda murmured cryptically.

Part One

*Love and desire are the spirit's
wings to great deeds.*

—Goethe

One

Athens, Georgia
Fall, 1859

Chase Tarleton pulled rein at the Athens Fancyware and
Drygoods store. He arched his stiff back, flexing his broad
shoulders, before sliding from his mount. Finally, his three-
month, cross-country journey had ended. What lay ahead he
didn't dare imagine.

Frozen in front of the store were two Southern belles,
properly decked out in their morning finery. With their
bavolet bonnets at a precarious angle, two sets of eyes wide,
they gaped at Chase, who was tossing his stallion's reins over
the hitching post.

He supposed he did look ominous, dressed in fringed
buckskin with his shoulder-length hair hanging loose. But a
quick glance at the women relieved him. They didn't look
frightened, just curious, and he wasn't offended by that. He
was accustomed to it.

"Ladies," Chase greeted in cultured tones as he bowed
slightly at the waist and doffed his John B.

Their nervous giggles followed him into the store.

Ladies! He rolled his eyes heavenward. Ladies were like
priceless paintings to Chase; objects to be enjoyed, but not

15

possessed. It wasn't the money; it was the emotional cost he couldn't afford—not after the way Leslie had died.

Inside the well-stocked store, Chase found no one in attendance. He wandered idly up and down the aisles, picking his way through a plethora of merchandise, but to no avail. He couldn't find what he wanted, which didn't surprise him. This was the third store he'd visited, and each time he'd gone away empty.

As he was about to leave, a portly fellow emerged from what Chase guessed to be the storeroom. The smiling man introduced himself as Jacob Culberson, the owner of the establishment. Jacob politely offered his assistance.

Chase studied the proprietor's expression warily, deciding the man's smile was genuine. Subconsciously, he swiped at his dusty bucksins. "Do you have any ready-made clothes that would fit me?"

Jacob studied the young giant. The only man he knew who was that big was Eli Tarleton, and since Eli was the richest man in North Georgia, Jacob always kept merchandise on hand for him.

"Back here," Jacob said, heading for the rear of the store.

Chase was pleasantly surprised when Jacob stood before a whole rack of clothes that fit his needs. In a few moments, he had made his choices, then he and Jacob headed for the front of the store. The door opened, admitting a sedately dressed matron and a redheaded, freckle-faced boy.

The child's eyes grew wide at the sight of Chase. "Look, Mama, a real Indian."

"Hush, Mark, don't be rude." The woman's cheeks flushed with embarrassment.

A chuckle rumbled from somewhere deep inside Chase. "It's all right ma'am. I'm sure Mark meant no disrespect."

He turned to pay the shopkeeper and gathered his packages in his arms.

"Come again." Jacob smiled at the Indian.

16

Chase opened his mouth to ask a question, then halted when he felt a small hand stroke his arm. Looking down, his pale blue eyes met the little boy's uncertain gaze.

"Never touched a real Indian before," the child whispered in awe.

Chase smiled as he looked into the little boy's guileless face. A scripture the Reverend Evan Jones had often quoted to Chase when he and his family were forced to travel the Trail of Tears popped into his mind:

"But the wisdom that is from above is first pure, then peaceable, gentle, and easy to be entreated, full of mercy and good fruits, without partiality, and without hypocrisy."

He saw the truth of these words reflected in the little boy's eyes.

Chase dropped onto one knee. On eye level with Mark, he ruffled the boy's hair. "How old are you, son?"

"Six and a half." The word *six* whistled through a gap where his two front teeth were missing.

Chase's throat felt tight. For a painful moment, he allowed himself to remember all he had suffered by the time he was six and a half. Mentally, he shook himself. Then he winked at the child.

"You're almost a man," he said.

Mark's narrow chest expanded with pride.

The door opened again, and Chase sensed trouble. He raised his head and saw two men standing in the doorway, one as fat as a pregnant bear, the other as skinny as a pelican's leg.

Their faces were shrouded in hate.

"Get away from that boy, breed," Fatty sneered, stepping into the store.

Chase straightened to his full height, his movement unhurried.

The newcomers' eyes widened as they looked up and up, finally reaching Chase's expressionless face.

17

"Damn, that's the biggest Indian I ever seen," said Skinny.

"That's the biggest *anything* I ever seen," concurred Fatty.

The air in the room crackled with tension. Chase didn't want to fight. He wasn't sure how his grandparents would receive him as it was. He certainly didn't want to have to explain his part in a town brawl when he met them for the first time. He decided to let the insult pass.

"Ma'am." Chase nodded, bidding the woman good day.

He turned to the proprietor. "Could you tell me how to get to the Tarleton plantation?"

Before Culberson could answer, Fatty grabbed Chase by the arm. "Don't turn your back on me, savage."

That word! In one fluid motion, Chase pivoted on the balls of his feet, swinging his powerful fist. With a crack that sounded like a rifle shot, he knocked Fatty to the floor, unconscious. Before Skinny could reach him, Chase stepped forward and threw another punch which sent his assailant tumbling to the floor beside his partner.

Mark jumped up and down, clapping his hands in delight. "Did you see that Mama? Did you? Can I go tell Papa? He won't believe it! Can I go, Mama? Can I?"

Chase winced. "I'm sorry you and the boy had to see that, Ma'am."

"They got what they deserved," she told Chase flatly. Then she called to her son's retreating figure, "Mark, you may tell your pa, but you come right back, you hear?"

The boy was already out the door. With a slight smile, Mark's spunky mother went back to her shopping, as if nothing had happened.

Chase shook his head. Women never ceased to amaze him. He turned to the shopkeeper and gestured to the felled men. "I'm sorry about the mess."

"It was worth it to see a fight like that. I've never seen the beat." He chuckled.

Chase was amused by the Southern expression he had

18

heard his mother use time and again.

"Where'd you learn to fight like that?"

His smile slipped away. Fingering the ruby ring he wore on the last finger of his left hand, he said, "Let's just say that I've had this sort of experience before."

The shopkeeper cleared his throat, embarrassed.

"Could you tell me how to get to the Tarleton plantation?" Chase asked again.

"Oh, yes, Towering Pines. Follow Front Street, that's the street right in front of the store, and go east 'til you pass Doc Hampton's place. It's the first farm you'll come to. The road that runs along his place dead ends into a thick stand of trees. There's a wagon trail that leads down to a lake that joins the two plantations. Mr. Eli's place is about two miles due east. You can't miss it."

Chase thanked the man, gathered his wrapped packages, stepped over Skinny's and Fatty's inert bodies, and walked from the store.

His deerskin moccasins made no sound as he crossed the store's front planks. Alert for more trouble, he placed the parcels in his saddlebags, retrieved Spirit's reins, then vaulted lightly onto the animal's back.

Once in the saddle, he raised his head and caught a glimpse of his reflection in the dry goods store's window. A strained smile lifted the corners of his mouth. It would never do to meet his grandparents looking like this. Grandparents! He still couldn't get used to the idea.

Maybe it was just as well; they might not like Indians any better than Skinny and Fatty did. After all, they were from Georgia. And Chase knew all too well how Georgians dealt with Indians. That, after all, was how he lost his *real* grandparents . . .

He tried vainly to ignore the bitterness rising in him and wheeled his horse about, heading east, toward the lake that joined the Hampton and Tarleton plantations.

Over the clatter of his horse's hooves, the laughter of children rang out. A dog barked. The town was bustling; all along Front Street the people of Athens went about their business. Finely dressed gentlemen and blushing coquettes rubbed elbows with dirt farmers and their runny-nosed families. And as a unit, they turned and watched the brooding savage pass by.

Two

Seated in a white wicker chair, Lacy Dawn Hampton settled her billowy skirts about her. Wistfully, she gazed through the arch of the Grecian-style gazebo at the beautiful blue lake in the distance. The water shimmered like a pool of liquid diamonds as well-fed swans glided across its glassy surface.

The secluded gazebo, situated at the edge of the immense lawn, was nestled in a garden, fairly bursting with late-blooming roses and heady gardenias. A magnolia tree filtered out the bright sunlight, casting dancing shadows about Lacy to the tune of musical breezes.

With the delicate movements ingrained by years of training, she patted her dress at her sides. She loved the gazebo. It was her favorite spot on Paradise plantation, a place where peace was often her companion, but not so of late. Her turbulent emotions had chased it away.

She breathed in the perfume of the blooms and thought of her blossoming womanhood. To her surprise, it had brought with it a measure of fear, insecurity, and confusion.

She worried her lower lip with her teeth. All her life she had been a content, peaceful child, albeit slightly spoiled. But now she was a stranger to herself. One minute she was satisfied to be Daddy's little girl, pampered and adored by

21

her family, and the next, she would yearn to experience life more fully. Whatever that meant. She supposed it had something to do with love. *Love!*

She thought of the love that flowed between Jared and Melinda, the oldest of her three brothers and his wife. Many mornings their faces would fairly glow. She sometimes caught Jared grinning at his wife, Melinda's responding blush hinting that something special had transpired in their bedroom the night before.

Although Lacy was too innocent and inexperienced to know exactly what it was, she did know that she wanted to feel like that, too. A flush of hot color burst upon her pale cheeks as she wondered if ladies of quality were supposed to have such wanton feelings and desires. Somehow, she doubted it.

She fingered the pleats of her gown, then flattened her downy soft hand over her heart in a dramatic gesture. Oh, glory! Little did it benefit her to desire such passion in life, for she lived with four men who seemed determined to keep her a little girl.

Besides her father and Jared, who hovered over her like two old setting hens, there were Brad and Jay. These two roguish brothers literally doted on her, spending every waking moment trying to keep her sheltered, innocent, protected . . . and ignorant. God, how she hated that!

She was quite convinced that if the Hampton men had their way, one day she'd be eighty years old and still sitting around with strange urges, not knowing what to do about them. Lacy balled her hands into fists and squealed.

She was so filled with frustrated energy that she jumped to her feet, swaying slightly from the weight of her caged crinoline, and left the gazebo, walking toward the lake. Its gentle waters often calmed her.

Sweeping her hoop skirt first this way, then that, she wound her way through the thick copse of trees that separated her from the shimmering water. Beneath the trees

22

it was a full five degrees cooler than in the sunlight. Slightly chilled, Lacy pulled her lace mantle more tightly about her shoulders.

It was a beautiful fall morning. All around her, brilliantly colored leaves fluttered in the air, drifting to the ground. Some were as golden as her hair, others the deep burgundy of Mammy Mae's cooked beets. Lacy smiled in spite of her tightly wound emotions and plucked a russet leaf that clung to her full-skirted gown.

If only she could have remained a child. Life had been so simple then. What a mass of conflicting emotions she had become. She longed for love, then wanted to be a child again.

"You can't have it both ways, Lacy girl," she chided herself aloud.

A slight breeze ruffled the lace of her sleeves and lifted a silken curl from her shoulders. It brought to her the sweet smell of water, along with a moment of tranquility.

Suddenly, she heard a splash, followed by a deep, husky gasp.

Lacy stood still, listening intently. Could it be Stuart's runaway slave, she wondered.

Her heart pounded; fear gripped her. A runaway would be insane to stop this close to civilization unless he was hurt. If that were the case, he could be dangerous.

She sucked in a deep breath and willed her heart to cease fluttering. What should she do? She knew she should leave, but perhaps she could help him. Nobody would have to know.

Taking a tentative step closer, she listened. More splashing. He certainly wasn't trying to be quiet, she noted with surprise.

Slowly, cautiously, Lacy moved toward the clearing. She could see patches of blue just ahead.

Abruptly, the splashing ceased. Lacy peered through the trees. Immediately her eyes grew wide, and she gasped. Standing in knee-deep water was a naked Indian.

23

"A savage. Oh, glory!" she exclaimed, awestruck. She clamped her eyes shut, knowing she shouldn't look at him. *Just turn around and leave,* she ordered herself. *Maybe just one peek,* she thought. Slowly, she opened first one eye, then the other.

She should have been frightened, but she wasn't. She was mesmerized by the beauty of his body. And there was so much of it to admire!

In a broodingly handsome way, Chase Tarleton, all six feet, four inches of him, looked positively dangerous. His blue-black hair, lightly swaying in the breeze, reached down to his shoulders. His moist skin was a dark, golden brown. To Lacy, it looked like soaked satin over steel. His broad shoulders were as wide as the horizon, his bulging arms as solid as the columns circling Paradise manor, his corded stomach as hard and flat as a Georgia pine.

Her perusal continued a downward course, causing her to wonder at her own boldness. Embarrassed, she caught herself just before she reached a dangerous level. She was inquisitive, but not that inquisitive. Once again, she closed her eyes.

The savage moved. The sound of swishing water aroused Lacy's curiosity. When she opened her eyes, she saw him walking toward shore. With each step, his thigh muscles bunched; resembling a stalking panther. Her mouth grew dry as all thoughts of maidenly modesty vanished.

Just then, she heard a horse whinny. The savage turned his head to the left, where a beautiful black stallion was grazing peacefully.

Lacy held her breath as he turned quickly in her direction. Did he see her? No. Surely, he wouldn't be standing there, facing her as naked as the day he was born, if he knew he was being watched.

She gripped the tree with white-knuckled fists. Her curiosity got the better of her, and her gaze slid lower. Black hair swirled around his navel and continued below.

24

A breath caught in her throat when something below his waist moved. Her mouth dropped open. What was that? And it was changing shape. She was fascinated.

The older girls at Miss Lucy Cobb's Finishing School had told her about *it,* but she hadn't believed them. She had thought they were teasing when they had told her what happened when a man got excited. Lacy couldn't imagine what had excited the savage.

As he turned his back on her, the abrupt movement spooked the resting swans. Their responding squawk jolted Lacy back to her senses—to the epitome of Southern womanhood.

She whirled, gathered her skirts into her arms and, in a flurry of silk, disappeared into the forest. When she reached the gazebo, she berated herself for a full fifteen minutes. Appalled, she could not believe that she had stared at a naked man like a common trollop. Humiliation and guilt flooded her.

Her daddy would have a stroke if he found out what she had done. She dropped her head into her hands and groaned in despair.

"Ah, come on now. Didn't you like what you saw?"

Lacy started at the sound of the deep, cultured voice. Sitting regally astride the black stallion, was the savage. He was no longer naked, but clothed in a scant flap of buckskin that was just damp enough to outline his considerable male attributes. Shocked, she couldn't speak.

"Are you all right?" he queried, noting her stricken look.

After a moment of strained silence, she cleared her throat and drawled, "I'm afraid you startled me. I thought I was alone."

Chase groaned inwardly. Lacy's lilting Southern accent sounded like golden honey pouring on a summer day. More like a caress than a sound, it reached out and stroked his heated flesh. He smiled with undisguised lust and absorbed her with his gaze.

As custom dictated, her hair was gathered thickly at the back of her head, arranged in a heavy, plaited chignon and trimmed with ivory satin ribbons. A few stray tendrils framed her oval-shaped face. Sultry, emerald green eyes held Chase spellbound. In their depths, he detected an innocent curiosity along with something else, something more potent.

Chase felt a familiar stirring in his loins. He had been traveling for three months, during which time he hadn't had a woman, and his abstinence was telling on him.

Unable to stop himself, he fixed his gaze on Lacy's body. Her waist was so tiny, he could circle it with his hands; her breasts were full for one so small. She gave the appearance of being young, but his eyes told him she was fully grown. The wasp-waisted beauty was playing havoc with his self-control.

She was dressed in an exquisite gown of pale peach silk. A lace mantle of darker peach rested in the curve of her arms. Chase knew little of fashion, but it was obvious that the young lady was acquainted with the finer points of costuming.

Lady! The word penetrated his lust-dulled brain. *Run man, she is a lady, even if she does like to watch strange men bathe in the buff.*

But Chase didn't heed his own warning. Without breaking eye contact, he slowly dismounted and padded across the thick green carpet of grass, moving with a stoic grace that belied his formidable size.

Lacy's heart pounded like a drum.

When he stood before her, she stared into his eyes. They were a beautiful shade of light blue, glassy clear, almost translucent, not Stygian dark as she had expected.

A surge of longing rushed through her virginal body; every frustrated feeling she'd ever known was intensified by his overwhelming presence. When a warm sensation uncurled low in her belly, a soft blush stained her face.

She had never been alone with a man before—certainly

never with one who was practically nude. Had he seen her at the lake? She panicked.

"What did you first ask me?" Her voice trembled.

"I asked if you were all right."

"No, before that."

"I asked if you liked what you saw." He raised an ebony brow.

The color drained from Lacy's face. She tilted her chin, striving for a look of innocence. "I'm sure I don't know what you mean."

He drew closer—so close that the heat from his bare body warmed her and his bare legs brushed the folds of her gown.

Looking down into her upturned face, he purred, "Sweet Peach, you don't have to put on airs with me."

Lacy jumped to her feet, suddenly enraged, her temper fueled by guilt and humiliation. "How dare you . . . you . . ." she sputtered.

The rapid movement caught Chase unaware. He lost his balance and tottered precariously. In an attempt to maintain his equilibrium, he gripped Lacy's shoulders more tightly than he intended.

"Don't touch me, you miserable lecher. My daddy will shoot you," she declared.

Chase threw back his head and laughed uproariously. "Lecher is it? Who watched whom take a bath?"

Lacy exploded. "I didn't watch you take a bath!" She stamped her foot, barely missing Chase's toe.

Chase stepped backward and held his hands up in a placating gesture. He found Lacy adorable, spitting and sputtering as she was. "Forgive me, Sweet Peach. You watched me walk naked from the lake and dry off. I stand corrected."

His lazy grin infuriated her all the more. "I didn't watch you. I heard a splash and thought you were a runaway slave . . . not a . . . a depraved savage!"

The grin froze on Chase's face; anger lit his eyes.

"Sorry to disappoint you, Your Highness," he said sarcastically. His tone was biting and hard. "But I'm not a savage, nor any man's slave. And if I were, you wouldn't live to turn me in."

She flinched as if he'd struck her. What had she said to anger him so?

The threat hung in the air as Chase advanced on Lacy. His massive frame dwarfed her, and his pale eyes were blue shards of ice.

"I wouldn't turn you in, in any case," she said softly.

He placed his hands on her shoulders once again. "I know you wouldn't," he mocked her sweet tone, then pulled her flush to his body. "Because I'm bigger than you." His breath was warm on her cheek. "And I'm stronger than you."

He caught a fleeting sign of fear in her eyes. Momentarily, his anger waned. Hooking a finger under her chin, he tilted her head back. Her scent, like sun-warmed roses, filled his nostrils, and he was enraged again. The heady aroma was a symbol of what he would never allow himself to possess: a soft, sweet-smelling *lady*.

"And I'm . . ." he began, but he couldn't think of anything else to say. So, suddenly, roughly, he pulled Lacy against his bare chest and hungrily plundered her mouth.

She gasped in shock as he thrust his tongue into her soft, moist cavern, deepening their kiss. She felt faint and clutched at him, engulfing his bare legs in her skirts.

To Chase's surprise, he forgot the source of his anger. The girl's unorthodox behavior clouded his mind and stirred something in his heart that he had spent months building impregnable walls against.

He tightened his grasp fractionally, then kissed her softly and gently, over and over, sipping, tasting, savoring her sweetness, until he was reluctant to stop. He stole her warm breath, and returned it to her, mingled with his own.

Finally, he released her.

Both thoroughly shaken, for a moment they stood staring

at each other.

Then Lacy emerged from the spell Chase had cast about her and did what every well-bred Southern lady had been taught to do in such situations. She drew back her hand and slapped his face, snapping his head with the force of her blow.

Eyes wide, she clutched at her throat, for she hadn't meant to hit him so hard. Under his bronze complexion, a perfect handprint was clearly discernable.

Chase raised his hand to his stinging flesh, and his expression grew passive. "You had better run back to your daddy, my Sweet Georgia Peach, before this *savage* does something that we'll both regret!"

"You already have," she whispered and hitched her skirts.

Seething, Chase stepped out of her path so that she could retreat. Inanely, he noticed that she had clocks embroidered on her stockings.

Then she was gone.

Three

Chase watched Lacy retreat until she was out of sight. He ran a shaky hand through his hair and willed his body to return to its normal state. He should have known he'd get stung by cavorting with a spoiled, self-serving prima dona. All ladies were alike, he reminded himself vehemently. And not for the likes of him!

He mounted his horse and headed back toward the lake, where he had left his gear. He wondered what the girl would do when she reached home. She'd probably sound the alarm to circle the wagons and prepare for an Indian attack, he mused wryly.

With a well-developed sense of will, Chase put all thoughts of the past unpleasantness aside and concentrated upon what lay ahead of him. When he reached the edge of the water, he slid from the saddle and set about *civilizing* himself.

He cut his hair with a hunting knife, then dressed in the new clothes he had bought for his first meeting with his grandparents. After he donned his white linen shirt, blue breeches, and black knee boots, he studied his reflection on the lake's surface. He was surprised to see that he had admirably made the transformation from a half-naked Indian to a well-tanned Southern planter. The realization brought with it a strange sense of guilt.

Reverently, he placed his breechcloth and moccasins into his saddlebags, along with his other buckskins. He wouldn't rid himself of his Indian trappings because his mother, Nelda Cruce, had made them, and they and his mother's ruby ring were all he had left of his old life. At least for now.

Spirit whinnied softly as Chase tossed his saddlebags onto the horse's back and mounted up. In less than an hour, he would reach Towering Pines. After his fight with the rednecks in town and his encounter with the young chit who had slapped his face, he hoped there wouldn't be another unpleasant confrontation.

He galloped along on the final leg of his journey at an unhurried pace, revelling in the scenery of his first home. The burst of autumn color infused him with a sense of peace; the bright crimsons, the gleaming golds, the deep russets washed over his soul. Nature always affected him that way.

But his peace was short lived. The loathsome word *savage* popped into his mind.

Why did she have to call him that? That was the one word that hurt him most.

When he'd gone to school in New England, they had called The People *Noble Savages,* an obvious contradiction in terms. But that wasn't the first time he'd run up against the derisive label.

In his mind the years fell away, like layers of an onion. Each formative event of his life was punctuated by the painful hiss of *savage,* until finally, he was transported back to a day twenty-one years before, a day that would always live in his memory, a day that would change his life forever. Upon this very land he'd first heard the awful name. With a measure of regret . . . he remembered.

It was May, 1838. The hot afternoon sun bore down upon the red clay of Georgia, melting away the cool of the day.

32

The federal militia resembled a sea of blue as it washed over the land, tearing the Cherokees from their homes.

In their ravaging, the army came upon the Cruce farm in North Georgia. Nelda Cruce and her sister, Neta, were watching their sons at play. Stalker, as Chase was called then, and his cousin, Little Spear, were playing with the neighbor's children, Brad and Jay Hampton. The militia posed no threat to the Hamptons, because they were white; for the Indian family, it was a different story.

The Cherokees had been given three years to vacate the state of Georgia voluntarily, and their time had run out. Now they would be driven from the land of their ancestors by force. It was to that end the militia descended upon Chase's home.

The frightened women, hearing the ominous sound of horses' hooves, ran for the children. Brad, Jay, and Little Spear huddled behind them in fear.

But Stalker didn't hide. When the regiment reined in before the wicker-framed house, he stepped protectively in front of his mother. He planted his feet and rested his tightly clenched fists on his hips like a brave sentinel guarding a castle. He was unwaveringly protective of his mother, for unlike the other boys, he had never known his father.

The action did not go unnoticed by Nelda. She swiped at her tears, and in an imitation of her small son, she squared her shoulders.

Working in the fields, her two brothers, Lone Wolf and Screaming Eagle, were unaware of the immediate threat to their family. Nelda knew that they would fight to the death before being driven from their home. She decided it would be better for the rest of the family to leave then and there, before the men returned.

As if reading her sister's mind, Neta cast Nelda an understanding look, and with her voice barely breaking a whisper, she said, "I'll go into the house and pack some food."

Before she could enter the house, a portly corporal cocked his rifle and barked, "Stop right there, squaw. You ain't goin' nowhere 'cept Injun country."

Wide-eyed with fear, Neta halted and turned to her sister.

Slanting her a reassuring look, Nelda addressed the commanding general. "Is this what the American government has come to, shooting women and children as well as stealing our homes?"

With icy disdain, General T. Henry Dykes replied, "Nobody's going to get shot as long as they do as they're told." Looking down his nose at Nelda, he continued, "And as for stealing your home, perhaps you should speak to Major Ridge about the treaty he signed, *Miss* Cruce."

Stalker was displeased with the general's disrespectful sneer. Raising his fists, he vaulted forth with a war cry bursting from his lip, prepared to do battle with what looked like the entire federal army.

"You little savage," Dykes shrieked as he kicked at the angry child. His abrupt movement frightened his mount, and the animal reared up, throwing the general to the ground.

From the fields, Stalker's uncles heard the ruckus. In haste, they mounted their horses and made for the house. Once there, they circled the regiment with blazing guns, hoping to draw the troops after them, while the others made for safety. They met with partial success; approximately half the soldiers followed them.

After getting his horse under control and remounting, General Dykes, who by this time was as mad as hell, roared to his remaining troops, "The rest of you men catch these women and children."

He snorted like a fire-breathing dragon and brushed the worst of the dirt from his coat. "This fiasco has taken enough of my time."

The two women were hauled roughly up onto the horses of their captors. Not knowing what would happen to their children, and with only the clothes on their backs, Nelda and Neta were spirited away to an unknown fate.

The two young Indians proved to be more difficult. With their friends whooping like braves on the warpath and running interference, they eluded capture for a good ten minutes. But finally, they, too, were carried off by the soldiers.

When they topped the rise of the hill in front of the Cruce farm, Stalker strained to look at the only home he'd ever known. Standing in the front yard were his two best friends, Brad and Jay Hampton, holding hands with tears streaming down their dirt-smudged faces. It was more than he could bear; he thrashed and flailed the soldier with his little fists.

"Stinkin' savage," the man hissed, throwing Stalker across his lap and pinning him there with a beefy hand.

There was that word again. Stalker didn't know what it meant, but he knew it wasn't good.

"I'm not a savage," Stalker yelled indignantly, before he bit down on his captor's flabby thigh. "Let me go. I want to go home," he shrieked.

The soldier cursed as he grabbed Stalker by his shoulder-length hair. He twisted the silken strands around his wrist and brought the child's tear-stained face close to his own. "Get a good look at this place, savage, 'cause it's the last time you'll ever see it."

"No!" Stalker screamed.

The last thing Chase remembered was the echo of *savage,* a crushing blow to the side of his head, and the ensuing darkness. The terrible memory of loss and humiliation hurt as much today as the actual occurrence had all those years ago.

"I'm not a savage," Chase whispered to no one in particular.

Why did she have to call him that? Didn't she know a man

had his pride, even if he was an Indian? Bitterness welled up inside of him. Chase damned the girl as he wiped the tears of remembrance from his eyes. He damned her for her thoughtless words and, most of all for being unattainable, for being a *lady*.

Then a satisfying thought was born. Chase straightened in his saddle. "I'm back. That bastard said I'd never see my home again, but I'm here."

Chase halted Spirit and looked around. Some of his pleasure drained away, for what he saw wasn't home.

Twelve dark green pines rose up before him, reaching their sharp branches toward the sky. Chase knew what lay beyond them, and it wasn't *his* home. It was Towering Pines.

His father, Evan Tarleton, had spoken of it so often that Chase felt he knew every rock and shrub on the entire four-thousand-acre plantation. He wound his way through the pines, until the house was in sight; it was just as he'd imagined.

Cradled in a forest of majestic pine, the dove gray manor was awe-inspiring. It was a two-story mansion, surrounded by a colonnade of sixteen white Ionic columns. There was a huge marble porch circling the front and both sides of the dwelling, and in the back, a covered walkway led to a small building that was obviously the kitchen.

As he rode up the long, winding lane, he tried to picture his father growing up in such a place. The stoic cattleman who had raised him from the time he was three years old just didn't seem to belong among such ostentatious wealth.

Maybe that was why Pop had stayed in The Nations after his stint in the army, Chase mused. Nervously, he patted Spirit's neck as he approached the house. The horse bucked and pawed the air, reacting to his master's uncharacteristic tension.

When he reached the porch, he dismounted, and a little Negro boy materialized from out of nowhere to take his horse. Chase thanked the child, handing him the reins, and was rewarded with a shy smile.

He then mounted the stairs, all but tripping over the dog that slept in the shade of one of the massive columns. Everything was peaceful. Chase suddenly felt painfully out of place.

He reached the massive front door, and it was opened by a wiry, gray-haired man whose wrinkled old face was the color of fresh coffee. The slave squinted against the bright sunlight flooding through the doorway.

Politely, Chase waited for an invitation to enter.

After a moment, when the old man's eyes grew accustomed to the glare, he looked at Chase. Still, he didn't speak, just stood there with his mouth agape.

Chase shifted his weight from foot to foot and cleared his throat. What was wrong with the man? He looked as if he'd seen a ghost.

Finally, as Chase was about to state his business, the man found his tongue.

"Dear gawd, it's Mistah Evan."

Four

"Welcome to Towerin' Pines, suh," the old man continued once he had composed himself. "M'name's Mose. You must be Mistah Chase."

The old man's voice was husky with emotion, and for a scant second, Chase thought he detected tears glistening in Mose's dark eyes.

His father had spoken of the family butler often, always with great affection. Chase smiled at the man who seemed more like a friend than a stranger. "Yes, Mose. I'm here to see my grandfather, Eli Tarleton."

The old butler ushered Chase into the foyer. "Yes, suh. He's been expectin' you. If you'll wait here, I'll go fetch 'im." He stole one last look at his master's grandson.

Before Chase could figure out how his grandfather had known he was coming, or, for that matter, how Mose had known he was a Tarleton, a person who looked more like a mountain than a man burst through the hall doors, catching Chase up in a bear hug.

"Well, hot damn, if you ain't the spittin' image of Evan, I'll eat my hat." Slapping him on the back, the old man beamed. "Son, I'm Eli Tarleton, your granddaddy."

Trying to regain his composure, Chase reached out to shake his grandfather's outstretched hand. "Sir, I'm pleased to meet you. I'm afraid you have me at a disadvantage. I didn't know that you were expecting me." His calm demeanor belied the turbulent emotions that were caused by coming face-to-face with his grandfather for the first time.

"Expectin' you? Hell, son, I've been waitin' on you for three months. Right after your folks died, some lawyer fella sent me a letter sayin' you'd be comin' as soon as you got the ranch all squared away." With a pained look on his face, the gruff old giant added, "It hurt real bad to hear that my boy was gone." Patting Chase's shoulder, he added, "I was real sorry to hear about your ma, too."

Chase inclined his head, acknowledging his grandfather's condolences, then realized they were not alone in the massive foyer.

A distinguished gentleman, who looked to be about fifty-five, stepped forward, offering Chase his hand. "Chase, I'm Adam Hampton, your grandparents' next door neighbor. Evan and I grew up together, and I'm proud to say that I considered him my best friend. I've missed him all these years."

Clasping Adam's hand firmly, Chase responded, "Dr. Hampton, sir, I'm pleased to meet you. My father spoke of you often."

"Well, he was a good man . . . and I'm glad to meet his son, finally. His last letter was about you. Actually, that's what Eli and I were just discussing. Your father had some very definite ideas about your future here in Georgia, and—"

Before Adam could continue, Eli motioned to him and said, "Doc, maybe we'd best let the boy get settled in before we start yammerin' about his future. And if we're gonna make it to that fancy shingdig at your place tomorrow night, we got some preparin' to do."

The conversation was interrupted when an elderly lady rounded the corner. Surprised by the men, she ran headlong into Chase, practically knocking the black lace cap from her silver-gray hair.

Since she looked as fragile as a china teacup, Chase was certain she had broken something. He reached out to steady her. "Ma'am, are you hurt?"

Looking up into Chase's eyes, she immediately grabbed him around the waist. "Oh, Mr. Tarleton! It can't be! Is this my baby's boy! Is this great big man my little Evan's son?"

Eli grinned so wide his face threatened to split. "Yes, Lizzie, this here's Evan's boy. And if you'll stop blubberin' all over him, I'll introduce you."

Obediently, Lizzie released Chase, stepping back. She was so short and he was so tall that she had to back up a bit to get a good look at him.

"Chase, this little lady is your grandmother Lizzie."

Chase automatically bowed and kissed his grandmother's hand. When she'd addressed Eli as "Mr. Tarleton," he'd been puzzled. Then he remembered that in the South some *ladies* addressed their husbands in such a manner.

"Ma'am, I'm pleased to meet you. I sure hope I didn't hurt you." Grinning sheepishly, he continued, "I've been told that running into me is sort of like running into a Brahma bull."

Looking more like a Southern belle than a gray-haired matron, Lizzie blessed Chase with a charming smile. "Lord, child, it'd take more than that to bust me up. I just hope I didn't hurt you."

Eli laughed heartily at the notion of tiny little Lizzie hurting a great big hunk like Chase. "Well, son, I think you've made your first contact with the fairer sex of the great state of Georgia."

Chase winked rakishly at his grandmother and declared, "If they're all as lovely as you, I'm going to like it here."

Beaming at Chase's compliment, Lizzie said, "Well, tomorrow night you're going to meet the loveliest girl in all of Georgia. We're going to a birthday party for Adam's daughter, and I just know that the two of you are going to hit it off."

Eli and Adam exchanged conspiratorial glances which

41

were lost on Chase. The mention of Adam's daughter brought vividly to mind the blond-haired girl who kissed like a courtesan and fought like a tiger.

Could the brat be Adam Hampton's daugher? I'll bet my ranch that tomorrow night will be anything but dull, Chase mused with mixed emotions.

Later that day, around two-thirty in the afternoon, Stuart Shephard's carriage approached Eagle Tavern. One of his drivers, a muscular slave by the name of Boyd, hopped to the ground, hurriedly opening the door for his master. Boyd knew all too well that Stuart beat his slaves for the smallest infraction, and he didn't intend to give Stuart an excuse to abuse him.

Meekly, he cast his eyes to the ground. Then, surreptitiously glancing at his hated owner, Boyd thought how deceiving appearances could be.

To the uninformed, Stuart looked like a handsome, upstanding, well-dressed member of polite society. He was a tall man, broad shouldered with a strong, masculine face. Although he was just over thirty, his face was creased with wrinkles. To a stranger the lines bespoke character, but in reality they reflected his hatred and bitterness against the world.

Just what Stuart had to be bitter about was beyond Boyd's imagination. The man possessed everything that a successful person could hope for: a moderately sized cotton plantation, an adequate number of slaves with which to run it, a respected position in Clarke County, and a powerful seat in the Georgia General Assembly in Milledgeville.

True, he wasn't as rich or as well liked as his uncle, Eli Tarleton, but as far as Boyd knew, he was Mr. Eli's only male heir. That should make him happy if nothing else did.

"Stay here with the carriage, boy!" Stuart ordered gruffly.

"Yassah," Boyd muttered humbly.

42

The tavern was almost empty that afternoon as Stuart swept into the dimly lit room. After his eyes became accustomed to the dark interior, he spotted the man he was there to meet.

Sitting at a back table, Beau Patton, a colleague of Stuart's in the Georgia General Assembly, was slugging down whiskey. Stuart and Beau had often been partners in various secret business ventures, most of them on the wrong side of the law. The scheme they were to discuss today was undoubtedly the biggest the two had ever attempted in terms of risk and reward. Stuart just hoped his friend was up to it.

Beau was smaller in stature than Stuart. Like his partner, he was attractive, but he was almost too attractive. Some would even call him pretty. His finely chiseled features, bordering on the effeminate, looked delicate and mild.

Stuart knew Beau's appearance was deceiving. Once while attending a meeting of the assembly, the two men had engaged a couple of whores for the evening. Before the night was through, Beau had almost beaten his girl to death, though neither man had lost any sleep over it.

A man as wealthy as Beau found it easy to cover his tracks. Secretly, Stuart wondered if Beau abused women to compensate for his less-than-virile appearance.

"When did you get back?" Beau questioned Stuart as the newcomer, withdrawing his hat and gloves, filled an empty chair.

"Last night," replied Stuart. "Barkeep," he called to the hefty old man behind the counter. "Would you please bring me a glass and a bottle of your best whiskey." Stuart was always polite to a potential voter.

Peevishly Beau called, "My friend wants a *clean* glass. The one you gave me was dirty."

Stuart rolled his eyes. Another tedious characteristic of Beau's was his obsession with cleanliness.

The two men sat silently, waiting for the liquor to be served. When the barkeep left, and Stuart was convinced they would not be overheard, he continued. "I wanted to meet with you as soon as possible and bring you up to date. Leonard, Will, and I have worked out an interesting plan that I think you'll approve of. Mainly, it depends on the two of us and some of our slaves."

"Well, what is it?" Beau asked impatiently. *It's just like Stuart to beat around the bush by being dramatic,* Beau thought. His hair-trigger temper was about to explode, but he knew better than to vent his frustrations on Stuart. Beau was no match for Shephard, so he'd just wait until later.

"We've decided to make it appear to the North that Southern planters are being influenced by the devil worshipping cult of Abbé Boullan and Adéle Chevalier."

"Are you talking about those two French Satanists?" asked Beau incredulously.

"That's right." Stuart said smugly, as if he'd accomplished a great coup.

"What do the Johnson idiots know about Satan worship?"

"Well, nothing! But they can read. I showed them the recently published exposé of the cult entitled, "The Temple of Satan." It tells all about the organization and practices of the group. Of course, I still had to come up with the plan." This last was spoken with an air of bored superiority.

"Well, I don't have time to read it, so give me a condensed version," Beau instructed wryly.

Stuart leaned forward, resting his elbows on the scarred table. "It was written by three investigators: Stanislas, de Guaita, and Wirth. They subversively penetrated the group of Satan worshippers by posing as followers of Boullan and recorded what they actually saw. They described Boullan as a pontiff of infamy, who was connected with the ancient city of Sodom. His Satanic rites involved sexual and scatological perversions and prayers to the sexual demons, incubi and succubi."

Stuart knew that Beau had heard of these sexual demons connected with medieval superstition.

"Actually, I believe in the succubi," Stuart confessed, keeping a straight face. He turned slightly in his chair; a deranged gleam burned in his clear blue eyes. "A beautiful succubus comes to me each night in my sleep. She looks just like Lacy Hampton. Soon I'm going to do to Lacy what I do to the little demon in my dreams, whether she wants me to or not."

Beau knew good and well that Stuart didn't believe in demons. He was a religious fanatic to the point of having delusions about being an agent of God. However, he didn't doubt that the man had demonic plans for Little Miss Goodie-Two-Shoes.

He shrugged. That was fine with him, for he had similar plans for her best friend, Celia Harrington, and was in the process of carrying them out. "Well, I can attest to the fact that actualizing your fantasies with a woman is a helluva lot more fun than dreaming about them."

Knowing about Beau's relationship with Celia, Stuart laughed lustily. "Yeah, yeah. Now back to the plan. I uncovered an old police record of another Satanic group operating in Paris almost two hundred years ago. It was written by the police commissioner of Paris, a Nicolas de La Reynie, who exposed the Satanic ring. He discovered that Madame de Montespan, a mistress of Louis XIV, was involved in it up to her heavily painted eyebrows.

"Because of her relationship with the king, the whole investigation was carried out in secret, and most of the three hundred and sixty members of the cult were arrested by *lettres de cachet,* eventually dying in prison without ever having a trial."

"Good God," exclaimed Beau. "How did you get hold of the report?"

"A friend in the French government sent me a copy. I've instructed Leonard to make it public as soon as we finish our end of the bargain."

"What does the document contain?"

Beau apparently wanted all the gory details. So, caught up in the perverse excitement of it, Stuart explained, "It details the various rites of the cult. It tells how they celebrated Black Mass over the body of a naked woman by cutting the throat of an infant, pouring its blood into a chalice, and offering prayers to Asmodeus and Ashtaroth, two leading demons mentioned in ancient Jewish and Christian writings. Then, it tells how the group subjected the woman to various kinds of sexual manipulation."

"Where can we join?" Beau joked.

"I'm serious. All this really happened."

"So am I."

Stuart took in the unholy gleam in Beau's eyes and continued his tale. "According to La Reynie, they discovered the bones of some two thousand babies buried in the garden of La Voisin, a fortune-teller who belonged to the group."

"All this is fascinating, but what does it have to do with us?" Beau always lost patience quickly and wanted to cut to the chase.

"It's vital to our operation," Stuart said with a condescending air. "After we beat a few slaves, cut Satanic pentagrams into their chests, and allow the ones who live to escape to the North, it will appear that there's a full-fledged group of Satan worshippers among the Southern planters.

"By the time the slaves arrive in Yankeeville, Leonard will have published La Reynie's secret report, keeping the recent excitement over the Boullan and Chevalier caper alive. By dropping a few well-placed hints to the rabid Abolitionists, he'll convince them that the South is involved in devil worship, mutilating and offering slaves in human sacrifice.

"The North will surely invade us if for no other reason than to put a stop to our damnable unchristian activities," Stuart sneered, practically out of breath from excitement as well as from his long speech.

Beau, amazed at how underhanded the scheme was, approved wholeheartedly. Caught up in Stuart's excitement, he summarized the rest of the plan. "Then we'll report the whereabouts of the South's major munitions depots to the Northern generals, collect five million dollars for our efforts, and head for England, where the rest of our holdings will be waiting on us.

"After the war is over, and the South's been soundly defeated, we can return and buy the whole state of Georgia if we want. Since by then we'll be the richest men in the South, we'll be able to control its destiny for the next half century."

"Beau, my friend," Stuart said. "I'd say you've summed things up quite admirably." Then his eyes clouded with mild disgust. "The only hitch I can foresee is that idiot Will Johnson, Leonard's brother. Leonard insists that he be in on the deal since he lives in Johnsonville, somewhere between Georgia and New England. It's a good place for us to meet, so I agreed to put up with him."

"I don't know about that. Do you think he can be trusted?"

"You can judge for yourself soon. We head for Johnsonville as soon as I can make the arrangements. We'll need to firm things up, and you can check him out firsthand. Personally, I think the man is totally out of his mind."

"Well, we can use him and then put him out of his misery," Beau said coldly.

"Sounds good to me. Before it's over we might want to put both Johnson brothers away. Then we'll have all the money to ourselves to invest during the war. Five million dollars goes a lot farther split up two ways than four. Besides, I don't like leaving witnesses behind."

Beau raised his glass in toast to Stuart and their nefarious plan. "Here's to our good fortune and the impending war between the glorious South and the idealistic North."

Stuart's glass clanked with Beau's. "With our wealth we can each buy a harem of succubi to sleep with every night," chuckled the larger man. "In the meantime, I have plans for a certain Southern belle, plans she just might not like . . ."

Five

Lacy crossed the veranda, elated to see the carriage of her best friend, Celia, coming up the oak-lined lane that led to Paradise. She hurried down the steps. A good talk with Celia was just the thing she needed to get her mind off the savage. She had thought of little else since yesterday, and that had to stop!

Before Celia's elderly driver could lumber down from his seat, Lacy jerked the carriage door open, and Celia stepped into her embrace. When Lacy hugged her friend, Celia grimaced.

"Cee Cee, what's wrong?"

"It's nothing. I just fell yesterday, getting off my horse, and bruised a few ribs. I'm a trifle stiff, is all," Celia said softly, failing to meet Lacy's eyes.

Lacy knew good and well that Celia would no more ride a horse than she would a goose. Still, she sensed that Celia didn't wish to talk about what was bothering her; so she let it pass.

Celia was relieved. "I've come to see if I can help you get ready for the ball."

The two young women made their way up the steps and through the doorway.

"Are you kidding?" responded Lacy. "Mammy Mae and

Aunt Reenie have all the house servants scurrying about like there's no tomorrow. They've forbidden me to lift a finger. Thank goodness you've come; I was dying of boredom," Lacy chattered. She took Celia by the arm and escorted her up the wide stairway to the second-floor gallery.

When they reached Lacy's bedroom, Celia stood in the doorway, admiring the room's beauty. It was a vision of elegance which reflected her friend's feminine personality.

The chamber was large, bright, and rectangular shaped. A sparkling crystal chandelier, suspended from the ceiling, lent it a regal air. The entire east wall was covered with mirrors behind which was a series of walk-in closets, containing Lacy's extensive wardrobe.

On the wall opposite the entrance, salmon-colored silk sheers hung from ceiling to floor, covering two sets of French doors that opened onto a private balcony, where lush coral and white rose bushes grew in profusion. The large, white-iron and brass antique bed sat on a dais in the center of the room, surrounded by a cloud of peach silk and satin. The shining hardwood floors were covered with deep bronze and bronze-beige oriental carpets.

At the far end of the room, two pale-peach moire Queen Anne chairs flanked a white, lacquered antique table. The girls entered the room and settled themselves in the comfortable chairs to enjoy the scented breeze wafting through the partially opened doors.

Lacy was pleased Celia had come. For as long as she could remember, they had closeted themselves in her room and talked. Through the years their meetings had changed in the sophistication of their dress and the maturity of their topic. Lately, it seemed, their topic was always the same: men.

But after her dismal confrontation with the savage yesterday, Lady didn't have much to say on that subject. Instead, she turned her attention to Celia's upcoming marriage. "Have you and Beau set a date for your wedding yet?"

Celia dropped her gaze to her lap and shuddered. "Yes, he and Father have. They've instructed me to ask if you would allow us to announce it at the ball tonight, since all our friends will be here."

Lacy studied her friend intently. "Why, of course you can. You know you needn't ask."

Suddenly, Celia burst into tears and buried her face in her hands. Her slender shoulders shook from her sobs, breaking Lacy's heart.

Lacy quickly gathered Celia into her arms. "Cee Cee, what's wrong? Is it the wedding? Is it Beau?"

Celia's voice was muffled against Lacy's shoulder. "Oh, Lacy, it is Beau. I don't want to marry him. He and Father have decided my whole life for me. I have no say about anything. I don't love Beau. I'm ashamed to say, I don't even like him."

"Well, glory!" Lacy exclaimed, holding Celia away from her by her shoulders. "Just tell your father how you feel."

Celia lifted her watery gaze to study Lacy's face. She loved Lacy, but realized that she was naive regarding the world.

"It's no use. Father owes Beau a great deal of money . . . money that he doesn't have. Beau will forgive him the debt if I marry him on March fifteenth. I have no choice."

Before Lacy could respond, a rap sounded at the door. She crossed the room and threw the door open.

There stood Brad, her handsome banker brother, leaning against the doorjamb, grinning from ear to ear. Without an invitation, he stepped into the room and bent at the waist in a gallant bow to Celia.

"Afternoon, Miss Celia. I was unaware that Lacy entertained such delightful company," he said as he straightened to his full height.

Lacy bit the inside of her cheek to tamp down a smile. *Now, why do I doubt that,* she thought as she looked at Brad's wide-eyed expression.

Lacy knew that Brad had always loved Celia as if she were

51

a little sister. But the predatory look on his face now was anything but brotherly.

Actually, Brad was startled himself. He had entered the room expecting to find two little girls having a hen party. To his surprise, the little girls had grown into women.

Celia rose and moved gracefully toward Brad. Suddenly, he forgot that his sister was in the room.

"Hello, Brad," said Celia softly.

Brad kissed her bare hand, letting his lips linger against her skin a second longer than necessary. Looking up, he detected a sadness in her eyes, saw the tracks of her tears, and felt the strangest urge to take her in his arms.

Mentally shaking himself, he turned to Lacy and engaged her in lighthearted banter, teasing her the way brothers do.

Celia didn't hear them, however. She was captivated by Brad. She watched him playfully cuff Lacy's cheek, causing his sister to giggle and wrap her arms around her waist.

"Don't make me laugh, Brad; my corset's too tight," Lacy gasped.

Chuckling, Brad shook his head.

Then he turned back to Celia. His deep brown eyes seemed to look clear into her soul. Losing herself in his gaze, she held her breath.

For what seemed like an eternity to Lacy, Brad and Celia stood silent, staring at each other. She felt like an intruder in her own room. Something odd was going on between her brother and her friend, and she wondered if they realized how silly they looked. Wide-eyed, Celia stood there, her hands clenched. And Brad looked like someone had hit him in the stomach, knocking the breath out of him.

Lacy cleared her throat, but was ignored. She tried it again, and two sets of eyes snapped in her direction.

"By the way, Brad, to what do we owe this honor?" Lacy asked.

Silently, Brad cursed the intrusion. "I came to ask if you were all right."

"I'm fine. Why would you think otherwise?" Lacy asked suspiciously.

"Yesterday on my way to the stables I saw you rushing across the lawn in a very unladylike manner," he replied and flashed her a dimpled grin.

Lacy groaned inwardly. She didn't want her over-protective brother to know what had happened at the gazebo.

"I was in a hurry to get home, that's all," she hedged.

Brad didn't buy Lacy's excuse, but he shrugged, offered each girl an arm, and said, "Please allow me to escort you to the parlor."

The girls slipped their hands through his arms and situated their full skirts, surrounding his legs with pastel silk.

With a broad smile, Brad led them downstairs.

Just missing Brad and the girls, Jared made his way up the thickly carpeted staircase, all the while scolding himself for acting like a hot-blooded teenager. He was behaving more like Brad than himself.

Earlier, while at his office, he had experienced an uncontrollable desire to be with Melinda. He knew that he had shocked his nurse when he had taken off like a possessed man, with a vague excuse that even Linni wouldn't believe.

"What the hell," he murmured. "What's wrong with a man wanting to make sure his pregnant wife is well, even if it is in the middle of the afternoon?" His lips spread in a lusty smile. He planned to do more than merely inquire about her health.

Quietly, Jared opened the door to their bedroom. He stood in the doorway, entranced by the sight before him. His wife lay sleeping in their bed. A soft smile was on her face. Though she was completely covered by a gown made of fine white linen and delicate pink satin, and was three-months pregnant, she stoked the fires of his desire.

Jared crossed the distance to their bed and stood looking down at his wife. Like butterflies in flight, Melinda's thick, dark lashes fluttered open, revealing passion-darkened eyes.

"Mmm, what a pleasant surprise. I was just dreaming about you," she purred, reaching for his hand.

Jared grasped her hand and lowered himself onto the bed. Heat spread through his lower body just thinking about what was to come.

"I thought you might need a doctor," he whispered suggestively. Then he took her in his arms and kissed her as he had a thousand times before. At that moment, Jared thought how wonderful married life was.

"How did you know . . . that I have a terrible ache right here," she returned breathlessly.

She took his hand and slid it slowly and deliberately beneath the hem of her gown, up over her sensitive thighs, to the warm center of her femininity. With her lips barely touching his ear, she whispered, "Do you think you have the cure?"

"Most definitely!" he laughed before he whispered against her hair, "You're shameless. You know that, don't you?"

She rose on her knees and pulled the nightgown over her head. "Yeah, and you love every minute of it!"

At that moment Jay passed by their bedroom. He heard the squeaking bed and his sister-in-law's throaty laughter. He grinned and shook his head. *Ah, wedded bliss; it does have its advantages,* he thought.

As he moved on toward his room, he reflected on his own life. He hoped to experience a love like that one day. But for the time being, there were others who needed him: men, women, and children who were powerless to help themselves. With that thought spurring him on, he entered his room and began preparing for the evening ahead.

Six

That evening, Lacy sat at her dressing table, staring into the oval-shaped gilt mirror while Mammy Mae towel dried her long, blond hair. The heady smell of gardenias filled Lacy's nostrils, for she had just stepped out of a gardenia-scented bath. The quartet her father had engaged for the evening had begun playing downstairs, and with each note, her excitement mounted.

She pulled her ivory satin wrapper more snugly around her small frame and thought about the man she'd met at the gazebo. She realized that her actions had been a bit unusual to say the least. After all, it wasn't every day one watched a naked man at his bath.

Truly, she had behaved like a hussy. Then when the poor man had called her on it, she had threatened to have her father shoot him and slapped his face. Giggling, she admitted to herself that the savage's only transgression was the effect his magnificent body had on her. If the evening ahead proved to be as stimulating, it would be a night she'd long remember.

"You look mighty pleased with yourself this evenin', chile," Mammy stated, smiling at Lacy's reflection in the mirror.

"Oh, Mammy, I'm so happy, I could burst." Lacy's

jeweled eyes flashed.

Mammy Mae patted Lacy's shoulder, laid her pearl-handled brush on the dressing table, and lumbered over to the large walk-in closet. She bustled about, collecting Lacy's clothes for the evening and congratulating herself on what a good job she and Doc Hampton had done in raising Lacy.

There was a knock on the door.

"I'll get it, Mammy," called Lacy.

When Lacy opened the door, she found her father standing in the hallway, holding three black velvet boxes in his hands.

"I've brought my girl a little something." Dropping a kiss on her cheek, he handed her the boxes. "Happy birthday, sweetheart."

"Daddy, what have you done?" Lacy asked.

Excitedly, she opened the gifts. In the largest box, she found an exquisite necklace of fiery emeralds and diamonds set in gold. In the second box, she found a matching bracelet, and by the time she opened the third box, her hands were trembling. Inside, she found earrings made of European-cut diamonds surrounded by fiery emeralds that matched her eyes.

She gazed up at her father, her eyes bright with unshed tears.

"Mammy Mae, come quickly. You've got to see this. My little girl is actually speechless!" Adam teased, to cover his own churning emotions.

From the moment he had entered the room, he had been struck by Lacy's resemblance to her mother. His heart felt as if it were being squeezed in a vise when he thought again how much he missed his precious Lysette. Had it really been eighteen years ago tonight that he'd lost her? After all these years, he was still tortured by the thought if he'd been a better husband she'd still be alive.

Mammy's gasp brought him back to reality. "Lawdy, Dr. Hampton, them sho is fine-lookin' jewels."

All at once Lacy seemed to come out of shock. Clutching the presents to her chest and throwing herself into her father's arms, she cried, "Oh, Daddy, they're so beautiful! Thank you! Thank you! Thank you, so much!" With each expression of gratitude, she kissed his cheek.

Adam was delighted to see his daughter so happy. "Whoa! All that gratitude can be hazardous to a fella's health."

Lightly pinching Lacy's cheek, he winked at Mammy and said, "Now, Mammy, you get this young lady dressed. We can't have her keeping our guests waiting."

Adam was still smiling when he reached his room. Isaac, Mammy's husband, who also worked for the Hampton household, had laid his immaculate evening clothes across the bed, but Adam didn't spare them a glance. His thoughts were on Lacy.

He walked over to the leather wing chair in front of the fireplace and sat down. He was determined to find Lacy a husband. She was simply too beautiful and loving not to have a family of her own.

Sure, she could have suitors waiting in line with the snap of her fingers, if she desired, but Adam wanted something more for her, a husband she could love, a husband who would recognize her innocent strength, a husband who would love her. Not just a man who thought of her as a pretty ornament on his arm.

He remembered Evan Tarleton's letter then. That was an interesting thought, Chase and Lacy.

"Doc Hampton, you best be gettin' dressed now. Folks are startin' to get here," Isaac broke into Adam's thoughts.

Quickly, Adam rose to his feet. Suddenly, he was anxious to introduce his idealistic daughter to young Tarleton. It should prove interesting.

Adam and Jared stood in the foyer of Paradise plantation, greeting their guests. Melinda stood by her husband's side.

When Lacy and her other brothers appeared on the second-floor landing, a hush fell over the crowd of exquisitely attired men and women who were congregated about the entrance. Adam followed their collective gaze to his three youngest children.

Escorted by a formally dressed brother at each arm, Lacy resembled a golden goddess escorted by two Greek titans. Adam's chest swelled with pride when he saw them. Lacy beamed back at her father, her eyes reflecting the glittering jewels she wore.

Just then, Isaac opened the front door to admit the latest arrivals. Lacy felt the cool night air on her bare shoulders and raised her view to see Eli Tarleton, Miss Lizzie, Stuart Shephard, and a handsome young giant enter the house.

Miss Lizzie was lovely, dressed in a deep lavender satin gown; a matching pearl-encrusted snood covered her silver hair. Eli and Stuart cut striking figures, dressed in black evening wear.

It was the newcomer, though, who caught Lacy's eye. He was extremely well-groomed and dressed like the others in black formal wear. His hair was neatly cut, just slightly longer than most, and rested lightly on his blinding white collar. He had medium-length sideburns that tended to emphasize the shiny blackness of his hair, and his tall, broad-shouldered physique was disturbingly masculine. She found him breathtaking.

Lacy smiled shyly at him, and he smiled back as if they shared a private joke. She was puzzled because he looked familiar. Replaying in her whirling mind every ball and cotillion she'd ever attended, she tried to remember where she'd seen him before. She came up empty.

Suddenly, a strange feeling came over her. Her heart began to pound, her mouth grew dry, and her legs turned to jelly. She swayed slightly against her brothers, who assumed that she felt faint from the excitement of the party.

Then, seeing that her face was flushed, Brad and Jay became concerned.

"Honey, are you all right? Do you need to lie down for a spell?" Jay questioned.

In a trembling voice, Lacy responded, "Don't be silly. You know what a goose I am. All the excitement has just made me a trifle unsteady, is all."

"Well, then," Brad encouraged lustily, "let's go slay 'em."

Having been distracted momentarily by her brothers, she looked back to see if the stranger was still eyeing her. To her disappointment, he was not. Miss Lizzie was introducing him to Rachel Jackson.

For some inexplicable reason this rankled Lacy. Practically leaning on her brothers for support, she made her way down the staircase, never taking her eyes off the stranger.

Then Eli's booming voice drew her attention. "Come here, you pretty little thing, and give me a hug."

Lacy's elegant silk gown swished as she hurried forward to greet the burly old man. Seeing Uncle Eli diverted her thoughts from the stranger, and for the moment, her senses returned to normal.

She had always had a filial affection for Eli and Miss Lizzie, and likewise, they had felt as if she were a part of their family. But that wasn't unusual in the South; lines of kinship were often blurred with close friends addressing one another as *aunt* or *uncle,* and families like the Tarletons and the Hamptons were often much closer than blood relations. Such thoughts were reflected on Lacy's lovely face.

She strained on tiptoe to place a maidenly peck on the old gentleman's weathered cheek, all the while aware of the energy radiating from her mystery guest. Without looking in their direction, she listened intently to the conversation between Miss Lizzie, Rachel, and the stranger.

Rachel, as always, was speaking in her husky voice, trying to attract male attention. "I'm so glad to meet you, Mr.

Tarleton. It's not often a man as handsome as yourself comes our way."

Chase recognized the lascivious gleam in Rachel's eyes. He had often been the object of lust for white women. He supposed they saw him as wild and exciting. They certainly ached to bed him.

But what stuck in his craw was that later, when they saw him on the street, they would turn the other way. He assumed that for them to acknowledge a savage in broad daylight would damage their precious reputations. They disgusted him, and so did Rachel. But he didn't let it show; instead he bowed respectfully over her hand.

Chase wasn't the only one who found Rachel's behavior disgusting. Lacy was incensed, though she was loathe to admit it. Granted, she and Rachel had never been close; however, she'd never felt such animosity toward Rachel before.

The woman's simpering sentiments made Lacy burn inside. She just couldn't stand the thought of Rachel flirting with this stranger. The redheaded heifer! She'd stand naked on top of Eagle Tavern, singing Dixie, if anybody would notice her, Lacy groused silently.

Shocked at the intensity of her feelings, she wondered why she should feel such extreme jealousy over a perfect stranger.

The disturbed look on Lacy's face caught her father's attention. He could tell she was eavesdropping on the conversation taking place between Chase and Rachel, and the look on her face was priceless. He knew a jealous woman when he saw her.

With matchmaking in mind, he tapped Eli on the shoulder. "All right, you old reprobate, stand back and let me introduce my Lacy to that grandson of yours."

Eli released Lacy and looked on proudly as Chase stepped forward.

Suddenly shy, Lacy dropped her gaze as if she were

interested in her fine silk-covered slippers.

Her father, who thought it cute that she was being coy, plunged ahead. "Chase, I want you to meet my daughter." Gently, he pulled Lacy forward. "Lacy honey, this is Eli's grandson, Chase Tarleton."

Chase bowed over Lacy's white-gloved hand. "Miss Hampton, how nice to meet you."

Not raising her eyes, Lacy dropped a slight curtsy. "And you, Mr. Tarleton," she breathed, but did not pull her hand back. Even now, she could feel the heat of his skin penetrating her glove. When Chase had touched her, she had felt a jolt of lightning shoot up her arm, down across her breasts, and finally settle into a warm ache in the pit of her stomach. With a faint smile on her face and unfamiliar sensations flooding her body, she gazed up at him through a thick fringe of dark lashes.

Chase stood studying Lacy with a fiery look in his eyes. Earlier, when he had seen her standing on the landing, she had looked like an ethereal vision, but up close, she was even more exquisite.

Her form was perfect, sheathed in a gold silk off-the-shoulder gown which left little to the imagination. Actually, with the exception of the soft mounds of flesh rising high above the fashionably low decolletagé, her gown was quite modest, though there was nothing modest about her emeralds and diamonds. They were a tangible reminder to Chase of how disparate their lives were.

Nonetheless, the silk fabric of the gown was so fine that it appeared to be a radiation of light rather than a tangible substance. Chase found himself envious of the material hugging her voluptuous curves.

He cautioned himself, realizing his need to be careful of such musings, lest his libido get the better of him. With difficulty, he dredged up the unkind words that she'd hurled at him the day before. Then, fortified by the sharp pain of remembrance, he tore his gaze from her body. But when he looked into her clear, innocent eyes, he found her incredibly sweet. Despite himself, he smiled.

Stuart Shephard, who had recently been courting Lacy, stood to the side, fuming that Chase could beat his time with a girl he considered private property. Spurred on by jealousy and his lustful plans for Lacy, he brushed past his newfound cousin as if he were a pesky flea and clutched Lacy's arm.

"Hello, Lacy dear. I think it's time we greeted your other guests."

More than a little put out at Stuart's high-handed manner, and unaccountably regretful to have been spirited away from Chase, Lacy retorted frigidly, "Good evening, Stuart. I agree. And if you'll excuse me, I'll do just that."

Then she swept away, her back ramrod straight, with a regal bearing that would do the most haughty monarch proud. Somewhat embarrassed, Stuart followed in her wake.

Miss Lizzie stepped forward and placed her tiny gloved hand on Chase's sleeve. "I apologize for Stuart, honey. I declare sometimes that boy acts like he was raised in a barn."

"There's no need to apologize. If I were sweet on a young lady as beautiful as Miss Lacy, I expect I'd be possessive, too."

Chase spoke congenially, but inside he was burning. When he'd met Stuart for the first time that day, there was something about him he didn't like. Then, when he'd learned that Stuart's plantation was the old Cruce farm, he was angered. Now that Stuart had spirited Lacy away from him, he was absolutely furious. But the only outward sign of his feelings was a slight tension in his jaw.

A young man stepped forward and claimed Chase's attention. "Hi. I'm Lacy's brother, Jay." He pointed to Brad and Jared. "And those are my brothers."

Jared and Brad identified themselves, grasping Chase's outstretched hand.

62

Something deep within Chase stirred when he shook hands with Brad and Jay. For a fleeting moment he was once again a frightened three-year-old Indian child, watching his two best friends wave goodbye.

The shock of seeing them after all these years was hard to conceal. He longed to tell them how he had survived his ordeal, and how his cousin, Little Spear, had died. Chase knew that Brad and Jay would feel a loss when they learned of his cousin's death; and one day he would tell them, and they would all grieve together.

Jay brought Chase out of his musings. "And this heartbreaker is Jared's wife, Melinda."

Chase bowed over Melinda's hand. "Charmed, Mrs. Hampton."

Melinda smiled sweetly at Chase. She saw in him a young man who could be the answer to Lacy's dreams. But if Rachel's reaction to him was any indication, Lacy would have to wait in line.

"Mr. Tarleton, if you'll allow me, I'll introduce you to our other guests."

Chase looked to Jared for permission to escort his wife into the ballroom.

Facetiously, Melinda assured her husband, "Don't worry, honey, I'll behave." Under her breath, for Chase's ears only, she muttered, "As if a pregnant woman could get in trouble."

Chase smothered a laugh while Jared called after the couple, "Chase, you see that she gets off her feet. Honey, I'm sure our guests will come to Chase and introduce themselves."

When Chase and Melinda entered the ballroom, he was awestruck by its beauty. Suspended from the ceiling by shiny brass chains were three magnificent crystal chandeliers dripping with hundreds of sparkling lavender teardrops. Their candlelight flickered and reflected off the gossamer gold silk wallpaper, reminding Chase of tiny bolts of white lightning.

The floor, whereupon elegantly dressed couples whirled to lively music provided by a string quartet, was made of the finest white marble shot through with sparkling gold veins. Placed around the walls were plush white velvet chairs, where somberly clad matrons perched, critiquing the behavior of the young belles and their beaux.

Chase led Melinda to one of the chairs, nonchalantly scanning the room for Lacy. He spied her among a myriad of male admirers. Chase thought it was no wonder men flocked to her, considering her flawless beauty.

But even though he appreciated her beauty, he was struck again by a sharp pang of anger. She had called him a savage, and that would be hard to forget. For the time being, he would give Melinda his undivided attention. Well, almost undivided. He would allow himself to watch Lacy out of the corner of one eye.

Melinda bit the inside of her cheek to keep from laughing. Rachel Jackson might have flirted her red-silk covered fanny off with Chase, but Lacy was the one who had caught his eye.

"Mr. Tarlteon, it's a shame for you to sit here with a married woman in a delicate condition, when the room is filled with the most beautiful belles in Georgia."

Choking on his laughter as he sat beside Melinda, Chase said, "Mrs. Hampton, you really are one of a kind." Resting his forearms on his knees, he angled a look at her. "But you're selling yourself short. You're just as beautiful as any single woman here."

"Mr. Tarleton, there are many advantages to being a married woman. For instance, one doesn't have to act coy and play silly little games to catch a man." Glancing around to see if anyone was listening, she whispered, "Of course, the way some of these old buffaloes gossip, even married women have to watch what they say."

Before Chase could respond, Lacy and a platinum-haired beauty approached them. He rose smoothly to his feet, smiling at the ladies.

With an enchanting smile, Lacy said, "Mr. Tarleton, I'd like to introduce my best friend, Miss Celia Harrington."

"Miss Harrington, it's a pleasure," said Chase. He thought the girl was pretty, but not as pretty as Lacy.

Celia nodded shyly. "Mr. Tarleton."

Chase shifted his gaze to Lacy. Suddenly she felt her heart pounding like a bass drum. He was the most handsome man she'd ever met. There was a mystique about him, like a primitive animal who wanted only to be wild and free. For some reason, she wanted to surrender herself to that primitive nature.

Chase would have given his weight in gold to know what was passing through Lacy's head at the moment. Her emerald green eyes pierced him to the core, unsettling him, playing havoc with his reserve. If she continued to stare at him like that, he wasn't sure he could be held responsible for his actions. It was ironic, but she made him feel like a savage.

Melinda cleared her throat in order to break the spell between Lacy and Chase. "Cee Cee, Lacy tells me that you and Beau have set a date for your wedding, and that you plan to announce it at the ball tonight."

"Yes. In fact, I was wondering when the appropriate time would be."

"I think perhaps after this next waltz," said Melinda. "I believe all the guests have arrived, don't you Lacy?" She tugged on Lacy's hand to get her attention.

"What—oh, I'm sorry Melinda, I didn't hear your question." Lacy blushed.

"I was asking if Celia and Beau should make their announcement after this dance."

"Yes, that would be great," Lacy replied with feigned enthusiasm.

"Speaking of this dance, Miss Hampton, may I?" Chase asked, using his most courtly manners.

When Lacy heard the deep timber of his voice, her legs

grew weak. "I'd be delighted," she said, placing her hand in his.

Chase led Lacy out onto the dance floor. The other dancers stepped aside in recognition of Lacy's first dance of the evening, though the enthralled couple was unaware of anyone else in the room. They were cognizant only of one another.

Chase raised Lacy's right hand and, circling her waist with his arm, gazed into her eyes. The rest of the world ceased to exist as they swayed to the rhythm of the waltz and the beat of their hearts. Everything—past and future—was lost for the moment.

For Chase there was no anger. There was only the present and the girl in his arms. "Miss Hampton, you're beautiful," Chase breathed against her cheek.

"Thank you, Mr. Tarleton," replied Lacy. She felt that strange tingling in the lower part of her abdomen again, but this time it was stronger.

"But I'm sure you've heard that before, with as many beaux as you have. Surely men are drawn to you like moths to a flame." He stepped back and looked into her eyes. "Though I might add, I'm not surprised."

If Lacy didn't know better, she would have sworn he was jealous. But that was preposterous. Any man as gorgeous as Chase must have women falling at his feet. Surely he was just flirting with her—two could play that game.

Batting her lashes at him, Lacy countered innocently. "Kind of like the way Rachel Jackson was drawn to you."

Chase laughed his appreciation. There was more to this young lady than a pretty face and a sumptuous body. "Yeah, kind of like that." He pulled her close again and lowered his head, breathing softly against her bare throat. "But she's not the flame I was drawn to."

Lacy's heartbeat accelerated while she revelled in the sensation that came from gliding across the floor in Chase's arms. She had danced with many boys before, but somehow this was different.

"I hope tonight never ends," she whispered to herself, but Chase heard.

He raised his head to look at her, but a movement at the back of the crowd caught his eye. Rachel Jackson and Stuart Shephard stood against the wall, naked jealousy and raw contempt written on their faces. It was the rapid fluttering of Rachel's red fan that had caught his eye. Behind that fan, she whispered something to Stuart. The hair rose on Chase's neck.

In a short while the dance came to an end. Reluctantly, Chase escorted Lacy back to Melinda and Celia.

During the dance, Beau and Celia's parents had joined the two women in anticipation of the coming announcement. It was obvious, to Lacy at least, that Celia would rather die than go through with it. She watched as Beau escorted Celia to the center of the room, calling for everyone's attention.

"Friends, everyone, may I have your attention, please?" Beau pasted on a smile that didn't quite reach his eyes. "Miss Lacy has been kind enough, on the occasion of her eighteenth birthday, to allow me and my dear Celia to share some very happy news with you, our dearest friends."

Celia stared at the floor, her hands clenched together in the folds of her gown. Beau's arm was possessively around her shoulders. He squeezed her in what appeared to be an affectionate caress. In reality, it was a painful warning that she'd better play the elated bride.

"On March fifteenth, Celia and I plan to be married in the Antioch Congregational Church."

Everyone rushed forward to congratulate the "happy" couple. Celia was hugged and envied by every quixotic female in attendance, but she was oblivious to it. She looked up and gazed directly into Brad's eyes.

When Brad had seen Beau and Celia step forward, he had sensed impending doom. Now he stood looking into the eyes of the woman he loved, and he knew it was too late.

"Damn," he muttered, cursing himself. For another second he stared into Celia's eyes, unable to hide the depth of his hurt; then he turned aside. "Bill, I could use a brandy. How about you?"

The gentleman being addressed gestured expansively. "Never let it be said that William T. Sherman allowed a man to drink alone. Lead the way!"

Seven

With the excitement of the announcement past, Lacy and her guests resumed dancing, but Chase wasn't interested. He stood apart from the other guests, watching Lacy dance with beau after beau, and felt the loneliness of an outsider.

"Chase, some of the men have congregated in the library for brandy and a smoke. How about joining us?" Jay spoke from behind Chase.

Tearing his gaze from Lacy, who was swirling gracefully around the floor with a tall, redheaded young man, he nodded his assent. He had enjoyed about all he could stand of watching Lacy in the arms of other men. Furthermore, he looked forward to spending time with his old friends—even if they didn't know his true identity.

When he and Jay entered the library, Chase saw Brad, Jared, Eli, Stuart, and Beau standing with a tall, thin, angular-framed gentleman. The impressive-looking stranger had auburn hair and appeared to be in his late thirties.

Chase and Jay were handed a snifter of brandy by a liveried servant as they walked over to the group.

Brad made the introductions, his Southern drawl a bit thicker than usual. "Chase, I believe you've met everyone here except my guest from Louisiana. This is Major William Sherman—" Brad winked at the distinguished gentleman and

69

added, "soon to be Colonel Sherman. Bill, this is Eli's grandson, Chase Tarleton."

The two men shook hands and exchanged greetings.

"Bill was just telling us that he knew your father when they were cadets at West Point together," Brad informed Chase.

"Yes, Major Sherman, my father mentioned you. I believe that he was in the class two years ahead of you, wasn't he?" Chase asked while lighting a cheroot.

"That's right. He was a fine man and a good soldier. In fact, a much better soldier than I." Sherman chuckled. "Did he tell you that I was a private the entire four years I was in school?" Sherman's hazel eyes snapped with delight.

"No, sir, he didn't. He did tell me, however, that you were an excellent student and that you even tutored him in some of his engineering classes," Chase replied with obvious admiration. He was glad to meet someone who had known his father.

"You are too kind. From my days at the Point, all I seem to remember is constantly bemoaning my lack of personal freedom and earning at least a hundred and fifty demerits a year."

"Well, you'll view being a troublesome student differently now that you're on the other side of the desk," said Jay. "It seems that those of us who were the most difficult students have a morbid curiosity about what our professors suffered and for some inexplicable reason become educators ourselves.

"Believe me, my students have more than paid me back for all the pranks I pulled in college."

Jay knew that Sherman had recently been appointed Professor of Engineering and Supervisor of the Louisiana Seminary of Learning, a military academy situated on the Red River near Alexandria, Louisiana.

"That's right, Jay," remembered Sherman. "You teach at the University of Georgia now, don't you?"

"Yes. But unlike your school, the university doesn't have

an official military aspect to its curriculum."

"Well, I personally plan to downplay the military aspect of the seminary," Sherman informed him, surprising the men.

Stuart had been standing by silently, observing the genial interaction between the Southern gentlemen and Bill Sherman. When he'd been introduced to the slightly bent gentleman, he couldn't believe the Hamptons had invited him. And now everybody was acting like the man was some kind of hero. Personally, he deemed it an insult to be under the same roof with a man who was not only a Yankee, but also the brother of John Sherman, the famous Abolitionist and congressman from Ohio.

Stuart mused, however, that Sherman's presence might be turned to his advantage. If he could get Sherman into a verbal battle of North versus South, it might enrage some of the important men in the room and persuade them to vote for secession when the time came.

"Tell me, Major, are you related to *black* John Sherman from Ohio? Is that perhaps why you are reluctant to train our Southern boys . . . militarily?" he cut in, with barely concealed contempt.

When Brad jerked his head in Stuart's direction the room started spinning. He had been drinking steadily ever since Beau and Celia had made their announcement, and he was in no shape to battle Stuart's bigotry.

"I'll thank you to keep a civil tongue in your head, Shephard. Bill is a good friend and a welcome guest in this home, and I won't have him insulted," Brad said.

He had been engaged in business with Bill Sherman's bank in San Francisco, Lucas, Turner & Co., and later with his law firm in Kansas, Sherman and Ewing, and he had always found him to be a man of exceptional honor. But more than that, he thought of him as a friend.

And he wasn't alone. He knew that Bill was well received in Louisiana, even by the most opinionated, slavery-sympathetic planters.

Then Brad realized that he needn't worry about protecting Bill. He knew Bill had a tuft of hair on the back of his head that invariably protruded whenever he got excited, and he noticed with some satisfaction that it was sticking straight out at the moment. William Tecumseh Sherman was a man who spoke his mind, and it appeared that Stuart was about to discover that fact.

Deceptively calm, Bill responded, "He's only my brother, and I don't care who knows it, though I, sir, am no Abolitionist. I'm merely a cross old schoolmaster."

He chose to leave Stuart's other leading question unanswered for the moment. He was known to advise his colleagues never to give reason for what they thought or did until they had to, for it could be that after a while a better reason would pop into their heads. Wisely, he took his own advise.

"Indeed," Stuart sniffed. "Then, I take it that you are in favor of slavery?" Stuart looked around the room, noting with satisfaction that he had the attention of all assembled.

"No, I am not. I am in favor, however, of the government of the United States of America," Major Sherman stated plainly.

"Do I take it, then, sir, that you are insinuating that secession is wrong?" Stuart goaded.

"Sir, I strongly object to the term insinuation. You may abuse me as you please, but I prefer to be accused of a direct falsehood rather than of stating anything evasively or underhandedly."

This was a foreign notion to Stuart, who, as a politician, relied heavily on the art of elusion and duplicity.

"As I tell all Southerners, Northerners, and insane politicians alike," continued Sherman, still speaking calmly, "I believe that the Union is supreme and secession is treason. If a dissolution of the Union is attempted, we shall have civil war of the most horrible kind."

Stuart stepped back expectantly, gauging the reaction of

72

the proud Southerners in the room.

Beau spat, sputtered, and fairly shrieked, "Is that, sir, a threat?"

Before Sherman could respond, Eli inserted, "No, that, sir, is a sad fact."

Stuart deflated like a punctured balloon. While he was quite comfortable taking on an outsider, he didn't care to challenge Eli, a man who owned more slaves than anyone else in the room, not to mention the fact that Stuart hoped to be the Tarleton heir. So he chose another point of attack by pressing the question that Sherman had left unanswered.

"If that is the case, Major Sherman, then how wise are you to train *our* fine Southern boys, who will no doubt be the first line of defense when the damnable Union brings about such a war? And do I take it that you will fight alongside *our* boys?"

"I plan, Mr. Shephard, to follow the motto that is engraved in marble over the main door of our seminary: 'By the Liberty of the Government of the United States, The Union—*Esto Perpetua.*' Whatever that requires of me, I will do. In the meantime, I consider it a great honor and responsibility to train and influence the fine young men of the South."

Begrudgingly, Stuart nodded his head. He recognized that Bill Sherman had gotten the best of him. His attempt to stir up trouble had failed miserably in light of the major's frank, practical explanation of his position.

Jared seized the lull in the conversation to change the subject. "Chase, Bill was telling us earlier that his first assignment was in Florida with the Seminoles. Wasn't your father's first assignment with the Indians, too?"

"Yes, Pop was assigned to the militia who escorted the five civilized tribes to Indian Territory." Chase's voice sounded a bit husky even to his own ears.

Still enraged at the Hamptons for inviting Yankee trash to the ball, Beau spoke without thinking. "Civilized!" he snorted. "Tell me, Chase, why did your old man stay out in the wilderness with that bunch of savages and mangy blanket heads when he could have come back home and lived with our kind?"

The color drained from Chase's face. He felt a rage that he hadn't known for some time. But before he had a chance to respond, Brad retorted baldly, "Probably because he had good taste!"

Brad knew that it was ungentlemanly of him to insult a guest, but ever since Beau's announcement of his engagement to Celia, he had wanted to throttle the little man. The least he could do was repay an insult for an insult. Besides, Brad had always felt a special affection for the Indians, ever since Stalker and Little Spear had been taken away.

Beau sneered, "Why, Brad, you Hamptons are such champions of the downtrodden, maybe you should go into politics."

Eli recognized the look of mounting rage on Brad's face. Putting a restraining hand on his shoulder, he boomed in his gravelly voice, "Adam has taught his boys to be too honest to be politicians."

Eli looked pointedly at Stuart and Beau. "You know the difference between a whore and a politician, don't you? When you pay a whore, you usually get what you pay for."

Everyone in the room save Stuart and Beau laughed, and Eli put on his most beguiling smile. "Present company excluded, of course."

Chase appreciated the support of Brad and Eli, but felt compelled to speak for himself. Stepping forward, he grabbed Beau's lapels. "You'd better watch what you say around me. If I were you, I wouldn't malign my father or the people he loved. It really wouldn't be healthy."

Beau paled. He decided to take Chase's advise and not tangle with him anymore. Still, he needed to get in the last word if he were to regain his honor. So, he turned on Bill Sherman. "You, sir, maybe one day we'll meet on the field of

74

battle, and you'll find that some Southern gentlemen won't tolerate Yankee trash calling us traitors." With that, he quit the room with Stuart in tow.

"Bill, Chase, my apologies," Brad offered.

"What asses," Chase muttered.

"Here, here," Jay agreed.

"You know what they say, Chase," Jared remarked as Chase raised a questioning brow. "Choose good friends, 'cause you sure as hell can't choose your relatives."

All the men laughed while Eli slapped Chase on the back, facetiously raising his glass in a toast to Stuart and Beau's momentous exit.

With all the excitement over, Chase felt drawn to the ballroom for another glimpse at Lacy. When he reentered the cavernous room, a little less reserved, thanks to the brandy, he caught sight of Lacy making her way out into the evening air. Scolding himself as he passed through the mass of whirling belles and beaux, he followed her through the garden doors.

Eight

When Chase's eyes became accustomed to the dark, he saw a pebbled path leading down to a lush rose garden. At first, Lacy was nowhere to be seen.

The lanterns at the edge of the garden provided pools of golden illumination that brought to his mind her translucent gown. He was confident that she had been swallowed up among the delicate bushes, so he followed the path. He tried vainly to convince himself that he wasn't following her for romantic reasons, but rather to ask why she hadn't exposed him as a savage.

Winding his way through the maze of flowers, he came upon a white wrought-iron bench in the middle of a clearing. There was just enough light for him to see that it was surrounded by yellow rose bushes, still heavy with flowers.

He saw Lacy sitting on the bench, and even though he still wanted to be angry with her, he was smitten. Silhouetted by a full moon, she was the most beautiful sight he had ever beheld.

She didn't detect his presence, so he stood there quietly, studying her as one would a priceless painting. His original intent for seeking her out fled his consciousness, along with the anger he had to constantly nurse while in her presence.

The heady scent of the blooms and her uncommon beauty

assaulted his senses. Her silhouette brought to mind a delicate ivory cameo his mother had often worn pinned at her throat. The thought of his Cherokee mother sobered him instantly. He was convinced that Lacy would disdain his mother because of her heritage, and it was more than he could bear. He turned on his heel to leave.

Hearing the crunch of gravel, Lacy looked up and saw Chase. "Mr. Tarleton," she called softly. Her pulse was quickened by his presence as she absorbed the magical night. The moon was full, the gentle breeze was sweet with the fragrance of roses, and the strains of a Venetian waltz wafted through the night air.

Chase turned, muffling a curse. He moved toward her with a sensual grace that belonged to an accomplished dancer.

Lacy experienced a sense of déjà vu. It was all so familiar: surrounded by flowers, her heart pounding in her breast, being stalked by a virile male animal. She found herself wondering what it would be like to be kissed by this handsome man in such a beautiful setting. If she could have seen the look of barely controlled rage on Chase's shadowed face, she would have fled.

"Did the belle of the ball have to retreat to the garden to escape her ardent admirers?" Chase asked, deceptively calm. Resting his foot on the bench beside her hip, he leaned down close to her face.

The pleasing smell of brandy tickled her nose. "Actually, yes. Dancing every dance has a tendency to make a lady weary, even if she is having a nice time," Lacy replied nervously. She snapped open a gilt-laced fan and stirred the breeze around her heated face. "Not to mention that it's a little rough on the feet."

Kneeling down on one knee, Chase lifted Lacy's right foot. *What am I doing?* he thought. *Seducing her?* What he really wanted was to throttle her. Maybe he wanted to humiliate her, like she had him. He wasn't sure.

His mysterious mood and provocative touch caused an unexpected reaction in Lacy. She sensed an element of danger, and something more. His warm hands felt good; they seared the flesh of her ankle, sending provocative tingles up the inside of her leg.

Halfheartedly retracting her foot, she said in a shaky voice, "Mr. Tarleton, don't, you'll ruin your clothes, kneeling on the ground like that."

Not to be deterred, Chase held Lacy's finely boned ankle and removed her slipper. "Shh, you let me worry about my pants. Just lean back and let me massage these poor, tired feet."

Without raising his eyes, he added, "And please, call me Chase." *Chase, not savage,* he thought bitterly, and tightened his grip.

He had fondled about every part of a woman's body, at one time or another, but rubbing his fingers across Lacy's silk-encased foot was the most exciting thing he'd ever done. A mixture of rage and passion surged through him. He tried futilely to concentrate on the rage and ignore the rising desire.

He shifted and placed both knees on the ground, then tilted his head back, still wondering what the hell he was doing. For a long moment, he looked up at the night sky.

He sucked in a deep breath and, concentrating on the warmth of Lacy's skin, increased the rhythm and intensity of his touch. Removing her other shoe, he sat back on his calves and rested her feet on his muscular thighs. The rage was gone.

His hands ventured up behind her calves as he wondered inanely if her stockings had clocks embroidered on them. He almost missed the low moan of pleasure that escaped her lips.

Rising on his knees, he nudged her thighs apart with his hips and leaned into her. Heat radiated from her body. Desperately, he wanted to brand her, to show her that he was

79

not a savage, just a man. And at least when it came to loving, he was as good as any man.

Something inside him burst. He engulfed her in his embrace and hungrily captured her mouth with his own. Kissing her with ardent passion, he tasted her sweetness. At every opportunity, he dipped the tip of his tongue in her mouth.

He could tell that she was an innocent who hadn't a notion of where such behavior could lead, and somewhere in the back of his mind, the voice of reason warned him to bring this risky torture to an end. But when Lacy encircled his neck with her slim, bare arms, all rational thought fled.

He deepened the kiss as his wandering hands traveled up the backs of her legs. The sensual pressure was virtually painful, and Chase cursed the material separating their bodies.

"Chase," Lacy whispered huskily. Strange, savage feelings swept her virginal body. Chase stroked her back and placed tender kisses on her eyelids, forehead, and cheeks; her breathing grew rapid, shallow.

"Uhm," Chase moaned, pulling the diamond-studded pins from Lacy's hair. He ran his fingers through her silken strands. He'd never felt anything as soft.

She tilted her head back and, ever so slowly, shook the cascading curls out, until they formed a glistening, gardenia-scented cape about her shoulders. She leaned back, granting him easier access to her neck.

Trailing kisses down the column of her exposed neck, Chase snaked his tongue out, and laved her pulse point. Almost mindless with passion, he ran the tips of his fingers down her throat, over her silken shoulder, and heated her bare skin. Once again he plundered the inner recesses of her mouth.

Leaning back, he looked into her misty green eyes. They were darkened with passion, as vivid as spring grass. Instinctively, she tightened her hold on him.

"Are you sure?" Chase breathed against her lips. He knew that he was far afield from his original intent, and the question was almost more to himself than to her. His words were an attempt to shock himself back into reality, but they met with little success.

Her answer was to hold him even more tightly.

He pulled away, shrugged out of his coat, and placed it on the ground. Using it as their bed, he lowered her onto her back. He leaned over her, placed his forearms on either side of her head, then looked into her eyes.

"I need to love you. Is that what you want?" His voice was thick with unfulfilled desire.

Lacy had never been in a situation like this before. She was totally innocent and unsure of what Chase meant. But since she considered herself to be in love with the handsome stranger—she'd fallen for him the first moment she'd seen him—she assumed he was just expressing the same sentiment.

"Oh, yes. I need for you to love me very much." She breathed the words into his mouth, wrapping her arms around his neck, drawing him close. She wanted him to kiss her again. She loved his kisses!

It occurred to Chase that perhaps Lacy wasn't as innocent and inexperienced as he'd first thought. After all, she had watched him bathe naked in the lake. Could she be another Rachel, and her innocent act just that, an act?

He feared he was rationalizing his actions because he was so deep in the throes of passion. But then, he lost his thought. If she didn't quit rubbing herself against the bulge below his waist, it would be a moot question anyway.

He groaned deeply and grew as many appendages as an octopus. Through the blood roaring in his ears, he heard Lacy moan low in her throat. He devoured her lips savagely and mapped her body with his heated touch, until finally he slipped his hand beneath the hem of her gown, dragging it up to her thighs.

Suddenly, over the muffled sounds of passion, a little girl's shrill voice pierced the night air.

"Aunt Wacy, are you out here? It's time to cut your cake. Aunt Wacy, answer me."

Breathless, Lacy rasped out, "Oh, my God, it's Linni."

"Who's Linni?" Chase looked down into Lacy's startled face.

"She's my niece," she answered.

After several tense seconds, she asked waspishly, "What the devil difference does it matter who she is? Would you look at me? My hair looks like I've been in a windstorm."

She tried to gather her clothes and her dignity about her. When she had heard Linni's voice, it was as if a bucket of ice water had been thrown over her. She knew it wasn't fair to be angry with Chase; but guilt and embarrassment made her peevish, and at the moment she was suffering from both.

For some reason, the enormity of what he had done caused Chase to react strangely; he doubled over with laughter.

This only served to inflame Lacy's volatile temper. "You idiot!" she whispered. "You don't have the sense God gave a goose. If we're discovered like this, our reputations will be ruined. And, more than likely, my brothers and father will fight each other over which one gets to blow your head off."

"Aunt Wacy, answer me. I can't find you!" shouted Linni again.

Chase's jaw twitched as he struggled valiantly to control his mirth. After shrugging into his coat and running his hands through his disheveled hair, he pulled Lacy's gown down over her ankles. Then he kissed her soundly, but quickly.

"You finish dressing and fix your hair, my Sweet Georgia Peach. I'll go run interference with our little intruder." Winking in a disgustingly attractive manner, he added, "And don't worry about me. I have a way with Hampton women."

"Oh, you!" Lacy hissed. She wanted to vent her anger, but

the name Sweet Georgia Peach distracted her. Someone had called her that before, but she couldn't remember who.

Chase was smiling when he walked nonchalantly from the garden. Standing halfway up the pebbled path, with her hands placed firmly on her chubby little hips, and with an indignant look on her cherubic face, was what looked to him like a miniature Lacy.

Looking into the handsome giant's face, Linni queried, "Have you seen my aunt Wacy?"

Chase exuded innocence and answered, "Why, little darlin', I don't know. What does she look like?"

Squaring her shoulders and lifting her dimpled chin, Linni proceeded to describe her beloved aunt. "She's got big green eyes, long curly yellow hair, is kinda small, and real pretty."

He hunkered down on one knee, then angling his head to one side, studied Linni intently. "You're teasing me. You just described yourself."

The child, thrilled with the comparison, put her dimpled hand over her mouth and giggled in delight as only little girls can. "Aunt Wacy is bigger than me," she explained seriously.

Then, remembering the importance of her mission, she said, "And I really need to find her. Mammy said to hurry so we can cut the birthday cake."

Chase gallantly offered Linni his arm. "Shall we go down to the garden and see if we can find her?"

Linni stared up at him as if he'd grown another head. "Wady's don't go walkin' with gentlemen without a . . . without a . . . a chapa . . . you know."

"Without a chaperone, darling," Lacy supplied as she exited the garden, gliding up the path toward the unlikely couple.

"Aunt Wacy," Linni squealed, thrusting herself into her aunt's arms. "I've been lookin' everywhere for you. Mammy sent me to find you. It's time to cut your birthday cake." Smiling sweetly in Chase's direction, she added, "This gentleman was goin' to help me, but I told him it wouldn't be proper."

"That's a good girl. A lady can't be too concerned about her reputation," Lacy told Linni and pointedly glared over the child's head into Chase's eyes, her temper still aroused.

Chase shrugged a thick shoulder negligently, as if he didn't have a notion of what she meant.

Kissing Linni on the cheek, Lacy said in a controlled voice, "Let's hurry inside before Mammy thinks we're both lost."

When they entered the ballroom through the garden doors from which she had exited a short time before, Lacy was relieved to see that Chase had the discretion to remain behind. Her anger eased a bit, but the name he had called her still rang in her ears.

While she made her way across the room to sit beside Melinda and Jared, Linni dashed off to tell Mammy that she had successfully completed her mission.

Lacy's kiss-swollen lips and passion-brightened eyes were enough to tell Melinda that Lacy had enjoyed more in the garden than a leisurely stroll. With a teasing smile, she declared, "My dear, I've been concerned about you. You've been gone so long I thought perhaps you'd been kidnapped."

Nervously, Lacy answered, "Was I really gone all that long? I was just taking in a breath of fresh air. You know how I love to walk in the garden."

Melinda knew it was bad of her to tease her sister-in-law. She really just wanted her to know that she had a confidante, if she needed one, a confidante who wouldn't be judgmental.

Discreetly, so that Jared wouldn't see, she reached over and plucked a piece of grass from Lacy's hastily arranged curls. With a knowing wink, she whispered, "Did you decide to take a nap along the way?"

Lacy gasped, but before she could explain, the quartet began to play "Happy Birthday." As the crowd sang, Lacy's nanny rolled out a lace-covered table that held a four-tiered birthday cake covered with peach-tipped roses.

All eyes turned to Lacy while hers locked with the potent blue stare of the handsome giant standing at the rear of the crowd. The name "Sweet Georgia Peach" rang in her ears. *Oh, glory,* she thought, the mystery of the name dawning on her. *Chase Tarleton and the savage are one and the same.*

She mouthed the single word, savage. Her breathing was shallow, the room began to spin, and her extremities grew numb. Before the song ended, she slumped unconscious into Jared's arms.

No one saw the look of pain and anger that flashed across Chase's face when he read her lips. It was obvious to him that she couldn't stand the thought of being mauled by a savage; she certainly hadn't seemed to mind his attentions when she had thought he was a rich planter.

Melinda read it correctly. "Good Lord, just looking at the man causes her to faint."

Celia, Beau, and Melinda stood clustered together at the bottom of the stairway while Jared carried Lacy to her room. When Rachel Jackson approached the group, Melinda excused herself and followed her husband.

"Dear me, I didn't know Lacy was such a delicate little creature. What some women won't do for attention," Rachel drawled sarcastically.

Celia turned on Rachel, ready to give her a tongue lashing, when Beau caught her eye. It was obvious that he shared Rachel's sentiments concerning Lacy, so she held her tongue. Unable to endure any more of their company for the evening, she braved Beau's wrath.

"Beau, if it would be all right with you, I think I'll stay here awhile longer and make sure Lacy isn't seriously ill."

Beau didn't like the idea of Celia spending any more time with Lacy than absolutely necessary. Lacy was a gently reared lady, but she was a little too independent to suit him.

85

He didn't want her giving Celia any ideas. He'd already trained Celia to be obedient—it had only taken a bit of physical persuasion—and he intended to keep her that way. His thoughts were interrupted by Rachel's sultry voice.

"Beau, since Celia's staying to see after her little friend, could I beg a ride home with you?" The bold look in her eyes promised carnal delights that both Celia and Beau recognized.

Celia wasn't surprised at how little she cared. She secretly wished that Beau would take Rachel home with him and the two of them would live unhappily ever after.

Beau had planned to refuse Celia's pathetic plea to stay with Lacy, but the expression on Rachel's face stopped him cold. Ogling Rachel's ample bust, he answered both women at once.

"By all means, Celia dear, you stay with your friend, and I'll see Miss Jackson home."

Hand in hand, Beau and Rachel left the house, without so much as a backward glance. Celia breathed a deep sigh of relief.

As soon as they were hidden in the darkness of his carriage, Beau took Rachel up on her nonverbal offer. He jerked her scandalously low bodice down around her waist and roughly squeezed a plump, white breast.

Unlike Celia, Rachel didn't whimper or cower. Laughing heartily, she reached down and grabbed him hungrily between the legs.

"Oh, you like it rough do you?" Beau grunted.

With a laugh straight out of hell, Rachel rasped, "I like it any way I can get it."

With that bold admission, and Rachel's full, soft body pressed against him, Beau's desire grew beyond belief. Lunging, he pinned her beneath him and drew her dark nipple into his mouth.

His sucking and vigorous rutting motion caused a painful ache to grow at the juncture of Rachel's plump thighs. Frantically, she fumbled with the buttons on his pants until she victoriously withdrew his swollen manhood. Discovering how inadequate he was, she experienced a moment of disappointment.

Then she fantasized about Chase, imagining how enormous and wonderful he would feel inside of her. Such thoughts excited her, even if it was Beau who would eventually satisfy her.

Rachel was a woman who would take a man whenever and wherever she could get him, so she never wore impeding undergarments below the waist. Beau gasped in shock and delight when, reaching between her legs, his intruding fingers met warm, moist flesh.

Rachel impaled herself on him, riding him hard. Grunting and jerking, they bounced the carriage up and down, all but unseating Joshua, the driver.

To Joshua, it sounded like the mating of two wild animals. The filthy language he heard coming from inside the conveyance embarrassed him, and he was a forty-year-old man with a wife and three children; he'd heard it all.

But even so, he didn't think the despicable act occurring inside was all bad . . . at least for tonight Miss Celia was safe. That was something.

Nine

The night was still and eerie, and there was fear and hatred
glowing on the shiny black faces of the spectators. The full
moon overhead hung suspended in a cloudless sky, casting a
gray pall over the thickly wooded landscape. Ringed by
stately pines, a clearing was illuminated by a multitude of
sputtering torches, and in the circle of light an all too
familiar scene was unfolding.

A frightened mulatto woman named Annie stood with her
calloused hands secured high above her head. Still dressed in
his formal evening attire, a handsome young man behind her
gripped a vicious-looking whip. When he let it uncoil at his
feet, his clear blue eyes took on a sadistic gleam, making
it difficult for those assembled to believe that he had ever
appeared handsome.

Purposefully, he stepped forward. His pale blue eyes
watered, and a seepage of spittle oozed from the right corner
of his twisted mouth. His heart hammered in his chest,
rendering his breathing erratic, and his tongue snaked out to
capture the moisture running down his chin.

He stiffened and stroked the whip. Looking around, he
noted the terror written on every face. His legs quivered in
anticipation, and his hands trembled with excitement.
Roughly, he ripped the girl's dress open, baring her slender

89

form to the waist.

Stuart Shephard loved beating his slaves. It aroused him to know that by the flick of his wrist he could tear chunks of flesh from their worthless bodies. To him they were lower than animals and not half as useful. He especially despised the light-skinned ones, who, like the unfortunate girl before him, evidenced the strains of their white ancestry through their fair complexions.

In his mind, he was an agent of God, commissioned to punish, and sometimes even destroy the mixed breeds. He quoted the good book to himself as he set about his "mission": "The sins of the parents' shall be visited on the children."

Stuart's ominous mumbling traveled the distance to Annie's ear. She trembled. She wanted to be strong, but she was so frightened. Even though she had endured more pain and suffering in her eighteen short years than most people experienced in a lifetime, she was nonetheless terrified. For this was different; this time she could die.

"Asmodeus . . . Ashtaroth," Stuart shrieked, failing to see the inconsistency of quoting the Bible in one breath and paying homage to demons in the next. Ruthlessly, he wielded the whip.

The first lash caught Annie on the right side of her back, laying the flesh covering her shoulder blade open to the bone. She bucked and screamed, but the sound was drowned out by the thunderous crack of the whip as it sliced into the tender flesh over her left shoulder.

Tears streamed down her face, and blood gushed from her back. She suffered yet another lash. Each stroke of the whip caused an all-consuming hatred, such as she had never known before, to well inside her heart. Knowing that she would soon lose consciousness from pain and loss of blood, she braved a look at the object of her hatred.

When Stuart jerked the whip back to his side, blood splattered on his crisp white shirt. He threw back his head and laughed hysterically.

Just then he saw Annie turn. He paused a moment. Then he thundered, "Asmodeus . . . Ashtaroth." Aiming carefully, he laid the whip alongside her face.

The bloody hide sliced the tender flesh just below Annie's cheek bone. Tears streamed down her cheek, burning the raw wound. She moaned in agony. Finally, with her back a sanguineous mass, a numbing blackness engulfed her.

Noticing her slump, Stuart called for her to be released. He knew from experience that once his victim could no longer feel the pain, his enjoyment ended.

Damn her, he cursed. She didn't last long enough for him to be satisfied; his loins ached fiercely. Later, he promised himself. Later.

Annie was lying on her side, and Stuart came to her in a few long strides. He kicked her in the stomach, rolling her over onto her back. When her blood soaked into the dry earth, her body convulsed with pain.

"Bethus, get your worthless hide over here and throw this whore in the shed," he growled, never taking his eyes from the abused girl. "And make sure you padlock the damn door."

Turning on the terror-sticken spectators, he spewed, "I better not hear tell of anybody givin' her food or water, either."

Sensuously, he stroked the blood-covered whip. "Cause I'd be glad to do the same thing to any of you jackals."

Jay crouched at the edge of the circle of light, trembling with rage at the macabre scene before him. He had arrived about the time Annie lost consciousness. When Stuart had kicked her in the stomach, Jay had pressed his face into the rough bark of the tree behind which he was standing. Nothing would have pleased him more than to give that filthy dog a taste of what he was inflicting upon the poor girl,

91

but for her sake, and many more like her, he remained hidden.

Jay had been actively involved in the Underground Railroad for two and a half years, and he knew that above all, anonymity must be maintained, for every time he helped a slave gain freedom, he risked life and family in the process. Because of the monumental risk, absolute secrecy was vital. Hence, participants in the railroad rarely, if ever, revealed their involvement to their families. He was no exception.

The only member of the Hampton household who was privy to his clandestine activities was Isaac; Jay's butler, dear friend, and competent connection. In fact, it was through Isaac that he had received word that a slave would need help tonight, and that slave was Annie. Standing behind the tree, he blessed Isaac for his intervention.

After Stuart stomped off toward the house, Jay watched Bethus gather the abused girl into his bulging arms. He noticed Annie's blood dripping off Bethus' smooth, dark flesh, and knew that he had to get to her soon, or she would die. Suddenly, his risk seemed of little consequence.

He searched the tortured faces of the crowd as they wandered away. It was obvious they were shocked and sickened at the brutality of the beating Annie had received, yet powerless to help her.

Hopelessness and rage mingled on their faces, setting fire to something ineffable that burned deep within Jay. He knew he couldn't satisfy their rage, but he could give them hope.

Jay waited until the torches were extinguished and all was quiet. Then slowly, under the cover of darkness, he made his way to the shed. Just before he rounded the side of the crude dwelling, he caught a glimpse of light. He held his breath and waited. The light was traveling in a straight line from the big house toward the shed. Hurriedly retracing his steps, he took cover.

Stuart made his way back to the shack where Annie lay unconscious. He unlocked the door and entered the room. Bile rose in his throat as the oppressive heat and vile stench of the filthy cubicle assailed his senses. Nonetheless, he was excited by the task before him.

He placed the dimmed lantern on the floor beside the girl's chest and withdrew a length of well-used cloth from his pocket. Lifting Annie's head, he secured a gag over her mouth. Even though she was unconscious, he couldn't risk the detection that her screams would cause should she awaken during this final act.

Stuart reached into his pocket and extracted a razor-sharp knife. The bright light that flashed off the cold steel was reflected by the maniacal gleam in his eyes.

Ruthlessly, he jerked the tattered, homespun dress down around Annie's waist. He sucked air through his clenched teeth when once again he felt hot blood rush to his loins. Slowly, meticulously, he carved a five-pointed star, the Satanic pentagram, into the soft flesh covering her breast bone.

When the knife first plunged through her sensitive skin, pain dragged Annie from the depths of oblivion. Through a haze of white-hot agony, she focused on Stuart's face. Then . . . mercifully . . . torpid darkness reclaimed her.

Stuart withdrew the gag from Annie's mouth, using it to wipe the blood from his instrument of torture. Sensuously, he stroked the knife while watching the blood ooze from her body. His breathing accelerated. He gasped and stifled a moan low in his throat when his body pulsed with carnal release.

On weakened legs, he crossed the room. He exited through the door, without looking back. Satisfied, in mind and body, he disappeared into the night.

Once again Jay approached the shed. In his hand he carried a crow bar to pry open the lock, but to his surprise, the lock was not secured. He couldn't spare the time to wonder about this strange happening. Instead, he threw the door open and rushed to Annie's side.

He was not prepared for the horror of her condition. Involuntarily, he retched in the soft dirt of the filthy shed. Then he covered her naked torso as best he could, lifted her slight weight in his arms, and quickly crossed to the door, unmindful of the blood soaking into his clean shirt.

Outside the shed, all was quiet. Jay realized that if he and Annie were discovered, Stuart could, and likely would, kill them. So he proceeded quickly, but quietly, to the clearing where his horse was tethered.

Once there, he retrieved a soft, clean blanket from his mount. With great care, he folded it around Annie's unconscious form. Then he mounted his horse with Annie cradled in his arms and headed for Paradise.

Through the murky haze of unconsciousness, shards of light penetrated Lacy's eyes. She squinted against the glare, blinded at first. Slowly, figures began to take shape. Staring down at her, their faces etched with worry, Jared and her father looked not unlike mourners at a wake.

"Sweetheart, how do you feel?" Adam whispered softly, as people are wont to do in a sickroom.

"Daddy, what happened?" Lacy asked. The last thing she remembered was Mammy bringing in her cake, her guests singing "Happy Birthday," then a blank. Wait, there was something else. Pale blue eyes popped into her mind. She recalled Chase's potent stare. She struggled to remember, and it all came back.

Groaning, she covered her eyes with her hand. *Oh, God! I must have fainted when I recognized him . . . how embarrassing!*

"Do you have a headache, princess?" asked Jared.

"No. I'm all right. I'm just a little tired."

"And no wonder with all the excitement you've had

today," said Melinda, entering the room, intent on removing the doting doctors. "Remember you two are working men who have to get up early in the morning," she reminded them. "Tomorrow, you'll have patients who are really sick— not healthy ladies who faint from the excitement of their eighteenth-birthday parties. Now hurry up . . . out of here, you two."

Lightly, she tapped their shoulders. "I'll see that Lacy gets settled."

After they had kissed Lacy good night, Adam and Jared turned her over to Melinda's care, albeit reluctantly.

Melinda shook her head when she noticed Jared surreptitiously check Lacy for a fever as he kissed her cheek.

"Thanks, Mel," said Lacy, sitting up in bed. "You know how those two get. It's nice to have two doctors in the family, but they do tend to worry overmuch."

Smiling wryly, she agreed. "You ought to be expecting a baby!"

Lacy's eyes widened.

"That didn't come out exactly right." Melinda giggled. "What I mean is, I'm lucky if your daddy lets me butter my own toast, he's so protective! And he's liberal compared to Jared!"

Lacy chuckled weakly, nodding her head in sympathy. The movement made the room spin before her eyes, and she groaned.

"You poor thing. We can talk more tomorrow. You need your rest. But first, I want you to tell me something."

Never one to mince words, Melinda asked the question that had been burning in her mind ever since Lacy had slumped into Jared's arms. "What happened between you and Chase Tarleton that caused you to faint at the sight of him?"

Blushing profusely Lacy lowered her eyes. She couldn't find her tongue.

"Lacy Dawn Hampton, look at me." Melinda gently

hooked her finger under Lacy's trembling chin. Slowly, she raised Lacy's head until she could look directly into Lacy's emerald eyes. She saw at once that they were round with confusion.

It tore at Melinda's heart. In her maidenly, white night rail, with loose curls cascading down her back, Lacy didn't look much older than Linni to Melinda.

With tenderness coloring her dulcet tones, Melinda declared, "Lacy honey, you're the closest thing in the world I have to a sister, and I love you with all my heart. You know that you can tell me anything, and I'll take it to my grave. Now, sweety, I'm asking you again, what happened between you and Chase?"

Thoughts were whirling so fast through Lacy's mind, it was virtually impossible for her to seize one and pin it down. She wished for the life of her that she knew what had happened between her and Chase. Oh, physically she *knew*, but emotionally she didn't *understand*.

"Mel, I don't really know what happened. We hugged and kissed and . . ." she whispered. "I know now that what we did was terribly naughty. Even if I do love him, I'm still a lady. And ladies don't act that way. But at the time, it seemed right . . . And anyway, he loves me, too."

Melinda's brow furrowed. She really didn't know what to say to Lacy. Her sister-in-law was so young and innocent, and Chase was a virile, mature man who, if she didn't miss her guess, knew his way around in bed. No wonder poor Lacy reckoned herself in love.

But even though Lacy was breathtakingly beautiful, it was difficult for Melinda to believe that a man like Chase Tarleton would fall in love at first sight, and then confess it to an innocent. Lacy must have misunderstood; she was more naive than Melinda had realized.

Melinda leaned over and covered Lacy's hand. "Honey, has your daddy or anyone ever had a talk with you about making love?"

Lacy's maidenly blush answered the question far more eloquently than words. Melinda then realized that some parts of Lacy's education had been grossly neglected for far too long, and she intended to see that that oversight was corrected. But not tonight. They were both too tired for that.

"I can tell there are some things you and I need to talk about. But you've had a full day. So let's get you tucked in, and we'll have a long talk tomorrow."

Melinda rose to her feet, tucked the blanket around Lacy, kissed her cheek softly, and left the room.

The sweet breeze wafting through the partially opened garden doors swept over Lacy's face, stealing a soft utterance from her lips, "Oh, Chase . . . who are you?"

Chase stood in the shadows on Lacy's balcony. He had arrived just as Adam and Jared were leaving the room. His first sight of Lacy, looking like a soft, fragile angel, had touched him deeply.

But involuntarily, he had erected a defense. His heart had been broken so many times in the past that he was convinced the healed-over scars had made the organ as tough as an old boot. Still, there was something about Lacy that penetrated it to the point of agony. And when he heard that she thought he loved her, he felt physically sick.

Where on earth had she gotten such a notion? he lamented. Either she was a consummate actress or the most innocent woman-child he'd ever known. His gut feeling told him the latter was the case.

If only things were different, maybe they could have a future together. Chase didn't dare hope. He wouldn't allow himself to dwell on "if onlys". He would never know a moment's peace if he did.

He had learned how futile that activity was in the months following Leslie's death. He was determined that he would not make the same mistakes with Lacy.

After composing himself, he entered Lacy's bedroom, silently moving over to her peach-silk-canopied bed. A pool of silver light, poured into the room, illuminating her beautiful face. The sight took his breath away.

From the rhythm of her breathing, he saw that she was already asleep. The poor thing was exhausted. She'd been through quite an ordeal, and he couldn't help but feel guilty. She looked so tiny and vulnerable that his arms ached to hold her.

In order to stifle her potential scream, Chase put his hand over her mouth as he knelt on her bed. She awoke instantly, terror filling her eyes. The dim lighting of the room prevented her from seeing his face, so Chase spoke quickly. "I won't hurt you. I just don't want you to scream. It's me, Chase." Feeling her relax, he removed his hand.

Lacy sucked in deep gulps of air, unable to speak for a moment.

Her warm feminine fragrance filled Chase's nostrils, bringing on an uncontrollable urge to finish what he had started in the garden. Balling his hands into fists, he regained a measure of control, then backed away from the bed and braced himself for a tongue-lashing. After all, he was a savage who had come uninvited into a maiden's bedroom, and he was sure she would be shocked. He didn't have long to wait.

"Are you insane? What are you doing in my bedroom? Do you know what would happen if my father found you in here? If he let you live . . . and that's a big if . . . you'd find yourself in front of a minister quicker than you could bat an eye." She started to say a firing-squad, but changed her mind.

"I don't know what proper behavior is where you come from," she continued, "but here in the South, there are certain rules of deportment, and from my vantage point, you've broken just about every rule in the book."

Lacy knew she was raving like a lunatic, but she had been

98

in the throes of a very erotic dream about Chase when he had awakened her. To find him practically lying on top of her was more than she could bear. Once again, guilt and embarrassment kindled her characteristically short temper.

For his part, Chase thought she looked adorable, blustering like a midwestern windstorm. "Well, honey, I offer my apology for behavin' like a disgustin' savage." He watched her closely for a reaction to the *savage* reference.

He was gratified; she had the grace to look ashamed. Tongue-in-cheek, he added, "It's just that when I get near such a desirable, 'even-tempered' young lady like yourself, chivalry is burned to a crisp by red-hot passion."

Starting to tremble when he mentioned passion, Lacy decided she'd better get rid of him. Truthfully, she didn't know which of them she trusted least. "What was it that you wanted, Mr. Tarleton? Or whatever your name is." Her voice wavered.

"Oh, it's Tarleton," Chase informed her as he raked her from top to bottom with an insulting glare.

Just then, they heard footsteps in the hall. Surprising them both, Chase grabbed Lacy and kissed her soundly.

"Sleep tight, Sweet Georgia Peach."

Chase slipped through the garden doors just as the bedroom door burst open.

Ten

Fear gripped Lacy's heart like the icy fingers of death when Jay rushed into her room, his clothes virtually covered in blood. "Oh, my God! What happened?"

With an intense look, Jay forestalled further questioning. "I don't have time to explain. Just get into riding clothes and meet me in the stable in ten minutes."

She responded to her brother's sense of urgency and was already on her feet, when he added, "And, Sis, it's important that you leave the house without being seen!"

Eight minutes and thirty seconds later, dressed in a jade green velvet riding habit, Lacy entered the stable to find Jay loading provisions onto the back of a packhorse. She saw her filly, Precious, already saddled beside Jay's roan stallion.

She hurried to his side. Once again she was cautioned to be silent. The lantern was turned low. It was obvious to Lacy that whatever they were about, it was highly secret.

Jay lifted Lacy onto Precious. Mounting his own stead, and holding to the reins of the packhorse, he led a very perplexed Lacy out into the darkness.

They walked the horses until they were out of earshot of the house. Lacy noticed that Jay was hugging the woods as if he didn't want them to be seen. When they were far enough away, he stopped and beckoned Lacy forward.

"Jay, what in the world are we doing out here in the middle of the night, acting like thieves? And whose blood is that on your clothes?" Lacy's nerves were strung as taut as the strings on a violin.

"I know that you have a million questions," he said, "but they'll have to wait."

Taking a deep breath to calm his emotions, he explained briefly, "You've got to help me save a woman's life. She's been brutally beaten, and she'll die if we don't get to her soon."

Jay spoke with more calm than he felt. Truthfully, he was scared to death, though not for himself. He had already made the decision to risk his own life helping slaves but if there had been any other way, he would not have involved Lacy in this. It was one thing for him to participate in the Underground Railroad, but for his sister to be put in such danger was unthinkable.

He had considered going to Adam or Jared, but he was fairly sure they would be legally required to file a report. He couldn't risk that and since Brad was uncharacteristically deep in his cups following the ball, Lacy was his only hope. He just prayed he had made the right decision.

Lacy watched the plethora of emotions flit across Jay's face. "Where is she and what is the extent of her injuries?" Lacy's voice was firm and calm, following Jay's example.

"She's at the old line shack," replied Jay. "Her back is in bad shape, and she has a bad cut on her chest. She also has a cut on her face, and I think she's in shock. She's lost a lot of blood. I brought ointment, bandages, and anything else I could lay my hands on."

From Jay's report, Lacy realized they had little time to waste. She lifted her reins and prayed that she was up to the task at hand.

"Well, Brother, don't just sit there; let's get going."

Jay took off at a fast clip with Lacy and the packhorse following close behind. They approached the line shack carefully; Jay was relieved that it remained just as he had left it.

Before he could dismount, Lacy was already off her horse, making her way up the steps. Inside the shack, she found a frail young woman lying on a cot in the corner of the sparsely furnished room.

When Jay came through the door, he saw that Lacy was removing the blanket in order to examine their patient. A dimly lit lantern on the table cast a hazy web across Annie's face. Her eyes were closed, and her dusky skin appeared drawn and clammy.

Jay stepped closer to the bed. He was pleased to see that Annie's bleeding had partially stopped. But one glance told him that her homespun dress had adhered to the blood-caked wounds. He was sure that wasn't good.

"Jay, you unpack the bandages, and I'll draw water. I've got to wash all this dirt and blood away and saturate her dress so that I can lift the cloth from her wounds without making them bleed again." Lacy seemed to read his thoughts. "Then we'll be able to see how badly she's hurt. Also, we've got to stop those deep gashes from bleeding. I don't know how much more blood she can spare. She'll no doubt get an infection, and we'll have to battle a fever." Lacy spoke more to herself than Jay.

He stood stock-still, staring at Lacy; he'd never seen this side of his sister.

"Well, don't just stand there like a ninny. Get moving," Lacy ordered.

She stepped forward and gave Jay a slight shove, softened by a reassuring smile. It was just as well that he didn't know she'd almost fainted when she first saw Annie's condition. One thing she had learned at finishing school was how to mask her true feelings. Every Southern lady had to be accomplished in that art.

She looked at the poor girl in front of her, pondering what it must be like to learn survival rather than the fine art of coquetry. Her throat burned with unshed tears when, for the first time in eighteen years, the real world stared her in the face. She wondered if perhaps she had been reared in a dream world, carefully constructed by those who loved her, where only the pleasantries of life were allowed to enter. It was an overwhelming feeling, one that brought with it a measure of guilt.

But she didn't have time for self-recrimination. She found an empty bucket in the corner of the room and, still wearing her fine kid riding gloves, proceeded to the well. She passed Jay unloading the supplies.

"Let me do that for you," he offered over the back of the packhorse.

"No," replied Lacy. "Go on and take the supplies inside. I can get the water. Don't pamper me."

She hurried past him, throwing over her shoulder, "Oh, and start a fire in the stove so that we can heat some water."

Jay shook his head. He never ceased to be amazed at his little sister. He must have known instinctively how capable she was or he wouldn't have sought her help. Yet, he hadn't expected her to be this competent. He only hoped that it would be enough and that together they could save Annie's life.

He tightened his hold on the bundle in his arms and hurried inside. Annie lay just as before. One day, he thought, he would kill the vermin who did this to her.

But for now, he would have to play the game, as if nothing had happened. To do anything else would jeopardize his work. Jay laid the packages on a rough-hewn table, thinking that his inability to exact revenge was the hardest part of his job.

Lacy and Jay soaked the cloth from Annie's back and gingerly cleaned each wound. Two of the nasty-looking gashes were deep enough to require stitches.

Lacy turned to the supplies on the table; her voice was

muffled. "We've got to stop the bleeding. Those two gashes need stitching."

"I'll do it. Just bring that lantern closer," Jay replied, rolling his sleeves up to his elbows. He wasn't sure that he could stick a needle through human flesh, but he felt sure that a lady with Lacy's sensibilities couldn't.

"No, I'll do it. I can sew better than you," she said flatly. "It's one of the few useful things in life that a Southern girl is taught," Lacy murmured quietly.

She squared her slender shoulders. "If I can embroider a pillow slip, I can surely use my skill to save this poor girl's life." She reached for the needles and thread. "We'll have to boil and cool these before we use them. While you're doing that, I'll clean the cuts on her chest and face."

When Lacy cleaned the blood away from the nasty slash below Annie's cheek bone, she was stunned. She hadn't realized the wound was so deep; her heart went out to the girl. Only another woman could understand the pain and embarrassment this disfigurement could cause.

For the next ten minutes, Jay and Lacy worked in silence. Then Lacy spoke softly. "Jay, what's her name?"

"Annie," he replied.

"She's so young and pretty. What kind of person would do this?" Lacy asked, but Jay didn't answer.

Lacy rolled Annie onto her left side so that they could have easy access to all her injuries. When Lacy cleared the blood from Annie's chest, she covered her as modestly as possible, then called out to Jay, "Come here a minute. I want you to see this."

He checked the pot on the wood-burning stove and crossed the room. "What is it? Does her chest need stitching, too?"

"No, I don't think the cuts are that deep. Look at that strange figure." Lacy gestured with a blood-soaked cloth.

"What the hell? It looks like the fool carved a five-pointed star over her breast bone," Jay seethed.

He returned to his tasks, and Lacy to hers, though they continued to talk across the room.

"What do you suppose it means?" Lacy asked.

"Damned if I know. Looks like a pentagram to me, but I guess it could be the symbol of some maniacal new secession group. They seem to be popping up all over," Jay said, cooling the sterilized needles.

"What's a pentagram?"

"It's a symbol used by devil worshippers."

"What? Surely it can't be that, can it?" asked Lacy incredulously.

"Who knows what that devil is capable of."

"What devil? Do you know who's responsible for this?" Lacy asked.

Jay drew his hand through his tousled hair. He had been dreading this moment, not knowing how much he should tell Lacy. Her safety could be determined by the extent of her knowledge. He had hoped she would just assume that he had come upon Annie by accident. But he couldn't bring himself to deceive his sister.

"Lacy, I'll be honest with you. I probably shouldn't tell you, but yes, I know exactly who the bastard was who tortured this poor girl and left her to die."

Lacy's hand flew to her throat. "Jay, you're not going to tell me that someone we know is responsible for this, are you?"

Jay laughed bitterly. "Oh, yes, we know him. We know him all too well!"

"Who is it?" Lacy asked.

"Stuart Shephard." Jay spat the name as if it tasted foul on his tongue.

Lacy fairly swooned. She couldn't picture Stuart doing anything this heinous. Lord, she had danced with him and laughed at his jokes just a few hours before.

He'd approached her on the dance floor and had apologized for his earlier behavior, saying he really hadn't meant to slight Chase, but that he'd just been a little jealous.

Being the silly little fool that she was, she had actually been flattered. He'd then kissed her hand, begging her to forgive him and agree to go riding with him in the morning. She had favored him with a smile and had accepted his invitation. How would she ever face him now without spitting in his face and tearing his hair out?

Just then Jay brought the sewing utensils over, distracting Lacy from her thoughts of Stuart. "Honey, are you sure you're up to this?"

"I'll be all right. Just hold the lantern high so that I can be sure I'm getting a tight stitch. It's the only way to stop the bleeding. Thank God she's still out. If she were screaming, I couldn't stick a needle in her."

Lacy's hands were surprisingly steady when she pierced Annie's soft flesh. The cut over Annie's right shoulder blade was so deep, she had to pull the edges together with her left hand and hold them taut while she painstakingly made each stitch. Sweat beaded on her brow, and she caught her lower lip between her teeth.

After closing the worst gash, she took a clean cloth and blotted the wound, pressing it gently to expel the collected blood through the stitches.

In a few minutes, she closed the second cut. Tasting the metallic flavor of blood in her mouth, she realized that in her concentration she had bitten her lower lip.

After bandaging Annie, she gently dressed her in a clean cotton gown. It swallowed the girl whole, looking suspiciously like it could have belonged to Mammy.

Jay was as relieved as Lacy that the work was done. He pulled two straight-back chairs close to the bed so that he and Lacy could rest their weary bodies.

"Do you think she'll make it?" Lacy asked hopefully, settling into the chair.

Watching Annie intently, Jay answered honestly, "I don't know. I'm no doctor; but it seems to me if she pulls through

107

the next twenty-four to forty-eight hours, she should be all right."

He slanted Lacy a glance and once again ran a trembling hand through his wheat-colored hair. "After she was whipped, she was thrown in the dirt like garbage. It will be hard for her to fight off infection as weak as she is from loss of blood."

Suddenly Jay looked much older than his twenty-five years. Lacy wondered how long he had been carrying burdens like this alone.

"Jay, do you want to tell me what this is all about?"

Jay knew that Lacy referred to something other than Annie. Slowly, he recounted his activities of the past two and a half years. He didn't glamorize his work on the Underground Railroad, nor did he overemphasize the danger he had faced. He just told her the facts, and it felt good to unburden himself.

Lacy came to the realization that her brother had been allowing everyone to think him lighthearted when he had actually been carrying a mammoth responsibility.

A burning desire to help in his work was born in her, and she hoped Jay would allow it. She wondered if her desire to become involved stemmed from a need to prove something to Chase, to prove to him that she wasn't the spoiled, bigoted brat he thought she was. But she put that from her mind.

"Jay, I want to help," she stated simply.

"Tadpole, just what do you think you've been doing the last two hours," Jay teased in an attempt to lighten the tone of their conversation.

But Lacy would have none of it. This was much too serious. "That's not what I mean. I want to continue to help in your work. And I want to continue to help with Annie."

When she could see by Jay's expression that he was going to accept her offer, she playfully hit him in the stomach. "And don't call me Tadpole . . . Jaybird."

"All right. You can help. But I want you to check

everything with me and accept my judgment at all times, no questions asked," he instructed.

Lacy saluted and chirped, "Yes, General."

"Honey, I know at first this seems exciting and glamorous. After all, the work we're doing is noble." Jay reached over and took Lacy's hand. "But it's dangerous work. Not to mention, it's illegal. And it's not just our lives we put at risk, but those of our family as well. The people we're trying to help trust us. But it's a sacred trust that's sometimes hard to live up to."

She looked over at Annie's abused body and sobered instantly. "I can do it. I have to do it."

Jay understood.

Then Jay informed Lacy more fully of Stuart's role in Annie's beating. He tried to persuade her not to go riding with Stuart. When she argued with him, saying that Stuart would become suspicious if she cancelled her date, he promised to allow them no more than thirty minutes and then come after her on some imagined pretext.

When that issue was settled, he returned to the house, leaving Lacy with Annie. He changed from his blood-stained clothes and, with Isaac's help, prepared some food for the injured girl.

Jay loaded everything on the back of the packhorse and left for the line shack while it was yet dark. He hoped Annie would awaken soon and be able to eat. It was important that she regain her strength quickly so that she could be taken to freedom. Until then, he and Lacy would share her care with Isaac.

In the distance, he saw the cabin, partially hidden by pine, oak, and poplar trees. With the sun behind it barely peeking over the horizon, it appeared so peaceful. He breathed a sigh of relief; so far all had gone well. Now, if only their luck would hold. . . .

Eleven

Just before sunrise Jay lifted Lacy into the saddle.

"Don't forget, Stuart's coming for me at nine o'clock. You're to rescue me no later than nine-thirty. I don't think I can bear his company for more than that," she reminded him.

"You could pretend you're sick, you know."

"No, that might make him suspicious," she said again. "I won't risk Annie's life."

Jay nodded reluctantly. He knew that when Lacy cocked her head as she did then, he was wasting his breath.

Stuart rapped impatiently on the front door of Paradise manor at precisely nine o'clock. He glanced about him uncomfortably. He always felt awkward at Paradise, and lately he'd felt downright unwelcome, particularly around Brad and Jay. Though he certainly didn't care!

He squared his shoulders, lifted his chin indignantly, and knocked at the door again, more forcefully this time. A scowl lined his face when Isaac opened the door.

For a moment Stuart thought he saw a look of pure hatred cross the butler's face, but then he dismissed the idea.

111

Although the Hampton Negroes were free, they were smart enough to know they were inferior to white men.

"Tell Miss Lacy I have arrived," Stuart ordered in a condescending manner, flicking an imaginary piece of lint from his sleeve as he entered the foyer.

Isaac would have given anything to stomp Stuart into the ground like the insect he was. The old man, who had just come from Annie's bedside, was sickened by her pitiful condition, but his stoic expression hid his true thoughts. With an imperceptible nod, he turned and climbed the stairs.

Sally, Lacy's personal maid, was putting the finishing touches on her mistress's hair when Isaac knocked at her door. "Come in," Lacy called hoarsely.

"Miss Lacy, Mistah Stuart is here to see you," Isaac informed her with a questioning look.

Lacy beckoned for Isaac to stay. "Sally, would you please tell Stuart that I'll be with him shortly?"

"Yes'm." Sally curtsied and hurried from the room.

When they were alone, Lacy whispered, "Oh, Isaac, Stuart asked me to go riding with him last night before I knew anything about Annie, and I accepted his invitation. I can't stand the thought of seeing him, but I've got no choice."

"Miss Lacy, I'll go down and tell him you're feelin' poorly if you want me to."

"I wish I could get out of it that easy. But I'm afraid if I act like something's wrong, he'll become suspicious. That could put Annie in even more danger."

Isaac trusted Lacy's judgment, but he hated the thought of her being around a man as evil as Stuart Shephard. He and Mammy Mae felt as if she were their child, almost as much as Adam's. They could never stand by and let anyone hurt her. Isaac knew that a black man was limited in what he could do to a white man; yet he'd risk anything to protect Lacy.

Lacy tried to put him at ease. "Don't worry," she said. "Jay's promised to rescue me from the monster soon after we start our ride. Surely I can endure a few minutes of his vile company."

Wearing a deep-bronze velvet riding habit and a peach jabot, Lacy descended the steps. She smoothed on her creamy, soft black kid gloves one finger at a time.

With a lascivious look, Stuart took in the sleek cut of her suit which accentuated her ample bust and incredibly tiny waist. Her mass of golden curls was pulled back from her beautiful oval-shaped face and tied at the nape by a matching velveteen ribbon.

She placed a smart-looking bonnet on her head, all the while avoiding his eyes.

Her proudly erect posture and blank expression infuriated him. He assumed she was still angry with him for his behavior at the ball, even though he had apologized. He knew he'd have to eat crow to get back into her good graces. If she weren't rich and beautiful, he'd tell her what he thought of her and her whole darkie-lovin' family. Then he'd take what he really wanted from her.

Stepping forward, Stuart took Lacy's gloved hand in his. "Good morning, dear. You look beautiful, as always." He bent at the waist and kissed her hand.

Lacy felt nauseous when Stuart touched her. Those hands were the same hands that had beaten poor Annie, who even now lay fighting for her life.

"Good morning, Stuart. It's certainly a beautiful day for a ride."

"That it is. I've taken the liberty of seeing that your horse is readied," Stuart said, ushering her out onto the porch.

Lacy ignored the hand he offered and mounted Precious with Isaac's help. Without a word to Stuart, she rode out ahead of him toward Towering Pines. Why she took that direction, she wasn't sure. She didn't even want to examine her motives at the moment.

Lacy found herself enjoying the ride, galloping across the gently rolling hills, out past the snowy white cotton fields. The land was so beautiful. Then her gaze settled on the largest field, teeming with slaves. Her mind went back to Annie and the man riding at her side.

Unable to endure Stuart's presence any longer, she urged Precious into a run and left him behind. The rushing wind blew her bonnet from her head.

It hit Stuart square between the eyes. Cursing, he sank his heels into his mount's flanks, but not before Lacy disappeared over a rise.

At the bottom of the hill, Lacy almost collided with Eli and Chase. They were sitting on their stallions at the edge of a large cotton field. She veered to the right to avoid hitting the men, but in the process lost her balance and tumbled from her horse.

In horror, the men watched her body slam to the ground and heard her head strike against a rock. In a blur of movement, Chase leaped from his horse and gathered Lacy in his arms.

She was unconscious.

Gently, he caressed her head. When he pulled back a bloody hand, he was shaken. He took his blue silk bandana from around his throat and pressed it to Lacy's wound.

Stuart topped the hill moments after Lacy's fall.

Chase was oblivious to everyone save Lacy and didn't notice his cousin's arrival, but Eli did. *Damn, that's all we need,* the old man thought.

Stuart dismounted, planted his feet, and held his arms akimbo. "Just what the hell happened here, Chase?" he asked disdainfully. "What do you think you're doing with that girl?"

Eli had never particularly cared for his dead sister's son, but he never thought he would see him more interested in his own feelings than in Lacy's well-being. He yelled in Chase's defense, "Dammit, Stuart! What does it look like? Lacy fell off her horse, and Chase is seeing to her."

Angry that Eli would defend this Johnny-come-lately, Stuart addressed Chase, "Well, you can take your hands off of her, boy. I'm quite capable of taking care of my *date.*"

Chase looked up at Stuart with something akin to murder in his eyes. "Get out of my way, Shephard. I'm taking Lacy back to Towering Pines, and once I'm sure she's all right, I'll be glad to meet you anywhere and beat your snooty little ass."

Stuart, red in the face, stood squarely in front of Chase and Lacy, refusing to budge.

Jay rode over the hill and approached the volatile scene. "What happened, Chase," he asked, ignoring Stuart.

"She's had a nasty fall, and her head's bleeding pretty badly. I'm taking her to Towering Pines since it's closer than Paradise," Chase replied.

"Good. I'll ride back to the house. I think Dad's still home." In a second, he was gone.

Chase rose easily with Lacy cradled in his arms. Eli offered to take her while he mounted, but Chase wouldn't release her. He placed his foot in the stirrup and held Lacy close to his chest, then effortlessly pulled up into the saddle. They rode off, leaving Stuart with a murderous look on his face.

Stuart clenched his fists until his knuckles turned white. One day he would beat Chase, but not in a fair fight. A man could get hurt like that. He would shoot him in the back. *That's not cowardice,* he thought. *Just using my head.*

Chase kicked the door open with his boot and mounted the wide staircase two steps at a time, clutching Lacy to his chest. He was beside himself with worry since she had not regained consciousness.

Lizzie met him in the upstairs hall and gasped when she saw Lacy's ghostly appearance. Recovering quickly, she hurried him into the guest bedroom across the hall from his own room, where he sat on the bed, retaining his hold on the injured girl.

Eli lumbered up the stairs and explained the accident to his wife. She stepped to the bed, placing her hand on Chase's shoulder.

"Honey, if you and your grandfather will leave the room, I'll loosen Lacy's clothes and settle her into bed. Then you can come in and sit with her until Adam gets here." She spoke softly and gently to her grandson, surprised at his anguish over Lacy's condition.

At first it appeared that Chase didn't hear. He held Lacy tightly in his arms. In a few moments he placed her on the bed and turned to his grandmother. "I'll be right outside the door. Please be careful with her."

Lizzie hugged him tightly. "I'll take good care of her. It'll only take a minute."

It seemed to Chase that he waited in the hall five hours rather than five minutes. For a bit, Eli feared he'd have to sit on the boy to keep him from rushing back to Lacy's side. But soon Lizzie opened the door and allowed Chase to pass.

Lizzie joined her husband in the hall with a puzzled look on her face. "Mr. Tarleton, what has gotten into that child? You'd think he and Lacy had been married for ten years the way he's carryin' on. Why, he barely knows her. It hardly seems proper."

Eli pulled his silver-haired wife into his arms, with a look of remembered passion. "Sometimes a man can fall in love with a beautiful woman on sight." He leaned back and winked. "I did."

Lizzie pulled from Eli's arms. "Mr. Tarleton, remember

116

yourself! Our neighbor's daughter is lying in our house unconscious. What would people think if they saw us standing outside her room carryin' on like two love-birds or something?"

Eli hooted with laughter and went to await the doctor's arrival, failing to see the faint smile that crossed his wife's face. She muttered to herself, "Silly ole fool. You'd think he was a fancy ladies' man or somethin'." But still her heart was pounding just a bit faster than usual.

Slowly, Lacy climbed from the cold, black pit of unconsciousness, experiencing a devastating pain that shot from the back of her skull to the front. The agony in her head shattered into a million razor-sharp pieces. The sensation was so overwhelming, she was flooded with nausea.

But as she drew closer to awareness, a soothing blanket hovered over her. It was in the form of a man's whisper. Along with it was a cool hand, caressing her brow. When warm lips replaced the gentle hand, Lacy opened her eyes, but the blinding light caused her to clamp them shut again.

"My head!" she groaned.

Chase jerked back as if he'd been burned, afraid his kiss had caused her pain. "Lacy," he whispered. "Can you hear me?"

Lacy nodded, unleashing again the fiery demons tormenting her brain. New waves of nausea washed over her, causing her to lean over the side of the bed and empty her stomach.

Chase had anticipated this possible reaction and had the chamber pot close at hand.

Lacy was too sick to know whether she'd hit the pot or the floor. At the moment, she didn't know whether she wanted to die from embarrassment or to end the pain. As long as she died, she didn't care.

Immediately, a young girl appeared to empty the offensive

receptacle. Chase walked over to a cherry-wood commode which held a blue-flowered pitcher. He filled the matching porcelain basin with cool water and dampened a cloth.

He then placed the cool cloth on Lacy's forehead and smiled when she moaned in appreciation. "Is that better?"

"Uhm," she breathed. Carefully opening her eyes, she focused on Chase's concerned face. "What happened to me?"

"You fell off your horse and hit your head. Eli and I thought you should come here to Towering Pines since it was closer than Paradise. Jay has gone for your father."

"Jay!" Lacy was alarmed at hearing her brother's name. It reminded her of Annie.

"I've got to go home," she said hoarsely and tried vainly to rise. Suddenly, the room began to spin before her eyes.

Chase pushed her back onto the bed. "Listen, Lacy, I expect it's going to be a few days before you can leave this bed. I don't intend to let anybody move you until I'm sure that you're able."

Ill or not, Lacy wasn't about to let Chase tell her what she could and could not do. "Listen, you ogre! Who do you think you are, God or something? Nobody orders me around, least of all you!"

"Well, maybe you'd prefer Stuart! After all, he was your *date*." Chase hated the feeling of jealousy that surged through him at the thought of Lacy preferring Stuart, or anyone for that matter. Why should he care? She was nothing more than a spoiled brat. His only concern for her was because he felt responsible for the accident. She had, after all, swerved to avoid running into him.

Lacy paled at the mention of Stuart. She looked around the room, seeing three of everything, including Chase. She asked the one in the middle, "Where is Stuart."

"I'm sorry, but your lover-boy isn't here yet. If you can hang on, he'll be along shortly."

Lacy was incensed with Chase's sarcasm. "You big ox! I

don't want Stuart any more than I want you! And Lord knows, I don't want you at all!"

Just then Adam entered the room, having heard Lacy's rebuff. "Princess, you must be feeling better already." He grinned.

Lacy turned to Chase. "You may leave now."

Looking like he wanted to choke her, Chase stalked from the room. Adam thought he heard Chase mutter something about "damn women," but he couldn't be sure.

"Jay told me you were knocked unconscious by a fall," Adam said, knowing better than to tease Lacy about Chase.

He placed his medical bag on the bedside table, opening it professionally while he talked. Only the trembling of his hands gave any indication of how upset he was that his daughter was injured. Lacy wasn't fooled by his nonchalant manner.

Adam wasn't the only man Lacy caused to tremble, however. As Chase made his way to the library, where his grandparents and Jay were awaiting word of Lacy, his legs felt unsteady. It amazed him that she could have such a marked effect on him in such a short period of time. Lord, before he knew her a month, he'd be howling at the moon.

When he entered the spacious room, he found Lizzie sitting before the fire in a plush, blue-taffeta Queen Anne chair. Jay stood at the sideboard, watching Eli splash brandy into two crystal snifters.

"I know it's a little early in the day for strong spirits," said Eli. "But with all the excitement, Jay and I needed a bracer. How 'bout you, son?" Eli had his eternal good humor intact.

Chase crossed to the large bay windows on the east side of the room, absentmindedly nodding to his grandfather. "Sure."

119

He looked blankly over the wide expanse of Towering Pine's front lawn. His mind was still upstairs with Lacy. Damn her hide!

Eli handed Chase his drink. "How's she doin'?"

"She regained consciousness," Chase responded vaguely. "She's just so tiny and frail, but her temper's intact." He sat in an oversized leather chair. "I wish she hadn't tried to avoid running into me. I feel responsible."

Eli studied Chase over the rim of his glass. He understood why Chase felt responsible for Lacy. He loved her. But he had a notion it would take a long time before his headstrong grandson realized it.

With feelings of guilt, Eli remembered the time Chase's father had experienced that kind of love for a girl. He'd been so excited when he'd shared his feelings with his parents. Their negative reaction that day had cost them their son. One day he would tell Chase all about it and ask his forgiveness—for that among other things. But it was too soon.

In a few minutes Adam entered the room. "She's going to be all right, but I think we should leave her here a few days."

Chase had mixed emotions about that bit of news. He wondered if her injury was more serious than he'd thought. His grandmother posed that question to Adam.

"No, it's just a precaution. She's suffered a mild concussion, and I don't want her to be jostled over the two miles between here and Paradise. Luckily, like most Hamptons, she has a hard head."

That her injury wasn't serious was a relief to Chase. Still, the thought of living under the same roof with Lacy was a bit unsettling. If Adam had known how Chase's loins were throbbing at the thought of Lacy sleeping across the hall from him, he would have spirited his virginal daughter away, bumpy road or not. At the very least, he would have fitted her with a chastity belt. Chase averted his gaze, finding it necessary to hide just how stimulating his thoughts had become.

Ever-attentive Eli understood Chase's problem and grinned. *Yep, if I don't miss my guess, that boy's just like his granddaddy.* Suddenly that thought wasn't completely comforting.

Twelve

It was midnight before things quieted at Towering Pines. Adam and Jay had remained with Lacy until around eleven-thirty. Shortly after they had left for Paradise, the Tarletons turned in, all but Chase.

He had stayed away from Lacy all day and at present was wearing a hole in his rug, pacing back and forth like a savage beast.

No matter how hard he tried, he couldn't get Lacy out of his mind. Knowing that she was just across the hall was driving him mad. He wanted to go to her, but there was much to consider: her reputation, for one thing; and her health, for another. But the most important consideration was that the chit thought he was a lowly savage. She'd probably just order him from the room again.

He tried to convince himself that he wanted to see if she needed anything. But deep down he knew his motives weren't noble. All he could think about was the softness of her body and the sweetness of her lips. He cursed himself for being a lecherous fool. It really wasn't like him to act this way. At least not with a lady.

Before he knew it, Chase was turning the knob on Lacy's door. Inside, he saw a single-globe gaslight hissing in the corner of the room, casting shadows over the big feather bed upon which Lacy slept. Although there were smoldering coals in the fireplace, the room was cold.

Chase crossed the room to stoke the fire, and tripped over a dark bundle lying beside Lacy's bed. With fear in her eyes, a young slave girl scrambled to her feet, purposefully melting back into the corner beside the hearth.

Chase assumed she was sleeping there to see after Lacy's needs during the night. Dammit! Why was she so afraid of him; and why was she lying on the floor? Surely in a house as rich as this a bed of some type could be found for the girl.

"Go to your own bed," Chase whispered. "I'm sleeping just across the hall. I'll listen for Miss Hampton."

"Naw suh! Miss Lizzie, she tole me to stay in here with the missy."

"Well, I'm telling you to go. It's too cold for you to sleep on the floor."

She was shocked that her master's grandson could care about a slave's comfort. Still, she hesitated to leave.

"You go on now," Chase said gently. "Miss Lizzie will understand. I'll tell her that I told you to leave."

Chase gritted his teeth; he didn't like to see slaves treated the way they were. It reminded him of the way his people had been treated.

Chase watched sadly as the girl left. She kept looking back at him as if he would change his mind.

He stoked the fire until it cast dancing shadows about the semi-darkened room. He moved silently and stood beside Lacy's bed. She looked so tiny and innocent, engulfed in the massive feather mattress. He was pleased to see that her breathing was stronger and that her cheeks had regained their healthy glow. She slept so soundly, he wondered absently if she'd been given laudanum.

Quietly, he knelt on one knee beside the bed and lifted her dainty white hand. Engulfing it in his own, he turned it palm-side up and marveled at its delicate softness. He had never

124

touched a hand so soft. The contrast of her petal-soft skin to his work-calloused hand was as marked as the difference in their upbringing.

Lacy had been coddled, spoiled, and adored by the inhabitants of her delicate world. How could she ever survive in a world other than her own? Again he was reminded of the impossibility of a future with this girl.

He lifted Lacy's hand to his lips, kissed it tenderly, and placed it beneath the covers. With his head bowed, he walked away from her.

Lacy screamed in agony as Stuart stripped yet another piece of flesh from her naked back.

He laughed maniacally as the vicious whip hissed through the air. Quickly circling the pole to which she was staked, he stood before her, trembling with excitement. His eyes were as red as the blood streaming down her back. His whip was a two-headed viper. When he cracked it against her cheek, the snakes sank their dripping fangs into her soft, smooth skin.

Lacy screamed uncontrollably as the snakes wrapped themselves around her shoulders, imprisoning her like two unbreakable vines.

Chase heard Lacy moaning from across the hall, and he jumped out of bed and into his pants. Before he could button them or don his shirt and shoes, her piercing scream reached his ears. He rushed across the hall and found her thrashing wildly about in bed.

Instinctively, he took her in his arms, allowing her to fight him like a cornered tiger. Realizing that she was in the throes of a horrifying nightmare, he crooned to her gently, attempting to awaken her.

He ran his hands soothingly over her shoulders and down her back. Slowly she stilled and grew relaxed. He tangled his fingers in the silken strands that streamed about her like a shimmering waterfall and breathed into her ear, "It's all right. You were just having a bad dream. I'm here now. I won't let anything hurt you."

Lacy awakened to find herself in Chase's strong embrace. She threw her arms around his neck. Her nightmare had been so real and frightening that she relished the comfort of his touch. Feeling safe and secure, she clung tightly to his broad, naked shoulders.

Chase grazed the tracks of her tears with the backs of his fingers. She was so incredibly soft, almost unreal. Overcome with the discovery, Chase rained kisses over her lidded eyes, down her blushing cheeks, and across her quivering chin. His warm breath evaporated her salty tears as it heated her face.

He felt her sift her fingers through the ebony curls that caressed his nape. Excited by her uninhibited response, he moaned low in his throat. He knew they were losing control again. He wanted desperately to stop, but couldn't.

Through the thin fabric of her nightgown, under which she wore nothing, Chase felt Lacy's ample breasts pressed against his naked chest. He cupped first one swollen globe and then the other and gently massaged her sensitive nipples between his thumb and forefinger until they were taut with need. He leaned over and suckled the aching tips through her thin gown.

Capturing her lips with a primitive growl, he quickly unbuttoned her gown. He bared her perfectly formed porcelain breasts, and lovingly mapped her body with his touch, kissing his way down the graceful column of her throat. With gentle bites he nipped the sensitive pulse-point at the base of her neck.

Feeling the rapid flow of blood through her veins, his control became virtually nonexistent. "Oh, Lacy, do you know what you do to me?"

His voice penetrated the spell he'd cast upon her. For a

fleeting moment, she realized the impropriety of wallowing in bed in the middle of the night with a half-naked man. But when Chase grew an extra pair of inquisitive hands and crooned to her in a passion-thickened growl, the definition of proper behavior eluded her. Now she didn't care to think, only feel.

The sensation between her thighs became almost painful. Even in her innocence, she knew that something wonderful could be done to relieve the tension building there. Chase deftly rolled her onto her back, covering her tiny body with his massive frame. Instinctively, she arched her hips toward his lower body.

The breath caught in his throat when her soft woman's mound ground against his throbbing member. Taking her head into his hands, he plundered her mouth with his tongue.

Her voluminous gown had ridden up to her waist in the tussle, giving him the opportunity to stroke her smooth, firm thighs. He paid homage to each leg, moving up slowly with his fingers, until they sifted through the silky, blond curls hiding her womanly pleasures.

Lacy gasped for breath and strained toward his inquisitive fingers, ecstatically grazing his muscle-corded back with her fingernails. He bent his head to lave first one passion-swollen breast and then the other.

"Chase," she sighed.

Wrapping his arms around her waist, he rolled onto his back, taking her with him, until she lay on top, her body nestled between his legs. He held her from him and slid her gown past her shoulders, settling it around her waist. With nothing between their bodies, she sat up and straddled his hips.

He groaned when her warm, moist flesh kissed his firmly muscled pelvis. He wanted to see her better, so grasping her waist, he held her upper body away from him again. The image he saw was permanently burned on his brain: a triumphant love goddess, rising high above her adoring mate. Silver moonlight filtered through the window at her back, causing the hair flowing around her naked torso to shine like a gossamer shawl.

"You're the most beautiful being God ever created," he said, staring into her passion-darkened eyes.

She fell on him and hugged him tightly. "No, you are!"

The sincerity of her response touched him deeply, when again he realized how achingly sweet and trustingly innocent she was. And he knew that what he was doing was wrong. Despite a need that was so savage he couldn't speak for a moment, he pulled back and captured her face in his hands.

The look on her face was one of pure adoration. He realized then that he could make her fall in love with him, but he also knew it wouldn't last.

They were too different, and she was too fragile to face the cruel world shackled to an Indian. Her adoration would turn to hate or even worse, to shame, and he couldn't bear the thought of her being ashamed of him.

He would rather never have her at all than have her and lose her like that. "I'm so sorry, honey. I have no right." Quickly and gently he rolled her off of him and stood unsteadily beside the bed, buttoning his pants.

She looked at him with hurt and confusion clouding her tear-filled eyes. Her lips were red and swollen from his kisses; her eyes were fixed and glazed with unfulfilled need.

She looked so utterly vulnerable and desperately abandoned that Chase had to clench his fists to keep from taking her in his arms again, vowing to protect her from the world. But the most hurtful thought was that she needed protection from him most of all. Drawing his hand through his disheveled hair, he whispered, "Please forgive me." With that he turned to leave.

A sob burst from Lacy's throat before Chase could escape

to the safety of his room.

"I hate you," she whispered pitifully.

"I don't blame you," he murmured and closed his door.

Lacy awakened to the pain of blinding sunlight. Her tear-swollen eyes burned as if she'd been out in the wind too long. The ache in her head attacked her with an unrelenting vengeance, and she wasn't certain whether the nauseating pain was a symptom of her head injury or the result of crying herself to sleep.

After Chase's shocking departure, she had been overcome with hurt, guilt, and embarrassment. His abandonment had almost broken her heart, to say nothing of its effect on her pride and self-image.

Oh, glory, how could she ever face him again? She wondered how he would react to her, and even worse, what he must think of her.

She didn't even know what to think of herself. All her life she'd been a very religious person. She studied her Bible, prayed daily, attended worship services weekly, and generally tried to live her definition of a Christian life. Then, why did she lose control whenever Chase came within three feet of her?

Groaning, she decided she had to get out of his house and back to Paradise. With a little luck, she thought, maybe her father would look in on her early and declare her fit to return home. Maybe she could even leave without seeing Chase again.

With these thoughts in mind, her eternal optimism returned. "I'll withdraw and let things cool off between us a bit," she declared to herself. "Then when we meet again we can just be polite friends who happened to share a silly moment of passion. Why, one day we'll probably even laugh about it."

Her head suddenly felt better, and the day looked brighter. But her good mood was to be short-lived.

A discreet knock sounded at her door. "Come in," Lacy called nervously.

Lizzie swept through the door in a flurry of jade-and-mauve-striped silk, smelling like sun-warmed lilacs. Her delicately lined face was lit with a brilliant smile. "Good mornin', sweetie. Did you sleep well last night?"

"Yes, ma'am, just fine," Lacy lied.

"Good." She reached over and patted Lacy's cheek sweetly. Lizzie looked about the room as if she expected to see someone else. "Now, where in the world is Ruthie?"

"Ruthie, ma'am?"

"Yes, dear. The girl who slept in here last night. I figured she'd have already helped you wash up and get ready for breakfast," Lizzie stated a little impatiently, obviously displeased at the girl's absence.

Lacy felt a moment of fear. Surely no one had been present when she and Chase had been behaving like dogs in heat. She couldn't even bear the thought of it. No, Chase must have planned her seduction and sent the girl away so that he could defile her in private. *I'll kill him,* she swore.

Lizzie saw the disgust in Lacy's eyes. "Honey, I know y'all don't approve of slavery, but I hope you won't be too offended if I ask you to allow Ruthie to attend you while you're here at Towering Pines."

"No, ma'am. It's not that. I appreciate all you're doing for me," replied Lacy. "I guess my head just hurts a little. I suppose I'm a tad out of sorts. Besides, I'm sure Daddy will come and take me home today. So I won't be needing to impose on you any longer."

"Oh, no, darlin'. Adam was here earlier and checked on you while you were still asleep. He didn't want to wake you because he said that rest is the best medicine for you right now."

Lizzie ran on and on. "He said to tell you that Jared will be over this afternoon to check on you, and that you'll need to stay here at least two more days. You know, honey, your daddy looks a mite peaked himself if you ask me. . . ."

Lizzie was still rattling on, but Lacy didn't hear a word she said past "two more days." How on earth would she avoid Chase in his own home for two more days?

She flattened her hand against her chest dramatically. *I'll just act as if I wish to have no more intercourse with him than a "how do you do?"* Oh, glory, she groaned to herself. *What a poor choice of words.*

Thirteen

Chase was spiritually renewed when he returned to Towering Pines from the lake where he prayed and greeted Grandmother Sun each morning, but his sense of balance was short-lived. He dismounted just as Stuart's horse was being led off to the stables. The man never had come to inquire about Lacy the day before.

Chase took the steps two at a time, halting just outside her door. He didn't want to eavesdrop, but he couldn't help himself. Although it was possible that Stuart's visit had nothing to do with Lacy, he wouldn't bet his life on it. One way or the other he had to know. Stuart's voice met him in the hall.

"Dearest, I was so distressed when I topped the hill yesterday and found that you had had an accident. Of course, I wanted to take you back to Paradise immediately so that your father could care for you properly, but that Chase person insisted on bringing you here. It makes one wonder why he'd be so desperate to whisk you away and install you in the bedroom just across the hall from his own."

He halted, to give Lacy a moment to consider the impropriety of the situation. When she just stared at him blankly, he continued, "Frankly, I'm shocked that Aunt Lizzie cares so little for your reputation that she would permit such a thing."

Lacy had felt sick when Stuart breezed into her room, dismissing Ruthie as if he owned Towering Pines and everything in it, including her. She had much on her mind and he had caught her unprepared. Even now her thoughts were jumbled.

She was dreading the moment she would see Chase again, after she'd thrown herself at him so brazenly. And she longed to return to Paradise so that she could help Jay care for Annie.

The last thing she needed was for this self-righteous woman abuser to browbeat her for occupying a room in the home of her father's closest friend. "Stuart, I know you have my best interest at heart," she began sarcastically, "but I assure you, that 'Chase person,' as you refer to your cousin, has been a perfect gentleman."

Stuart made a rude sound of disbelief while Chase stood outside in the hall grinning cheekily. If she considered him to be a perfect gentleman, he wondered what it would take to be considered a randy rogue. He wasn't sure he had the stamina!

Still smiling, Chase tapped lightly on the door. Lacy called for him to enter.

"Why, Stuart, how nice to see you. I didn't know you were here." He sauntered over and slapped Stuart on the back, a tad more forcefully than necessary.

"But I must caution you, you really shouldn't be in Miss Hampton's room alone so early in the morning. We wouldn't want her reputation to suffer, now would we?"

Lacy hid a satisfied smile behind her hand.

Stuart lifted his indignant chin in a sniff. "Indeed! Then what, may I ask, brings you here?"

"Cook asked me to check to see if Miss Hampton is ready for her breakfast."

"Since when did slaves impose on their masters?" Stuart taunted.

Chase refused to be ruffled. "Well, it really isn't an imposition since I was coming up to my room anyway. It's just across the hall, you know." He paused for emphasis. "Besides, I don't consider myself anybody's master," he concluded forcefully.

Since Stuart didn't have a reply for such a foreign notion, Chase turned to Lacy for the first time since he'd entered her bedroom. His voice softened, and they both remembered the evening before. "Miss Hampton, are you ready for breakfast?"

When Chase looked directly at Lacy, her face glowed with embarrassment and anger. "I will be in a moment. Please tell Cook I'll be down as soon as I can locate my clothes. I assume Miss Lizzie and Ruthie put them around here somewhere."

"Do you really think you should come downstairs?" Chase asked, genuinely concerned. "I'll be glad to bring a tray up to you."

Stuart was insulted at being so pointedly ignored. Lacy addressed Chase. "That's kind of you, Mr. Tarleton. But I'm sure Ruthie will see to it."

Chase's eyes narrowed. So the brat did want a slave to do her bidding. He bowed slightly. "Good day, then." With a sideways glance at Stuart, he quit the room.

Lacy was napping when she was awakened by a squeal in the hall. "Aunt Wacy, where are you?"

Linni bounded into the room with Jared close behind. Before they got to the bed, Chase walked in and knelt in front of Linni.

"Well, hello there, Miss Hampton." He winked at Jared over Linni's head. "I knew I'd caught your eye at the ball the other evening. You have come to court me, haven't you?"

Giggling, Linni replied in her most grown-up tone, "Wady's don't come to court gentlemen. Me and Daddy

135

came to see Aunt Wacy and bring her some clothes."

Chase pretended to be disappointed at this announcement. Worried that she'd hurt his feelings, Linni reached out a dimpled hand and patted his cheek. "But you can stay and visit with us if you want to," she said sweetly.

Chase sketched a bow to the little enchantress, thinking that she was definitely going to be a heartbreaker, just like her aunt Lacy.

Pleased with his response, Linni bounded across the room and threw herself onto the bed beside her beloved aunt. "Aunt Wacy, are you all right? Papa and Uncle Jay told Daddy that you bumped your head."

Lacy hugged her niece tightly, running her hands through the silken blond curls that were so much like her own. "Yes, sweetie. I'm just fine. Miss Lizzie and her family are taking good care of me."

"Can I stay and be your nurse while Daddy goes to Athens?" Linni asked hopefully.

"Sweetheart, Aunt Lacy has a headache and needs her rest," said Jared. "You can go with me to Athens today and help Nurse Smithers."

"I don't like Nurse Smithers," said Linni. "She takes her teeth out after lunch, but won't let me take mine out."

Lacy grinned. She didn't like Nurse Smithers either. Besides, she thought that Linni's presence might serve as a buffer between herself and Chase. "Jared, she'll be fine, really. I'd love to have her. And you can pick her up this afternoon on your way back to Paradise."

Chase wasn't fooled. He knew what Lacy was thinking, and truth to tell, he agreed with her. They didn't need to be alone together, since neither of them had a great deal of restraint.

It had been a long time since he'd been around a little girl like Linni. He found himself looking forward to spending some time with her. "It'll be fine, Jared," said Chase. "Eli is occupied today, so I'm going to be at loose ends. When

Lacy needs to rest, Linni and I can keep each other company, if that's all right with her."

Grinning, Linni hopped off the bed and placed her tiny hand into Chase's.

Jared laughed. "Well, if you're sure. Oh, by the way, Lacy, Jay said to tell you he'll be over as soon as he can get away from the university."

With the formalities over, Linni addressed the men seriously. "Now, if you gentlemen will go out, I'll help Aunt Wacy put on some of the clothes mommy sent."

Jared and Chase did as they were bidden. But as they left, the men heard Linni exclaim, "Isn't Mr. Tarleton a nice gentleman? I bet he doesn't take his teeth out."

Chase noticed that Lacy didn't comment.

Later that day Chase sat in Eli's office studying the plantation ledgers as his grandfather had requested. Though he'd been at Towering Pines only a few days, Chase had learned a great deal about its operation. It was the largest and richest cotton plantation in Georgia and had been in the Tarleton family for over thirty years.

Eli pointedly informed him that Towering Pines had always been run by a Tarleton, and that when he and Miss Lizzie were gone, Chase would be the only Tarleton left. Chase knew what his grandfather was leading up to. He obviously expected him to take Evan's place as the next Tarleton heir. But he had mixed emotions about it.

He leaned back and rested his head on the desk chair. Suddenly, he was homesick. The only life he'd ever really known was on the Circle C in Indian Territory. Both of his parents had called it home. Evan and Nelda had poured their blood, sweat, and tears into the ranch, hoping to carve a new life out of the wilderness. For the most part, their dream had become his dream.

At the same time, he felt an attraction to the rolling hills of

Georgia. His parents had been born here, and if it hadn't been for the tragedy of the Indian Removal under Andrew Jackson, they would have died here.

Chase rubbed his ruby ring thoughtfully. Maybe his visit here would help him decide where he really belonged. So far, however, it had only raised confusing questions, mostly concerning Lacy Hampton. In the scheme of things, did she occupy a place in his life? Common sense told him no, but his heart said yes.

Chase's musings were interrupted by a strong knock on the door. "Come in," he called.

Jay entered the room with a congenial smile on his face. "Hi, Chase. I've come to see Lacy. I thought I'd stick my head in to see how you're faring."

The men shook hands.

"I'm just fine. I'll show you upstairs and kidnap Lacy's little nurse so that you and our patient can have some privacy."

"I didn't know Dad had gotten her a nurse," Jay stated.

"Oh, yes. And she's quite efficient."

When Chase and Jay entered Lacy's room, Linni was chattering like a squirrel.

"Well, well, it looks like you're in good hands, Tadpole," Jay said, chuckling.

Lacy had been deep in thought when the men entered her room. She had been sitting in a chair by the window for a long while, looking blankly out at Towering Pines while Linni chattered endlessly.

One good thing about little girls, they could talk nonstop, without ever receiving a response. Lacy had no idea what the child had been saying. She had been too busy thinking about a certain raven-haired gentleman who made her toes turn up with the heat of passion.

To look up and find him staring at her with undisguised desire caught her off guard. After a long pause, she composed herself and said, "Hi, fellas. What are you two up to?"

"Jay would like to visit with you, so I'll steal your nurse away and introduce her to a special friend of mine."

Jumping up, Linni turned to Lacy. "Aunt Wacy, do you think you'll be all right if I go with Mr. Tarleton?"

Lacy ruffled Linni's hair and winked at her. "Well, since Jay's here to take your place for a while, I guess I'll be all right. But you be a good girl and mind Mr. Tarleton, okay?"

"Yes, ma'am." Linni took Chase's hand and looked up at her uncle. "Uncle Jay, you call me if Aunt Wacy needs me."

"I will, sweetheart," said Jay, grinning.

After Chase and Linni had gone, Jay fastened the door securely and dropped into a chair close to Lacy. "I thought you'd like a report on Annie."

"I've been going out of my mind with worry," said Lacy. "She's still alive, isn't she? Stuart hasn't found her, has he?"

"She's regained consciousness, is eating a little, and is slowly regaining her strength. She's fighting the infection better than I thought she would, and thankfully, for the moment at least, she's safe. In fact, I haven't seen any sign of Stuart or anyone else even searching for her."

"That doesn't figure," puzzled Lacy. "But I guess we should be thankful she's not being hunted."

Nodding his agreement, Jay stifled a yawn. The dark circles under his eyes showed that he had been burning his candle at both ends. He looked like he was about to drop from exhaustion.

Lacy leaned forward. "I feel so guilty about leaving you to carry this burden alone. How are you able to care for Annie and meet your classes, too? I know you need me. I've got to get out of here so that I can help you."

"No, hon, it's all right. Isaac found someone to help me. In fact, I've been thinking that it's best you're here. If my actions are discovered, no one will think of you as a possible accomplice. You'll have an alibi for all except that first night. And since half of Clarke County saw you faint at the ball, I doubt you'll be suspected."

After Jay left, Lacy sat pondering. She could see the wisdom in his words, but she still needed to get away from Towering Pines . . . or rather away from Chase.

She was beginning to feel more for him than she wanted to, and quite frankly, it frightened her. She knew that she was too young and inexperienced to handle this situation. At first she had been disturbed only when the handsome savage was near. Now she was deeply stirred whenever she even thought about him.

The strange feelings and urges she'd been experiencing for months were nothing compared to the intense passion and desire she felt since meeting Chase. She was a novice in the matter of love, and she truly didn't understand such feelings.

She did, however, recognize the potential disaster they foreshadowed. They caused her to lose control and behave in a manner that could bring shame to herself and especially to her family. That latter possibility caused her great concern.

Lacy flattened her hand over her chest as if it ached. There was nothing as important to her as her family. She'd rather die than hurt them. Oh, glory, if she could just go home!

Groaning, she leaned forward and peered out the window. On the lawn below, she saw Linni with a precious, chubby black child. They were wallowing all over Chase.

He looked like a felled giant flat on his back, being attacked by midgets. The children squealed with delight when he rose up on all fours, imitating a bucking bronco.

Linni climbed onto his back with her skirts and petticoats flying. Almost out of breath from laughing, she circled his neck with her short little arms.

The slave-child, Jeffy, jumped up and down, cheering as Chase bucked and swayed, giving Linni the ride of her life. When she was dislodged, Chase caught her up in his arms and planted a sound kiss on her cheek. Then he set her on her feet and told Jeffy that it was his turn to ride.

Jeffy's dark eyes lit up with anticipation when he shyly climbed up onto Chase's strong back. Lacy could feel the child's excitement from where she sat. His look of pure joy was virtually tangible; it reached out and touched her. She stood to her feet.

She watched as Chase imitated a wild horse again. He seemed to be having as much fun as the children, if not more.

"Hold on," he called to Jeffy, who was laughing so hard he was tottering precariously from side to side.

Playing with the children reminded Chase of the days when he, Brad, and Jay had been carefree and innocent. Days before they had learned of such things as race, color, prejudice, and hate.

Suddenly, he raised his head and looked up at the window of Lacy's room. She stood like a statue. For a second, their eyes held. In her emerald gaze he detected a look of sweet acceptance. Then she was gone.

Fourteen

On Saturday Brad awakened early, despite the fact that he was suffering from a devastating hangover. When he sat on the side of the bed, the room started to spin. Groaning, he held on to the mattress until the world righted itself. Then he dropped his head into his hands.

Ever since the night of Lacy's ball, when Beau and Celia had announced their engagement, he had visited Eagle Tavern following supper each night. It was always the same. He would sit alone at a back table, tossing down one drink after the other. The family was worried about him, and he was disgusted with himself. He had to snap out of it.

He walked slowly to his closet, mindful of his brandy-swollen brain, and chose a dark blue jacket of superfine with sky blue pants and waistcoat.

He hoped the contrast of his powder blue linen shirt with a navy silk cravat would make his complexion appear a little less green. After running a brush through his thick ebony hair, he went downstairs. When he passed through the kitchen, the smell of country ham was almost his undoing.

"Mistah Brad, you sit down and I'll bring you your breakfast in a jiffy," Mammy Mae offered.

"No, thanks, Mammy. My stomach's a little queasy today," Brad said weakly.

Mammy Mae just shook her head as Brad left the house through the back door. She knew that what was ailing him had little to do with his stomach and more to do with his heart. But she had confidence that he'd be all right.

While he rode into town, Brad agonized over Celia. He was haunted by the sad look he had detected in her eyes. She certainly didn't look like any young bride he'd ever known. Why wasn't she happy to be marrying Beau? Obviously there was something wrong. But what? Damn! Brad kicked his horse into a gallop and tried to concentrate on something else, anything else.

He arrived at the bank about eight-thirty and retreated to his office, where he sat down behind a gigantic, oak rolltop desk. He took out his unopened mail and thumbed through a stack of letters until he found the one that had come from a Mr. Judson Stephens of the Bank of England.

Quickly tearing open the expensive beige envelope, he read:

July 1, 1859

Mr. Brad Hampton
The Bank of Athens
Athens, Georgia
USA

Dear Mr. Hampton:

With regard to your inquiry of April 2, 1859, I can affirm that the Bank of England is indeed the bank in question. We appreciate our good customers, Mr. Stuart Shephard and Mr. Beau Patton, for recommending our services to you, and as with them, it will be our pleasure to receive your gold deposits. We are at the service of all our customers, both domestic and foreign.

Given the unsettled political conditions in your

country at this time, we are suggesting to all who use our services that they ship their deposits by special courier. We look forward to being of assistance to you.

Respectfully,
Judson Stephens, Esq.
The Bank of England

Brad reread the letter and placed it in a drawer on the left side of the desk. He locked the drawer with a small key which he returned to his vest pocket.

He, of course, had no intentions of shipping gold to the Bank of England, but it appeared that Beau and Stuart were doing just that. He had written his letter of inquiry only to satisfy a nagging suspicion about them.

In his letter, he had stated that he had great respect for Beau Patton and Stuart Shephard, who had recommended their overseas bank to him. Ostensibly, he just wanted to confirm that it was indeed the Bank of England where they did business before sending his first shipment.

Brad drew himself out of his comfortable chair and walked aimlessly through the bank. He felt the need to move around. He always thought clearer when he was on the go. Something important and perhaps even sinister was afoot, that much he knew. And unless he missed his guess, Stuart and Beau were firmly in the middle of it.

He had been suspicious of the two for some time now. On occasion he had caught them speaking in quiet tones until they saw him coming. Then they'd clam up as if they didn't want him to overhear their conversation. Once he had overheard the words *foreign bank,* which had made him even more curious. He knew that if they were using the services of a foreign bank, it was probably in England because they spoke only English. Hence, his letter to the Bank of England.

What puzzled him the most was that both Beau and Stuart

were very verbal supporters of the movement to secede from the Union, never losing an opportunity to proclaim such. Constantly, they preached that the South had nothing to fear from the North. If they really believed this, why were they shipping their gold to England? Brad was even more curious now that he had received Stephens' letter.

His stomach chose that moment to remind him of his overindulgence last evening. Perhaps a breath of fresh air would help. He opened the door of the bank and stepped outside. Placing his hand on his stomach, he looked down.

Accidently, he bumped into someone. The collision set the demons loose in his brain again, and for a moment the two ladies in front of him looked fuzzy.

The one he had run into was gasping for breath. Although the collision was very slight, the lady paled, as if she were in great pain. Damn, did she have a hangover, too?

Brad's vision cleared, and he saw that the injured woman was Celia. He grabbed her arm to support her. "Cee Cee, my dear, I'm so sorry. Are you hurt?"

Celia, accompanied by her friend, Mary Bruster, was both shocked and pleased to see Brad. Her tender side forgotten for the moment, she responded, "Oh, Brad, hello. No, I'm not hurt. I just have a small bruise on my side that's a little sensitive, that's all."

She stood staring at him for a moment before she remembered her manners. "Do you know my friend, Mary Bruster?"

"Yes, I've known the Brusters for some time. How are you, Mary?"

"I'm fine, Brad." Mary fluttered her long, sooty eyelashes in a futile attempt to attract his attention. She was no different from any other girl in Clarke County; she considered Brad Hampton to be extremely desirable.

Unmoved, Brad returned his gaze to Celia. He stared into her beautiful blue eyes as she gazed into his.

Embarrassed that she had been slighted, Mary continued, "Brad, I wish you would come by the house soon. Daddy has been asking about you lately."

"I'll do that. Give him my regards, won't you?" Brad said without looking in her direction.

"I guess we had better go," Celia said reluctantly. "We still have several items to pick up." All the while, her eyes were fully fixed on Brad.

Mary gave her a little nudge to bring her back to reality. She didn't like what was going on between Celia and Brad. Celia already had her man. It wasn't fair that the county's most eligible bachelor was looking at her as if he were smitten. Mary knew by the look in his eyes that Brad wouldn't notice her as long as Celia was around, so she decided to leave her seduction of him for another day.

Finally, Celia turned to Mary and smiled. Then the two of them moved down the street. When they reached Child's Jewelry and Fancyware store, Celia chanced a glance in Brad's direction. With a slight wave of her hand, she disappeared inside the store.

Brad stood there for a few moments after she was out of sight. *God, how beautiful she is. And she's too good for Beau Patton, the crook!*

Then Brad's head cleared. If he could prove that Beau was a crook, he could rescue Celia from his clutches, her knight in shining armor and all that. Suddenly, he felt a new sense of purpose. Smiling hugely, he moved on down the street.

Fifteen

The sun cast a rosy glow over Lacy's room as Ruthie slipped inside. Quietly, she hurried over to the fireplace, retrieved the poker, and stoked the fire.

"It's all right, Ruthie, I'm awake," Lacy said in a sleep-husky voice.

Ruthie jumped. "Lawdy, Miss Lacy, you scared the life outta me."

Lacy smiled and stretched. "I'm sorry, Ruthie."

"You want me to help you with your bath or are you wantin' breakfast?"

"I'll have breakfast, please."

Ruthie curtsied and rushed out of the room. She left the door slightly ajar, and Lacy craned her neck, trying to see across the hall into Chase's room. She almost fell out of bed, but not before she determined that his door was closed. He was obviously back.

Every morning she had been at Towering Pines, Chase's routine had been the same. He would leave before sunrise— she never knew where he went—then he would come back and have his breakfast. Before going about his business for the remainder of the day, he would stick his head into her room and inquire politely if she needed anything. Then she wouldn't see him again until evening.

The past two nights he had dined with her. As always, he treated her cordially, nothing more.

They sat talking for hours after supper, and had established somewhat of a truce. He told her about being raised in Indian Territory—she didn't think anybody else in Georgia knew about his ancestry—and she told him what it was like to be reared as a lady in the South. While he shared his exciting tales of living off the land, she reminisced about debutante balls and spring cotillions.

Their pasts varied markedly, but they found a common ground in their belief in the equality of people. Lacy didn't reveal her involvement in the Underground Railroad, however, but she felt sure he would approve. Still, a person couldn't be too careful.

He remained distant, and it was obvious to Lacy that something was bothering him. He had not tried to kiss her after that first night, and she thought it just as well. She acted like a trollop whenever he made advances, and she was grateful that he exercised restraint even if she couldn't. Though his self-denial wasn't particularly flattering to her.

"Mornin,' sweetie," Lizzie greeted as she swept into the room in a gray watered-silk dressing gown.

"Good morning, Miss Lizzie."

"Your daddy was here last night after you retired and asked Chase if he'd bring you home today."

For a moment, Lacy experienced a pang of regret. She wondered if she'd see Chase once she left here. Then something Lizzie said caught her attention.

"I'm sorry, Miss Lizzie, would you repeat that?"

"I said that you've been cooped up so long that I told Chase to take you on a nice picnic on your way back to Paradise. He plans to leave within the hour, so you hurry and get ready now."

Lacy's heart pounded, and she was speechless; but Lizzie didn't notice. With an affectionate pat on Lacy's cheek, she left the room to speak with Cook about preparing their food.

Lacy hopped down off the bed and flew to the closet.

"Here's your breakfast," Ruthie said, looking around for Lacy.

"I'm not hungry, thank you," Lacy called from inside the closet. "I'm going home today."

"Will you be needin' my help gettin' ready for that picnic?" Ruthie grinned slyly.

Lacy turned and looked suspiciously at the smiling young woman.

Ruthie chuckled at the expression on Lacy's face. She would be sorry to see Lacy leave. Still, she had seen the way Lacy and Chase looked at one another . . . when the other wasn't looking, that is. She wouldn't be at all surprised if the young master brought Lacy home as his wife one day—at least she hoped he would.

"Here, you come on over here and eat a bite, and I'll get your things together."

Lacy did as she was bidden, then dressed with the greatest of care. She pulled on the latest in French fashion, a pale peach and cream robe Gabriellé. She admired the one-piece dress. It was made of twenty yards of the finest silk, closed with pearl buttons in the front from neck to waist, and three buttons at waist level in the back. It was covered from collar to hem with fragile, handmade beige *point de gaze* needlepoint lace.

Carefully, she smoothed the gown down over her slightly rounded hips. At her throat, she secured a delicately carved, cream and peach antique cameo that had been passed down from generation to generation through her mother's family.

Then Ruthie styled Lacy's hair. She pulled the golden curls together, neatly securing them at the base of Lacy's neck with a matching peach satin ribbon. With the tip of her finger, Lacy loosened curly tendrils. As they whispered over her forehead and caressed each side of her face, she sighed deeply.

Ruthie placed a narrow-brimmed bonnet of the same

material as Lacy's dress atop Lacy's head. Expertly, Lacy tied the streamers in a big bow to the side of her chin. Standing before a full-length beveled mirror, she critically studied her appearance.

Her cheeks had regained their healthy blush; her emerald-green eyes, fairly snapping with anticipation, stared back at her.

"You look just fine," Ruthie complimented. She handed Lacy a matching reticule and parasol. "Now, you sit over there by the window where the light is just right. When Mr. Chase comes in to get you, he'll be struck plumb blind."

"Ruthie!" Lacy giggled and shook her head, but she hurried over to the chair by the window just the same.

Unbeknownst to Lacy, across the hall, Chase was dressing just as carefully. At Eli's insistence, he had visited Eli's tailor in Athens during the past week and had bought an entire new wardrobe. Fortunately, most of his things had been completed and delivered the day before.

Now lying on his bed were fawn-colored breeches and a dark brown jacket of superfine to match. Placed beside his jacket was a brown and cream embroidered vest and a blinding white linen shirt. Tossed carelessly on top of the shirt was a simple brown silk cravat. Chase stood, clothed only in his drawers, checking the new clothes and wondering how he'd gotten talked into taking Lacy on a picnic.

All week long he had suffered nine kinds of hell, lying awake each night, knowing that Lacy was so near yet unattainable. Somehow, he had found the strength to remain in his room. With restraint that he didn't know he possessed, he avoided taking advantage of a very tempting situation. Now he would have to spend the afternoon with her alone. That was asking a bit much of a man as lusty as he.

He hoped he could trust himself to remain a gentleman. He gave himself a stern look in the mirror, reminding himself of a young lady named Leslie; then he dressed in his new clothes. The bed creaked from his weight when he sat down to put on his boots.

When he stood before his mirror and brushed his blue-black hair, he noticed a slight tremor in his hand. He wasn't surprised. He just wondered if it was due to thoughts of his past with Leslie or his future with Lacy.

Chase pulled the covered buggy up beside a crystal-clear lake. The hardwood trees that ringed the lake were heavy with gold, red, russet, and orange leaves, looking like a giant patch-work quilt that had been thrown carelessly by the hand of God. In the middle of the stand stretched a small clearing that bordered the lake. The cove was completely cut off from the outside world. It was a perfect place for a lovers' tryst, Chase thought uncomfortably.

"Oh, Chase, it's beautiful!" Lacy breathed, interrupting his dangerous train of thought.

"Not half as beautiful as you," he said gallantly as he handed her down from the carriage.

"Thank you," Lacy said. She was momentarily dis-comfited. She wasn't accustomed to idle flattery from Chase, but she knew how to play the game. Batting her lashes and pasting on a sweet simper, she assumed the role of a coquette. "Kind sir, you are good for a girl's ego." Her drawl was slightly intensified. "I'm afraid you have spoiled me. What will I do after you take me home? I know. You'll have to send over at least a compliment a day by messenger or I shall surely perish."

"Maybe today will never end," Chase said cryptically.

He offered Lacy his arm and escorted her to a secluded spot that was cushioned with lush green grass and sheltered by a massive oak tree. Then, taking blankets from the rear of the carriage, he made a soft pallet under the tree and chivalrously seated Lacy upon it.

Finally, he retrieved the large picnic basket that Cook had filled with fried chicken, potato salad, fresh bread, fried apple pies, crystal, china, silver cutlery, and white wine. He placed it beneath the tree. While he spread the food around them, Chase surreptitiously studied the picture Lacy provided.

The sun was filtering through the foliage of the stately oak, causing shafts of light to reflect off of her silken curls. Her partially shaded face looked to him like hand-fashioned ivory porcelain. Her peach-colored cheeks were delicately smudged, and her lips resembled two pale pink rose petals bathed in morning dew. Lips like that were created for kissing.

He shifted uncomfortably and cleared his throat. "I'm starving. How about you?"

Lacy smiled. "Uhm."

In silence, they picked at their food, neither of them truly hungry. After they had partially repacked the basket, Chase handed Lacy a goblet of wine.

"Thank you."

With his own glass cradled between his palms, Chase leaned against the tree. Once again, he studied Lacy intently.

She shifted uncomfortably under his potent stare. He was so close she could feel his warmth through her sleeve. The breeze carried his spicy scent to her, and she shivered.

"Are you chilled?" he asked as he set his wine aside and removed his jacket.

"No," she answered simply and offered him a tremulous smile.

His brow creased with confusion as he placed his folded jacket beside his hip.

The silence was deafening, but neither of them spoke. They were aware of every breath the other drew. So much so, that after a moment they were breathing in unison.

"Why?" he asked softly.

Though his voice was low, Lacy jumped. "Excuse me?"

"Why?" he asked again.

"Why what?"

"Why haven't you told anybody that I'm an Indian?"

"Why should I?"

"Well, because," he answered, exasperated. The spell that had hovered over them was broken.

Lacy was unaccountably put out with him for ruining a perfectly beautiful moment. "Because why?" she asked, stiffening her spine.

"Because you know."

"I know many things, but that doesn't mean I have to shout them to the world, does it?"

"You're just being difficult," Chase snapped. He didn't like Lacy making little of something so important to him. "This is important. I would think at least you'd want to inform my grandparents that their grandson is not what they think he is."

"Maybe you are what they think you are, or maybe you sell them short, or maybe you just sell yourself short."

"What's that supposed to mean?"

"You're so smart, you figure it out."

Lacy turned her back on Chase; she found his suspicious attitude irritating. It was almost as if he thought she had an ulterior motive for keeping his background a secret. Truth to tell, his being an Indian just didn't seem very important to her.

Chase moved so quickly that Lacy pressed her side into the tree. But when he knelt in front of her, and his faded blue gaze met her eyes, she relaxed a bit.

"I just can't figure you out."

"Not many can," she whispered, watching him warily.

"I'm sure." He smiled slightly, then cradled her jaw in his palm. "I need to know why you're keeping my secret."

Lacy rolled her eyes heavenward, but Chase kept his hold on her face. She covered his hand with her own. "Chase, I didn't even know it was a secret. I assumed if you wanted people to know that you were half Indian, you would tell them."

155

She raised her hands, palms up, and he released her.

"What difference does it make anyway? We're all half something. I'm half English; do you care?"

Chase took his place on the blanket beside Lacy, and she rested her back against the tree. He stretched his legs out in front of him and looked out over the water. With pain evident in his voice, he said, "It's not the same, and you know it."

"It is to me."

For a long moment, they were both silent.

"Do you really mean that," Chase whispered incredulously.

"Of course I do."

Without saying a word, Chase turned toward Lacy and removed her bonnet. If only he could believe what she said! She had sounded so sincere.

He placed his hand at the base of her neck and pulled her face forward. He looked into her eyes, then covered her mouth with his own. As tender as a sigh he kissed her, gently at first, then more boldly. He slipped the tip of his tongue between her slightly parted lips and groaned; she tasted of mint and cold tea. It was so good.

His blood ran hot, and he felt as if every part of his body was vitally alive. Somewhere in the back of his mind, he remembered his promise to act the gentleman, but the vow was too far back, drowned out by the rush of blood pounding in his ears.

He kissed her deeply, savagely devouring her lips, until they were both gasping for breath. When he pulled back, he stared her full in the face.

"Thank you for saying that," his voice came out in a harsh whisper.

The look of sheer gratitude on Chase's face touched Lacy deeply. Tears pooled in the corners of her eyes when at that moment she realized the pain he must have suffered, the rejection he must have experienced. How could she understand that? She who had always been pampered and adored; she who had never known rejection at any level.

Then the word *savage* sounded in her ears, and it was her voice that she heard. Had she really been so unfeeling as to call him that, that day at the gazebo? Pain twisted in her stomach, and she knew she had to make amends. So, she wrapped her arms around his neck and lifted her face to his.

He took what she offered. He pressed his lips to hers, moved them slowly across her cheek, and then clutched her to his chest. Murmuring words of seduction, he buried his face in her hair and lowered her to the blanket.

Light filtered through the gently swaying oak, casting wispy shadows across Lacy's face. With the tips of his fingers, Chase traced each shadow. He marveled at the texture of her skin and the look in her eyes.

What he saw there surprised him. Her look was raw, primitive, savage . . . yet wholly innocent. He slipped the pins from her hair, murmuring to her softly. Groaning, he covered her pliant body with his own, and he knew he was lost. His hands roamed everywhere at once; he couldn't have stopped if he'd wanted.

When he fitted her ample breast in his palm, teasing the tip through her fragile gown, he was flattered by the sentiment that bubbled from deep within her.

"Oh, glory!" she groaned.

Sixteen

When Chase captured her face between his hands and slowly placed his mouth on hers, Lacy was sure she would die. She held on to him as if he were the only solid element in a world that threatened to spin out of control, a world that she had never traveled through before, a world of vital sensuality, where the virile man above her was her only guide.

A kaleidoscope of colors flew before her eyes as he kissed her long and deep. Her heart raced in rhythm to the thrusting of his tongue, and she writhed beneath him when his hands moved down over her neck, seeking out every vulnerable point of her highly sensitized body.

He mapped her soft curves with adoring hands. The finely embroidered lace of her dress felt rough against his fingertips, in contrast to the soft flesh beneath the dress. Deftly, he unbuttoned her gown. He sucked in a deep breath when he uncovered the transparent chemise that covered Lacy's breasts. The filmy garment, brushing the backs of his fingers, left little to his imagination, and the sight of it was so intimate that it gave him cause to wonder at his actions.

Then he pushed the thought aside and massaged her warm flesh through the silk. When he shoved the offending material lower, he nibbled at her rosy peaks, feeling them rise against his mouth. Mindlessly, he slid a muscled thigh between her firm legs. The action caused their breathing to accelerate in tandem.

The spell that he was weaving about her was so potent she barely noticed the cool air soughing against her bare flesh, sensing only Chase's lips as he traced each inch of flesh he uncovered.

"Oh, Chase," she groaned.

He had been so long without a woman, and longed so desperately for Lacy, that Chase had to fight to maintain control. His hands trembled when he remembered that she was an innocent. It excited him beyond belief, yet it frightened him. He stilled for a moment, wondering if she knew what she was consenting to. He wondered if he knew what he was doing.

His hand rested on her rapidly rising chest; he could feel her heart pounding beneath his palm, and he looked deep into her emerald eyes. The depth of unfulfilled desire that he saw there was his undoing. Overcome, he fused their lips together once again.

Lacy had been romantically kissed a total of five times in her life, but never before like this. He captured her soul each time he assaulted her eager lips.

She had never felt so alive and in touch with her emotions as she was at that moment, cradled in Chase's arms. His long, hard body seared her flesh through his thick layers of clothing. She wondered absently what it would feel like to lie next to him flesh to flesh.

She squirmed ever closer to his heat, and boldly tracing the flexing muscles of his massive shoulders, she slipped her hands beneath his vest. He leaned back to help her shed him of the restricting garment.

The affectionate smile on her face caused his heart to catch. "I want to see all of you," he said huskily.

They were like two individuals who had been stranded in

the desert without water. Frantically, they tore their clothes away. In a scant second, they were lying below the proud old oak, flesh pressed to flesh from top to bottom.

They were beyond rational thought, just a writhing mass of uncontrollable desire. The late morning coolness was muted by the warmth of the passion flowing between them.

Chase raised himself up on one elbow and leaned over Lacy's gloriously nude body. He had traveled this country from coast to coast, but had never beheld such beauty in his life.

He deemed her perfect in every detail. Her face was that of an angel; her breasts were firm and full above her incredibly small waist. Her legs were lovely in form, and her most secret place was a beautiful, slightly distended mound of silken blond curls. His pale eyes and dark hands worshipped every inch of her body, setting her on fire.

Lacy's hands roamed over Chase's back, then lower; she raked the tips of her nails over his flexing buttocks. She had a vague memory of seeing him nude beside the lake at their first meeting. But she didn't remember him being so beautifully male.

The sight of his taut body, rippling with massive muscles, was almost as provoking as the sensual assault of his roaming hands and adoring lips. She knew that she should be appalled at lying nude under a man in broad daylight, but for some inexplicable reason she wasn't.

When Chase held her and kissed her, it felt right. He was tender, loving, and for lack of a better word, respectful in his treatment of her. There was nothing shameful in the way he loved her. It was as if she had been born for no other reason than to love and be loved by him. And she matched him, caress for caress.

Chase, almost mindless now with need, knew that he would have to take Lacy soon in order to retain his small grip on sanity. He had never before experienced such emotions. He was buffeted by feelings of overwhelming arousal, aching tenderness, fierce possessiveness, and all-encompassing desire.

This little slip of a girl had shattered his foundation, and here beneath the tree, she controlled him completely. He sensed that she couldn't wait much longer either, so he slipped between her thighs. Instinctively, she opened up for him.

He rasped, "Honey, open your eyes and look at me."

Trustingly, she obeyed.

"I want to make love to you now, but it's not too late to change your mind."

Lacy had no intentions of changing her mind. She wanted him too desperately. "No," she whispered thickly.

Knowing that it was Lacy's first time, Chase didn't want to hurt her. But he'd never been with a virgin before, so he didn't know what to expect.

Gently, he labored with the seat of her passion until he aroused her even further. The act served to excite him as much as it did her. He drew a deep, shuddering breath and poised himself, feeling as if her heat would surely melt him.

Slowly he slipped into her, groaning low in his throat at the feel of her warm, moist tightness. His strong legs trembled, but he halted several times, allowing her un-initiated body to adjust to the feel of him. Finally, he encountered her protective sheath, and sucking in a great breath, he held himself still.

Tenderly, he leaned forward and kissed her as she arched against him, splitting the barrier. His mouth muffled her cry of surprise and pain. For a moment, he saw the agony in Lacy's dark emerald depths. His heart constricted as one lone tear slipped down her cheek, but then his body thrust instinctively. He rocked slowly and sensuously inside her, and all pain was forgotten. She found his rhythm, and the two moved as one.

Lacy was astounded by what they were doing. It was as if a curtain had been lifted, bringing the world into focus. *So this is what put that smile on Melinda's face,* she mused. *No wonder!*

Her entire being was on fire. She was completely captivated by Chase as he labored lovingly to stoke the flame that was burning throughout her body. Her world was absolutely consumed with this gorgeous, delicious-tasting man who made her feel things that were beyond belief. Matching him boldly thrust for thrust, she flew with him above the clouds to a place that was all brilliant light and tactile sensation.

Chase was shocked at what a tigress his little peach was. She didn't behave like a gently reared virgin. No, she acted like a ravenously hungry woman. And there was nothing more exciting to him than to know that the woman he wanted desperately returned his feelings. And the way Lacy was panting and writhing beneath him, there was no doubt that she wanted him, too.

Chase wanted their lovemaking to last forever, but he knew that his control was rapidly burning out, evaporating from the heat of Lacy's passion. But he was determined that she reach fulfillment first. He slipped his hand between their bodies and rapidly massaged the bud of her desire.

Lacy dropped her head back to the blanket, and her eyes glazed over in ecstasy. Short, rapid breaths escaped from between her parted lips.

Just as she approached the pinnacle of completion, Chase leaned forward, covered her mouth with his own, and with one deep thrust carried them both over the edge. They lay pulsing in one another's arms, Lacy's sheath tightened around Chase's proud manhood, drawing the life from inside his body.

In all their passion, they were gloriously oblivious to the fact that they had an audience. Stuart Shephard, hiding behind a clump of trees, was shaking from head to toe, his face virtually purple from the violent hatred that he felt. Watching the loving couple cling to one another's perspiring bodies in the aftermath of their passionate experience, he had never wanted to do violence to another human being as much as he did then.

He growled low, "Enjoy it while you can, trash, because I swear before God and the devil that this day will be your last. I'll give you today, but tomorrow you will die. And I'll glory in feeding your dead bodies to the vultures."

Stuart had arrived at Towering Pines not long after Lacy and Chase had departed for their picnic. Earlier in town, Jared had told him that Lacy was well enough to return to Paradise, and he had invited Stuart to supper that evening to welcome her home.

Stuart was so pleased at the prospect of finally getting his property—as he thought of Lacy—away from Chase that he decided to go to Towering Pines, spirit Lacy away, and spend a romantic day with her.

He was irritated to learn that she'd already left with Chase. He intended to find the absent couple, dismiss Chase like a lowly servant, and then proceed with his plans.

When he noticed the buggy tracks veer off the main road to Paradise, he naturally followed them. He never expected to come upon the scene that lay before him.

Even now, the sounds of their desire drifted to him. But he couldn't watch them again. He crept away to where he had tethered his horse.

As he went, he comforted himself with the thought that the beating he'd given Annie would be considered a loving caress compared to what he was going to give Lacy for playing him for a fool. Although he never gave her credit for having brains or courage, he had, however, considered her a lady. Now he knew that such was not the case. She was just another low-life, immoral slut who needed punishing. And he would be God's agent for justice.

He jerked his horse's reins when he mounted. His teeth clenched as he thought of Chase, whom he hated even more than he did Lacy. Things had been all right until he showed up, but still that didn't excuse Lacy. He would punish them both severely in God's name and cleanse the earth of their vile presence.

Stuart rode away from the quiet cove, already making plans for a fatal retribution, plans that he intended to set in motion at Paradise that night.

Seventeen

Chase and Lacy perched side-by-side on a low divan in the library of Paradise manor. Since their arrival twenty minutes earlier, the couple had strained to sustain a light conversation, to avoid any awkward long silences. Though their passion had been sated more than once during the afternoon, they were on edge. Even now the rising sap of desire coupled with the deepening of their relationship disturbed them both.

The tense mood permeating the room was interrupted by a soft knock on the library door. Rising from her seat, Lacy drifted across the room to open the door.

Her graceful movement caused Chase's blood to stir all the more, and his expression grew pensive. He had never been so affected by a woman before, and he was disturbed.

The opened door revealed Linni, grinning sheepishly. When she saw her beloved aunt, she sprang to life like a frog on a hot rock. "Aunt Wacy, I didn't know you were home! I've been taking a nap with Mommy. Nobody told me you were here."

Lacy knelt and hugged Linni to her chest. "You didn't think I could stay away from my little angel or Mammy Mae's cooking for very long, did you?"

Linni giggled at being lumped in with Mammy's cooking as the reason for Lacy's return.

"Speaking of food, it's about time for tea. I'll run and ask Mammy to set it up in the great parlor while you entertain our guest." Lacy winked at Linni.

When Lacy straightened, Chase was at her side. He placed a warm, strong hand under her arm for support, and his unexpected touch thrilled her. She turned to him automatically.

Raising a tanned finger, Chase brushed back an errant curl from her forehead. With slightly parted lips, he stared at Lacy's still-swollen mouth.

She leaned toward him. Both, reliving their passionate afternoon, reacted to the overwhelming attraction they felt for each other. They forgot their little visitor when Chase lowered his mouth to Lacy's.

When their lips were so close that their breath mingled, Linni wedged her wiggly body between them. "Mr. Tarleton, did you come to court me today?"

The two lovers jumped apart as if they had been burned. Shakily, Chase dropped to one knee and hugged the blond-headed doll who had brought him back to his senses. "Now, why else would I be here?" he said with a big smile.

Watching Chase charm yet another Hampton female, Lacy raised a perfectly arched eyebrow, thinking, *Why else indeed?*

One by one the Hampton family congregated in the parlor for tea. For Lacy, it was a happy occasion. She had returned safely to the bosom of the family she loved, was sitting shoulder-to-shoulder with the man of her dreams, and had the whole evening ahead in which to enjoy them all.

Her gaze traveled around the elegantly appointed room, settling on her aunt and her sister-in-law. Miss Reenie and Melinda were already dressed for supper, and they looked as if they could grace the pages of the fashion magazines that

Lacy read religiously.

Miss Reenie, wearing a rust-and-cream-striped dress, smartly made of rustling moire taffeta, would do justice as a fashion plate from *Magazin des Demoiselles.* Her tawny hair was secured in a rust-colored snood; russet topaz teardrops dangled from her delicate lobes. Lacy sighed, wondering if she would be as lovely as her aunt when she was in her forties.

To Lacy, Melinda looked like an earth mother in her jade-green watered-silk creation. A narrow, white satin sash circled her torso just below the bust line. Her thick shiny hair was styled neatly in a knot and ringlets which complemented her heart-shaped face. Her jewelry of jade was sparse but sufficient for the simplicity of her gown. She would do well in *Englishwoman's Domestic Magazine,* Lacy decided.

Wiggling at her mother's side, Linni looked as if she had been spit-shined and polished. Lacy winked when she caught her niece's eye, and to her delight, Linni winked back.

Shortly before tea, Linni and Chase had romped and played. Linni had returned resembling nothing so much as a chimney sweep after a hard day's work. Mammy Mae had taken her in hand, transforming her from dirty ragamuffin to spotless angel in a time that was nothing short of miraculous. How Chase had managed to be none the worse for wear baffled Lacy.

She shifted her gaze to him. They sat together on the low periwinkle and rose brushed-satin sofa, aware of every breath the other drew. They appeared to be listening to Jay replay the humorous events that had occurred at Paradise during Lacy's absence, but they were not.

Jay was interrupted when Isaac discreetly entered the parlor and handed Lacy a note. She sensed something was wrong. Before reading the missive, she pulled a delicate lace handkerchief from inside her sleeve and dabbed at the perspiration on her upper lip. When she opened the note, she recognized Stuart's handwriting immediately. She read:

Dearest Lacy,

I am elated to learn that you have finally returned to Paradise. Jared has kindly invited me to share supper with your family tonight. I look forward very much to seeing you.

The reason for my letter is to inform you that I plan to ask your father for your hand this evening. I thought it would be prudent and courteous to be forthcoming with my intentions. I feel assured that you will welcome the idea of becoming my bride. In any case, I ask that you consider this proposal seriously.

Until this evening
Your love,
Stuart

Lacy reread the note intently while the others looked on. When she finished, she rose from the sofa and excused herself.

"I suddenly feel rather tired," she said to her family. "I think I'll go up to my room and lie down for a few minutes."

There was stunned silence in the room.

Chase worried that their amorous activities of the day had been too much for her. He experienced a sense of guilt and tried to catch her eye. But with her head bowed, Lacy hurried from the room.

Melinda and Miss Reenie followed close behind.

In the meantime, Jay retrieved the note which had fluttered to the floor when Lacy left the room. He uttered a silent oath when he finished reading it.

That evening the Hampton men and Chase gathered around the supper table, wondering if Lacy would be able to join them. Stuart strolled into the room, and they all stilled.

"Hello, Dr. Hampton." He offered Adam his hand.

"Stuart." Adam shook his hand.

"I'm here to see Lacy," Stuart said without greeting any of the others.

Surprised at Stuart's rudeness, Adam's voice was cool. "Lacy is still not feeling well. But we hope she will join us at some point in the evening."

Stuart purposefully kept his back to the corner where Chase lounged with a dark scowl on his face.

To relieve the tension in the room, while they waited for Lacy and the other women, Adam and Jared engaged in shoptalk. They were discussing a patient of Jared's who was scheduled for surgery the following week.

"We've got to talk to Crawford Long about the proper use of anesthesia," Adam said. "It's the coming thing, and we're all going to have to learn how to use it."

"Do you think we could meet with him early next week?" Jared questioned, anxious to avail himself of this remarkable discovery.

"Could be. I'll send around a note Monday morning to see if he has time," Adam responded, furtively glancing at Chase's dark expression.

Stuart was bored with any subject that didn't directly affect him, so he blurted out, "I've lost another one of my Nigras. She ran off a few days ago, and I'm going to go lookin' for her. Don't suppose you'd want to help me, would you, Chase?"

Chase schooled his expression and just stared at Stuart. The tension in the room was so thick, the men scarcely noticed Miss Reenie and Melinda move quietly inside.

Every muscle in Jay's body grew taut as he ground out, "Why did she run off, Stuart?"

"Damned if I know," Stuart said, shrugging his elegantly clad shoulders. "I treated her like a queen, and this is the thanks I get. Now I'll miss several days from work because some do-gooder helped her get away. Everybody knows that darkies are too dumb to escape without help."

With great effort, Adam overlooked Stuart's racial slur. "Haven't both you and Beau lost several slaves recently?"

Brad stiffened when Beau's name was mentioned. He watched Stuart closely and noticed a hard glint come into his eyes when he responded to Adam's question.

"Yes, we have." Stuart's tone was strangely accusing. "But this is one slave I'm not going to lose. I've gathered a group of men together, and tonight we begin combing the woods to find her. I expect her campfire will alert us to her whereabouts, and I'll have her back by morning."

Jay turned away lest Stuart see the horror on his face. Somehow he had to get Annie out of the county right away, but he couldn't take her himself. He was already committed to helping a family of slaves escape the very next night. He couldn't jeopardize a whole family for one girl. Yet he couldn't stand by while Stuart caught her either.

Jay's look didn't escape Chase's notice. He stared unblinking into the professor's troubled eyes.

Lacy, who was just then coming through the hallway, overheard the distressing conversation about Stuart's slave. Shaking, she entered the room to see Jay and Chase staring at each other. Looking first at Jay, then at Chase, a thought took seed. But first she had to get through what she knew was going to be a trying night.

Lacy had rested and composed herself after reading Stuart's note. Then she'd taken a bath in rose-scented water, meticulously applied a light application of fine French cosmetics, and dressed in an exquisite off-the-shoulder gown of melon-colored organdy.

When Stuart saw Lacy, he stepped forward and grabbed her arm as if she were a succulent pork chop for which he was a starving mongrel.

Jay slanted Chase a look only to see that his ice-blue eyes were murderous. Still, Chase's parents had trained their son to be a gentleman, so Chase remained passive.

Stuart knew full well that Chase was seething with jealousy at his possession of Lacy, so he played it for all it was worth. He leaned down to Lacy's ear and fairly purred, "Darling, I trust you received my note this afternoon." It was a statement, not a question.

The color drained from Lacy's face while she directed her troubled gaze to the floor.

"Princess, I want you to sit by me tonight," Jay said seriously, daring Stuart to object.

Lacy smiled her thanks to Jay and hurried to his side.

Stuart glared daggers into Jay's back as he seated Lacy, wondering if perhaps he should get rid of Jay after he finished with Lacy and Chase. Frankly, he had always hated the young professor. He even suspected him of being involved in the disappearance of slaves. *Yes,* he plotted, *he'll have to go, too.*

Meanwhile, Lacy sat staring at her plate while Brad and Jared seated the other ladies. Adam beckoned the servants to begin serving.

Lacy sat through dinner without eating, oblivious to everyone and everything around her. Her mind was racing ahead to the moment when Stuart would press her for an answer to his abhorrent proposal of marriage. She feared his reaction to her negative answer.

Her fear was not for herself, but for Chase. Having seen the violent looks passing between the two men, she dreaded the confrontation that was sure to come. Somehow, she had to see Stuart alone, politely refuse his proposal, and send him on his way before he created a scene. She had a feeling that if Stuart started something unpleasant, Chase would finish it without much diplomacy.

When dinner was over, Stuart hastened to Lacy's side. Leaning over her shoulder, he asked within hearing of all, "Dearest, would you care to take a walk in the garden?"

Chase's stare burned a hole through Lacy as she whispered, "Yes."

173

She rose and looked directly into Chase's crystal blue eyes. She hoped to see understanding; instead she saw only hurt. Completely at a loss, she decided to go with Stuart and be done with him. She would explain her actions to Chase later, hoping he would forgive her.

On leaden feet, she accompanied Stuart through the French doors out into the crisp night air.

In the dining room, the air was thick with tension.

"Ladies, if you will excuse us, I'll take Chase and the boys into the library for an evening brandy." Adam smiled weakly.

Miss Reenie and Melinda smiled sympathetically in Chase's direction, simultaneously nodding their heads at Adam. After the men had exited the room, Miss Reenie looked at Melinda. "Oh, glory," she said, borrowing her niece's oft-uttered expression.

Outside, with the moonlight guiding their way, Stuart led Lacy to a white wrought-iron bench at the entrance of the meticulously manicured garden. Neither of them appreciated the beauty of the evening because of the tenseness of the moment.

Stuart was no fool. He knew that Lacy would rather drink poison than marry him. But he didn't care. Marrying her was not what he was about. He wanted, rather, to punish her and Chase mentally for what they'd done that afternoon, before he punished them physically.

Acting the perfect Southern gentleman, he began, "Darling, you know what I wish to ask you."

When Lacy opened her mouth to stop him from continuing, he placed a long finger over her lips. "Shh, dearest, let me finish."

Lacy leaned back on the bench and clutched her hands in her lap. Nausea surged over her, and she was glad that she'd not eaten her supper.

"Lacy, I think you're the most beautiful woman I've ever seen, and I count it a great honor to be in your presence."

With every insincere word Stuart uttered, Lacy's panic rose, until it threatened to consume her. She didn't know how much more she could stand. In her mind's eye, she kept seeing two things: Annie's bloody back, and the pained expression on Chase's face. Trying to ease her mind, she sat rigidly and listened with half an ear to Stuart's rambling. Then he caught her attention.

"May I go in and ask your father for your hand?" he questioned flatly.

"Stuart, you are a very kind man whom I'm very fond of," Lacy lied baldly. "But I don't think I'm quite ready for marriage at this point in my life." She held her breath, awaiting Stuart's response.

"Dear Lacy, you are eighteen years old, are you not?" he all but sneered. At the moment, he recalled the sight of Lacy's tiny white body writhing beneath Chase's massive bronze frame, and his resolve to be gentle hung by a delicate thread.

"Yes, Stuart, as you well know from attending my birthday party scarcely a week ago, I am eighteen," Lacy replied sarcastically, her facade of civility cracking somewhat.

"Well, then, I should think that it's high time you took a husband and started a family," Stuart suggested with a lascivious grin. "You and I have been a couple of sorts for some time, and I think I deserve to be rewarded for always playing the gentleman. Your body is delectable, my dear, and it hasn't always been easy for me to keep my distance.

"So far I have managed to tamp down my ardor from doing the things I have been dreaming about, but now I would like to make you my wife. I'm convinced that once you have a taste of my body, you will be glad that you accepted this honorable proposal."

That did it! Lacy was so filled with disgust that her control snapped. She knew Stuart's proposal was anything but honorable. She recognized the difference between a man expressing affection and a cad proposing lust.

But before she could slap Stuart's despicable face, he was snatched from her side by a large, tanned hand.

Lacy jumped to her feet. She gasped and clutched her skirt in her fists. Chase held Stuart with one hand by the nape. Stuart looked like a pathetic puppet dangling from the strong arm of an avenging giant.

And from the black look on Chase's face, she knew he had heard Stuart's filthy proposal. But just as he drew back a fist to pound Stuart's fear-whitened face, Jay placed a steadying hand on Chase's rigid shoulder.

Jay searched Chase's face until he saw the uncontrollable fury leave his eyes. Then, as if he were of no more consequence than a filthy rag, Chase threw Stuart to the ground.

Jay stated decisively, "Stuart, Lacy is tired. You'd better say good night."

Chase stepped protectively between Lacy and Stuart, much like a young Stalker stepping between his Cherokee mother and the federal militia.

Turning on his heel, Stuart stomped away without a word.

Lacy collapsed onto the bench and heaved a sigh of relief.

In an instant, Chase knelt at her side. Placing his hand beneath her chin, he lifted her bowed head. The two gazed into each other's eyes, feeling no necessity of words.

Once the shock of seeing Lacy walk through the garden door with Stuart had worn off, Chase had realized that she was meeting with him alone in order to avoid a scene. While the other men had enjoyed their brandy, Chase had excused himself to search for Lacy and Stuart. His plan had been to stand nearby, undetected of course, and make his presence known only if Stuart got out of hand. Well, he had gotten out of hand.

Chase drew a deep breath. It was a good thing that Jay had followed him when he left the library, for when he'd heard the way Stuart was talking to Lacy, he'd wanted to kill him.

It never ceased to amaze Chase how quickly civilized men, including himself, could turn savage when someone they loved was threatened. And that was how he'd felt, savage. It was a sobering thought.

Jay and Lacy's eyes met over Chase's head. Understanding passed between them, and they nodded in agreement. Jay was the first to speak. "Chase, there is something we need to ask of you, but it carries a great deal of risk."

Chase's mind was still filled with Lacy, and it was hard for him to make sense of Jay's words. Finally, he realized that Jay was asking a favor of him. Chase nodded, encouraging Jay to continue.

"Before you agree so quickly, maybe you'd better hear us out," Lacy said and placed her hand on Chase's arm.

He realized then that he was still kneeling in front of her.

"All right," Chase agreed and took a seat beside Lacy on the bench, placing a comforting arm around her shoulders.

The night was peaceful with the moonlight filtering through the gently blowing trees. Lightning bugs flickered like minute burning candles all around them, and somewhere in the distance a grasshopper made a low chirping sound by rubbing its front legs together. But the tale of horror that Jay and Lacy related to Chase was in marked contrast to the comforting sights and sounds of nature.

"About a week ago, Stuart beat one of his slaves—a girl by the name of Annie—almost to death," Jay began. "When I found her, I took her to an old shack about twenty-five minutes from here. Lacy and I treated her injuries as best we could. She's much improved, but we've got to get her out of here before Stuart finds her. We need someone to help her escape to the Underground Railroad safe house in Hiawassee."

"Is she the slave that Stuart said he and his men are going to search for tonight?"

"Yes, and I'm afraid the poor girl doesn't have much of a

177

chance," Lacy interjected. "Stuart is supposed to be a big woodsman and tracker—at least that's what he claims. I'm afraid he'll find her if we don't hurry," she continued.

"I would take her myself, but the lives of others depend on me. There is a whole family of slaves that I have to help escape tomorrow night. Will you help her?" Jay asked.

Chase's face grew thoughtful. "Why me?"

"Many reasons. One, you've just traveled cross-country, so I doubt you'll have any trouble finding your way to the safe house. Also, you're not from around here, so I can trust you. And you hate Stuart as much as I do."

Chase couldn't argue with that. "We need to get her out of that shack as quickly as we can," Chase said suddenly, accepting the challenge to help the girl. "Stuart will look there for sure. Take her to the gazebo by the lake. Stuart won't ride up that close to your father's home in the middle of the night.

"I'll meet you there before daybreak. Annie and I'll be out of the county before first light. In the morning, one of you can give me instructions about where to meet the Underground in Hiawassee."

Jay clasped Chase's hand firmly. "Thanks, for everything. I suppose you two would like to be alone," Jay continued, "so I'll run now and see you in the morning."

Before Chase or Lacy could say anything, Jay was gone.

Hand-in-hand, the couple moved deeper into the garden, both lost to their private musings. In unison, their hearts pounded, each young lover anticipating the moments ahead; Lacy with all the exuberance of first love, and Chase with all the dread of a man forced to break her tender heart.

They walked in silence, looking up into the clear sky above. To Lacy, the twinkling stars looked as light as the morning dew, but to Chase, they appeared as heavy as his heart, their ponderous weight threatening to hurl them from the sky.

When they reached the clearing, Lacy turned to Chase, her hand still clasped in his. Warmly, she looked into his expressionless eyes. "Thank you," she whispered and flattened her free hand against his broad chest.

"For what?" he asked, past the lump in his throat.

"For rescuing me from Stuart . . . for Annie . . . for being you"—she dropped her gaze, and her voice barely broke a whisper—"the man I love."

Chase clenched his teeth until his jaw ached. This was going to be harder than he thought. But it was for her own good, he reminded himself, strengthening his resolve. He had decided to end his affair with Lacy; he cared about her too much to carry it any further. Sooner or later, a true gentleman would capture her heart. Then she would think she was stuck with a savage and hate him. He couldn't allow that to happen. He just wished he hadn't stolen her innocence.

"Lacy, look at me," he instructed gently.

Slowly, very slowly, Lacy raised her head. She looked him full in the face, unable to find her love reflected in his carefully controlled expression.

Chase knew the words he would utter in the next few moments would change their relationship forever, as would her reaction to his rejection. But still, he plunged ahead.

"You don't love me; you just think you do."

Lacy jerked her hands to her sides as if Chase's flesh had burned her palms. "And what gives you the right to tell me whom I do and do not love? Are you so wise and all-knowing?"

"No, honey, I'm not wise and all-knowing. If I were, I would know how to explain this to you without hurting you." He tentatively reached forward and placed his hand on Lacy's shoulder. "And I don't want to hurt you, sweetheart. I want to be your friend."

Lacy stumbled backward, out of Chase's reach. "Friends! Do you do what we did this afternoon with all your friends."

"Please let me explain. I swear I don't mean to hurt you; I'm trying to save you."

"Don't flatter yourself! You haven't hurt me."

The sparkling tears in her eyes told Chase differently, but he remained still.

"I was just toying with you." Lacy's laughter had a hollow sound. "Do you really think I could fall in love with a half-breed . . . a . . . a savage?" When the words left her mouth, Lacy wished desperately that she could recall them.

Before her eyes, the tender look on Chase's face hardened into a horrible mask. Lacy's hand flew to her throat, and she sucked in the cool night air. A nauseating wave of guilt flooded over her, but her wounded pride wouldn't allow her to retract the vicious words that she knew had mortally wounded Chase's heart.

Before walking off, Chase spat coldly, "That's just as I thought, Miss Hampton. But if I might impose on our friendship one last time, I have a request of you." He clenched his fists at his sides, and towering above Lacy, he ground out, "You stay the hell away from me!"

Lacy stood motionless until she could no longer hear Chase's booted footfalls against the marble walkway. Then, with the pieces of her broken heart scattered at her feet, she dissolved into tears.

Eighteen

When Chase returned to Towering Pines, he found Eli in his office, relaxing before a crackling fire with a snifter of fine brandy clutched in his hand. After the scene with Lacy, Chase wasn't up to seeing anyone, but it couldn't be helped.

He still planned to take Annie to safety, but he didn't quite know how to tell his grandfather that he would be leaving Athens in the morning. Knowing that the old man was thrilled to have him at Towering Pines, he couldn't bear to hurt his feelings. Unable to tell him the truth about his mission, Chase couldn't quite bring himself to lie either. He hoped that in the course of their conversation he would think of something.

"Hello, son. Fix yourself a drink and come sit with me a spell." Eli smiled up at his grandson, indicating the chair to his right.

"Thank you, sir," Chase replied.

After splashing a small amount of aromatic amber liquid into a cut-crystal glass, he folded himself into the chair at his grandfather's side.

"Did you have a nice evening with the Hamptons?"

"Yes, sir. They're a fine family." Chase shifted nervously in his seat.

"Yeah, they're fine folks. That Lacy is a pretty little thing,

181

isn't she?" Eli swiveled in his chair to catch Chase's expression. When his grandson's cheeks reddened, he stifled a chuckle. He misread the reason for Chase's discomfiture.

"Yes, sir," Chase murmured, downing a healthy swig of brandy.

He couldn't shake the pain that had plagued him ever since her hateful words. He had truly wanted to save her from himself, but did she appreciate it? Why he should care what the brat thought was more than he could fathom.

Eli recognized that he was making Chase uncomfortable talking about Lacy, so he decided to change the subject. There was something important he needed to discuss with Chase; he reckoned this was as good a time as any.

"Son, I've got something to talk over with you. I hope you'll be pleased."

Intrigued, Chase pushed his impending trip and hurt feelings to the back of his mind, giving Eli his full attention.

"I've noted with pleasure the interest you've taken in Towering Pines since you got here. I hope it'll come as no surprise to you that Miss Lizzie and I plan to leave everything to you when we're gone."

Chase's mouth dropped open. His grandfather had hinted that he hoped he'd run Towering Pines someday, but he hadn't thought of it quite like this. The idea of inheriting everything that generations of Tarletons had worked for was a bit overwhelming.

"Sir, I don't know what to say. . . . I haven't been here very long, and I have the Circle C to think about." Also, he didn't want to be this close to Lacy, but he didn't say that.

"I know you do, son, and I appreciate the fact that you feel an obligation to carry on where your folks left off; but I just want you to know you have a home and a heritage here, too."

Eli looked at Chase with such hope in his eyes that the young man was deeply moved. Chase hadn't known what he would find for himself when he came to Georgia, but whatever it was, this wasn't it.

Reaching over, Eli laid his old, weathered hand on his grandson's arm. "Son, everything I've got should be Evan's, but he's gone. So now it's yours. If you'll let me, I'll show you how to run this farm like my daddy taught me. It's the finest plantation in Georgia, and I think you're the man to keep it that way."

Chase knew that times were changing in the South, and that no one would be able to keep Towering Pines as it had always been. Truthfully, he wasn't sorry. But he couldn't tell his grandfather that. Men like Eli wouldn't understand.

Instead, he asked, "What about Stuart? Surely he expects to inherit from you, doesn't he?"

"Stuart has already inherited my sister's share of the Tarleton estate and has proven himself unworthy. I've got my suspicions that he's cruel to the slaves and doesn't love the land like he should.

"I don't like to speak ill of family, but I've got to be honest and tell you that Stuart Shephard loves two things: himself and money. Even if you don't take Towering Pines, God forbid, it won't go to Stuart."

When Chase remained silent, Eli continued, "I want you to think about this carefully, and if you decide to accept your daddy's inheritance, I'll begin training you right away. Then, when you're ready, I'll turn it all over to you, and Miss Lizzie and I will live out our remaining years quietly."

Eli watched his grandson's face carefully, trying to read his thoughts, but it was futile. Chase's face remained expressionless.

After a long while, Chase addressed his grandfather. "Sir, do you mind if I take some time to go away and think about all of this?"

"Son, you take as long as you want. Towering Pines has been here for generations, and I reckon it'll be here when you get back."

Setting his empty glass on the table beside his chair, Chase solemnly shook his grandfather's hand. "I'll leave before

183

daybreak. I'll be back when I work things out in my mind."

On silent feet, he left the room.

Chase returned to his room for a few hours' sleep after making the necessary preparations for the ride through the mountains to Hiawassee. There, he hoped to hand Annie over to the Underground Railroad for safe passage to the northern United States or Canada.

He knew that the trip would take several days at least, and the mountains would be rough travel for the girl. The nights would be cold in the higher elevations, even though the temperatures in Athens were still extremely pleasant. He had packed his saddlebags accordingly.

Chase undressed, blew out his lamp, and stretched out on his feather bed. He had better enjoy the next few hours because once he and Annie left Athens, there would be no such luxuries.

In the moments before sleep claimed him, he thought about what lay before him. He had no doubt that he could get through the posse without detection. It had been his experience that most white men were ignorant of the ways of trail life; he had a feeling that Stuart and his men were no exception.

Still, he worried about Annie. He would feel better when he was able to determine the extent of her injuries for himself. She had undoubtedly lost a great deal of blood and would be in a weakened condition. He would probably have to help her all along the way.

But if it was necessary, he would protect Annie's life with his own. Even though he was half asleep, his lips spread in a smile; it was ironic that a future plantation owner would think of protecting a slave with his life. He fell asleep with the smile on his lips.

He awakened before sunrise and concentrated on the task

at hand. After donning his buckskins and moccasins, he slipped quietly from the house.

Once in the barn, he retrieved the buffalo coat he had brought from The Nations. One never knew when such a coat would come in handy, and even though Chase preferred to travel light, with a woman along, he knew that would be impossible.

He stored the heavy coat on his packhorse and double-checked the supply of food, blankets, cooking utensils, and weapons he had packed before retiring. Finally, after tying a small sack of gold coins around his waist, he slipped his rifle into the scabbard on Spirit's back. He didn't know what perils might await them on the trail, but he wanted to be prepared for any contingency.

Chase gracefully mounted his horse and rode away from Towering Pines, leading the heavily laden packhorse behind him. In a few minutes, he arrived at the gazebo where Lacy, Annie, and Jay were waiting. His approach was so quiet the trio failed to hear him.

"It's time to go," he said in a soft voice.

As one, the three swiveled around to face him. Lacy refused to meet his gaze. The other two gaped at the sight of the virile young man sitting astride his magnificent stallion.

When he moved, his corded muscles rippled against the velvety-soft animal skin of his snug-fitting clothes, giving him a primitive look. Jay was shocked that his cultured friend was so ruggedly masculine. Gone was the sophisticated, intellectual gentleman. In his place was an Indian brave who looked to be one with the wilds of nature.

Retreating behind Lacy, Annie peeked curiously around her shoulder. She had never seen a white man quite like this before. Chase looked like he could eat nails and spit bullets.

Lacy spoke coldly. "Finally, you're here."

Jay jerked his head in her direction, wondering at the animosity in her voice.

"We were afraid that Stuart and his bunch would find us before we could leave. Annie and I considered leaving you behind," she taunted.

Chase turned to Lacy. She was dressed in a black velvet riding habit, expensive black leather boots, and a flowing black cape which was tossed carelessly over her saddle. She had dressed Annie in a similar black broadcloth costume with the exception of one item.

"What in hell do you have on your hands?" Chase spat at Lacy.

Lacy clenched her teeth. "Yellow Swedish leather gloves. What in hell do you think?"

"Lacy!" Jay was shocked.

"And what do you mean, we?" Chase ignored Lacy's fashion information and her unladylike language.

"I've decided to go with you," Lacy remarked flatly. "Annie is still sick from her beating, and she needs medical treatment. I have to be along to care for her. Besides, she won't go with you alone."

Lacy purposefully left the insulting taunt hanging in the air.

Chase bristled. Through clenched teeth he growled, "You aren't going."

Annie ducked her head behind Lacy, hiding from Chase, while Jay looked from Chase to Lacy, his jaw loose on its hinges.

Lacy drew herself straight. "I most certainly am!"

Chase slipped from the saddle, closed the distance between himself and Lacy, and leaned down in her face.

"Hell no, you're not! I don't intend to risk this girl's life by hauling a spoiled, self-serving brat with yellow gloves over those mountains!"

Lacy looked ready to explode, but before she could speak, Jay intervened. "Chase, Lacy can ride well. She won't be a burden."

186

Chase was unmoved. His eyes were still trained on Lacy's face.

"Annie needs her, and she'll be afraid without her," Jay said, then wedged himself between Lacy and Chase. "Chase, your cousin did this to her."

That bit of logic penetrated Chase's reserve, but Jay was unaware of this. Desperately, Jay asked, "Lacy, don't you have any other gloves?" Personally, he thought Chase was making a big deal of Lacy's clothing, but one never knew a man's quirks.

"Yes." Lacy glowered at Chase. "Lavender kid!"

Chase cursed, finally able to get a word in. "Mount up!"

Jay was still hopelessly confused, but relieved to see that Chase had relented.

Deep in the recesses of Chase's mind, a part of him was pleased that Lacy was going along. The thought of spending several days in the wilderness with her excited him. Fool that he was!

At the same time, her presence worried him, for reasons other than his wounded pride. His job would be doubly hard now that he had two women to care for instead of one. And if anything happened to either of them, he would never forgive himself.

Mounting up, he questioned a bewildered Jay, "Does *she* know where we're supposed to be going?"

Lacy seethed. The ape couldn't even call her by name. Not that he'd ever called her Lacy anyway; it was always Sweet Georgia Peach, or honey, or sweetheart, or some other syrupy address. But she didn't think he would be doing that anymore, and she hated to admit that it bothered her more than a little.

"She does. I've drawn you a map to Hiawassee. I understand that Harriet Tubman is there picking up other runaways. She'll be at a safe house down by the creek."

Turning to his sister, Jay instructed, "Princess, show

187

Chase the map."

Jay felt better. He knew Annie was in good hands and was convinced that Chase could handle most anything, with the possible exception of Lacy and her fashion choices.

He did fear, however for his sister's reputation. Although Chase was a perfect gentleman, when it became widely known that Chase and Lacy had spent their nights together unchaperoned—as they would once they turned Annie over to the Underground Railroad—they would have to marry.

No self-respecting Southern gentleman would dare marry Lacy after she spent the night with a virile young man like Chase, her considerable beauty and large inheritance notwithstanding. She would be considered soiled goods.

Jay had lain awake all night feeling guilty for putting his innocent sister into such a position, but with the life of another human being at stake, Lacy's risk seemed small in comparison. After viewing the tenseness between them now, however, he doubted Lacy and Chase would find marriage a viable solution.

Lacy solved the problem. She too had lain awake during the night, but her time had been well spent. Knowing that Jay would be leaving for parts unknown with a group of slaves, she had come up with an explanation for both of their absences.

"Jay, I have a letter for Daddy that I want you to put on my nightstand before you leave this morning."

Jay opened the letter and read:

Daddy,
   I am so distraught about Stuart's proposal that I need to get away. Jay has offered to take me to Cousin Billie's in Chattanooga for a nice long visit. Forgive me for not saying goodbye, but we needed to get an early start. I love you and will contact you soon.
   Your daughter,
   Lacy

A satisfied smile lit Jay's face. "You're a sneaky little wench, you know that?"

For the first time since Chase's arrival, Lacy smiled. "I take after my brother."

"Which one?" Jay threw back rhetorically, then walked over to Annie.

She had climbed atop a gentle gelding. "Annie, Chase is a good man. He'll take care of you and see you safely to freedom," he reassured the frightened young woman, patting her slender hand. "You can trust him."

"Yes, sir, Mistah Jay." Her voice broke when she whispered, "I thank you for all you did for me." With tears in her dark brown eyes, she leaned down and squeezed Jay's hand. "Thank you for all my people, Mistah Jay. God bless you."

Jay cleared his throat over the lump rising there and faintly nodded his head.

"Well, let's be off. The sun'll be up before we know it," Chase said, settling into his saddle in preparation for the long, grueling trip.

Lacy, settled atop Precious, drew alongside him, but she didn't spare him so much as a glance. Her attitude irritated Chase and convinced him that it was going to be a long, hard trip. And he wasn't even taking into consideration the difficulties of trail life!

"Chase, you watch your back, you hear?" Jay called. He stood beside the gazebo until the trio was out of sight. Quickly, he walked back to the manor house, feeling the enormity of the secret life he led.

Part Two

I raise my eyes unto the hills;
from where does my help come?

Prayer of Chief John Ross
Georgia, 1838
Outset of the Trail of Tears

Nineteen

Chase led the two women over the fields, toward the mountains. They had traveled less than two miles when he stopped. He turned to the women abruptly. "Do just as I say without question. Get off your horses and follow me into this gully."

Quickly, they dismounted. Chase led Spirit and the packhorse down into a shallow gully. When he whispered something into Spirit's ear, the great stallion lay down flat on his side.

He then turned his attention to Precious. He wrapped his right arm around the mare's head and placed his left hand on the side of her massive jaw. Gently, he twisted the horse's head until she went down beside Spirit. She struggled to rise, but Chase held her down.

"Lie over her neck," he whispered to Lacy, "and put your hand over her nostrils." His lips twitched suspiciously. "And lose those damn yellow gloves."

Without acknowledging his last remark, Lacy did as she was instructed.

Annie flinched when Chase stepped close to her, but he didn't notice. He repeated the procedure with her mount, then stepped away. Annie lay over the gelding's neck and placed her trembling hand over his nostrils. Sweat popped

193

out on her brow, and she sucked in volumes of air through her mouth. Luckily, her mount proved more docile than Precious.

Lacy could see that the young black woman was suffering, and she was deeply worried about her. If Annie opened her wounds and lost more blood, she could die. But if she was captured, she would suffer something worse than death. Lacy sighed resignedly; this was the lesser of two evils.

Annie and Lacy didn't know what was happening, but they had the uneasy feeling that they were about to be discovered. Lacy reached over and clasped Annie's trembling hand. In silence, both women prayed.

Chase quickly pulled up handfuls of dry grass from the sides of the gully and spread them over Lacy, Annie, and the three horses. He then repeated the earlier procedure with the packhorse, covered himself and the reclining animal with grass, and waited.

Shortly they heard the sound of horses' hooves, pounding against solid earth, and the muted voices of Stuart and his men. The men rode up to the edge of the gully. The morning darkness and the layer of grass hid the people and the horses below.

"Damn you, Bart. You led us over here to look at a ravine filled with dry grass." Stuart's voice was clearly recognizable.

Annie's eyes teared, and she bit her lip to stifle a cry of terror.

"Sorry, boss. I sure thought I saw four horses over this way. Guess my eyes are getting a little dim in my old age."

"You're damn right they are," replied another man irritably. "From now on we'll listen to Stuart. He's the best tracker and hunter in these parts, so let him run the show."

Lacy and Chase recognized Beau's voice.

"Let's get out of here," Stuart spat in disgust. "I'll catch that worthless Nigra if it's the last thing I do."

His subsequent threats were swept away by the cool

morning breeze as they rode off in the direction from which they'd come.

After a while Chase and Spirit rose in unison. Chase helped Lacy and Annie do the same. Immediately their horses rose, snorting clouds of white smoke, anxious to get out of the gully.

A slightly shaken group mounted up and rode off into the darkness, heading toward the North Georgia Mountains.

Their near encounter with the men who were combing the woods for Annie made Lacy realize that this trip was not going to be an enjoyable lark. For the first time, she understood how much danger they were in. One mistake on her part could prove fatal for Annie.

She glanced at Annie and was relieved to see that she sat her horse well. Lacy fervently hoped Annie's strength would hold until they stopped for the night, whenever and wherever that would be. She looked around, and even though she was only minutes from her home, her surroundings were unfamiliar.

She was surprised at the route Chase was traveling. She had ventured north many times with her father and brothers, but they had always meandered around farm houses and traversed through towns, following the main roads.

But Chase led them quickly and quietly through the woodland. Lacy saw no flickering lights from civilization, and fortunately they encountered no one. It was as if the three of them were all alone in the world.

Somehow, she felt uneasy. After all, what did she really know about Chase? Other than the fact that she had given him her innocence, and he had dumped her like a pail of overripe garbage.

"Mr. Tarleton, where are you taking us? Don't you think we'd better follow the road?" Her voice sounded more haughty than she intended.

"What's the matter," he asked sarcastically. "You afraid a half-breed savage is too ignorant to find his way?"

Stiffening her spine ramrod straight, Lacy refused to answer his insult . . . and jerked her bright yellow gloves back on.

Despite their heated exchange and her smoldering anger, when dawn came, Lacy was overwhelmed by the magnificent scenery. The bright-colored autumn foliage glistened in the caressing rays of the early-morning sunlight. The mountains were topped by fluffy, white clouds, softening the vivid colors.

She detected a certain wildness here that wasn't to be found near her home. Nature burst to life with the sounds and sights of birds, squirrels, and a thousand other creatures that made their home in the rolling hills of Georgia.

And in the midst of it all was Chase. Lacy slanted him a glance. She had never known a man like him. He was as much a part of the landscape as the timid young fawns that peeked at them from behind the trees. If she had not been following him closely, he would have vanished in the panoramic beauty of nature. But she'd die before she let him know she was impressed.

Occasionally Chase would stop, turn his head as if listening to something intently, then move on. At first Lacy wondered if he had all his horses harnessed; then she suspected that he wasn't addled at all. Rather, he appeared to hear noises she and Annie didn't hear, and smell aromas they didn't smell. Despite her misgivings, this provided her a strange sense of security.

Chase was well aware that Lacy watched him, but he ignored it. Passing through the high country, a blissful peace washed over him. His thoughts drifted back to his Cherokee mother whose beautiful face he pictured, just as if she were inches away. He could feel the warmth and contentment of her spirit, and as always he drew strength from it.

God, how he missed Nelda and the Indian ways she had taught him. His early days with her came alive now that he was among the hills and the forest. The mountains of North Georgia were full of her spirit and that of the Cherokee people. He looked from Annie to Lacy and wondered if the women sensed it. Probably not. He caught Annie's eye and smiled. She dropped her gaze, but not before Chase saw her lips turn up at the corners.

Though she had said nothing along the way, Annie's fear of Chase was dwindling. It was her physical condition that occupied her mind. With every step of her horse, fiery pains assaulted her back and chest. Her face was almost healed, but the scar would always be with her. She hoped she wouldn't bleed anymore or become too weak to ride. She desperately wanted to be no trouble to her companions, since they had done so much for her.

She was ashamed of her earlier reaction when Lacy informed her that Chase Tarleton would take her to safety. She feared the Tarletons because they were wealthy slave owners. She had begged Lacy to go with her, so Chase Tarleton wouldn't hurt her.

But, now that she was actually on her way to freedom and had met Chase, she wasn't quite as frightened. Still, she planned to stay close to Lacy.

They rode hard all day without stopping for lunch because Chase knew that the first part of their trip would be the most dangerous. If they were caught, it would be close to Stuart's plantation. His object was to put as great a distance between them and Shephard as possible.

Finally, they stopped for the night southeast of Gudalu-lu, Mount Yonah. The bald, rocky face of the mountain loomed up large before them.

The women, quite stiff, slid gratefully from their horses. For a split second, Lacy held on to her horse's mane, afraid her legs would not support her.

Then Chase took her horse, and she looked away. He led the animals behind an outcropping of trees at the foot of the

197

mountain and dropped their reins, surveying Gudalu-lu. He was pleased to see the huge landmark again after so many years.

Although he remembered a few things about Georgia, the preponderance of his knowledge came from his mother. She had described virtually every nook and cranny of the North Georgia Mountains. Listening carefully to the wind as he unsaddled the animals, he could still hear her haunting voice, telling the Cherokee stories about the mystery of their ancestral home, passing down to her son what generations of Cherokee mothers had passed down to generations of Cherokee sons and daughters.

The thought of Cherokee sons and daughters strangely brought Lacy to mind. Chase leaned his head on Spirit's back.

When he and Lacy had made love, he thought he would never be unhappy again, that somehow the loneliness he'd known over the past three months—the loneliness he'd known most of his life—was behind him. He had thought that he and Lacy would be one forever.

But when he'd heard the awful things Stuart had said to her, he realized he was no better. She was a lady for God's sake, and he'd rutted with her beside the lake like a randy goat. Was that any way for a man to treat a lady like Lacy?

Why couldn't she understand? Why couldn't she know that he had to sever their relationship. Didn't she realize that she deserved better? She couldn't let it go, couldn't imagine that he had her best interest at heart. She had to hurt him, to humiliate him. And he'd been as prickly as a pear with her ever since.

"Women!" He clenched his teeth against the emotional pain. "You stay away from those fillies, boy." He clutched the stallion's mane in his hand. "They'll do nothing but break your heart." Spirit whinnied indignantly as if he agreed.

Lacy and Annie stood where they had dismounted their horses, numb with exhaustion. Unaccustomed to long hours

198

in the saddle, they ached in places they didn't even know they had.

It was hard to tell which suffered more. Annie was more familiar with hard times than Lacy, but Annie's poor state of health had left her almost as drained as the aching girl at her side.

"I'll fix us something to eat," she offered. Even though she still suffered from Stuart's abuse, she felt that it was her duty as a black woman to serve the other two.

"I'll do it. You just rest," replied Lacy, starting in the direction Chase had taken the packhorse. But something she'd detected in the tone of Annie's voice stopped her in midstride.

"We're all equal out here, Annie," she said softly, startling the girl. "Chase and I don't intend for you to serve us."

"I can't let you wait on me. I wasn't brought up like that." Annie walked over to Lacy and looked at the ground, obviously discomfited by all Lacy had done for her already. "You rest, Miss Lacy, I'll see to the chores."

"No you won't, Annie," Chase's voice brooked no argument. He had heard just the last bit of the women's conversation, when Annie told Lacy to rest.

Lacy swung around to face Chase. He had slipped up on them and scared her out of ten years of her life. Just like an Indian! "Oh, glory," she whispered silently and put her hand to her throat.

He interpreted the look on her face as one of guilt. "Did you plan to come along and then let your patient wait on you?"

"But—" Annie wanted to clear up the misunderstanding.

"You don't have to take up for her, Annie. I didn't want to bring her along in the first place; but I did, and I sure don't plan to let you cosset and coddle her all the way to Hiawassee."

Lacy was wounded that Chase would think so little of her. But she'd walk over hot coals before she'd explain herself.

She shot Annie a look that communicated don't tell him anything, then placed her hands on her hips and glared at him.

Annie excused herself to go into the woods to tend to her personal needs. Lacy followed.

Chase felt a moment of regret at hurting Lacy's feelings. He really didn't think she'd allow Annie to wait on her. After all, there must be a little starch in her drawers; she'd ridden hard all day without a word of complaint. But his frustration and wounded pride had set his tongue in motion, and he hadn't been able to stop it.

Why hadn't she said something, defended herself, fought back, screamed at him? Maybe she just didn't care about his opinion. That was a depressing thought.

By the time the women returned to camp, Chase had started the fire and was frying sliced potatoes in a skillet. When the food was crusted black, the three filled their plates in silence.

Lacy poured them all a cup of coffee, and Annie brought the bread from the provisions. When Lacy handed Chase his coffee, she appeared to look right through him, increasing his feelings of guilt.

After they had eaten their fill and cleaned up the mess, Chase laid out blankets for the three of them. When he came to Lacy's bedding, Annie noticed that he patted it down especially well.

Lacy was busy getting the supplies she would need to change Annie's dressings. She was afraid that the hard ride had opened Annie's wounds, and she was anxious to check. Chase made himself scarce, aware of Annie's modesty.

Quickly and competently, Lacy cleaned the wounds, applied a soothing salve, and dressed them with fresh bandages. Annie thanked Lacy and took to her pallet. She was asleep almost as soon as her head hit the blanket.

But Lacy was restless. Chase had said they would have to extinguish the fire right after supper, so she took a small pail of water over to the fire to drown it. When she tilted the bucket, Chase stayed her hand.

Lacy looked up and detected a warmth in Chase's eyes. Despite her promise to ignore him out of existence, she met his gaze. A slight smile started to form at the corner of her lips, then froze in place.

She remembered that he had all but accused her of abusing Annie. Thoughts of the awful things Stuart had done to his slave came to mind. Was that what Chase thought of her? She jerked her hand away, spilling water over his deerskin moccasins.

He took the bucket from her, and with a blank expression on his face, he poured the water on the ground, then tossed the bucket away. "Cherokees don't put out fires with water."

He sprinkled dirt on the blaze until it died.

"How should I know how to put out fires? I've always had servants for that!" She threw at him.

Chase moved over to his bedroll. He was too tired to spar with Lacy anymore. He smothered a grin as she stomped over to her blanket, threw herself on the ground with a muffled groan, and jerked the blankets up above her head. Her abrupt movement uncovered her shapely derriere. Chase moaned and tried to concentrate on the stars shining above him.

The night was clear, and he could see Gil' LiUtsun'yi, shining brightly in the sky. He thought of the Cherokee version of how the Milky Way came into being. He smiled into the darkness when he remembered his mother telling him about the giant dog.

Before he fell asleep, he wondered what Lacy would think of the tale. How he wished she could understand the old ways of his mother's people, understand and appreciate the Indian part of him. Then, they might have a future together. But that would never happen! He sighed deeply.

The sound carried across the space to where Lacy lay. Unwittingly, she parroted his sigh. The day had confused

201

her, Chase had misunderstood her, and she had been frightened out of her wits; but she felt more alive than she had ever felt in her life. She knew she wasn't as worthless as Chase thought she was; still she had a long way to go. Somehow she'd show him!

She flopped over onto her back, and her muscles screamed in protest. If she tried very hard, she could learn something on this trip. If nothing else, she could learn her own limitations. And for a girl who had been smothered all her life, that was a valuable lesson.

But if she and Chase didn't quit fighting, she would be too distracted to notice anything else. She promised herself to speak to him, to establish a truce of sorts, and then finally, gratefully, she fell asleep.

Twenty

The next morning, after breaking camp in near silence, they continued their trek north. Lacy's resolve to speak to Chase melted in the light of the early-morning sun.

Before noon, they passed by Nacoochee. Chase stopped just inside a clump of trees that bordered the picturesque valley. He could see Indian Mound about a mile away, and he was flooded with deep emotions, which were reflected in the grim look on his handsome face.

Lacy rode up beside him and saw his pained expression. "What's wrong? Are we in danger?" she questioned, casting a nervous gaze in Annie's direction.

"No," said Chase. "Many Cherokees lived in these mountains." He turned in his saddle, gesturing to the panoramic vista that lay before them.

His voice hardened; he wanted to let her know what her people had done. He twisted his ruby ring as he spoke. "Twenty-one years ago we were driven from our home and forced to travel nine hundred miles overland to a place we had never seen." His face was ashen and hard as he relived the suffering of his people. "Up ahead is where they herded us, where we were held under armed guard."

"I'm sorry," Lacy breathed. And she was sorry. She knew the Cherokee had lived in Georgia at one time, but she didn't know the circumstances of their removal. Still, she herself had done nothing to them, and she couldn't understand why Chase seemed to hold her personally responsible. But sensing the depth of his pain, she held her tongue.

Chase moved on without further comment.

Annie had spoken little on the trip thus far, so when she spoke, Lacy and Chase were surprised.

"I wish there had been someone to help your people, like you and Miss Lacy are helping me now."

Chase smiled. He hoped this meant that Annie was growing to trust him. He stopped and turned toward her.

"There were some, Annie. Men like Henry Clay, Daniel Webster, and Davy Crockett tried to help, but it was a lost cause. Andrew Jackson wouldn't listen to them. Even on the trail, many of the soldiers who accompanied the Cherokees to Indian Territory were kind to us.

"My people tell of a man named John Burnett, who was a private in the army. Many nights he gave up his coat to a sick Cherokee child. I vaguely remember the night he gave it to me." Chase had a faraway look in his eyes. "I remember how warm it was."

His expression darkened then. "But some were brutal, like Ben McDonal. He was a teamster. I don't remember him myself, but Mama told me all about him. He lashed my grandfather one day with a bullwhip for no reason at all. Papa was old and feeble, and he damn near died from the beating that animal gave him. John Burnett saw the whole thing and gave McDonal what he deserved with the butt of his hatchet."

Suddenly, Chase dismounted and moved ahead a short distance on foot. When he came to a small grave nestled in the midst of the trees, he fell to his knees.

The grave was so small Lacy and Annie knew it had to be that of a child. They wondered if Chase had had a brother or sister die during the Removal.

Reverently, Chase brushed aside the leaves from the small

stone to reveal a few symbols of the Cherokee language carved into its face. Chase stared at it in deep meditation while the women remained on their mounts.

"My cousin is buried here," he said. "He died twenty-one years ago when one of General Winfield Scott's men struck him in the head with his fist. He was only six years old when it happened. I wasn't sure I could find his grave." His voice broke, and he looked away, obviously embarrassed by his show of emotion.

They soon left Nacoochee Valley, and Lacy was glad to put the place behind them. For some reason, she couldn't bear seeing Chase hurt. She had heard that a woman's first love was always special to her. That must be the reason she felt his pain almost as deeply as he.

Later that day they passed Tray Mountain on the right. While moving slowly around its base, Chase issued stern instructions to Lacy and Annie. "From now on stay close to me."

The two women didn't know the reason for his comment, but whatever the cause, they would do as he said. They knew the Blue Ridge, with all its beauty and majesty, was no place for the likes of them. The tall peaks, fascinating in their pristine beauty, were frightening. Teeming with hazards, this untamed land could consume a person in the blink of an eye, and they were wise enough to recognize it.

The threesome rode hard again all that day. At sunset, they made camp and ate a light supper before they fell asleep. Although Lacy was unused to sleeping on anything harder than a feather bed, in her exhaustion she slept like a baby. All thoughts of her talk with Chase were again forgotten.

The next morning, the women learned the reason Chase cautioned them to stay close. When they awoke he was nowhere in sight. Lacy assumed he had gone out hunting or scouting, so pulling herself out of her warm cocoon, she

205

started breakfast. Almost immediately Annie joined her and asked about Chase's whereabouts.

"Has that big, handsome man of yours abandoned us," Annie questioned uncharacteristically, only half teasing.

"You know better than that," Lacy admonished as she reached over to give Annie's arm a playful swat. "Chase wouldn't dare leave us . . . and why do you say he's my man? Last time I checked, Chase Tarleton was his own man. Not to mention that that big, handsome man would like to strangle me most of the time." Lacy opened her eyes wide in imitation of Annie.

Annie laughed, feeling good for a change to have something to laugh about. "I know he wouldn't leave us. But I'm not so sure he ain't your man. I've seen how he looks at you."

Wanting to bite her tongue as soon as the words were out, Lacy asked, "How does he look at me, Annie?"

"'Bout like he could eat you up."

Lacy secretly hoped that what Annie said was true. She rolled her eyes heavenward, and reminded herself that Chase didn't want her and she was an idiot to think otherwise.

The conversation was making her uneasy. "I'll be right back. I'm going down to the stream to get some water for coffee."

"You be careful now, you hear."

Lacy made her way down the path that led to the stream. She smiled gaily and swung the bucket as she went. This trip was turning out to be less hazardous than she thought at first. Annie's health was much improved, the scenery was breathtakingly beautiful, and with Chase for a guide, nothing could possibly go wrong. Now, if she could just protect her heart from that big, handsome man, all would be well.

She reached the stream and lowered her small pail into the water. Just then she heard a ferocious growl behind her. She turned and saw an enormous black she-bear not fifteen feet

206

away. "Oh, glory!" she squeaked.

Lacy surveyed the area for a possible avenue of escape. She was surrounded by insurmountable obstacles. The bear blocked her way back to camp, to her right she saw a heavily wooded ridge that was too steep for her to scale, to her left was a precipice that fell off abruptly into a small canyon, and behind her the stream flowed swiftly down the mountainside. The bear growled again, and the hair raised on the back of Lacy's neck.

Suddenly, Chase appeared from out of nowhere. He had arisen early that morning and gone downstream to greet Grandmother Sun as was his habit.

On his way back to camp, he had heard Lacy going down to the stream. When he smelled a *yonv* in the vicinity, he began running. He perched himself on the upper ridge above the path and sized up the situation.

He knew the *yonv* had recently eaten, for he could smell blood on her breath. Nevertheless, she could be in an ugly mood if she thought Lacy was depriving her of water. He had nothing but his hunting knife with him, so he wasn't quite certain what to do.

Then the bear growled again. Chase noticed Lacy cringe at the vicious sound. He jumped from the ridge and landed between Lacy and the bear.

"Thank God," Lacy breathed.

Chase stood erect with tensed muscles. He set his face hard against the bear, which was startled by his abrupt appearance. The *yonv* growled ferociously, but Chase stood his ground. With eyes glaring at the bear, he seemed almost to communicate with her. For a long moment the bear stood blinking at Chase; then abruptly she turned to the precipice and lunged down the mountainside.

Chase turned to see Lacy's face dripping with tears of fright. Before he took a step, she threw herself into his arms. He caught her and held her tightly. "It's all right now," he soothed huskily.

Every inch of his body was alive with the feel of her. He was flooded with strong desire. Trembling, he tightened his embrace until Lacy's feet cleared the ground.

Annie rushed down the path with a frying pan held high above her head. Her eyes darted about in search of the bear. When she saw Chase and Lacy together, that they were all right, she sighed relief.

"I declare, it scared the wits outta me when I heard that bear growlin'. I could just see Miss Lacy bein' breakfast for a grizzly!" she said, still holding the pan over her head.

At the sight of Annie prepared to do battle with a frying pan, Chase and Lacy burst into laughter. Reluctantly, Chase relaxed his hold on Lacy.

She stepped back, embarrassed that she'd thrown herself at a man who had used her and then discarded her. The thought didn't hurt as badly as before, however. He had risked his life for her, and that had to mean something.

"Annie, there aren't any grizzlies in these mountains, just black bears," Chase informed her, his gaze never leaving Lacy. While he was inordinately pleased that she'd run to him, he knew that that show of affection didn't change anything. He could never have her, and he would have to keep his distance.

Chase's look didn't escape Annie's notice. Just ahead of Lacy and Chase, she ambled back to camp, muttering to herself, "If that young'un gets gobbled up, it won't be by a bear."

"Did you say something to me, Annie?" Lacy asked, a bit winded from the excitement, bear induced and otherwise.

"No, just talking to myself."

Later that morning, they traveled farther up into the mountains, following an old Cherokee trail. The dark forest, dense with foliage, and the memory of Lacy's encounter with the bear had unnerved the women. They were determined to stay close to Chase. They sometimes whispered to each other when he stopped to listen to the sounds of the forest or sniff the wind, wondering what he could possibly be searching for.

He heard them and was amused.

That afternoon they passed through Unicoi Gap. They could see Brasstown Bald rising up on the left. Chase knew that everyone believed Tray Mountain was the highest peak in Georgia, but as he sat below Brasstown Bald, he thought it looked as if it were higher. After a moment, he moved on.

He didn't want to stray too far west. He thought it best to avoid the Underground Railroad that ran between Dahlonega and Blairsville and contact it in an area that was seldom used.

Late in the afternoon, Chase stopped once again to listen and sniff the breeze. For an unusually long time he remained silent, attune to the forest around him. Finally, turning to Lacy and Annie, he said, "Tonight we will stay with friends."

They soon came upon a clearing where three small cabins had been built. Several Cherokee men and women were scurrying about, performing their evening chores.

Chase, Lacy, and Annie had approached so quietly that even the Indians had not sensed their presence. When they emerged from the woods, the Cherokees were frightened.

Chase knew that they feared detection by white men. For twenty-one years, they had lived in fear of being caught and imprisoned, and to see strangers bearing down upon them was frightening.

When the oldest warrior reached for his bow, Chase spoke to him in the Cherokee tongue. "I am come," he greeted.

The Indians looked in amazement at Chase and his female companions. After a long silence, the old warrior raised his hand in a gesture of peace, saying "You are; it is good."

Chase knew then they were welcome. "We'll be safe here tonight," he said. "You'll get to sleep indoors in a bed for a change."

Lacy looked at Chase's face to see if he had meant it as a slur, if he still thought of her as a pampered brat. But he turned back to the old man before she could see his expression. Stiffly, she dismounted.

Chase slipped from Spirit's back, and a painfully thin, bronze-skinned child took the reins. He knew his stay with these people would be both pleasant and sad. It had been too long since he had been with his mother's people; he missed them. But the village was obviously poor, and it hurt him to see their poverty.

Chase followed the men over to a fire. He chuckled when he realized that Annie and Lacy were right behind him, his two little shadows. When he sat, they sat.

In Cherokee, he introduced himself as Stalker, the son of Nelda Cruce. The older ones had known his mother and the Cruce family well. They even remembered the little Stalker who had been taken away by the soldiers. To have him back among them was a good omen.

But they were overcome with grief when he told them of the brutal death of his grandparents, Little Spear, and his aunt Neta, and of Nelda's recent death from typhoid pneumonia.

With a sense of dread, Chase inquired on the health and whereabouts of his uncles. The information was sketchy, but the old warrior who had raised his bow said he had heard they had gone far to the north, beyond the Great Mountains in their attempt to escape the Removal. The last word he had received was that they were being persecuted by an evil white man near Johnsonville, Tennessee.

Then a young maiden approached them and showed Annie and Lacy to a cabin. She provided the women with a warm bath and a hot meal.

When she dressed for bed, Lacy allowed herself the luxury of sleeping in a gown. She pulled the fragile garment, made of virtually transparent linen, over her head. Around her neck, she wore a blue necklace of glass beads that had been

210

given to her by the young girl who was now making her bed.

Lacy smiled at the lovely young woman. She admired the beauty of her smooth skin, her high cheek bones, and her clear, black eyes. She wondered if that was what Chase desired, a black-eyed Indian girl, not a pale, blond, green-eyed girl who irritated him at every turn, a lady who wore yellow and lavender gloves.

She slid between the covers and smiled. Truth to tell, she had two pairs of black gloves packed in her saddlebags, and she only wore the outrageous gloves to irritate him. But had she irritated him too much? Her smile faded as she wondered where he was. Was he laughing with a black-eyed maiden, doing with her what he'd done to Lacy by the lake? Squeezing her eyes shut against the mental picture, Lacy turned toward the wall.

She tossed and turned long after Annie had fallen asleep at her side. Finally, she eased out of bed and wrapped a light blanket around her shoulders. She told herself that she wasn't checking on Chase, just going outside for some night air.

The outside fires burned dimly in front of each of the cabins. There was no one to be seen. The grass was damp on Lacy's bare feet, and she hiked her voluminous gown up to her knees to keep it from getting wet. Slowly, she walked to the edge of the light.

"What are you doing out here?" Chase whispered.

Lacy jumped; she hadn't heard Chase's approach. When she turned around, she was surprised to find him standing directly behind her, much closer than she'd thought. His special scent filled her nostrils, saddle leather with the slightest hint of woodsmoke. It was a pleasant smell, a masculine smell, a smell that set her heart to pounding.

"I couldn't sleep," she said nervously and stepped back from him.

Chase followed her close enough to feel the heat of her body radiating through the wispy thing she wore for a gown.

211

It didn't look sturdy enough to serve as a handkerchief, much less proper covering for a body as tempting as Lacy's. The blood rushed from his rapidly pounding heart to his swelling loins.

"Was there any particular reason why?"

"No, I just couldn't sleep." The way he was stalking her, Lacy doubted he had been with another woman. She was inordinately pleased.

Chase caressed her cheek, marveling at the nearly transparent look of her skin. It was almost as transparent as her gown. Groaning silently, he then dropped his gaze to her full, sensuous lips and touched a calloused fingertip to them. Slowly, he trailed his finger down her neck until it rested on the Indian necklace nestled between her breasts.

"Beautiful," he murmured.

"Singing Wind gave it to me."

Chase smiled, and his teeth flashed white against his dark face. "I wasn't talking about the necklace."

Lacy swallowed deeply. She wondered at the change in Chase's mood.

He ran his thumb over her slightly parted lips; her breath felt warm, and he scolded himself for pursuing her. But here in the village was the first time he had felt truly safe since he had left Athens. He didn't have to worry about Stuart; the lookouts of the village were on alert.

He could leave the worry to someone else for a change. But this gave him too much time to think, too much time to remember how good Lacy had felt when he'd plunged his life-giving force within her.

He slid his hand around to the back of her neck and drew her mouth to his. The kiss was gentle, stroking, reminding, coaxing, rewarding.

The blanket dropped to the ground when Lacy's arms encircled Chase's neck of their own free will. She strained toward him, and felt his hardness against her belly. He was so solid, so hot, so familiar, and for just a moment, she could

212

almost believe they were beside the lake, sharing love and satisfying desire. She moaned from the strength of the memory.

Spurred on by Lacy's response, Chase dropped his hand to her chest. He fitted one full breast into his palm, molding it to form a perfect globe, all the while drawing sweet nectar from her lips. His other hand lay possessively against her buttocks, all the more arousing for its inactivity.

When finally their embrace ended, Chase and Lacy stepped apart. Unbidden, the reality of the last few days returned. They knew what they wanted, but were powerless to attain it.

Lacy just hoped the animosity that had colored their relationship was gone. "I'd best get to bed now," she said weakly. She waited, but Chase didn't speak. "Good night, Chase," she breathed.

Chase watched her until she was safe inside the cabin. Then he let out the breath he had been holding.

"Good night, Sweet Peach," he whispered.

Twenty-One

The next day dawned bright for Lacy. She was relieved that she and Chase had bridged the gap, at least partially. After thanking their hosts, she and Annie stepped from the cabin. Her eyes immediately sought Chase.

He was walking their way, but something was wrong. He wouldn't meet her eyes.

"You'd better mount up. We have a long way to go today," he said cooly.

Lacy's face burned when she remembered what had passed between them in the moonlight. Maybe he just wanted her after dark, to satisfy his manly needs. In the light of day, he couldn't be bothered with her.

Damn him! She would learn her lesson one day. She would learn that she couldn't give herself to him physically because he wouldn't give himself to her emotionally. And as much as she hated to admit it, that was what she wanted more than anything.

She saw how he loved his people, how they were as much a part of him as the stars were a part of the night sky. Was it too much to want him to love her like that? Did he hate what she was that much? He hated bigotry when it was directed toward the Indians, but was it any different when he directed it at her?

215

And what was she? A spoiled, self-serving prima dona? No! But that's what he thought. She had tried so hard to change his impression of her. The last two days she had ridden until she thought she would drop, had bathed in an ice-cold creek, worn the same clothes, eaten burned potatoes, half-cooked bacon and hard, tasteless biscuits, and been practically devoured by a bear. And she had never once complained.

The stupidity of it all was that she had done it so he could overlook her family's wealth. Well, she couldn't help the accident of her birth any more than he could help his. And she was sick and tired of apologizing for it!

Sitting on her horse, she stuck her tongue out at Chase's retreating figure. She knew it wasn't very mature of her, but she just didn't care.

Chase was unaware of Lacy's action, but the old warrior he approached had noticed. He stifled a grin and nodded when Chase stood before him.

Chase handed him a gold coin. He knew it was probably worth more than all the village's worldly possessions, but it was important that it not look like charity. So he patted the old man's frail shoulder and said simply, "For the children."

The man's faded eyes misted, and once again, he nodded.

Throughout the day Chase was lost in thought. For the first time since he'd begun the trip, he was wholly unaware of the beauty surrounding him. His tortured mind claimed all of his attention.

The few hours he had been in the Cherokee village had served to remind him of his Indian ancestry, and how the Indians had been impoverished by Southern society. When he compared the poor Indians to Lacy's fabulously wealthy family, he was disheartened.

He wondered if Lacy's love for him was strong enough to overcome such diversities in background. He muffled a derisive laugh, thinking that he was taking a hell of a lot for granted. Lacy didn't really love him. Quite the contrary!

But she had come on the trip. Did she want to be with him? Maybe she just thought of all this as a great adventure and him as some fascinating creature. Such notions tormented Chase's mind for a greater part of the day. He had many questions and few answers.

The next day, they reached Hiawassee. After dark they slipped down to the creek where the Underground safe house was located. A black man named Lazarus lived there.

Frogs, crickets, and other night creatures were in full chorus along the creek bank, rendering their footsteps inaudible. Chase gestured with his hand for the women to wait at the corner of the cabin while he knocked on the door. He rapped two short strokes, paused, and then three short strokes. According to Jay, that was the secret signal at this safe house.

After what seemed an eternity, the door creaked open. Inside, Lazarus's black skin melded with the dark interior of the cabin. But the whites of his eyes reflected the brilliant starlight. "What do you want?" His shaky voice was a mere whisper.

"We need your help," Chase replied. He beckoned Lacy and Annie to come into the open so that Lazarus could see them. "We've been told that Harriet Tubman is here helping slaves in trouble."

Lazarus swung the door open and stepped out onto the porch. Sizing up the situation, he said apologetically, "You've just missed her. She left yesterday with her baggage and won't be back for two or three months." He turned to Annie. "I'm sorry."

By *baggage*, they understood he meant runaway slaves. Chase reached out his hand to the old man. "Thank you. We won't bother you further."

Lazarus nodded, shook Chase's hand firmly, stepped back inside, and closed the door.

Chase looked at Lacy and Annie. "We might as well leave. We can't do any more here."

They left Hiawassee and made camp some two miles to the east.

Lacy was disappointed, scared, and angry with Chase for the way he'd been ignoring her. She struck out at him. "If you'd gotten us here a day earlier, we wouldn't be in this fix."

Chase was astounded. "If I hadn't had to drag you along, I would have gotten here on time."

So I'm right, she thought. *He still thinks of me as a burden.* "How dare you use me as a reason for your failures? You big oaf."

"I guess we'll have to go back," Annie said, fear evident in her voice.

"No we won't. I'll take you to safety myself. We don't need him," Lacy said.

Chase laughed bitterly. "You couldn't take anybody anywhere. You're such a spoiled brat, you'd probably break a fingernail making camp and go all to pieces. Not to mention that you'd get lost before you traveled ten feet."

"You're so full of yourself, Chase Tarleton! If you're so smart, then tell us, where do we go from here?"

"I'll take Annie over the Smokies to my uncle's village. But you had better catch a train back to Daddy, because I don't think you can make it. And I'd hate to leave such an even-tempered young lady all alone on the trail," he sneered sarcastically.

"Where Annie goes, I go. And I'll keep up. Before it's over, you'll eat your words, just see if you don't."

Lacy jumped up and walked away from camp.

"Don't go too far, princess. I might not rescue you again, if a bear tries to make a meal of you."

Lacy's muffled oaths reached their ears, and Chase turned

to Annie with a huge smile on his face and winked. She coughed to cover her laugh.

For several days they traveled up into the Great Smoky Mountains. The scenery was breathtaking to all three of them, though the tension between Chase and Lacy was thick.

Chase led them past Clingman's Dome on toward Newfound Gap. The going was rough for the women, but it was safe. Not having seen a living soul since they left Hiawassee, it seemed that except for the teeming wildlife darting here and there, they were all alone in the virgin forest.

At night they always managed to camp near a mountain stream, since the mountains were richly supplied with water. The soothing, bubbling brooks lulled them to sleep at the end of each tiring day.

Chase was gentle and kind to Annie and cooly polite to Lacy. He wasn't really angry with Lacy. He just thought it a good way to keep her at arm's length. He could see that she was struggling under the burden of traveling through the mountains, yet without complaint. He hoped her anger with him would keep her occupied so that she wouldn't notice how hard the trip truly was.

Annie was still sore and somewhat weak from her wounds; both she and Lacy were rump weary from excessive riding.

Chase felt sure they were safe from capture, so he stopped often for them to rest. At every opportunity he pointed out landmarks of note to the women, telling the stories of the Cherokee and the beginnings of their life in the hills. Lacy pretended not to care, but he knew she was interested.

One afternoon Chase turned to Lacy and Annie. "We're close to a Cherokee village."

They traveled on another thirty minutes, when they came to a clearing in the mountains. Before them was a fairly large

Cherokee village composed of about ten cabins. Lacy noticed that the structures all seemed to be in a good state of repair. It was obvious that the people who lived here were carrying on a normal way of life, in spite of their hiding from white men. And they seemed to be having some sort of celebration.

"They're celebrating the Green Corn Ceremony," Chase explained before Lacy even asked. "I'm sorry we've interrupted them, but it's too late to turn back now."

The Indians halted their activities when they spied the three newcomers. Several of the men approached them with suspicious looks clouding their swarthy faces.

"We have come in peace," Chase said in the Cherokee tongue. "I'm sorry that we have interrupted the Solut-sunigististi. I am Stalker, the son of Nelda Cruce, of the *a ni wa yah* "(Wolf)" clan of the great Cherokee nation. I have come from Indian Territory bringing greetings from our people. The golden-hair girl with me is my woman. We are helping the black woman escape from bondage."

When the group looked curiously at Lacy, she wondered what Chase had said.

An old warrior, who appeared to be the chief, stepped forward. "I am War Eagle of the *a ni ka wi* "(Deer)" clan. We are glad to hear from our brothers who were driven from us. I remember Nelda Cruce and the little Stalker before they were taken on the Trail of Tears. You are welcome to come among us. We invite you to join us in the celebration. Your women will be cared for by our women." He turned to the other men and spoke to them rapidly.

Chase turned to Lacy and Annie. "We're welcome here. I'm going to participate in the Green Corn Ceremony with my people. You must stand quietly aside with the women. They'll see to your needs." Quickly dismounting, he padded to the circle of men in the center of the village.

Lacy was a bit put out at what she considered Chase's high-handed manner, but she was getting used to it.

Shrugging her shoulders, she and Annie joined the women who were standing on the fringe of the ceremonial circle.

The Indian women appeared to be ready to serve the men whenever asked. Lacy and Annie looked on in wide-eyed amazement and were soon caught up in the excitement of the moment.

Lacy tried to imagine Chase being reared in a village like this. It was certainly different from Paradise! But still nice. All the cabins appeared to have been recently plastered with red clay. Cedar twigs were tied to the posts of the cabins, giving a festive appearance to the whole village. It reminded Lacy of Christmas.

In the middle of the town the men sat cross-legged on the ground. One warrior stood in the center of the group, addressing them. Chase had taken his place among them as if he had always lived there. Lacy could scarcely take her eyes from him.

To Annie's surprise, one of the men in the group was black. He was dressed like an Indian and seemed to understand their language. From all appearances he belonged to the group. This unexpected surprise heartened her, making her feel that perhaps she would be welcome after all.

When the speaker finished, he took his place among the men. An attendant arose, took a large bowl containing a dark-colored liquid, and drank from it. Passing it among the rest, they did likewise.

After a while one man rose, crossed the clearing to the edge of the village, and began to retch. Slowly others followed until all the men had vomited and returned to the circle. Lacy was horrified. Even her cooking hadn't produced that result.

This act was repeated twice more that afternoon. By evening all the men were gaunt and weak, except Chase. His considerable size gave him an advantage. But the next part of the ceremony had an affect on him. The men took clay

221

pipes from their buckskin shirts and smoked a strong-smelling substance which weakened even Chase. Finally, they retired for the evening to separate huts, away from the women.

"Welcome to our village," a beautiful Indian girl greeted Lacy and Annie in perfect English. "I am Morning Star, the daughter of War Eagle. I know you are worried about your man, but he will be all right tomorrow. As for tonight, you are to stay with me in my cabin. In the morning there will be much work for us to do in preparation for the great feast. Come and I will show you where you are to sleep."

The girl's soft speech was like water rippling over smooth pebbles in a stream. Lacy felt a twinge of jealousy as she looked at the beautiful young woman. Chase loved his Indian ancestry so much she was sure he would prefer having someone like Morning Star. And no doubt the girl was very capable, used to a hard life.

Lacy tried to resent her, but when she looked into the young woman's guileless eyes, seeing only kindness, she chided herself for her negative thoughts.

"Thank you," Lacy said. "I'm Lacy Hampton, and this is my friend, Annie."

Morning Star and Annie nodded to each other.

Lacy continued. "You're right. I am worried about Chase." Though she'd die before she let him know it. "That black stuff they drank looked dreadful. What is it?"

"It is *pasa,* a bitter emetic that helps our men purge themselves of impurity. The Green Corn Ceremony represents a new beginning which we celebrate each year. It is important for the men to rid themselves of the past year's impurities."

Morning Star talked as she walked toward one of the cabins in the village while Lacy and Annie followed. After casting a sideways glance at the cabin where Lacy knew Chase to be, she followed Morning Star inside.

The dwelling was immaculately clean and in order.

Morning Star led them to a second room, where a small bear oil lamp illuminated the interior. The small cubicle contained a bed made of blankets spread over a straw mattress. Thanking her for her hospitality, Lacy and Annie, without even taking time to undress, lay down on the bed, totally exhausted from the day's activities.

As Morning Star extinguished the lamp and left, Lacy lay awake, thinking about Chase. She hoped he would be all right. His drawn face continued to torment her mind until she was lost in sleep.

The next morning, Morning Star awakened them. "I have clothes for you. The women will join the celebration today in the last sacred dance, and you are invited to dance with us. Since we all wear our finest clothes, I have found some suitable for you. You will keep them as a gift from the Cherokee people."

She handed Annie a beautiful, soft, beige deerskin dress with matching moccasins. The dress was fringed on the sleeves and around the hem.

Annie accepted the clothes and held them close to her breast. With tears in her eyes, she whispered, "I've never had anything as fine as this in my whole life. Thank you, Morning Star."

Morning Star was pleased with Annie's response. Next she turned to Lacy. "I have a dress for you that I think will look beautiful with your yellow hair." She brought out a magnificent, white fawn-skin dress that was as soft to the touch as fluffy cotton. Like Annie's, it had fringes on the sleeves and the bottom of the skirt. It was decorated with blue translucent beads that reminded Lacy of Chase's eyes.

Lacy was at a loss. With all her father's wealth, she had never bought a dress as lovely as this. She held it close, smelling its earthy aroma and feeling its smooth, soft texture. "Morning Star," she breathed. "In all my life no one has ever given me a nicer gift. I will always cherish it."

"I'm glad you like it. And now here are headbands to go

with your dresses." She handed Lacy and Annie beaded headbands made of the same material as their dresses.

"Both of you will look beautiful today," she said sincerely. "When you finish dressing, come outside. The final part of the celebration will begin soon." Morning Star rushed out like a child on Christmas morning in search of Santa's stash.

Annie and Lacy donned their new clothes and readied themselves for the day's festivities. Lacy brushed her hair until it shone like liquid gold, flowing freely down her back past her tiny waist. As a finishing touch she slipped the headband over her hair, onto her forehead. Then, turning to Annie, she helped her with her hair and headband.

When they stepped outside, Chase was standing on the porch. "You both look beautiful, like a moonlit summer night and a glorious sunrise." Both girls blushed outrageously. Chase then bowed and walked away.

Twenty-Two

The women of the village were busily washing the cooking and eating vessels when Lacy and Annie joined them. The men resumed their places in the circle to continue the ceremony.

Lacy's heart was as light as a feather. She cherished the words Chase had spoken. It seemed but a moment later to her when the sun passed its midday cycle and started to decline. She saw a priest appear in the circle of men, dressed in white buckskin.

She moved closer to see everything clearly. The priest wore a waistcoat that fitted around him like a skirt and a headdress of white swan feathers. He took a piece of dry poplar wood with a hole partially drilled in it. Into the hole he fitted a circular stick that could be turned rapidly by being rubbed briskly between the hands. He turned the stick for a few minutes, and a small flame burst forth. He added pitch to the flame and fanned it with birds' feathers.

When the fire was well lit, the priest placed it into an earthen vessel which he set before the assembled crowd. While he made yet another speech, the women drew near. In a few minutes, an attendant took a flaming brand outside to the waiting women, who then took the brand and started new fires in their cabins and cooking pits.

At this point another assistant rose and began to dance rhythmically around the sacred fire. Two others beat drums in rhythm to his movements. Soon all the men were dancing. Then the priest beckoned the women to enter the circle and join in the dance.

Morning Star took Lacy and Annie by the hand and led them into the midst of the dancing Indians. Lacy was soon caught up in the rhythm of the drums, swaying to the primitive beat along with the others. Her golden hair fell down over her shoulders and brushed her white fawn-skin dress, giving the appearance of early-morning sunlight shining on a white cloud.

Chase watched her out of the corner of his eye. In all his life he had never seen anything more beautiful than Lacy participating in the ancient ceremony of his people. For the moment, he could almost forget their differences—almost believe that her heart was as Indian as his—almost but not quite.

That evening they celebrated with a great feast: meat, fish, vegetables, and fruits of various kinds. Smoking their pipes, the men talked of the glorious olden days when Cherokee land extended as far as the eye could see.

Everyone seemed at peace. And Lacy, too, felt that contentment. She sat close to Chase, listening intently, even though she did not understand what was said. It was the spirit of the words that touched her. More than ever, she wondered about the Indian way of life. That indefinable element that was wild and free, yet calm and stable. It didn't need to be articulated to be experienced. And as they sat, not speaking, just feeling each other's presence, she and Chase met on a common plane, and something real passed between them.

Annie sat next to Lacy, lost in thought, watching long, red and purple fingers in the sky. Suddenly, the black man walked up in front of her and said boldly, "My name is Jeff

226

Jinkins. I couldn't help but notice how beautiful you are, when you danced with us this afternoon."

Annie jerked her dark eyes around in shock. She was at a loss for words. Finally she responded. "I'm Annie. These are my friends, Miss Lacy Hampton and Mr. Chase Tarleton."

Jeff greeted Chase in the Cherokee tongue, asking him if both Annie and Lacy were his women. Chase assured him that one woman was enough for him. Reaching down, Chase laid his hand on Lacy's shoulder. Again, Lacy wondered what he had said about her.

"Why is the beautiful black woman traveling with you?" Jeff queried.

"Annie was a slave back in Georgia. My woman and I helped her escape to Hiawassee. We were told that Harriet Tubman would be there, but we were too late. She left the day before we got there. Now we're crossing the mountains, hoping to find a place where Annie can stay."

Looking into the man's dark eyes, Chase felt a flicker of recognition. He could have sworn he'd seen him somewhere.

"It wasn't too many years ago when I was in the same fix myself," Jeff said to Chase, kneeling before Annie. "Nearly froze to death in these mountains and would have if it hadn't been for these Indians. They found me and nursed me back to life. I told them that I had worked for an Indian family once. That was enough for them to make me one of their tribe." Jeff related the story with obvious affection for his adoptive people.

With a sense of recognition nudging him even stronger, Chase asked, "Who were the Indians you worked for?"

"I worked for a fine Cherokee woman who lived close to Clarke County Georgia, back before they ran all the Indians off. Her name was Nelda Cruce. Actually, I worked mostly with her brothers, Lone Wolf and Screaming Eagle."

Chase's mouth swung open on its hinges during Jeff's explanation. He jumped up and grasped Jeff by the

227

shoulders, pulling him to his feet. "Jeff, Nelda Cruce was my mother. I'm Stalker. Don't you remember me?"

Jeff peered into Chase's eyes for a long while. "Well, I'll be. You've growed a mite since I saw you, but I remember you. You were the little Stalker that was always playing around the house with your little cousin and those two little white boys. I can't remember their names."

"They were Brad and Jay Hampton." Chase pointed to Lacy. "Lacy's their sister."

Jeff looked at Lacy and laughed out loud. He asked in English, "You mean to tell me you're Dr. Adam's little gal?"

"Yes," Lacy affirmed, a bit bewildered.

"Well, I'll be. Back when I ran off from my white master, your daddy was the only one I trusted. I told him what I was goin' to do, and he gave me some money to help me get away. Looks like the Hamptons have been helpin' black folks for a long time." He winked at Lacy. "And now Dr. Adam's little gal is up to the same tricks her daddy was."

Lacy was shocked to learn that her daddy had helped slaves escape. This was wonderful; she couldn't wait to tell Jay.

Jeff sat down beside Annie and joined her in watching the sun go down. Soon the night creatures produced a cacophony of sounds to celebrate the end of a perfect day. When darkness settled on the peaceful village, the four sat in companionable silence before a flickering fire, absorbed with thoughts of their uncertain futures.

Finally, Annie and Jeff separated and turned in for the night. An hour later, Chase walked Lacy to her cabin. Standing on the step above Chase, Lacy looked down into his face.

"I want to thank you for today."

"Did you enjoy yourself?" he asked.

"Yes, but it was more than that. Seeing the Cherokee like I did today . . ." she sighed, not really knowing how to continue. "I really don't know very much about you, do I?"

"I guess not. And I don't think I know very much about you. I guess we never really gave ourselves the chance. Everything moved so fast with us, and then it was over."

Lacy detected a sadness in Chase's voice, and felt the same. "Do you want it to be over?"

"I don't know. For me, I don't, but for you it might be best." He hadn't thought he and Lacy would ever have this conversation, but the day had wrought a change in them. When he'd seen her dancing with the other women, he realized she wasn't so very different. After all, she was just a woman, and he was just a man.

"Can't you let me decide what's best for me? If nothing else, can't we at least be friends?" Lacy asked, hopefully.

"We can try."

When Lacy stuck her hand out to him, Chase chuckled. He grasped it, then pulled her to him. Gently, he touched his lips to hers.

She rested her hand on his cheek. "Good night, Chase," she said, with the moisture of his kiss shining on her lips.

"Good night, Sweet Peach." He smiled.

The next morning Chase awakened early. He left his cabin in search of War Eagle. He found the old chief warming his aching bones in front of a blazing fire.

Chase joined him, sitting on the ground, and warmed his hands before the fire. "I'm trying to find my uncles, Lone Wolf and Screaming Eagle. I was told in a Cherokee village to the south of here that some of our people fled far to the north years ago in order to escape the Removal, and that they are being persecuted. Do you know of this?"

"Yes, I have heard of this." War Eagle nodded. "It is true that many of our people fled far to the north, high up in the mountains. I have also heard that a white man who is the sheriff of a place called Johnsonville discovered their location. He steals their deerskins and their women. Since he is the law and can do anything he wants, our people have suffered much at his hands."

"Do you know if my uncles live among these people?"

"That I can't say. I do know that they went north years ago with the others."

Both men watched the dancing fire in silence. Finally, rising to his feet, Chase said, "We'll be leaving this morning, Chief. We appreciate your hospitality. We would like to give you something in exchange for the gifts you gave us." With that he handed the chief several pieces of gold.

The old man took the coins in his hands and looked at them closely. "My brother is very generous. This is a great deal of money. It will provide food for the bellies of our children and blankets to keep our women warm when the snow piles deep."

Respectfully, Chase clasped the forearms of the old chief in a demonstration of friendship. He looked toward the cabin where the women had slept and saw Jeff Jinkins and Annie walking away from it, hand in hand. Lacy and Morning Star, who had just come outside themselves, were watching the couple, smiling.

Chase padded over to Lacy. "It's time to leave," he said. "War Eagle has given me more information about the possible whereabouts of my uncles. I think they may need my help."

Lacy turned to Morning Star. "Thank you, Morning Star. I will remember you as long as I live. I hope someday we will meet again."

With tears shining in her eyes, Morning Star choked out a weak reply. "My heart is full of you, Lacy, and of your friend, Annie. I hope a good spirit will guide you on your journey."

Chase loaded the packhorse with provisions and saddled the filly and the gelding while the women said goodbye. Annie and Jeff returned from their walk, still holding hands.

Annie came to Lacy and Chase. "Miss Lacy, Mr. Chase, I wonder if it would be all right if I stayed here with Jeff. He says this is a wonderful place to live, and he wants to take care of me."

Lacy and Chase exchanged looks. "We want you to do whatever you think is best. If you want to stay with Jeff, Chase and I will be happy for you," Lacy said, hugging her friend with motherly affection. It would be hard to leave Annie behind. She had been concerned with the girl's welfare for so long, she would feel an emptiness without her. Still, she rejoiced that Annie had found happiness.

"Well, if you don't care, I think I'll stay," replied Annie softly.

Chase shook Jeff's hand. "You take good care of her."

"I will." Jeff stared at Annie wistfully, reassuring Chase and Lacy that she was in good hands.

After Chase gave Annie a quick hug, he and Lacy turned to leave. Chase handed the gelding's bridle to Jeff. "Here, Jeff. You and Annie keep the gelding. He might come in handy someday."

The gelding was worth more than Jeff and Annie had ever owned in their lives. "Thank you, Mr. Chase," said Annie. Before she finished, her voice broke. Her eyes sparkling with tears, she waved goodbye.

War Eagle and several of the men walked along with Chase and Lacy until they reached the edge of the village. Chase stopped and held up his hand. "I go," he said in Cherokee.

"You do," War Eagle replied in the usual Cherokee farewell. Then he added, "Be careful, my brother, it's *gola.*"

With that reference to the cold season, Chase led Lacy out into the forest. It would be very cold before long, and he would soon have to hunt for their food. Glancing over at Lacy, it dawned on him that this would be their first night alone. All he had to remember was that they were just

231

friends, not lovers.

As if reading his mind, Lacy blushed and looked away. She wondered if he would attempt to make love to her, and if he did, what her reaction would be. Friends, she reminded herself; they were just friends.

From the corner of his eye Chase saw Lacy's blush and smiled.

of water over to the fire to drown it. When she tilted the bucket, Chase stayed her hand.

Twenty-Three

Brad sat behind his cluttered desk in his office at the Bank of Athens. Ever since the ball, he had thought of little else than Celia, and it was driving him to distraction.

He rested his elbows on his desk, knocking papers to the floor, and dropped his head in his hands. Try as he might, he just couldn't drive the tormenting picture of Celia's sad eyes from his mind.

He had to know what was wrong. If Lacy had been around, he would have asked her, but blast it, she was off in Chattanooga. He'd have to find out on his own.

He left the bank and headed for Celia's home. Her parents owned a house on the corner of Hancock and Pulaski. It was only a few blocks from the bank, and since the sky was clear and the day was unseasonably warm, Brad walked.

He headed north on Lumpkin, passed Clayton, Market and, when he came to Hancock Avenue, turned left. Passing Hull he came finally to Pulaski Street. On the corner of Pulaski sat the Harrington home.

Brad had not seen Celia's home recently and was surprised to find it in a state of disrepair. The front door was loose on its hinges, the porch steps were rotting, and the porch itself was sagging. In addition the whole structure was sorely in need of a good coat of paint.

Brad sauntered up the front walkway, feeling more than a little foolish now that he'd arrived. What was he going to say: *Excuse me, Celia, but why do you appear to hate your fiancé? Wouldn't you much rather have me?*

Quickly, Brad turned around and headed back down to the walk. Before he could make his getaway, however, Celia's mother opened the door. "Brad," she called in surprise. "Please come in. I'm so glad to see you."

Pasting on a smile, Brad turned around and made his way back to the door. "Thank you. I was just in the neighborhood and thought I would stop by and say hello to Cee Cee."

Brad stepped inside. Mr. Harrington rose from his chair, and the men shook hands.

"Come in, son," he said with a warm smile. "We're delighted that you've dropped by. But Cee Cee isn't here. She's staying at Beau Patton's place while he's up north. She's seeing to the plantation for him."

"How are the two of you doing? I've missed seeing you around," Brad said, trying valiantly to hide his disappointment.

"We're doing all right," Mr. Harrington replied weakly.

It was clear from the way he spoke that he was not telling the whole truth, but Brad didn't pry.

"Well, I'm sorry I missed Cee Cee. Please tell her that I came calling."

"Won't you stay awhile?" Celia's mother asked.

"Thank you, but I need to hurry back to the bank."

Brad walked slowly back to his office. He wondered if the plight of Celia's parents was the cause of her sadness. Or did it have something to do with Beau?

Later that day, Brad decided to leave work early and stop by Beau Patton's plantation on his way home to Paradise. It was probably a good idea to talk to Celia while Beau was gone. It struck him that Beau might be the possessive type.

He rode his buggy out to the Patton plantation and was greeted by an old Negro slave woman who had been in the

234

Patton family as far back as Brad could remember.

"How are you today, Sarah?"

"I'm doin' just fine, Mistah Brad. I'm sorry you rode all the way out here, 'cause Mistah Beau ain't here."

"I knew that before I came. I'm really here to see Miss Celia. Would you please tell her that I'm here?"

"Yes suh, I sho will, Mistah Brad. But I don't think she'll be able to see ya." With that, she hastened into the house.

In the meantime, Brad climbed down from the buggy and waited. Sarah's last remark aroused his curiosity.

After a short while Sarah returned. Her eyes were large and darted about nervously in her dark face. "I'm sorry, Mistah Brad, but Miss Celia says she's too busy to see folks today. Mebbe you can come back when Mistah Beau is here and see 'em both."

Brad was surprised and more than a little hurt by Celia's rebuff. The Celia he knew would have been out there the instant she was told that he had come calling. He turned to Sarah. "I'm going in. There's something wrong here, and I'm going to find out what it is."

"Thank you, Mistah Brad," replied Sarah gratefully. "I was hopin' you'd say that."

Brad bounded up the steps two at a time and rattled the door knob. It was locked. "Cee Cee, open this door; it's Brad," he shouted impatiently.

Inside he heard Celia's quiet voice plead, "No, Brad. Please go away. I can't see you now."

"Cee Cee," he shouted back. "Get away from the door." He raised his booted foot, slammed it into the door, and broke the lock.

Inside, Celia was sitting in a chair in the corner of the foyer. When Brad thrust his large frame through the opening he had created, she pulled a scarf low over her face so that he couldn't see it.

Brad stepped through the door, pulled off her scarf, and said, "Cee Cee, what the hell's going on? Oh, God, what has

235

that monster done to you?" Then he let forth with a string of oaths that caused Celia's face to burn. Right then and there Brad swore that he'd wring Beau Patton's scrawny little neck.

Celia's face was black and blue around her eyes and across her narrow jaws. She had obviously been given a severe beating.

Brad knelt in front of her and regained his composure. "Cee Cee," he said softly. "Did Beau do this to you?"

She sat there with tears glistening in her eyes, holding on to Brad like a lifeline. Slowly she nodded her head.

He took her hands and drew her to her feet. Then he led her to the parlor, where he sat down in a chair and pulled her into his lap.

"Now, tell me everything," Brad said firmly but kindly. He knew that Celia was scared and humiliated, but he needed for her to confide in him. He rubbed his hand down her back.

"I want to help you, Cee Cee, but I can't unless you talk to me. I promise I'll make everything all right." When Brad's voice faltered, Celia began to sob as if her heart would break.

She cried against his shoulder for a few minutes while he tried to console her. Finally, wiping her eyes, she spoke in a quivering voice. "Brad, I'm in a bad position. Daddy owes Beau a lot of money, and he can't pay it back. Beau says he'll take away everything Mother and Daddy own unless I marry him. I hate him with every ounce of my being, but I can't let him destroy my parents."

She sobbed again.

Brad noticed that her injuries were worse than he'd thought. It was an effort for her to even sit up in his lap, so he pulled her close to his chest, cradling her broken body.

"Baby, it's you I'm worried about, not your folks. I'm sorry to hear about your father's problems, but he'll be all right. When I went by there today, it was obvious something was wrong. That's why I'm here now, to offer my help. If your father owes money, I'll help him."

Celia relaxed against him. Brad continued, "What I don't understand is why Beau beats you. If he's gotten what he wants, why does he feel the need to hurt you?"

"Beau hides it very well, but he's a cruel man. If my father knew that he beat me, he would force me to leave him. But he doesn't know. No one can imagine Beau doing something like this. Well, that's not completely true. Beau's slaves know all too well. They are so afraid of him they won't even tell *me* how vicious he is. I just know he is mistreating them in some way or another. I'm afraid that he even tortures them. Oh, Brad, please help me. I don't believe I can go through with this. I can't live in the presence of such evil."

That was all Brad needed to hear. "Sweetheart, you don't have to ask for my help again. I'm here for you."

Brad tapped Celia's nose much as he had when, as children, she and Lacy had followed him around. "I've always been here for you. I promise you Beau Patton will never touch you or your family again. Now, let's get your things together. I'm taking you out of this hellhole. You're going back to Paradise with me."

"Thank you, Brad. I knew I could count on you." Celia burrowed deeper into Brad's arms. He had always been her hero, so it wasn't a surprise that it was he who would rescue her from Beau's evil clutches.

Celia had been beaten so severely that Brad had to carry her into Paradise. Despite the strange looks the couple received from Mammy and Isaac, Brad sailed right past them into the guest room located across the hall from his bedroom.

Celia was so embarrassed by her battered condition, she buried her face in his chest. Breathing in his manly smell of fine cigars and spicy cologne, she tingled from the roots of her hair to the bottom of her feet. Until she healed a bit, Celia didn't want to see another living soul, except Brad of course.

Brad crossed the elegantly appointed room and laid his precious cargo in the center of a very large, ivory, velvet-covered bed. Never losing eye contact with Celia, he stretched out beside her. Very gently, he pulled her into his arms.

A myriad of emotions flooded through Celia, but she didn't pull away. She had been reared a chaste Southern lady and had intended to remain such until her wedding night. But her romantic notions had died a cruel death a few short months after Beau Patton began courting her.

At first Beau had appeared the ultimate gentleman. He had been soft spoken, considerate, and above all, respectful. Then her father's business suffered a setback, and he was forced to approach Beau for a loan. Celia wasn't sure what kind of deal the men struck that afternoon, but when her father returned from his business meeting, he informed her that she and Beau Patton were unofficially engaged.

In her romantic dreams, Celia had always imagined herself married to Brad, so when her father informed her that she must marry Beau, she objected quite strenuously. It was one thing to allow Beau to court her casually, but something different altogether to consent to be his wife. When Celia finished pleading and crying, her father merely shook his head sadly and retired to his room.

That evening, as usual, Beau arrived to escort Celia to dinner at the Franklin House Hotel. But instead of going into town, Beau took Celia to Raven, his plantation. He led her into the parlor and closed the doors securely behind them. When Celia objected, saying that it wasn't proper for a single lady to visit a single man unchaperoned, Beau became abusive.

He grasped her arms and roughly hauled her across the room. He threw her lengthwise onto the sofa and fell roughly on top of her. She scratched two bloody trails down Beau's face, kicked and bucked, but she failed to dislodge him. The more Celia fought, the better Beau liked it.

Since then she had learned to lie as still as a corpse while he coldly and heartlessly raped her. Her mind withdrew further and further while she died a little each time she was abused. The external damage from Beau's beatings was obvious, so she had been forced to tell Brad about that. But the internal damage Beau had inflicted was easily hidden. This she could share with no one.

As she lay in Brad's arms, she wondered if he suspected Beau had raped her. She feared that Brad might see her as used goods and think less of her when he learned of her shame. She looked up at him, afraid she would see disgust in his eyes. But all she saw was love.

Brad gazed deeply into Celia's crystal blue eyes as if he were spellbound. Overcome with tender feelings, he dropped a feather-soft kiss on her forehead. When he raised his ebony-tousled head, he saw her eyes fill with moisture. He felt as if an iron fist gripped his heart.

He shifted to his back, placed his arm around her shoulders, and pulled her tightly to his side. In a soothing parental voice he crooned, "Now, tell me the whole story."

Painfully, Celia poured out her sordid story of physical abuse at the hands of Beau Patton. As she spoke, Brad had to draw upon every bit of self-control he possessed not to explode into a million fiery pieces. To think that anyone would deliberately harm this delicate creature was beyond his comprehension. Beau Patton deserved to fry in hell, and Brad planned to send him there soon.

When Celia finished telling Brad every despicable deed Beau had committed against her, including his violation of her, she was emotionally and physically drained. He knew that she needed rest, but wanted to reassure her that nothing she had told him damaged his respect for her. He proceeded carefully so as not to offend her.

"I'm sorry that Beau hurt you like he did. I want you to know that you are precious to me and always will be."

"Then, you don't think I'm bad?" The hopeful look in

Celia's misty eyes pulled on Brad's heartstrings.

"Bad? Not at all. If anything, I think more of you for having endured the hell that bastard put you through."

Brad's temper had gotten away from him. He thought it a terrible habit to use foul language, especially in front of a lady. He repented, "Cee Cee, please excuse my language. I don't usually curse in front of ladies."

A timid smile spread across Celia's face. "So you still think I'm a lady?"

Brad's captivating smile answered Celia's question.

Twenty-Four

The morning sun kissed the eastern sky as Lacy stretched like a lazy feline, snuggling closer to the coals that simmered at her side. Burrowing deeper under the cover, she sought to reclaim the peacefulness of contented sleep, but her rest was disturbed by the feather-soft tickling of her nose. Eyes tightly closed, Lacy wrinkled her nose, swatting like a kitten worrying with a ball of yarn.

Kneeling at her side, Chase stifled a chuckle while he rubbed a silken strand of Lacy's golden hair between his thumb and forefinger. Since tickling her nose had failed to arouse her, he dropped a soft kiss on her smooth cheek, trying to keep it friendly rather than passionate.

When her thick, tangled lashes fluttered open, Chase saw his thoughts reflected in Lacy's gaze.

"Good morning, pal," he teased. "I thought you were going to sleep the day away."

"Well, I'm traveling with a slave driver, who doesn't seem to know when to stop." Lacy's smile showed that she wasn't really complaining.

"How would you like to stay around here today and not move on just yet?"

Thrilled at the prospect of spending a whole day with one hundred percent of Chase's attention excited and worried

241

Lacy at the same time. As long as they were in the saddle all day, it was easy to remain aloof. But she didn't think she could trust either of them to stick to this *friend* thing otherwise. Nevertheless, a day of rest was too good to pass up.

"That sounds wonderful to me."

Chase leaned down and brushed Lacy's tumbled hair from her eyes. Not unlike what her brothers would do. "Good."

Lacy was moved by Chase's affectionate act and the tenderness she saw in his sky-blue eyes.

That afternoon Chase and Lacy approached a small clearing in the woods. The space was about two hundred yards wide. Chase motioned for Lacy to remain quiet. Across the clearing, there was a small herd of white-tail deer feeding on fallen acorns.

In one hand Chase carried a bow and a quiver filled with razor-sharp arrows. In the other hand he held another item that resembled a deerskin folded into a small bundle.

"Stay here and watch the deer," he whispered. "I'll be back in a few minutes." With his equipment in hand, he disappeared into the forest.

Lacy stood silently, looking out over the clearing. The deer in the wilds were a beautiful sight. "Just like Chase," she whispered.

The does were busy eating, while two bucks locked horns, challenging each other since it was the rutting season. Soon a third buck appeared on the far edge of the clearing. He shook his head back and forth, striking limbs in the trees and making a strange sound.

The fighting bucks stopped to look at the newcomer. One of them trotted toward the intruder, prepared to lock horns with him. Suddenly the intruder straightened. Lacy gasped. It was Chase. Before the deer could bolt, he shot an arrow right through its heart. The other deer and the does quickly bounded out of sight and disappeared into the forest. Soon Chase returned to Lacy, carrying the felled buck over his shoulders.

Lacy laughed. "That was great. You looked just like a buck when you were bent over."

"It's an old Indian trick," Chase said, pleased that Lacy seemed so at ease with him. Chase dropped the buck to the ground and unfolded the deerskin.

"See how the antlers are hollowed out in the back to make them light and easy to carry. I place the deer head over my head like this." He took the deerskin and placed it over her head. "The rest of the skin falls down over my back. When I bend over, I look enough like a buck to deceive one into charging me. Of course, this works only in rutting season."

He grinned cheekily. "During that time the males are irritable and easily excited. Without thinking, they charge. It's only a matter of shooting one after that. Any Cherokee hunter is accurate with his bow for at least forty yards, sometimes more."

Lacy shook her head and handed the skin to Chase. She was still blushing from Chase's reference to the rutting season. "You amaze me," was all she said as she turned to walk back to camp.

Chase picked up the deer and hurried to catch up with her. He had meant to tease her with the reference to rutting males, but it had backfired on him. It took his mind in a direction that he didn't want it to go, and what it did to the rest of his body didn't bear examining. He needed to occupy his mind elsewhere.

"Have you ever heard the Cherokee version of the origin of the Milky Way?" Chase asked rhetorically. Knowing that she hadn't, he told it to her.

"One time long ago, the Cherokee noticed that something was stealing their cornmeal at night. The People met and discussed what to do. Finally, a wise old warrior made a suggestion.

243

"He said that everyone should arm themselves with rattles, drums, and other kinds of noisemakers and hide behind the millstone. That night a giant dog appeared from the west, glowing with a silvery sheen. He began eating the cornmeal that The People had laid on the ground the day before. But the dog was so big the old warrior was afraid to do anything. After a while he gained his courage and started shaking his rattle. Then they all shook rattles, beat drums, and shouted.

"The giant dog was so frightened that he ran around the millstone and leaped into the air. The meal that he had eaten poured out of his mouth. It left a white trail pouring across the sky. This is what the white man calls the Milky Way. But the Cherokee call it Gil' LiUtsun'yi, which means, 'Where the dog ran.'"

"Thank you for telling me that," Lacy said, then walked ahead. In a moment she stopped and turned, saying, "I really do enjoy hearing about your people. I hope you know that."

For Chase the sun was just a bit brighter, the wind a bit fresher, and life a bit sweeter. He hadn't realized how much he wanted her approval, how much he needed it. It was a disconcerting discovery. Still, he revelled in the day ahead. Side by side they worked, skinning and cleaning the deer. They laughed, talked, touched as often as they could, and cast furtive glances at one another. Wanting it to be so much more, but not knowing how, they kept reminding themselves that they were just friends.

Twenty-Five

The next several days were uneventful except that the riding was harder and the weather colder. Much of the time Lacy was colder than she'd ever thought possible, but she never complained. It took all the blankets they had to stay warm at night. Chase thought of suggesting that they share their body heat, but he didn't dare.

Instead, he kept a fire going at night to keep them warm as well as to discourage wild animals. He feared that bears might come into the camp looking for food, even though they would hibernate soon. There was also a threat posed by wild fox. A hungry fox could be vicious. But then so could a deprived lover, he reminded himself.

About mid-afternoon a few days later, Chase suggested that they stop early to make camp. They camped beside a beautiful waterfall that cascaded down from a craggy cliff above. Much of the water had frozen on the way down, giving the appearance of sparkling glass. The cliff curved around in such a way as to block off most of the north wind, so it was a perfect place to camp. When Lacy began gathering sticks for the fire, Chase pulled out his bow.

"I heard a turkey gobble a ways back. I think I'll go see if I can get him. Some wild turkey would be real tasty tonight." Chase winked as he slipped his quiver over a shoulder.

"That sounds wonderful," Lacy enthused. "I'll fix some coffee while you're gone." She rubbed her hands together, and after cupping them, she blew her warm breath into them. "It's going to be another cold night."

"I won't be long," Chase said. Then he threw over his shoulder, "Don't go far from camp." In a moment he was out of sight.

Lacy walked over to the stream and filled her bucket with crystal-clear mountain water. After setting in on a rock, she started the fire. Once it was blazing, she poured a good helping of coffee into the bucket and placed it close to the flames.

The aroma of hot coffee wafted through the crisp air as she retrieved the blankets from the packhorse and prepared their beds. She tossed Chase's big buffalo coat on top of her blankets. He had insisted that she use it, and with the nights getting so cold, she decided it was no time to be heroic. She had accepted it gratefully.

Chase had been gone for about half an hour when she heard a twig snap. Glad that he had gotten back so soon, she turned around to see what he had bagged for their supper. The scream that tore from her throat echoed over the cliff.

She saw a huge man, apparently a prospector, standing on the edge of the camp. He must have weighed three hundred pounds if he weighed an ounce. An enormous sheepskin coat, making him look even bigger, partially hid his filthy homespun clothes.

He looked like he hadn't had a bath for months or even years. The right side of his jaw was puffed out with a recently chewed-off plug, and his reddish-brown, scraggly beard dripped with tobacco juice. His hair, stringy and dirty, hung down to his thick shoulders while a flea-infested raccoon-skin cap barely kept his greasy strands from impeding his view. A long, rusty rifle rested in the hollow of his arm. In all of Lacy's life, he was the most frightening thing she had ever seen.

"Well now," he croaked in a coarse, gravelly voice. "What have we here?" His eyes narrowed to lustful slits as he raked Lacy from head to toe. When he licked his lips, brown-stained saliva trailed down his filthy beard.

Lacy felt nauseous. She had no doubt what he wanted from her. In a trembling voice, she said, "My husband is hunting and will be back in a minute."

"Sure he will. I suppose yer husband don't hunt with no gun." He pointed a filthy hand toward Chase's rifle. It was resting in the long holster, still attached to the packhorse's saddle.

Lacy gauged the distance to the carbine. Her thoughts of reaching for it must have shown on her face. "Don't even think it, lady," the filthy man croaked.

"You know what I think?" he continued. "I think mebbe you ain't got no husband, and that yore jest out here all by yerself with no man to take care of you." He grinned, revealing broken, black teeth. "'Ceptin' mebbe me."

"That's not true," Lacy stammered. "My husband hunts with a bow. He doesn't need a rifle to kill game. He left his rifle for me in case wild animals attacked the camp." Lacy didn't stop to consider why she referred to Chase as her husband. She was too busy tamping down her hysteria.

The miner found Lacy's comment about wild animals hilarious. He laughed heartily until he choked on tobacco juice. Then he addressed her other claim. "So he don't need no rifle to hunt? What is yer husband, some kind of Injun or somethin'?"

The filthy man's stomach shook as he laughed again at what he thought was a clever joke. "You 'spect me to believe that a nice white girl like you is married to an Injun?"

He took a menacing step toward her, and his foul breath sickened her. She looked around for an avenue of escape. A sheer wall of mountain had her hemmed in from behind and to her left. The stream cut off her escape on the right, and the man was blocking the only other way. It reminded her of the bear scare, but somehow this was worse.

In absolute terror, she screamed with all the power of her lungs, "Chase . . . !"

The man was on her in an instant. He grabbed her by the arm and slapped her across the mouth. Lacy tasted his filth and the metallic flavor of her own blood. If he hadn't been squeezing her arm with his meaty fist, she would have crumpled at his feet.

Hysterically, she screamed again and again. He doubled up his powerful fist and beat her about the face, but the more he beat her, the more she screamed. Finally, she was too weak to struggle.

He didn't think she was telling the truth about her husband, but he didn't want to take any chances. Even his dull mind knew it was unusual for a beautiful white girl to be up in the mountains alone. So, with little effort, he dragged her limp body away from the camp, deep into the forest, and up over the mountain to the north.

Sighting the turkey, Chase closed for the kill. It was a big, handsome gobbler. Lacy would be pleased, he thought like a love-sick schoolboy. He raised his bow and aimed; then he lowered it. Something wasn't right. He detected a slight alteration in the chirping of the birds. His instincts told him that nature wasn't quite in balance.

He stood there motionless, listening. The gobbler appeared to hear nothing unusual. It continued to peck at seeds on the ground. A squirrel inched its way around to the far side of a tree, but showed no alarm. Still, Chase couldn't escape the feeling that something was wrong.

Lacy! He whirled around toward camp, spooking the turkey. Chase's hair stood up on the back of his neck, his lip curled slightly, and a low moan issued forth from his throat. He could taste the fear of losing her in his mouth. He started running, dashing over streams, and jumping small canyons.

When he reached camp, he saw that Lacy was gone. He found a man's footprints where he had dragged Lacy off into the forest. He looked at his gun, but then decided to leave it. He didn't want to shoot the man who had taken Lacy; he wanted to kill him with his bare hands.

Chase dropped his bow and quiver and started tracking them. He moved through the forest in total silence. Not a twig or leaf moved as he passed. His eyes blazed with fire, and his animal instincts came to the surface as he stalked his prey with the cunning of a panther, looking not unlike a wild creature himself.

Each time Lacy regained her strength, she struggled, and each time she suffered shattering blows for her effort. The last blow again brought the taste of blood to her mouth. Then she fell unconscious.

Her abductor picked her up and threw her over his broad shoulder like a sack of feed. For a big man, he exhibited great speed and agility. He covered a long distance in a very short time. Soon he came to the side of a mountain that rose straight up from the forest floor.

Grabbing a long rope that dangled down from a ledge, he struggled up the mountainside, still holding his limp bundle. When he reached the ledge, he was breathing hard. He threw Lacy to the ground and dropped down beside her.

The soft ground shook and Lacy moaned, regaining her senses. She thought only of escape.

The big man studied her bruised and swollen eyes, craftily reading her mind. "Don't try it, lady. You ain't goin' nowhere. There ain't no way up or down 'cept by this rope." Sneering, he pulled the rope up and coiled it at his feet.

Unable to give up so easily, Lacy looked around her. A small cabin built out of logs was situated on the mountain ledge, making it virtually unreachable. Clouds of blue smoke swirled up from the chimney into the frothy mist that had

249

settled over the mountaintop. If she hadn't been in fear for her life, Lacy would have thought it a lovely setting.

Suddenly, the cabin door burst open, and another man emerged. If possible, he was more terrifying than his partner.

"That you, Lim?"

"Yeah, Buck. Look what I brung up fer supper," Lim roared, pointing to Lacy.

Buck was wearing a wooly sheepskin coat and filthy homespun clothes like his partner. Tall, slim, and completely bald, he had an extremely large mustache that curled around both sides of his mouth. He had obviously been drinking heavily from the jug in his hand, for he was weaving. When he saw Lacy, he grinned from ear to ear, revealing a mouthful of black teeth.

"Good God, Lim, let's get her clothes off right now. I ain't had no white woman in years."

Lacy whimpered. She tried to get up and run, but Lim pulled her down into his lap and imprisoned her against his smelly body. His foul, musty breath ruffled the tendrils on Lacy's forehead.

"Dammit, Buck, let me catch my breath fer a minute or two. There's plenty of time."

Buck took a long pull from his jug and belched loudly. "All right, Lim. But let's git her in there fast. I got a hankerin to see what she tastes like 'tween her legs. She looks good enough to eat to me." He laughed at the look of pure revulsion on Lacy's face.

She sobbed. She couldn't believe that men like these existed. Dogs and pigs were better than they were. She wanted to be strong, but nothing in her life had prepared her for this. She prayed that Chase had heard her call. He was her only hope. But until he got here, she would fight. She didn't intend to let these two animals rape her without inflicting some damage of her own.

Suddenly, Lim grabbed Lacy by the hair and dragged her into the dim cabin. She bucked and twisted, trying to gain her feet, but was unable to. Lim yanked her through the door and threw her onto his filthy bed.

Facedown on the blankets, Lacy nostrils were filled with the odor of dried urine and Lim's sweat. She grabbed her stomach and retched. A scrawny, gray cat came out from under the bed, leaped up beside Lacy, and began to lick up the contents of her stomach.

The two men hooted with laughter. "Even ol' Cockroach thinks she's good enough to eat," Buck slurred. "Before we git through with her, there won't be nothin' left." He took another pull from his jug.

"Gimme that jug, you bastard," growled Lim. "If you finish it before I git my half, I'll kick your ass all over this mountain." He snatched the liquor from Buck and drained the jug. When he turned back to Lacy, his yellowish eyes lit up like a crazed tiger.

"Come here, bitch. I aim to have ya right now," he yelled as he stumbled over to Lacy. Lacy screamed at the top of her lungs, convulsing with fright.

Suddenly, an eerie moan sounded outside the cabin. The two men, although under the influence of alcohol, were still keen of hearing. They looked at each other.

"What's that?" asked Lim, a slight quiver in his voice.

"I dunno," replied Buck, casting furtive glances from Lacy to the door. "Probably just the wind."

They stood motionless, listening. Again a low moan carried through the walls. Lim crossed over to the window and peered out. "There ain't nothin' out there," he growled. "The liquor's just got us skittish."

"Mebbe so. But I'm goin' out there for a looksee," said Buck. With that he stepped outside the cabin.

Lim turned back to Lacy. "Don't worry, lady. Nothin' can git up here without that rope hangin' over the cliff. We'll take good care of you." He scratched the bulge in his pants with a filthy paw.

"Buck, what is it?"

There was total silence.

"Dammit," he swore. "Now I'll have to go see fer myself." He went to the door and stepped outside.

As soon as he disappeared, Lacy ran to the door for some fresh air. The stench inside the cabin was more than she could bear.

When she stuck her head through the door, she saw Buck lying on the ground. His throat was slit from ear to ear. Blood poured out of his jugular veins in pulsating streams. Lim's face was ashen white.

"What the hell's happened to Buck?" he asked the empty air.

"The same thing that's going to happen to you," came a deep voice from the side of the cabin. Chase stepped into plain view when he spoke. His eyes were flashing red in his granite-chiseled face.

Lim drew his knife. His lips quivered with fear as he looked around for a way to escape. One look at Chase told Lim he was overmatched.

Chase was tall, broad shouldered, and muscular beyond anything he had ever seen. He stood straight with nothing in his hands, although a knife hung at his side in a deerskin sheath. He had a slight smile on his lips. It was the smile that scared Lim the most.

Lim leaped forward, swinging his knife. Chase side-stepped, pivoted on one foot, and crashed his fist into the side of Lim's head. Lim yelled in pain as he went down. Struggling to his feet, he rushed Chase with his bearlike arms outstretched in front of him. Again Chase sidestepped and struck the big man a tremendous blow to the back of the head as he flew past.

Lim lay facedown in the dirt. Crossing over to him, Chase yanked him up by his long, dirty hair. Blood oozed out of his nose and ears, soaking his tobacco-stained beard. With the back of his hand, Chase struck him again. Lim's head broke through the window of the cabin, strewing glass on the floor inside.

Lim looked up at Chase through glazed eyes. He then realized what this was all about. The white girl was this man's woman.

Lim roared, spitting blood with every syllable. "You bastard, yore too late. I done had the whore. And she begged for more!"

His remark shook Chase, that and the sight of Lacy's beautiful face, now bloody and battered. To think of this foul beast touching her drove Chase crazy with rage.

He grabbed Lim by the crotch with one hand and by the throat with the other. He lifted him high over his head as if he were weightless, walked to the precipice, and with a mighty heave threw him over the cliff. Lim screamed all the way down until his body was dashed to pieces on the jagged rocks below.

Chase turned in time to catch Lacy as she flew into his arms. Her tears and her mouth were all over his face. "Oh, Chase, I'm so glad you came. And God help me, I'm glad you killed him . . ." Lacy's last words trailed off inaudibly as she swooned.

Trembling, Chase put his arm under Lacy's bottom and raised her to his chest. He made his way back to camp, clutching her to his breast. He couldn't escape the feeling that he had failed her. But he could make sure that it never happened again.

Then he marveled at the changes that had come over Lacy since they left Athens. Imagine, she was glad that he had killed a man. Maybe there was a little savage in everyone. . . .

Twenty-Six

The night air was frigid when Chase returned to camp carrying Lacy. She was still unconscious. In sympathy for the abused woman, the forest inhabitants appeared to have ceased all sound, though Chase was painfully unaware. His only concern was sheltered in the circle of his arms.

Seeing Lacy's battered face caused his stomach to cramp with guilt; the possibility that she had been raped rendered him frozen with shock. But with a control he didn't know he possessed, he pulled himself together and set about caring for her. He cleaned her cuts and applied a healing salve over them. After washing the filth of the men off of her, he dressed her in a clean gown and wrapped her in his buffalo coat. Then he laid her on her blankets and sat close by.

It was the next morning before Lacy awakened. Her first sight was of Chase; he was leaning over her, tucking the coat more tightly about her shoulders. It was obvious from his disheveled appearance and bloodshot eyes that he hadn't slept a wink since her rescue. Her heart was strangely warmed, but she was uncomfortable with his nearness.

Chase was unaware that Lacy was awake, so he reached out to smooth the hair away from her face. When she flinched and drew back in fear, his heart ached. He was sure she no longer trusted him since he had killed two men, even though she had praised him at the time. She had been in shock. It hurt him to think that she now really considered him savage.

"How do you feel?" he asked softly, not wanting to look into her eyes, afraid of what he'd see.

"I've been better." She tried for a weak smile. She had seen the pain in Chase's eyes, but she couldn't help it. After what she had endured, she just couldn't be close to any man. She knew that Chase would never hurt her, he had saved her, he was a good, kind man, but what she knew with her head and what she felt in her heart weren't always the same.

"I'll get you something to eat," he said, rising.

"No thank you, I'm not hungry. I just need to rest."

Lacy burrowed deeper in the covers, clutched the buffalo skin under her chin, and squeezed her eyes shut. Chase's deep sigh caused a lump to rise in her throat.

For the rest of the day, Lacy lay around camp, recuperating. Chase went about his daily schedule, hunting, cooking, caring for her, and as often as possible, leaving her alone. He had grown as pensive and withdrawn as she, and most of the day, they barely spoke.

The next morning Chase expressed concern about the dark clouds hanging ominously in the northern sky. The sun's radiant beams slowly turned into reddish gray streaks as the sky became more overcast.

"Stay wrapped up," he told Lacy quietly and handed her another blanket. Then he turned and walked into the woods.

Gusts of cold air raced down through the valleys and around the stately pines, blowing his hair out behind him. A buck standing like a marble statue at the base of the mountain showed no interest in his presence. No squirrels scurried about; all was still except for an occasional call of a crow which broke the deafening silence of the frigid forest.

Chase returned to Lacy. "We're going to have a blizzard. We'd better prepare for the worst. We'll do well to have some shelter."

"All right," returned Lacy with slightly chattering teeth. She was as frightened at the prospect of being enclosed in a small area with Chase as she was of the coming blizzard. Despite her fear and discomfort, she asked, "What can I do to help?"

Her face was shiny red from cold, tears of fear and uncertainty were frozen to her cheeks, and in spite of her best efforts, her body quaked. Chase knew when he saw her shiver again that he'd better hurry.

"You're not able to help. Just stay under those blankets and try to keep warm."

Chase moved over to the edge of camp where four evergreens grew in close proximity to one another, forming a rectangle in the middle. Two of the trees were cedars, one was an Appalachian spruce, and the fourth was a yellow pine.

Intrigued, Lacy rolled over onto her side and watched Chase gather their gear and place it in the midst of the trees. Quickly taking a rope, he cut two long sections from it. He looped a length of it around one of the cedars, and with his considerable weight, he bent the tree. Then he secured the length of rope around the top. Next, he bent the pine opposite the cedar in a like manner and attached the two with ropes. When he pulled them tightly together, he formed a branchy archway. He repeated the process with the other two trees. When he finished, all four trees converged at the top, forming a teepeelike shelter with an area of approximately one hundred square feet in the middle.

Lacy was astounded. Where did he come up with these ideas? She rested her head on her palm and continued to watch as he took a small hand axe and cut the lower branches from the trees on the inside. He lay these branches on the ground, forming a soft floor for the structure.

Next, he searched the surrounding area. In record time, he cut down four additional coniferous trees of about the same height and leaned them against the structure, practically enclosing the entire area with thickly leafed trees. He strengthened the shelter by weaving long slender branches, which he cut from hardwoods, into the bases of the conifers up to several feet high. Finally, he looped the remainder of the rope around the whole structure, pulling it all together tightly.

By then the snow had begun to fall, first in flurries, then in heavy sheets. Chase crossed over to Lacy, and before she could resist, he lifted her effortlessly in his arms and carried her to the structure. Once there, he crawled through the opening. Inside, he set her to her feet and retrieved her bedding. Then he prepared her bed.

"You lie down, and I'll gather wood and build a fire."

Chase hurried out of the enclosure. He stopped and sucked a deep, cleansing breath through his teeth. He ached inside. Lacy had trembled from head to toe when he took her in his arms, and it wasn't from the cold. God how it hurt.

But he didn't have time for self-pity. The snow was already piling up, and it appeared that they would be snowbound for some time. He gathered a large amount of wood, trimmed each branch and passed it through the opening of the shelter. Then he stepped inside.

He slanted Lacy a look. She was lying on her side, facing the wall. So that's how it would be? She was going to ignore him. He hoped fervently they would not be snowed in long.

After stacking the wood in a neat pile and starting a blazing fire, he spoke softly to Lacy. "I'm going to check on the horses." There was no response.

He shrugged wearily and stepped outside. He found the horses in a clearing on the other side of the mountain. He thought about hobbling Precious and the packhorse, but then decided not to, for in this weather the horses needed to be free to fend for themselves. He didn't think Spirit would allow the others to stray too far from camp anyway.

Chase lifted his face skyward and closed his eyes. The snow was coming down hard now. The fluffy flakes caught in his hair and eyelashes, swirled around his legs and, in contact with his warm body, melted and saturated his clothing. When he opened his eyes, he saw the wind driving the snow hard, forming drifts.

He checked one last time to make sure he had completed all the tasks necessary for their safety. Satisfied that he had done everything he could, he crawled back into the shelter, covering the opening behind him.

Lacy was just as he'd left her, only she was shivering even more. He stoked the fire and went to her side. "The wind's blowing through the branches of the conifers now," he said. "But I don't think that will last long. Soon the snowdrifts will block the draft, and we'll be warm." There was no response. He sat on his bedroll close to the dancing flames, drying his cold, wet clothes and watching the smoke filter through a small opening in the structure.

Before long his prediction came true. The snow accumulated on the sides of the trees, stopping the flow of wind into the shelter. The fire, now burning brightly, heated the inside of their little house, giving rise to a rosy glow on their faces.

Chase put a pot of coffee on the fire and prepared something for them to eat. They had plenty of smoked venison, and with an assortment of nuts that he had collected along the way, he filled their plates.

"Would you like something to eat now?" Chase asked, hoping that Lacy wouldn't continue to ignore him.

"I'm not hungry," she said without turning toward him.

It was obvious from her voice she had been crying, and if there was anything that panicked Chase, it was a crying woman. He had to do something, but what? He didn't dare touch her, because she was scared to death of him. But he couldn't just let her lie there and cry.

They had yet to discuss what she'd actually suffered at the hands of the prospectors, and Chase assumed the worst. The thought of those beasts raping her filled him with such rage that he was glad he had killed them. He only wished he could

259

do it again, and this time more slowly, more painfully. Maybe he was a savage.

A muted sob from Lacy cut through the curtain of white-hot rage that had fallen over Chase's eyes. She was so tiny and vulnerable . . . and so distraught, he had to do something. So he did what he usually did when a woman made him nervous; he talked.

Chase teased, "So you want to know everything about me, huh?"

He waited for Lacy to respond to his inane attempt at humor. He couldn't see her watery smile, and when she didn't respond verbally, he continued. "Originally my family lived in the North Georgia Mountains not far from Indian Mound at Nacoochee. When my grandparents were too old to care for their farm, my mother moved to Clarke County. Then my aunt Neta and my two uncles, Screaming Eagle and Lone Wolf, moved there, too. They all lived there, working the farm together.

"It was then that my father, Evan Tarleton, met my mother. They eventually got married. The bigotry of white men who wanted to remove the Cherokee to Indian Territory kept them from being married at first. I was three years old before I even knew my father, though our families lived on adjoining land."

Chase looked into the fire, twirling his mother's ruby ring as he talked.

He paused then, wondering if Lacy had fallen asleep. When he didn't resume speaking right away, she turned over onto her back.

"Where was he?" she whispered, without looking at him.

"At West Point. Mama said he didn't know about me. It was on the Trail of Tears that they finally married. Pop was an army officer, serving with the troops that escorted us to Indian Territory. After he saw the terrible injustice the Cherokee were made to suffer, he didn't want to live with white men any longer; so he married Mama before we reached The Nations, and later when his commission expired, he resigned from the army.

"Then they bought some land and build the Circle C—C for Cruce of course."

Chase raised his chin proudly. "We have the best horses and cattle money can buy, and the Circle C is one of the finest ranches in the West. Pop saw to it . . . before he died."

He paused and cleared his throat. "I hope to go back there one day and run the ranch, just like he did. It's being taken care of by a friend of mine, but that's not right. It's my obligation. I know that now."

Chase said this last as if he were revealing something of import to himself.

The wind howled outside. Lacy shivered, whether from cold . . . or shock . . . or the thought of Chase returning to Indian Territory without her, she didn't know.

But he didn't notice. Darkness had fallen outside, casting their structure in shadows. Their fire provided more warmth than illumination, little more than an amber glow.

"I remember living with my mother on Papa's farm. It wasn't far from Paradise, and Brad and Jay used to come over and play with me and my cousin, Little Spear—his was the grave I showed you at Indian Mound."

He was looking in her direction now, though she couldn't see his face. His back was silhouetted against the fire, his features in shadow, and all she could make out was his shape. She wanted to see his face, for his voice sounded strange, almost wistful.

"The four of us were playing together the day the soldiers came to take us away. I can still see Brad and Jay running interference for us," he said softly. "It took the soldiers several minutes to catch us."

Lacy raised up and spoke tentatively, as if she would retreat at any movement he made. "I've heard Brad and Jay tell about the time when they were playing with their Indian friends. I used to cry at night when I thought of how those

261

little boys were taken away from their homes. Brad and Jay still say that with the exception of when Mother died, that was the saddest moment of their lives. They have continued to wonder through the years what happened to Little Spear and . . ."

"Stalker," Chase whispered.

"That's right. His name was Stalker," Lacy said, amazed. "Chase, are you Stalker?"

"Yes, my Cherokee name is Stalker. Chase is supposed to be an approximation of it. Mother gave it to me in Indian Territory when I started to school. She thought that Chase sounded more civilized."

Even in the darkness, Lacy detected his pain.

"Why didn't you tell Brad and Jay who you are?"

"I didn't want to tell them I was Stalker until they got to know me as Evan Tarleton's son."

"But why?"

"I think I've talked about myself enough tonight. In fact, I don't think I've talked about myself this much at one time ever! And you, young lady, need to get some sleep."

He leaned over to tuck the blankets around Lacy more tightly, but to his dismay, she shrank back against the wall as soon as he reached out to her. He let his hand drop, confusion ruling his mind, then lay down on his bedroll.

"Good night, Lacy," he said softly.

"Good night, Stalker," she whispered.

Stalker fell asleep, strangely soothed by the howling wind outside . . . and the perplexing young woman resting at his side.

Twenty-Seven

The next morning the sky was clear, and the sun was shining brightly when Chase crawled outside. A sparkling winter wonderland lay before him. In awe, he looked all around him. The drifts of snow reached to five feet in some places. Spirit and the other horses were standing a short distance from the shelter, warming themselves in the morning sun.

The day that followed was much like the one before. Chase provided for Lacy, but they barely spoke. He could see that she was suffering, not physically so much, but emotionally. And he didn't know how to help her.

Thus, they continued for five days. Then, on the fifth night, Lacy had a nightmare, reliving her traumatic experience. When Chase tried to comfort her, she cowered away from him, and he left her alone.

The morning after her dream, Chase suggested that they move on. He thought perhaps putting as many miles between Lacy and the scene of her despoiling as possible would help her heal, emotionally at least.

She agreed.

The next few days were uneventful. They continued their trek through the mountains, looking for Chase's uncles. Gradually, Lacy relaxed, and they talked about benign subjects. Sometimes she would even smile in that little-girl way of hers, reminding Chase for all the world of Linni.

But occasionally, her eyes would fill with tears, and Chase knew she was thinking about what she had suffered. Still, he didn't push her. He never mentioned her assault, and neither did she. He figured when she got ready to tell him about it, she would. And he still thought she feared him for killing her abductors.

One day toward evening, Chase heard the faint sounds of a village and smelled their cook fires. It was an Indian camp.

Chase hastened his mount, hoping against hope that his uncles would be among the villagers. Lacy followed in his wake.

When they reached the outskirts of the village, the scene before them was disheartening. The wicker huts were in bad disrepair, barely able to keep the cold wind out. Chase halted and turned to Lacy.

Then something attracted his attention. At the far end of the village there was a commotion. Chase maneuvered into a position where he could see what was happening.

Two white men, dressed in deerskin coats, had one old Indian man on the ground and were kicking him in the head and stomach with their pointed boots. The old man, still conscious, was groaning in pain. A handful of women and children looked on in horror, keening eerily and praying to Grandfather pitifully.

Spirit, feeling Chase's thigh muscles tense, instinctively leaped forward into a full gallop. The white tormentors looked up just as Chase reached them, but it was too late. He was all over them like an enraged grizzly bear. One of the men was tall and muscular with red hair; his partner was short and fat with flowing blond hair.

Chase slammed his fist into Red's face with such force that it sent him reeling to the ground, senseless. He then buried his fist wrist-deep in Shorty's belly.

The man bent over gasping for breath, his thick jowls

turning grayish-white for lack of oxygen. When he looked up, Chase smashed him in the face with a full swing, knocking him on his rear. Blood splattered down the front of his coat.

Chase taunted through gritted teeth. "Get up, you miserable pig. You don't seem as brave now as you did when you were kicking the old man."

Enraged, Shorty rose unsteadily to his feet, brandishing a hunting knife at Chase, waving it back and forth in a futile attempt to frighten his enemy. With a sinister smile on his bloody face, he couldn't wait to feel Chase's flesh close around the cold steel. He intended to make this stranger pay for what he had done to him and his friend.

Suddenly, with the quickness of a rattlesnake, Chase grabbed the man's wrist and twisted it. The short man flipped over onto his back. At the same time, the still air was split by a loud snapping of bones.

"Get up you yellow-bellied snake before I kick your teeth in," Chase hissed.

Shorty slowly rose, supporting his broken arm. He spat out a mouthful of blood on the ground as he weaved unsteadily on his feet. His lip curled in a sneer.

"You damned savage. Don't you know who you just knocked down? That's Rob Johnson, Will Johnson's son, and I'm Ben Black. When Will finds out what you've done, he'll kill you along with the rest of these foul-smelling blanket heads."

With lightning speed, Chase backhanded Ben across the face. His head jerked sideways, and frothy blood poured from his lips. "As for your friend, he really doesn't frighten me much lying around unconscious like that. If his old man's not any tougher than he is, I'm not too worried about him either. In any case, you'd best throw him across his horse and ride out of here before I kill you both."

Chase's voice was quietly menacing, his eyes as hard as steel, combining to convince Ben he had better do as he was told. Painfully, he managed to hoist Red over his mount. Climbing aboard his own horse and favoring his wrist, he rode out of the village without another word.

Chase turned his attention to the broken man lying on the ground. Already the women were seeing to his wounds. Lacy came riding up, having watched the encounter from a distance.

Chase cursed softly. Would she ever see him as anything but violent now? Dammit! This was violent country, and a man had to do certain things to survive. But he had no hopes that anybody as refined as Lacy could understand that.

Lacy dismounted and rushed to the wounded Indian's side. Hoping that someone among the Indians spoke English, she said, "Let's get him inside. He's in shock, and the cold will only make it worse."

Chase's eyes widened. That was the most spirit she'd shown since her attack. And it was in behalf of an Indian. He was pleased.

An old woman stepped forward. "Follow me. We will take him home, where I can care for him."

Chase bent down, hoisted the old man effortlessly, then motioned for the woman to lead the way.

As they walked, she told Lacy proudly, "I am Dawn; this is Running Fox, my husband. He is our tribe's *didanvwisgi*, medicine man."

She led them to a small cabin in the center of the clearing. Inside the structure all was clean and in order, but the house itself was badly in need of repair. Gaps in the walls allowed wind to blow into the cabin. Lacy shivered, feeling the cold air on her neck.

Chase reverently laid the Cherokee holy man in the center of his bed. The old fellow groaned as he opened his eyes to stare at Chase. His face was ghostly-pale and drawn. He didn't speak.

Dawn addressed Chase gratefully as she knelt by the bed next to her husband. "If you had not come when you did, they would have killed him. The best thing for my husband now is to stay warm." She pulled well-worn animal skins up over his bony shoulders. "Soon the men of the village will return from hunting. They will know what to do for him."

Chase nodded. "I am Stalker and this is Lacy. Why were those men here?"

"They come here often, steal our deerskin, and take them to Will Johnson. He sells them and keeps the money for himself. Meanwhile, we don't have enough money to buy food for our children. Our husbands have tried to stop these men, but they are not able. This time they are off hunting for deer to replace the skins the greedy white men have stolen. Running Fox is too old to hunt anymore, so he stayed behind with the women and children."

She fingered her husband's coverings. "When we told the white men that we had no skins, they beat Running Fox and accused us of lying. Now I'm afraid of what Will Johnson will do to our people when he learns of the fight."

Both Chase and Lacy stood solemnly, listening to Dawn's tale of woe. Chase hoped that Lacy would realize that he had done what he had to. Because he would do it again! The Cherokee were truly a defeated people, uprooted from their homes, living in desperation, and he had to help them.

"I'm so sorry this happened to your husband," Lacy said. Even though she'd had no part in it, the acrid taste of guilt was strong in her mouth; she was ashamed of what the whites of Johnsonville were doing to the Cherokee. "I wish we had gotten here sooner and spared your family this tragedy."

Tears rolled down Dawn's wrinkled cheeks. "Your eyes are good and kind. I'm glad you have come. We have little, but what we have we are proud to share with you."

"Thank you, but that may not be necessary," Chase said. "I'm looking for my uncles, Lone Wolf and Screaming Eagle. Are they among your people?"

She turned to Chase, sympathy evident in her dark eyes. "Your uncle, Lone Wolf, lives here with us. But Screaming

Eagle is dead. Will Johnson's men killed him when he raised his hand against them."

The look of grief and disappointment on Chase's face reached out to Lacy. She walked over to him and stood at his side.

Chase had wanted to see his uncles again and tell them about their parents, their sisters, and the things that had happened to the family since the Removal. He had also wanted to help them, if possible, return to a more civilized way of life, so they might enjoy the peace and comfort they had been denied for so long.

Now, because of Will Johnson, it was too late for Screaming Eagle. As Chase vowed to avenge his uncle's death, to make Will Johnson suffer as he was now suffering, he felt a gentle hand touch his arm.

He looked down into Lacy's face, not surprised to see her standing beside him. He noticed the telltale bruises against her pale complexion, and it occured to him that a person didn't have to be Indian to suffer at the hands of white men. He touched her cheek, but neither of them spoke. Words weren't necessary.

Twenty-Eight

The tender scene was interrupted by a noise outside. Chase stepped to the door of the cabin and saw six Indian warriors returning from the hunt. They were all older men, slumped on the backs of their saddleless horses, looking weary from riding all day.

The youngest of them, a man in his middle forties, looked in Chase's direction while Dawn related the events that had just transpired, including the part about Chase saving the *didanvwisgi* single-handedly.

He dismounted and strolled over to Chase, stopping in front of him. He peered intently into Chase's face for a long while, searching. Slowly a smile lit up his broad face. Lone Wolf recognized the young hero's striking resemblance to Evan Tarleton.

"Stalker," he asked in the Cherokee language. "Is it you?"

"Yes, Lone Wolf, it is I. I have come."

"You are; it is good," replied Lone Wolf, pleased that Chase had offered the traditional Cherokee greeting. He smiled, and the skin around his eyes crinkled. It was good that his sister had taught her son the ways of their people.

With the formalities past, the two men embraced warmly. It had now been almost twenty-two years since Nelda and little Stalker had been taken away by the soldiers and Lone

Wolf and Screaming Eagle had fled to the mountains. In all those years, Lone Wolf had never ceased wondering about the fate of the other members of his family.

"Tell me about your mother and our family," said Lone Wolf eagerly.

The villagers slipped away, and Chase told his uncle of the deaths of his grandparents, his aunt, and his cousin. Finally, with great pain, he told about his parents. "Mother died about a year ago of the same illness that had claimed my father. Both were taken by what the white man calls typhoid pneumonia."

"I'm sorry to say that Screaming Eagle joined the rest of our family in the spirit world three weeks past," said Lone Wolf after a moment. "But he did not die from disease. He died at the hand of Will Johnson's men." A fierce hatred for the white man was evident in Lone Wolf's voice.

Just then Lacy emerged from Dawn's cabin, and Chase held out his hand to her. She walked over to him and placed her hand in his. "Lacy, this is my uncle, Lone Wolf. Lone Wolf, this is my friend, Lacy."

"Your friend is a rare beauty," Lone Wolf said to Chase, then turned to Lacy. "You remind me of another beautiful white woman I knew once long ago." He spoke with a wistful smile on his face. "Tell me, child, who is your father? I used to know many white people before the Removal of the Cherokee. I might know him."

"Adam Hampton. He's a doctor in Clarke County."

Lone Wolf's eyes glistened like diamonds. "Yes, I know him. Your father is one of the few men in Georgia I respect."

Lacy thanked Lone Wolf for the compliment in her father's behalf.

"Come, you will be our guests in my home."

They followed Lone Wolf to his cabin. He lived alone without wife or children. Lone Wolf hurried about preparing turkey, hominy, squash, and nuts for their evening meal. In a matter of minutes they were sitting at a roughly

270

hewn wooden table with a typical Cherokee dinner in front of them. After they had eaten, Lone Wolf pulled out a long pipe in anticipation of his evening smoke.

"Uncle, save your pipe for another time. I have something I think you might like better." Chase removed two cheroots from his shirt pocket and handed one to his uncle.

Lone Wolf savored the smell of the thin black cigar for a moment. "It's been a long time since I enjoyed a good cigar." Smiling, he continued facetiously, "That's one thing from civilization I've missed!"

When the cigars were lit, Chase and his uncle sat silently, puffing heartily. Blue-white curls of smoke escaped through a small hole in the roof.

Lone Wolf looked at Lacy. "How's Miss Reenie?"

Lacy and Chase looked at each other in surprise. "She's fine. Do you know my aunt?"

"Yes. She and I were good friends once." Lone Wolf's voice softened as he spoke. "Sadly, since I am an Indian and she is white, there could be no future for our friendship." It was unusual for Lone Wolf to speak of matters of the heart with anyone, but with Chase and Lacy it was different. "Seeing the two of you together brings back memories."

Lacy and Chase avoided one another's eyes. Both wished that they were truly together.

"Why don't you come back to Clarke County with us?" Chase asked after clearing his throat. "I'm sure you will be welcomed by my father's family."

"Chase, have you told your grandfather that you are half Cherokee?"

"No," answered Chase. "But I plan to tell him as soon as I get back. Lacy and I left Athens suddenly in order to help a slave girl escape to the North. I wanted to tell him, but there was no time."

"How do you know that this white man will accept you when he finds out you are an Indian?"

"I don't know . . . for sure," Chase answered honestly.

271

"But Eli Tarleton is a good man, and I just have a feeling that my Indian blood will mean nothing to him." Chase surprised himself that he spoke with such conviction. All along he had doubts about the way his family would accept him, but for some reason his doubts were waning.

"But if they reject me, I own a fine ranch in Indian Territory, where there will always be a place for you. It is called the Circle C, named in honor of my mother's family, your family, the Cruces. If my father's white family cannot accept my Indian blood, I will return there, and you can go with me."

Lacy's heart ached. She had sat quietly, listening to Lone Wolf and Chase, and when Chase said that he might leave Georgia, she realized just how much he had come to mean to her. She couldn't imagine what life would be without him. He obviously didn't feel the same toward her, however, or he couldn't talk about leaving Georgia so casually.

Lone Wolf sat in the doorway, watching the long shadows of night fall over his village. The sun was now sinking fast, the mountains looming up dark in the foreground. The cold air began to seep through his buckskins, which he pulled more closely together. "Stalker, I cannot leave my people as long as they are oppressed by Will Johnson."

"I've heard that this man steals your deerskins and sells them for himself," said Chase.

"It's worse than that, Nephew. Will Johnson takes our deerskins as his own, but that isn't enough; he also takes our women. After he's violated them, he gives them to his men to do with as they please. When they are allowed to return to us, they are as good as dead."

Lacy gasped in shock as Lone Wolf continued his agonizing report. "We are powerless to fight him. He has many men while we are so few. He has reduced us to a handful of warriors by killing all who raise a hand against him. Screaming Eagle was hung as an outlaw for trying to protect a sixteen-year-old girl who was being raped by

Johnson's son. As the sheriff of Johnsonville, the man controls everything and everyone in it. The problem you came upon today was caused by his men demanding more deerskins from us than we have. Now he will return in force to make us pay dearly."

Chase rose to his feet and glanced over at Lacy. When Lone Wolf had mentioned rape, she had paled visibly. He wished that his uncle had not been so graphic.

Feeling the weight of the Indian village heavy upon his shoulders, he sighed. "I didn't know things were this bad." He strode to Lacy's side and placed a reassuring hand on her shoulder. This time she didn't flinch.

He turned to his uncle. "I think I'll pay Mr. Johnson a visit and help him change his attitude toward the Cherokee."

Lone Wolf smiled. The look in his nephew's eyes bode ill for his enemy. "I think maybe you can persuade Will Johnson to change. I don't think he's ever met an Indian like you."

"Thanks for your vote of confidence, Uncle," said Chase. "In the meantime, it would be best for you to move your people out of here. We can't risk Johnson and his men coming here, looking for vengeance before I've had a chance to finish with him. High up in the Smokies is a Cherokee village that you must try to reach. I'll give you directions. War Eagle, their chief, remembers you. He'll welcome you and your people among them. You should be safe there until I come for you."

"Yes, I know War Eagle. We will be safe with him." He turned to Lacy, "Will you go with us, to be safe?"

In unison, Lacy and Chase said: "I will stay with Chase," and "Lacy will stay with me."

Lone Wolf smiled.

Twenty-Nine

Early the next morning Chase made camp in a dense forest two miles outside of Johnsonville where he was satisfied that Lacy would be safe until he returned.

"I should be back before noon," Chase said as he mounted Spirit.

Lacy walked over to him and laid her hand on his thigh. "Do you really have to do this? Now that Lone Wolf has moved his village, Will Johnson can't hurt them."

"I know you can't possibly understand." He covered her hand with his own. "But it's just not right for a person to run a man off his land. If Lone Wolf and the others stay away, then Will Johnson has won. He's run them off like mad dogs, and their pride will never recover."

"I understand more than you think," said Lacy, dropping her hand to her side. It hurt that Chase still thought of her as insensitive. Still, if Will Johnson got the upper hand with Chase, it would be the last time she'd ever see him. "Is pride worth risking your life over?"

He reached down and touched her cheek gently. "You worried about me, Sweet Peach?"

"No, I'm worried about Will Johnson," she said sarcastically and slapped his leg. "Of course I'm worried about you, you big oaf. After all, you did save my life!"

Chase's teeth flashed white against his swarthy complexion. "Well, don't worry, you can't get rid of me so easily. I'll teach Will Johnson a well-deserved lesson and be back in time to cook you a decent dinner."

Lacy rolled her eyes. The conceit of some men never ceased to amaze her. But she chuckled when she said, "Well, don't go too hard on poor ole Will . . . not to mention the dozen or so well-trained gunmen that'll be aiming at your back."

Chase leaned down and planted a soft kiss on Lacy's mouth. Still bent over, his face close to hers, he promised, "I'll have pity on the poor slob."

Then he rode off, smiling all the way to town.

On the outskirts of Johnsonville he came to a general store. He threw his reins over the hitching post and crossed the boardwalk. When he stepped inside the dimly lit store, he saw the propietor, a portly young man, standing behind the cash box.

"Good morning," said the propietor, without looking up. "What can I help you with today?" Then he saw Chase. Shocked by his size, his face turned ashen white.

"I need some new clothes," said Chase. "I'm an undertaker and need to look presentable." An hour later, when Chase left the store, he wore a black suit and tie, black pointed shoes, black top hat, and carried a cane.

While he walked down the street, he looked over the town. He wanted to know where everything was located in case he needed an escape route. Contrary to the bravado he'd exhibited with Lacy, Chase was no fool and knew he'd have to be careful if he expected to survive.

The small town consisted of six wooden structures, all boasting the name of Johnson. To Chase's right was the Johnsonville Saloon; next to it was Sheriff Johnson's Office and Jail, then the Will Johnson Hotel. On the left was the Will Johnson General Store, the Johnsonville Bank, and finally the Will Johnson Livery Stable.

Chase turned into the sheriff's office and introduced himself to a deputy who was slumped behind a low desk.

"Hello, sir. My name is John Dungen. I'm new in town and would like to see Will Johnson. I understand he's the sheriff here." Chase offered his hand to the deputy.

The deputy, a tall, lean fellow of about forty, jumped up from his chair, grasped Chase's hand, and shook it like a dog would a rabbit.

"I'm Deputy Jurden; not Jorden, mind ya, but Jurden. Everybody wants to call me Jorden, but I ain't no Jorden; I'm a Jurden," he said in a staccato voice.

"Well, Mr. Jurden," Chase emphasized, "I'm glad to meet you. By the way, you don't look like a Jorden to me. If I had to guess your name, I'd say right off it was definitely Jurden and not Jorden."

"Don't ya talk purty. Ya say m'name jest right. I sure 'preciate that. I hate it when folks call me Jorden. Don't know why nobody never gits it right," the simpleton rambled on, then abruptly, "Are ya a precher 'r somethin'?" He peered at Chase intently. "Ya sure do look like one t' me."

Chase broke into the deputy's rambling before he could launch into another speech. "Mr. Jurden, I've come looking for Sheriff Johnson."

"Well, I'm 'spectin him back here dreckly. Whatcha want with 'im?"

The deputy's speech was so peculiar Chase wasn't certain he understood everything he said. Linni was easier to understand that Jurden.

"I'm an undertaker. I thought I might set up business here, but I want to talk to the sheriff first and find out if it would be worth my while."

"Hot ziggidy," said Jurden, rubbing his hands together. "That's jest what this town needs, a good undertaker. We ain't never had one of those, and the way folks keep dyin' off around here—I'm glad ya ain't no preacher. Now that ya got m'name right, I want ya to stay healthy."

"Is there something wrong with being a preacher, Mr. Jurden?"

"They sure is. Why, Mr. Will, he purely hates preachers. Now, hows 'bout a cup of coffee while ya wait fer the sheriff?"

"Thanks. That sounds good." Jurden's attention span was so short that getting information from him was like pulling hen's teeth. Chase folded his long length onto a splintery bench protruding from the wall. "Why does Mr. Johnson hate preachers?" He shifted, striving to get comfortable yet avoid the spiky splinters.

"Why, he hates 'em, that's all they are to it." It was obvious to Chase the deputy was quoting a frequently expressed sentiment. "He thinks all preachers are goin' straight to Hell. I think sometimes he'd like to hep 'em git there," the deputy whispered like a conspirator as he poured black coffee into two dirty cups. "But he leaves 'em alone so long as they leave him alone, and bleve ya me, they leave him alone. Mr. Will, he don't put up with nuthin', and folks 'round here knows it. But now since yore an undertaker, that'll be all right."

Suddenly the door was thrown back on its hinges and banged against the wall. Will Johnson swept into the room. He was nothing like Chase expected. He looked more like a buffalo than a brigand. He was too heavy by half, and his huge jowls were red from hard drinking and barely suppressed rage. His bushy eyebrows practically met in the middle, forming a thick, dark line over his nondescript, beady eyes. His receding hairline was in stark contrast to the shaggy mane of dark, greasy hair that flowed over his frayed collar.

If ever a man needed facial hair, it was Will Johnson. His features were so ominously chiseled, his was a face even a mother couldn't love. His smile was a sneer; his gaze was a glare. One look at Will Johnson convinced Chase that this man was capable of anything.

Chase rose to his feet.

Johnson took one look at Chase and said, "Jorden, who's the stranger?"

"Now, Sheriff, I've told ya m'name's Jurden, not Jorden," protested the deputy inanely.

"Shut your damn mouth, you idiot. I'll call you anything I like. Now, who is this?"

A muscle twitched in Chase's jaw as he fought to control his temper. "I'm John Dungen, Sheriff. I'm an undertaker. Thinking of settling here."

"Mister," said the sheriff harshly. "You look like a damn preacher to me. If you are, you're in the wrong place. I don't have no truck with preachers. If you're one of them, you had better get out of my town while you still can."

Without emotion, Chase responded, "Mr. Johnson, I assure you I am no preacher."

Johnson's eyes became slits as he gave Chase the once over. "So you're an undertaker?"

Chase nodded.

"Yeah. Well there's lots of spies around these days. And preachers are the worst kind. If you're lying to me, I'll hang you."

Chase had about decided that a man as crazy as Will Johnson was not worth the effort it would require to punish him. Chase fought for what he believed in, but a paranoid bigot could hardly be considered a worthy adversary. All of a sudden the past didn't mean much to him, only the future. Lacy was right. Now that Lone Wolf and his people were on their way to War Eagle's village, Will Johnson couldn't harm them. All Chase wanted to do was return to Lacy as soon as possible.

"Mr. Johnson," he said politely. "It's been good meeting you, sir. And you, too, Mr. Jurden. I think I'll just walk

279

around town and meet a few other people. I'm sure I'll be seeing both of you again real soon." He started for the door after a gentlemanly bow.

Just then the door opened, and Stuart Shepard and Beau Patton entered the room. Chase froze in his tracks. Stuart spoke to the sheriff without noticing Chase. "Will, we're supposed to meet with Leonard Johnson at the hotel in thirty minutes."

At that moment he became aware of the newcomer and peered intently into his face. At first he didn't recognize Chase, not expecting to see him in Johnsonville; then his eyes widened.

"Tarleton, what the hell are you doing here?"

Chase stood motionless. The blood was pounding in his head, drowning out all sound. The name Leonard Johnson opened a festering wound in Chase's mind. The red curtain of rage slowly subsided, leaving Chase to face Stuart and Beau. Inwardly, he cursed himself for not wearing a gun.

"Tarleton?" said the sheriff. "His name's not Tarleton. He's John Dungen, a new undertaker in town. Are you drunk again, Shephard?"

"I don't know what the bastard told you, but he isn't an undertaker. He's Chase Tarleton." Stuart ground out his words, infuriated that this local yokel would question him.

"That's right, Will," Beau supported. "Stuart ought to know. He and Chase are cousins."

Immediately palming his gun, Will raised it behind Chase's head. "Boy, I told you not to lie to me. Now I know you're a damn spy and probably a preacher to boot." He struck Chase on the head with the butt of his gun, rendering him unconscious.

When Chase awakened, he found himself locked inside a dark, musty cell. He was lying on his stomach on a bare cot with his hands shackled to the iron bed railing above his head. The rusty shackles bit into his wrists, and his head ached something fierce. He could hear Will, Stuart, and Beau discussing him in the front office.

"He must have discovered our plan and come here to spy on us," Stuart said. "We can't let him go free now. We can't be sure how much he knows."

"Don't worry, Stuart," the sheriff said. "I'm gonna hang him tomorrow. Nobody lies to Will Johnson and lives to tell about it."

"Now, Sheriff," Jack Jurden whined. "He seems like a right nice young feller to me. Mebbe it's jest a misunderstandin'."

"Shut up, Jorden, or I'll hang you, too."

"Jurden, not Jorden," the deputy muttered under his breath.

Stuart looked through the bars, grinning sadistically. "Tell you what, Will. If you're going to hang him in the morning, why not let me have a little fun with him first?"

"What do you have in mind?" the sheriff asked.

Stuart lifted a razor strap off a nail on the wall and said, "I think I'll punish the dog for spying on us. Back in Georgia, I had planned to shoot him in the back, but giving him a good whipping and watching him hang is even better."

"Fine by me."

Beau's eyes lit up. "Go ahead and give him a strapping."

The sheriff retrieved the key from his desk and opened the cell door. "Hey, you in there. Yeah you, liar. Stuart's got a little surprise for you this afternoon; then we'll hang what's left of you tomorrow."

Chase glared at Stuart as he entered the cell. His eyes burned into Stuart's skull. "If I were you, I'd be careful with that strap," Chase warned.

"You don't scare me, Cousin. You'll cry like a baby before I get through with you." With that he swung the strap, hitting Chase across the neck.

Chase didn't so much as flinch. Each time Stuart wielded

the strap, he hit Chase in a different spot.

Stuart was strong, and his face reddened from excitement, not exertion. The hatred he'd suppressed ever since Chase arrived at Towering Pines was unleashed, making him mindless with violence.

Suddenly, Chase swung his legs to the floor, lifted the bed by the railings, and slammed it into Stuart's middle, penning him against the bars of the cell. Stuart screamed in pain as his ribs cracked. Chase backed up and rammed him again. Again Stuart screamed from the white-hot pain.

Will Johnson drew his gun and shot past Chase's head. "Back off or my next shot won't miss," he growled.

Chase retreated a step, lowered the bed to the floor, then sat on it. Stuart, doubled over in pain, was gripping the bars of the cell for support.

Beau stood to the side watching the whole incident with a twisted grin on his face. It was obvious to Will that Beau was not going to help his friend.

The sheriff opened the door, reached in nervously, and jerked Stuart out. He locked the door, then threw the key on the desk.

After Stuart caught his breath, the sheriff barked, "Let's get out of here. Leonard's waiting for us at the hotel." Without waiting for an answer, he turned to Jurden.

"Jack, you watch the prisoner closely. Nobody, and I mean nobody, is to get into this jail while I'm gone. Do you hear me?"

"Yes, sir. I'll watch 'im like a hawk. They won't be nobody git past me." Secretly, Jurden was in awe of his prisoner. Stuart had treated the deputy like dirt since he'd come to town the day before, so it did Jurden's heart good to see him get his comeuppance.

Will, Beau, and a pale Stuart left the jail, headed for the hotel.

Chase felt whelps burning his neck, back, and legs where

282

Stuart had strapped him. He had been ready to leave this place peaceably. But not anymore. Now that he knew Leonard Johnson was involved, he had to see it through.

He wasn't too concerned about getting out. He was mad enough to tear the bars out of the walls if he had to. But if he hoped to make good on an escape, he'd have to get free from his shackles first.

"Mr. Jurden," he called softly. "I'm beaten up pretty bad. If I could just get out of these shackles, I could rest a little easier. Do you think you could see your way clear to free my hands?"

"I don't know," replied Jurden dubiously. "The sheriff told me to watch ya close. He didn't say nuthin' 'bout takin' them shackles off."

"That's true. But he didn't say anything about not taking them off either. Besides, I can't go anywhere as long as I'm behind these bars, so what's the harm in allowing me to be free inside the cell?"

"Well, I guess that won't hurt nuthin'. Ya seem like a decent feller to me. Here's the key." He pitched the key to the shackles through the bars onto the bed.

Chase nudged the key up to his hands with his chin and quickly unlocked the shackles. He couldn't believe he had talked Jurden into releasing him so easily. The poor man had a kind heart. Later he might even talk him into opening the cell. Chase frowned when he thought about what Will Johnson would do to the deputy when he found out he had released him.

But Chase couldn't help it. He was facing a rope in the morning, and he would do whatever he had to do to avoid that. But for the time being, he thought it best to leave things alone. By nightfall Jurden would be less skittish and more likely to listen to him. He could probably get him to open the cell freely. Chase didn't want to hurt the deputy, so he hoped to gain his confidence and get his cooperation.

Chase turned over onto his side, facing the wall. What he needed most now was rest so that he would be ready to escape when the time came. He figured he'd have a busy night ahead of him.

But he couldn't sleep. His thoughts were on Lacy. She must be worried sick by now. God, he hoped she stayed at the camp. If Stuart found out she was here, there was no telling what he would do to her. He might even realize she'd had a part in saving Annie. Chase shuddered at the thought.

Thirty

When Chase didn't return by mid-afternoon, Lacy knew something was wrong. She panicked. If something had happened to Chase, she couldn't—well, she just wouldn't think about that now.

"Here's your chance to prove you're not the flighty twit he thinks you are," she encouraged herself as she mounted Precious bareback for the short ride into town.

She saw the general store situated on the edge of town and decided it was as good a place as any to start her search. She bowed her head and walked inside. A plump gentleman came forward to greet her.

"Can I help you, ma'am?" he asked cheerfully.

"I hope you can," she sniffed while she drew a delicate handkerchief from inside her sleeve. Dramatically, she dabbed at her moist eyes. Worry about Chase made crying easy.

"My husband is recently deceased, and I require the services of an undertaker. Please tell me if you have an undertaker in Johnsonville." She affected her most helpless look.

"As a matter of fact, ma'am, we don't, not unless the young man who was by here this morning settles here."

"Could you please direct me to this young man?"

"Well, ma'am, that might not do you much good. About an hour ago, Miss Lillian Johnson came by here and told me the sheriff had him locked up. Seems like there was something about him being a spy or a preacher or something."

"Oh, my," said Lacy. "I could use an undertaker and a preacher. I'll run see the sheriff. Thank you for the information."

Lacy left the general store more frantic now than ever. She looked the town over, trying to decide what she could do to get Chase out of jail. In a moment, it came to her.

She made her way toward the back of the saloon. The tinny sound of the piano, mingled with sounds of drunken male laughter, was accented by the high pitch of female voices. Apparently Johnsonville was a rowdy place, if the saloon clientele was any indication.

When she reached the back of the saloon, she saw what she expected; stairs leading up to the rooms on the second floor. She suspected that dance-hall girls occupied the rooms. From them she'd borrow the necessary clothing needed to put her plan into action.

She quietly climbed the stairs and listened at the first door for movement. When she heard nothing, she slowly opened the door and slipped inside. In a cluttered closet she found what she needed. Quickly changing her clothes, she mussed her hair and drenched herself with cheap perfume. When she finished dressing, she looked into the mirror and wrinkled her nose distastefully. In place of a gently reared Southern belle, she saw a provocative painted floozy, who smelled to high heaven.

She waited until darkness fell over the town. Then she crept down the steps and hurried to the jail. She said a quick but heartfelt prayer, then quietly stepped inside.

Her heart caught when she saw Chase lying on a cot in the cell. Despite his injuries, he was on his feet in an instant. His face spread in a grin when he recognized her.

Jack Jurden, nodding his head in slumber, reclined in the chair behind the desk. Stirring, he opened one eye to see who had come in. When he saw Lacy, he jumped like he had been shot.

"Ma'am, whatcha doin' here? This ain't no place fer a lady."

Lacy blinked her long, sooty eyelashes, sashayed over to the desk, swinging her hips from side to side, and smiled seductively at the deputy.

"Somebody told me that the sheriff in Johnsonville was a good-looking man. But I didn't expect to see anyone as handsome as you," she drawled in a husky voice.

"I'm not the sheriff, ma'am. I'm Jack Jurden, the deputy." He coughed, sputtered, and turned red with embarrassment.

In the back, Chase had to bite the inside of his jaw to keep from laughing at the way Lucy turned Jurden into mush.

The deputy never had been able to keep his wits about him when it came to women. He just fell all to pieces. Even ugly ones shook him. But he'd never seen a woman as pretty as this one. The very sight of her made him feel faint. Sweat popped out on his brow, and his heart pounded against his ribs.

"Well, Mr. Jurden, I think you are a handsome man, sheriff or not," Lacy said, looking him over hungrily. She stepped around the desk, sat on top of it, then slowly crossed her legs, showing an enticing amount of bare flesh.

With eyes as big as saucers, Jurden backed away from her. He knew he couldn't handle the situation. All he could do was get away from her. Lacy slid off the desk and stalked him. He backed up to the bars of the cell just as she had hoped he would. Before he realized what was happening, Chase slipped an arm around his neck.

"Quick, the key's in the desk drawer," Chase whispered.

287

Lacy retrieved the key and opened the cell door.

Chase slowly eased Deputy Jurden into the cell. "Just get into the cell and keep quiet and nobody will get hurt," he said to the fearful man.

"Yes sir, Mr. Dungen. I won't tell a soul what happened if ya don't want me to."

"I appreciate that," Chase said as he locked the door.

Chase grabbed Lacy's hand and pulled her to the front of the room. He hugged her close, pressing her against his body, burying his face in her hair.

"You're something, you know that?" he murmured.

Lacy angled her head back and smiled up into Chase's face, inordinately pleased with his praise.

"You saved my life. They were going to hang me," he told her.

She raised her hand, soothing the angry red whelps on Chase's neck. "Maybe I'm not such a worthless piece of baggage after all," she whispered.

"I never thought you were," Chase returned honestly.

Lacy raised a questioning eyebrow, reminiscent of Chase's action the very first time they met. "You didn't?" Her tone implied that she wasn't buying a bit of it.

"Well, maybe for a while." He grinned sheepishly. "But not lately."

"You mean to tell me that I risked my life to prove my worth to you and it wasn't necessary. I risked my life for nothing?" Lacy feigned exasperation.

"No, you risked your life for me. Besides, seeing that walk was worth it." He leaned down and kissed her, holding her as if he would never let her go. But he had to. The sheriff could come waltzing in at any moment.

While Chase searched through the saddlebags that he took from Spirit and brought into the jail, he explained about Will Johnson. He was dressed in fringed buckskin, soft moccasins, and a beaded headband. Then he smeared

288

on war paint.

"Stuart and Beau were in Johnsonville when I got here this morning," he continued his tale.

"Do you mean Stuart Shephard and Beau Patton?" Lacy asked incredulously, intrigued at the red and white stripes Chase was painting on his handsome face.

"One and the same. They were meeting with Will Johnson and another man from up north, Leonard Johnson."

Lacy noticed Chase's hands shake when he spoke the name Leonard Johnson.

"Do you know what they're up to?"

"I have no idea." Chase walked over to her.

"What are you going to do," she asked, not at all frightened by his savage appearance. This was Chase; he was anything but frightening to her now.

"What I came here to do," he answered cryptically. "You stay here with Jurden, and if you hear anybody coming down the boardwalk wearing hard shoes, go out the back way. If all goes well, I should be back before you and the good deputy can get fully acquainted."

"Don't worry, I'll take good care of her," Jurden called gallantly.

The humor of Jurden's offer to care for Lacy was not lost on Chase and Lacy.

"I appreciate that, Jurden," Chase said, his voice trembling with barely suppressed mirth.

Turning their backs on Jurden, they grinned at one another. Lacy spoke softly behind her hand. "Are you sure his quiver is full of arrows?"

Chase pressed his lips together and glanced back toward the cell. "Not altogether."

Lacy peered around Chase's shoulder, and Jurden waved at her.

She waved, pulled back, rolled her eyes, and instructed Chase warily, "Hurry back!"

He picked up his tomahawk and stepped through the doorway.

"Be careful," she whispered once he was gone.

Chase went directly to the saloon and peered through a side window. Several men stood at the bar drinking whiskey. A dance-hall girl was singing beside an old piano that was being played by a gray-bearded fellow. He appeared to be about half drunk as he pounded out an unrecognizable tune.

In the center of the room, around a circular table, sat Stuart Shephard, Beau Patton, Will Johnson, and Leonard Johnson, deep in conversation. Intent on their discussion, they were oblivious to the music and the activities of the others around them.

Chase backed away from the saloon and hurried over to the hotel. Instinctively, he glanced toward the jail. When he was satisfied that Lacy was safe, he climbed the side stairs of the hotel to the second floor and stepped through a door, into the empty hallway. An oil lantern burned dimly at the far end of the hall, casting eerie shadows on the faded walls. He counted five rooms on each side of the hall.

He wondered which one belonged to Leonard Johnson. The fact that Leslie's father was meeting with Stuart and Beau was intriguing. It was a matter that Chase could not just walk away from.

He had suffered great humiliation from Leslie Johnson's father in New England when his Indian ancestry had come to light. Leonard had blamed Chase for Leslie's suicide, and Chase had accepted the guilt.

Any man would blame himself if the woman he loved killed herself. Chase still felt the queasiness of guilt rising even now. If he had only told her of his Cherokee blood at the beginning, maybe she would still be alive.

He stopped at each of the doors in the hall to listen for sounds from within. The hotel was presently unoccupied. He searched each room, futilely examining the contents, until he entered the room at the far end of the hall. It was Johnson's. He recognized the vaguely familiar smell of his special blend of pipe tobacco.

In the corner lay two black leather satchels filled with clothes and toiletries. Chase searched them carefully, hoping to find an explanation for the alliance between Leonard, Stuart, and Beau.

In a false bottom of the smallest case, Chase discovered a stack of letters tied together with a faded strand of yellow grosgrain ribbon. His stomach churned when he recognized the ribbon as the one Leslie had worn the last time he'd seen her.

He thumbed through the letters. There were two in particular that caught his interest. One, obviously from Stuart, was addressed to Leonard Johnson; the other, addressed in a feminine hand, had the name Chase printed on the front of the envelope.

Chase quickly opened his letter and read:

June 23, 1856
Dearest Chase,

Because of my father I cannot marry you. I want you to know that this doesn't mean that I don't love you. I have many problems, my love, but you are not among them. I will try to explain what is in my heart so that you will never blame yourself for what is about to happen.

I've come to accept what I've actually known for a long time. My father is losing his mind. He used to be kind and good, but two years ago he changed. I don't know if my mother's death is what caused it or not, but whatever the reason, he is not the same person I knew and loved as a child.

I thought I could help him, but now I know that I can't. Tonight, after I told him about us, he violated me. He said vile things to me. He said that if I had no more pride than to give myself to a savage, he would use me, too. Something inside me has died.

I don't know where to turn. I'm faced with the prospect of turning my own father over to the authorities or of allowing this to go on. I had hoped we could build a life together, but, Chase, I can't bring myself to marry you now that I have been defiled by my own father. My only choice is to end it all. Please forgive me.

With eternal love,
Leslie

Chase sat staring blankly at the floor, profoundly shaken. For years he had blamed himself for Leslie's death. Now, in a matter of minutes, he discovered that he was not the cause.

He was relieved that the fault was not his, but was saddened when he thought about the pain that Leslie had suffered during her final hours.

Then he thought of Lacy. She had been defiled; would she kill herself, too? He had to get back to her, make her discuss what those miners had done to her, so he could help her bear it. But first, he had a job to do.

White-hot fury burned in his breast. He thought of the vile crime Leonard Johnson had committed and the abuse that the Cherokee had suffered at the hands of Will Johnson and his men.

Then he remembered the other letter he held crushed in his hand. It read:

October 15, 1859
Leonard:

Just a note to confirm our plans and set the meeting in Johnsonville as we discussed earlier. Here in Georgia all is going according to plan. I have prepared one slave girl with a pentagram. She has been "rescued" and should reach the North shortly. When she surfaces, make sure to publicize the devil worshipping practices of the Southern planters. If war is to break out, we need an issue that all the god-fearing Yankees can rally behind.

In the meantime, Beau and I will continue to stir up anti-Northern sentiment in our region. The war commission meets next week, and we will be apprised of the projected locations for the munitions depots in the South. Speak to the Northern generals in our behalf and tell them that the information they seek is forthcoming. Make sure they know the price is five million and non-negotiable.

Beau and I will meet you and Will in Johnsonville, as we agreed. If all goes well, the country should be at war within a year, and we will be in England before the first shot is fired.

I caution you to keep a tight rein on your brother and proceed slowly. If you have need to contact me, go through the usual channels. Burn this letter after you've read it.

Stuart

Obviously Leonard hadn't taken Stuart's advice to burn the letter. No doubt he was planning a little extortion of his own. With the information Chase now possessed, he would see to it that neither Stuart nor Leonard would succeed in their nefarious scheme. He and Lacy had to get back to Athens fast.

"Is everything going according to plan, Johnson?" Stuart leaned back in his chair, striking a match on the bottom of his gleaming Hessian boot, while he studied Leonard's face.

"Of course it is. Didn't I tell you I would take care of my end?" Leonard answered peevishly.

"Just see that you do!" Beau spat.

"Hey, that's no way to talk to each other when we're about to be five million dollars richer. Let's celebrate!" Will said, studying each man at the table carefully, before breathing a sigh of relief.

"Sheila, get over here with a fresh bottle of whiskey before I kick you out in the streets where you belong."

A girl behind the bar hurried over to the center table with a full bottle clutched in her trembling hands. "You don't have to talk to me like that, Mr. Will. Just tell me what you need. I'll be glad to wait on you."

"I believe that girl's got some spunk," slurred Beau, a little tipsy from four rounds of drinks. "Come here, sweet thing, and sit on my lap." He chuckled as he grabbed her greedily and pulled her down.

When he put his hand up her dress, she tried to get away, but he held her in a viselike grip. "Your bottom's soft and silky," he said, grabbing her painfully.

Mortified at Beau's groping, Sheila freed herself from his grasp and slapped him soundly across the mouth. "I'm a barmaid, not one of your slaves," she shouted, tears clouding her vision. "I don't have to take this kind of abuse from the likes of you."

Beau jumped out of his chair, grabbed her by the hair, and bent her over the table. Stuart, Leonard, and Will sat watching, unconcerned.

She squirmed on the table, but he held her down with his full weight.

"I ought to poke you right now in front of all these men for slapping me." Still holding her down, he took out a knife and sliced her dress from neck to hem. Stuart, Will, and Leonard looked on with growing interest.

"Get her!" howled Leonard.

Beau ripped her chemise off, baring her to the waist. He cut the string that was holding her lower undergarments secure, revealing her private parts. She screamed and fought, but without success.

Beau was too strong for her, and his ire was up now. Hot blood pulsated through his body. He was determined to rape the barmaid, or by God he'd die trying.

Suddenly, the back door burst off its hinges with a tremendous noise. Chase had been watching from the window until he virtually went mad with rage. Not one more girl would suffer as Lacy, Leslie, and God only knew how many Cherokees had, not if he could help it!

He kicked the door in with his foot and went straight to Beau. He hit him in the face with the blunt side of his tomahawk, instantly breaking his nose. With a backward swing he struck Stuart in the jaw; then with another swing he caught the back of Will's head.

Leonard ran like a coward, but Chase quickly caught and slammed him against the wall. He slumped to the floor, unconscious.

The men at the bar pulled their guns on Chase and began firing. But he was so quick, they couldn't draw a bead on him. He was on them like a demon. He leveled the whole bunch in a matter of seconds.

When everyone in the room was down except for the women and the piano player, Chase yelled, "Get out of here and take as many of the others as you can."

He stood beside the wood-burning stove, waiting for them to vacate the saloon.

Will looked at Chase through a haze of pain, not recognizing him as the prisoner he had locked up earlier. One by one he dragged Leonard, Stuart, and Beau outside. The others, moaning and groaning, crawled out the best way they could.

Foolishly, Will returned one last time with his gun in

hand. He aimed and fired at Chase. But he was too groggy to be accurate.

As he fired, Chase took his tomahawk, threw it, and with the blunt side hit the big man in the chest. The blow sent him reeling back out the front door.

The saloon, now empty, had two main support posts. Chase hoisted the axe used to split wood, and chopped the first post in two, closest to the front door. The front part of the building sagged. Then he took a few swings at the second post.

After stoking the fire in the stove, he backed to the rear entrance, then threw the axe with all his strength, cutting the second post in two. As the building crashed in, he leaped to safety. The saloon was soon a flaming inferno.

Chase picked out several choice firebrands. He threw one into the hotel. The old timbers caught fire, and the entire structure went up in flames. He threw the remaining firebrands into the bank, the livery stable, and the general store. Only the jail was spared for the sake of Jurden and Lacy.

By this time, the town was in total panic. Men were running everywhere, some to save the animals housed in the livery, some in an attempt to obey the orders croaked out by Will Johnson, to save the money in the bank.

Chase watched the pandemonium for a few seconds, then walked down the middle of the street toward the jail. Inside, he found Jurden and Lacy, both white as sheets.

Lacy ran to Chase and threw herself into his arms. Then she stepped back and raked him from top to bottom with her eyes, reassuring herself that he was unharmed.

"I've gotta get you away from here," he told her.

He walked over to the cell, and unlocked the door, letting Jurden out.

The deputy stared in amazement.

Chase took a piece of paper from his desk, scribbled a few

words on it, and tacked it up on the wall just inside the door.

He turned to the wide-eyed deputy. "Goodbye, Jurden. I suggest that you get another job. Working for Will Johnson is a little dangerous if you ask me." Chase winked and put his arm around Lacy. Together, they stepped out into the night.

No one spared the Indian and the painted floozy so much as a glance as they walked down the street amidst the burning rubble. Unnoticed, they disappeared into the forest and were swallowed up by the darkness.

Back in the jail, Jurden looked at the note Chase had left nailed to the wall. He read aloud: "This time, Johnson, you live. The next time you harm a Cherokee, you die."

Thirty-One

Brad arrived home from work early and turned his horse and buggy over to a servant. He rushed inside, anxious to see Celia. It had been weeks since he'd taken her from Beau's plantation, and he knew that tongues were wagging about them as far away as Carroll County. But he didn't care. All that mattered to him was keeping Celia safe, and to do that she had to remain at Paradise.

He found Celia alone in the library, reclining on an embroidered sofa. An opened book rested in her lap.

She wore an Alma organdy gown. Its low decolletagé revealed firm alabaster swells, and her body, though very slight, aroused Brad to a feverish pitch.

"Brad," she greeted softly.

"I missed you," he said as he removed his hat and gloves and placed them on a side table.

"I'm glad. I've missed you, too," she replied, blushing. "In fact, I was just thinking about you."

"What were you thinking?"

Casting her gaze lap-ward, Celia didn't notice Brad's rakish grin. It was more than obvious to him what she'd been thinking, and unless he was off by a mile and a half, it was the same thing he'd been thinking.

"I was just thinking about your work at the bank," Celia

299

answered coyly. "I find banking so interesting. I think I'd like to learn more about it someday."

Brad was certain the little minx had not been thinking about his bank. He crossed over to the sofa and clasped her hand in his. "Celia Jeanette Harrington, you're not very good for a man's ego. I hoped you were going to say you had been thinking about me, not about my work at the bank."

"Well, I've been thinking about you, too," she said, blushing all over again. "It's such a nice day, I thought it would be wonderful if we could enjoy it together."

The expression on her beautiful face portrayed a passion that Brad did not miss. He looked deeply into her eyes. They exuded warmth and desire. He touched her soft face with his fingertips, moving them slowly downward, across her slightly parted lips.

Her mouth quivered at his touch with an unmistakable invitation to be explored. Very deliberately he lowered his face and slanted his lips over hers.

Then he picked her up in his arms and effortlessly carried her up the stairs into her bedroom. He kicked the door closed with the heel of his boot and laid her down on the bed. Luckily, they met no one along the way. Brad was desperately aroused, but he didn't want to scandalize the family, or embarrass Celia.

Celia sighed. This scene was reminiscent of the day Brad had rescued her from Raven plantation. But unlike that day, Celia now had no reason to cry. She wanted only to smile— smile at the incredibly handsome man whose brown eyes were devouring every inch of her.

For what seemed an eternity, Brad hovered above Celia, adoring her ethereal beauty. He had in mind to introduce her to the joys of lovemaking as it was meant to be. In his mind, Celia was still a virgin. What Beau Patton had done to her was not lovemaking but physical violence. And Brad was mindful that Celia was still affected by the atrocities she had suffered.

Very carefully, so as not to frighten her, Brad placed a tender kiss on her lips. He groaned low in his throat when he felt her urgent response. Deepening the kiss, his hand lightly grazed Celia's sensitive breast. Beneath the thin fabric of her tight bodice, he felt her nub tighten with excitement.

He deftly unbuttoned the front of her gown. With her platinum hair fanned out over the pillow and a shy smile gracing her heart-shaped mouth, she looked like a heavenly being. Brad was convinced that God must have used Celia as his model when creating his court of angels. As if she were holy, he gently loved her.

Celia appreciated Brad's gentleness. She knew he would never hurt her. He cared for her too much. Still, being in bed with a man was a little threatening after what she had endured. She had to let Brad know, however, that she wanted him. Taking his tanned hand, she placed it beneath her chemise, covering her alabaster breast.

Her provocative gesture all but shattered Brad's control. Hungrily, he plundered the velvety recesses of Celia's mouth, his breath mingling with hers. His steamy kiss caused them both to forget the past. Their conciousness was limited to the circle of one another's arms and the glorious moment.

Brad sprouted another set of hands as he made short work of peeling away Celia's confining clothes. He feasted his eyes on her naked body, like a starving man. She was so incredibly tiny that for a moment Brad feared his solid form might injure her. But when she raised her silky arms to circle his neck, he forgot everything save the feel of her flesh burning into his.

While Brad tantalized every inch of Celia's snow white body, she brazenly removed his shirt. He stood to remove his breeches and boots and then lay down, full length, against her.

The late-afternoon sun, filtering through the windows, illuminated Brad's bronze body. To Celia, he looked like a Greek god. And the contrast of his corded muscles against

301

her soft white flesh was strangely erotic. When his full arousal made contact with her hip, she instinctively ground against it. Brad moaned low in his throat, pleasing Celia inordinately.

Uncharacteristically bold, she pushed Brad's shoulders to the bed. Angling herself above him, she rubbed her breasts across him, delighting in the feel of his hair-roughened chest. Passion-darkened, chocolate brown eyes blazed into sultry, ice blue eyes as Celia tilted her head, placing a passionate kiss on Brad's lips. Mocking her lover's previous activity, Celia's mouth and hands traveled the length of his beautifully male body.

Brad was almost in shock. He had planned to go slowly and gently with Celia, but she was seducing him like a practiced courtesan. He was on fire for the little temptress, loving every minute of it, but if he didn't regain control soon, he would be incinerated.

Worming his way on top, his male instincts took over. Brad, who had made love to countless women, was extremely accomplished in the art. But he had never experienced anything like this. Making love to this child-woman, whom he had seemed to love forever, touched him in a way that no other woman ever had. He and Celia weren't merely satisfying carnal desires. They were giving a part of themselves to one another that neither had given before.

"Brad, please!" Celia rasped. There was an ache in her center that only Brad could appease.

Brad asked thickly, "Please what, honey?"

"Please love me!" Celia answered breathlessly, straining toward her love.

With a sensual smile that would make demons blush, Brad fitted himself between Celia's slender thighs. He rested his forearms on either side of her head while touching the moist tip of his proud manhood to the entrance of her most intimate place.

Celia arched her back slightly, closing her eyes in anticipation.

Huskily, Brad spoke, "Honey, look at me. I want to see your beautiful blue eyes when I make you mine."

Celia felt a tingle low in her belly at Brad's provocative statement. Doing as she was bidden, she saw such love and desire flashing from Brad's deep brown pools that she thought for a moment she might well drown.

Suddenly, Brad thrust himself into her warm center. She moaned primitively, clutching his flexed buttocks with her greedy hands.

Impatient for her, Brad's first few movements were rapid and forceful. Then, exerting great control, he settled into a sensual rhythm, capturing her kiss-swollen lips.

Brad wanted to savor the experience and love Celia completely. He was so mindless with desire that he could plunge over the edge at any time, but he didn't want that. He wanted Celia to experience the wonders of love, too, before he claimed his prize.

Passion crackled around them as if they were in the midst of a violent thunder-storm. Their hearts pounded in unison; their bodies labored as one. With Brad gliding in and out of Celia at a maddening pace, they shared themselves totally: body, soul, and spirit.

Finally, Brad's plans to take it slow disintegrated in the heat of their desire. In the midst of their feverish coupling, Brad and Celia shuttered in simultaneous release.

Mindful of Celia's delicate size, Brad shifted his weight, positioning himself at her side. When her breathing slowed, Celia gazed into Brad's eyes for a split second, then looked away in embarrassment.

He gently lifted her chin until she was once again gazing into his eyes. "Cee Cee, I know you're embarrassed, but you don't have to be. I don't ever want you to be embarrassed around me again. What we just shared was not shameful, no

303

matter what you've been taught by society or been made to feel by Beau's abuse."

Celia cringed slightly at the mention of Beau's name.

"Honey, making love isn't evil . . . not if two people care for one another," he continued. "Don't you know what you mean to me?"

Celia smiled, hugging Brad closely to her chest. She didn't trust herself to speak. She just wanted to be held. Brad sensed as much and willingly obliged.

Thirty-Two

Chase and Lacy returned to camp in silence. Once there, Lacy washed off the cheap perfume and heavy cosmetics she had applied for her part in Chase's jailbreak. After disappearing into the underbrush with her well-packed saddlebag in tow, she dressed in a Naccarat bloomer costume. The scandalous breeches didn't really suit with riding boots, but she couldn't help that. They were the only shoes she'd brought.

Next she unstopped the scent bottle that hung suspended from her neck chain and dabbed on a few drops of lavender. The tart fragrance made her feel deliciously feminine again. To complete her toilette, she arranged her thick mane of golden curls in a low braid.

While Lacy dressed, Chase washed the war paint from his face. He was kneeling on his haunches by the fire—still dressed in buckskins—when Lacy emerged from the shadows. Her delicious scent reached him first, and he looked up expectantly. He dropped his gaze and feigned great interest in the fire.

Lacy knew he was dying to tease her about her unorthodox costume. *What self-control he must be exerting!* she thought. *After all, it's not every day that one sees a woman dressed in a man's necktie, basque jacket, flounced*

305

skirt, and baggy trousers. And all in the most adoring shade of tangerine . . . deep in the Smoky Mountains, no less. She stifled a grin.

"Come over by the fire where it's warm," Chase instructed, his lips twitching.

"Definitely!" Lacy hurried over.

Chase straightened up, rubbed his lower back, then sat down on a log by the fire, making room for Lacy to join him. For a while they sat in companionable silence, staring at the dancing flames, then finally Chase spoke.

"Lacy, about what happened in town . . ."

"What *did* happen in town? Did I just imagine it or was it burning? Did you do that?"

"Yes, I had to. I had to stop that man—he was hurting innocent people—the only way I knew how. With a man like Will Johnson, money means power, and power means the ability to do anything he wants, to anybody he wants. The only way to stop him is to impoverish him. And that's what I did."

Lacy sat quietly, considering what Chase had said. She fully agreed with him. She was thinking about how she would like to do the same thing to Stuart—impoverish him and take away his power. Chase interrupted her thoughts. He spoke so softly, she had to ask him to repeat himself.

"I said if that makes me a savage, then so be it."

"Who said you're a savage?"

"Isn't that what you're thinking?"

Lacy wanted desperately to tell Chase to go to blazes and refuse to defend herself, but the outcome of this conversation was too important. She knew now that she loved him with all her heart, just as she knew that their time together was short. It was now or never. Once they got to Athens, who knew if they'd ever see each other again?

"No, my dear misguided *friend*. That's not what I was thinking."

Chase was so distraught that her words didn't register. He

had admitted his feelings for Lacy as well—at least to himself—and it was imperative that he make her understand his violent actions.

He turned to her. "Tonight when I left you in the jail, I went to the saloon. Beau was cutting the clothes off a barmaid. He was exposing her for everyone to see. If I hadn't stopped him, he would have raped her right there on the spot. And Will, Stuart, and Leonard Johnson were cheering him on. Just waiting to take their turns at her when Beau finished. Surely after what you've suffered, you can see that I had to stop them."

"After what I've suffered?"

The look on Chase's face was one of such anguish that tears came to Lacy's eyes.

"After what those men did to you," he said thickly.

Lacy reached for Chase's hand. "Chase, those men didn't rape me. Is that what you thought?"

"What? Of course it's what I thought. Thank God." He pulled Lacy into his embrace. "The thought of those animals hurting you has almost driven me crazy . . . and then tonight when I read Leslie's letter . . . and knew that you'd suffered the same thing she had . . . and the way she died . . ." Chase kissed the top of Lacy's head and shuddered.

"What are you talking about? Who's Leslie?" Lacy tried to tamp down her jealousy. Was it Leslie's ruby ring that Chase cherished so?

He straightened his leg and pulled two letters from his pants pocket. Without a word, he handed her Leslie's letter.

It was yellowed with age, and Lacy felt a moment's hesitation when she noticed the feminine scrawl on the envelope. After she'd read the letter, she raised her questioning gaze to Chase.

"When I was a student in New England, I had a girlfriend." He gestured to the letter that Lacy clutched in her hand.

"At first I didn't tell her that I was half-Indian. I know that

307

was wrong." Chase chastised himself. He turned to Lacy. "That's why I never hid my true background from you. I didn't want you to be another Leslie."

Lacy smiled sadly.

"Shortly after graduation I told her that my mother was a Cherokee Indian." He cleared his throat, not really wanting to go on. "Then I asked her to marry me. She didn't say no and she didn't say yes; she just said she'd tell me the next day. It seemed to me that she wanted to accept my offer, but she needed to discuss it with her father first. The next morning, when my best friend, Sam, came to my room, he told me that Leslie was dead. She had committed suicide."

Lacy felt pity for Chase's suffering, yet it hurt so badly to think of him asking another woman to be his wife. She was ashamed of her petty jealousy; the woman was dead.

"Later that day Leslie's father drove me away from his house, shouting obscenities at me because I was a savage."

Lacy thought of the first time she'd called Chase a savage and understood why he'd become so angry.

"I left New England that day. I believed Leslie killed herself because she couldn't accept the fact that I was part Indian. Ever since then I've lived with the guilt of her death.

"That's why I was so distant to you, always ridiculing your clothes and telling you to go home to your daddy. When what I really wanted to do was hold you close to my side and never let you go."

"Did you really?"

"Of course I did." Then he smiled rakishly. "And I didn't want to be your *friend,* pal."

Lacy giggled self-consciously. But her giggles turned into moans of ecstasy when Chase drew her into his arms and kissed her with all the passion he'd suppressed since that magical day beside the lake.

The letters were forgotten then. Chase circled Lacy's waist and shoulders with his arms and carried her to his bedroll.

He lowered her to the blankets and covered her with his body.

The night sounds around them grew dim, drowned out by the hot blood that pulsated through their fiery bodies. It rushed through their ears and swelled their sensitive organs of love. Through their clothing, Chase ground his sensitive manhood to Lacy's throbbing core. They grew frantic with need.

They had been denied for so long, for too long. Chase ripped away only the clothes necessary to join their bodies. Then he buried himself in her depths, as he had dreamed of doing every night since he'd known her.

His thrusts were fast and sure, his breathing rapid and labored. Lacy arched to meet him, and Chase murmured words of love in Cherokee. Lacy gasped his name over and over, massaging his flexing muscles.

Then with a final surge, Lacy and Chase were flung from the earth, careening into the dark night sky, to a place where lovers travel, never alone, only with someone they love.

Chase came up on his elbows, cradled Lacy's face between his hands, and gazed down into emerald green pools that were swimming with love. He was unable to speak.

"I love you, Chase Tarleton," Lacy gasped, still out of breath. Free for having said it.

"And I love you, Lacy Hampton," Chase said finally. Then he looked at the tangerine bloomers he'd removed from her and carelessly tossed on the ground just minutes before.

"You and your fancy bloomers"—he nuzzled her neck— "and those god-awful yellow gloves."

Lacy giggled again. "Yellow Swedish leather if you please. And what about my lavender kid ones?"

Chase sat up on his knees and proceeded to divest Lacy of her remaining clothes. Through the buckskin shirt that he pulled over his head came a muffled "those, too."

309

Then he lunged for Lacy, and everything but their rising desire was forgotten. This time they made love slowly. Not one inch of either lover was neglected. Until at last, they were physically exhausted and thoroughly sated.

Chase pulled his buffalo coat over their naked bodies, and they lay awake long into the night, too overcome by the power of their discovery to sleep—saying the things that lovers say, that no one else will ever hear. Finally, they fell asleep in one another's arms.

Lacy awakened in the night to the feel of something heavy moving deep within her. She gasped in ecstasy when Chase claimed her mouth. The veil of sleep evaporated quickly, and she strained closer to the hot, solid mass above her.

His calloused hands felt rough massaging her straining peaks; his hair was soft sifting through her fingers. Caught up in the erotic web he was spinning, she wrapped her legs around his waist and arched to meet him.

"Oh, glory," she moaned when he touched her inner core.

Down inside his thick chest, Chase laughed. But when she slid her hands over his back and lower, his laughter turned to groaning.

His thighs bunched and his buttocks tightened each time he drove into her. When she clutched him to her center deliberately, he pressed her down into the blankets, over and over again. She met him, and matched him, rhythm and force; then finally passion burst over her, like the tide rushing to shore.

The second time she awakened, it was morning, and Lacy was cold. She reached over and patted the bare blanket where Chase had slept. It felt like ice. Quickly, she snatched her hand beneath the covers.

"Good morning, Sweet Peach," Chase called in a sleep-husky voice.

Lacy opened one eye and saw Chase heading in her direction, his arms loaded with firewood.

"I'm cold." She pouted prettily.

"Uhm, I can't have that." He dropped the wood beside the fire pit and hurried to her side. Dropping a kiss to her lips, he tugged on a blond curl.

"I'll start a fire, and then we can have breakfast. We've got a long way to go today."

She tried to capture him and pull him beneath the cover, but he was too fast and more fully awake then she. Instead, he lifted the cover and popped her bare bottom lovingly.

"Get a move on, woman."

"Oh, glory," she groaned and pulled the covers over her head.

"Now, none of that." Chase chuckled.

Lacy mumbled from beneath the buffalo robe. "I declare my rear has calluses from sitting on a horse."

"No, it doesn't." He grinned and lifted the robe again. She looked up at him, a maidenly blush staining her cheeks. "And I'm in a position to know. Besides, after a little ride this morning, you can kiss that saddle goodbye." Chase winked.

That aroused Lacy's interest. She was for anything that would get her out of the saddle. "What?"

"We're going to take a little train ride."

"Where?" she asked excitedly.

"Home," Chase answered.

Lacy grew silent then, wondering what would become of their newfound love once they reached Athens.

Thirty-Three

Lacy dressed in her well-worn, black velvet riding habit for the ten-mile ride to Bristol, a town on the Tennessee-Virginia border. She would be glad to get back into silks, but she wasn't anxious to see the trip end. She would miss Chase desperately.

Chase looked up at Lacy from underneath Spirit's belly, where he was tightening the cinch.

"The fog is too thick. It'll be dangerous going until we get out of these mountains. I think you should ride with me until then."

Lacy's heart pounded at the thought of sharing Chase's mount.

Chase lifted Lacy aboard, pausing with his hands resting around her waist. He noticed that she was unusually quiet, but he made allowances. He had kept her awake most of the night with his lovemaking. Was it any wonder that she was sleepy? But it had the opposite effect on him; he felt positively invigorated.

So much so that he didn't notice the sadness clouding her eyes when she reached down and brushed a stray tendril of ebony hair off his forehead.

He caught her hand in his and pressed his lips to it. Then he looped the reins of Lacy's mare and the packhorse around

313

his wrist, and vaulted into the saddle behind Lacy. Wrapping a strong arm around her middle, he pulled her close to his body. When she leaned into him, he smiled.

The first thing they did when they arrived in Bristol was check the horses and gear at the livery stable. Next they went to a general store to buy clothing suitable for train travel.

Lacy was preoccupied for the time being and forgot her worries. It had been months since she'd worn a dress that felt good to her skin, one that was completely clean, so she made the most of it.

She bought two gowns in the latest fashion, with the front hem slightly raised. Naturally, since her feet would show, she had to have matching leather slippers. Not to forget matching petticoats to be worn over an artificial crinoline. In addition to silk chemises, drawers, corsets, parasols, and colorful bonnets.

The dress she chose for the trip was a periwinkle and lemon-striped confection, complemented by a broad-brimmed periwinkle bonnet topped with yellow rosebuds. When she chose white lace gloves to replace her well-worn yellow Swedish leather ones, she smiled, tucking her old gloves in a lemon-colored reticule. They would always serve as a reminder of the barriers she and Chase had knocked down on their romantic trip through the Great Smoky Mountains.

Chase rented a hotel room in which he and Lacy could bathe and dress. He bathed first while Lacy had her hair styled in the hotel salon. After she had bathed and dressed, she met him downstairs in the lobby of the hotel.

He had forgotten just how beautiful she truly was.

"You are too gorgeous to be real, Sweet Peach," Chase said.

Lacy's heart was aching, but she played the coquette. "Why, thank you, kind sir." Twirling her silk parasol, she drawled softly for Chase's ears only, "It's going to take some

314

doing to get used to this corset again."

"I don't know why you wear all that garb. You certainly don't need it, and you're much more accessible without it." Chase winked roguishly.

Lacy thought of the evening before and blushed. Chase chuckled and, taking her arm, escorted her to the buggy waiting to take them to the train depot.

When they arrived, he purchased tickets on the East Tennessee & Virginia Railroad. He also made arrangements for their horses to be retrieved from the livery and loaded into one of the cattle cars.

The train would take them through Chattanooga to Atlanta, where they would then switch over to the Georgia Railroad for the short ride to Athens.

Before long they heard the steam locomotive blowing its mournful whistle in the distance. It thundered into the depot, spraying steam out both sides like a giant dragon. When Lacy and Chase found car eight, which was designated as a "Ladies' Car," they took seats close to the back door.

"I hope you don't get too cold being near the door," Chase said, pulling Lacy close to his side. "I thought being near the door would give us a little ventilation. These trains can almost suffocate a person at night," he explained apologetically.

Lacy smiled and snuggled closer to his side. She actually thought the accommodations quite nice, though the air felt a little dry. Their car, being a "Ladies' Car," was one of the best on the train. It had cushioned seats that reclined, a toilet on one end, and a drinking-water tank on the opposite end. She noticed both a single candle and a small wood-burning stove at front and back.

Lacy reached inside the small watch-pocket of her gown and pulled out a delicate timepiece. It was seven thirty P.M.; they were leaving half an hour late.

Chase adjusted the reclining seats so that they would be more comfortable. With all the stops between Bristol and Atlanta it would be many hours before they arrived at their destination in spite of the fact that the train would move along at a rapid clip of some twenty-five miles an hour. Between all the stopping and starting, the poor ventilation, and the fact that the car had some forty or fifty passengers, Chase doubted they would get much sleep.

"Chase, did you love her very much?" Lacy asked out of the blue.

"Who, honey?"

"Leslie. Did you love her very much?"

So that was why she'd been so quiet. "It's hard to explain," he said, bending over and tossing his hat between his knees as he spoke. "I think we were more in love with being in love than with each other. We were just kids." He straightened and palmed Lacy's chin. "I never felt anything for her like I feel for you. I've never loved anybody like I love you."

Lacy's breath caught in her throat. She was drowning in his pale blue eyes. "Do you really love me, really?"

"Of course I do. Why else would I want to marry you?"

"You want to marry me?"

Chase nodded and did something he'd never done before. He blushed. "You mean I didn't tell you that? Are you telling me I didn't ask you to marry me?"

Lacy squealed and threw her arms around his neck. "Of course you didn't, you silly man. Would I have moped around all day like a long-in-the-tooth spinster if you had?"

Then Chase kissed his not-so-long-in-the-tooth spinster until they were both gasping for air.

"Wait a minute." He held Lacy at arm's length. "I know I asked you to marry me. Last night, the first time we . . . uh—" he looked around to see if anyone was listening, then whispered, "The first time we . . . when we were finished, you know. I know I asked you to marry me then."

Lacy's cheeks flamed. She knew he meant when they reached sexual fulfillment the first time last night, but she didn't remember him asking her to marry him. Surely, she would remember that!

"Well, if you asked me, what did I say?"

Chase burst into laughter. He leaned down and placed his lips against her ear. Breathlessly, he panted, "Chase, Chase, Chase."

She swiped at his arm, mortified.

Then it came to Chase. Truly, at that ecstatic moment he *had* told Lacy of his love, and he had even asked her to marry him; but he had spoken the words in Cherokee. No wonder she didn't remember!

Wiping tears of laughter from the corners of his eyes, he asked—in English—, "Will you, Lacy Hampton, be my wife?"

Lacy's soft whisper made Chase the happiest man in the world. "Yes."

Soberly, he slipped his ruby ring from his finger and grasped her hand. When she pulled back a bit, Chase's eyes clouded in question. "Was it Leslie's?" She had to ask.

Chase smiled fit to shame the sun. "Sweetheart, my father gave this ring to my mother—this ruby ring—on their wedding day to remind her of the red clay of Georgia."

He tightened his hold on her and slid his mother's ring on her left hand.

"I love you, Stalker."

"And I love you, my Sweet Georgia Peach."

Suddenly subdued by the depth of their feelings, Chase gathered his betrothed in his arms, and with her head resting against his heart, she fell asleep.

At the next stop, Chase excused himself and left the car to see that the horses were faring well. After finding all in order he returned to his seat beside Lacy.

When he sat down, he noticed that a Hasidic Jewish

family of four had boarded the train, taking their seats a few rows in front of them. The man wore a black suit with a black top coat, accentuated by a starched white shirt and black tie. A black broad-brimmed hat sat squarely on his head, allowing a strand of curls to hang down on either side of his face. His beard and mustache were trim and neat.

His son, a boy about seven, was dressed exactly like his father, including side curls and top hat. His wife was modestly clad in a gray dress, a gray bonnet, and black high-top shoes. The youngest of the family was a little girl of three. She was an exact replica of her mother. Chase and Lacy smiled at the family and snuggled together in their seat.

Shortly after leaving the station, the conductor made his way down the aisle, collecting tickets from those who had just boarded. "Tickets," he said to the Jewish family.

The husband looked up somewhat bewildered. *"Ich spreche nein English,"* he said hesitantly. The conductor had no idea that the gentleman's strange utterings were German for "I don't speak English."

"Give me your tickets," ordered the conductor, "or get off the train."

The Jewish man, frightened by the volume of the conductor's voice, looked around for someone to help him understand what he was supposed to do.

The conductor was more provoked than ever. "I wish these damn foreigners would stay in Europe where they belong."

Chase rose quickly from his seat, making his way down the aisle to the conductor. "Hold on there, sir," he said. "The man doesn't speak English. Give him a chance."

The conductor, who was still looking down at the Jewish family, replied arrogantly. "Don't tell me to hold on. I'll do as I please on my own train." Looking up, he saw Chase standing a good six inches taller than himself and much more massive. "All right. See if you can make him

318

understand," the conductor stammered. It was obvious that he wanted no part of Chase. Lacy grinned behind her gloved hand, watching the exchange.

Chase spoke to the Jewish man in German. "Sir, the conductor wishes to see your tickets."

"Ya," said the man. "I have them right here." Taking them out of a leather satchel, he presented them to the conductor. The conductor handed them back unceremoniously before passing on down the aisle. Chase remained to talk with this new German friend for a few minutes.

"Have you just arrived here from Germany?" Chase asked.

"Yes. We've been here about a week. We've been visiting my wife's uncle. Now we're on our way to Charleston to see my brother. He belongs to the old Congregation Beth Elohim there and is caught up in the Reform movement. I thought that a visit from me might keep him on the straight path." He chuckled.

"From your dress I take it that you are Hasidic."

"Yes. I'm a disciple of Israel Baal Shem Tov."

"Ah, 'The Shechinah permeates all stages of life, from the highest to the lowest,'" said Chase, reciting the only phrase he could remember from Israel Baal Shem Tov.

"Good," replied the Jewish man. "I see that you have been reading from the master."

"No, not really," confessed Chase. "I've dabbled a little in Jewish literature, but I'm really a novice. And when it comes to Kabbalah, I confess I'm lost."

"You are an interesting *goi*," he replied.

Chase smiled, wished the man a good night, and returned to his seat beside Lacy.

The night passed slowly. Chase and Lacy dozed to the tune of the train clanging against the rails, never releasing their hold on one another. Occasionally Chase would open one eye to see the dark fields pass by; then he would doze again. Shortly after leaving Chattanooga, the train made a routine stop.

Two men boarded the car and sat in the rear two rows behind Chase and Lacy. They wore bib-overalls, sported full beards, and reeked of foul body odor and alcohol.

Chase cursed under his breath. He hated for Lacy to have to endure the smell, but as long as the men behaved themselves, he couldn't very well ask them to leave. They were, after all, paying passengers.

The two men were apparently unlucky prospectors from Dahlonega who had not been smart enough to get out of the business before the mines played out. Passing a half-empty whiskey bottle between them, they cursed their sorry fate for all to hear.

Still, they showed no signs of violence, so Chase decided to go back to sleep. He touched his lips to the top of Lacy's head then drifted off. He was awakened shortly by one of the men, who had raised his voice.

"Those damn Amish are everywhere. Look at the old crow with his black hat. He thinks he's better than the rest of us."

Chase looked heavenward for patience when he realized that the drunken imbecile was referring to the Jewish gentleman he'd conversed with earlier. Would men never learn to live and let live?

The next sound Chase heard was the little Jewish boy saying his evening prayers. Standing in the aisle, he repeated them quietly in Hebrew, all the while moving his head up and down with jerky movements as if he were saying yes. Chase smiled.

"Baruch Adonai Elohenu . . . ," the child continued in a slow monotone.

"Hey you, Amish, there, stop that mumbo jumbo or I'll skin you alive," the biggest of the two drunk miners yelled. His partner took a swig from the bottle.

The little boy, oblivious to the man, continued his prayers.

320

His mother and father had no idea that the shouting in the rear was directed at them.

The big miner jumped up, yelling again. "Hey you, Amish. I'm talking to you. You answer me or I'll teach you a lesson right here on this train."

The miner hurled a few more obscenities in the direction of the boy, then slumped into his seat. His partner handed him a freshly opened bottle of whiskey. Taking it, he drank a big swig. In a few minutes, when the liquor was flowing freely through his veins, the miner resumed his harassment.

"You Amish think you're better'n everybody else. I'm gonna knock your teeth out."

He staggered down the aisle, yelling as he went. When he got alongside Chase and Lacy, Chase elbowed him in the groin. The injured man doubled over, cursing and howling.

By this time, everyone on the train was looking back at the yelling miner. Their stares and Chase's size intimidated him for the moment. Falling over his feet, he went back to his seat.

The Jewish family was alarmed when it became clear that the frightful man was shouting at them. They had no idea what the miner said, but by the look on his face, they knew it wasn't good.

Chase noticed their panicked expressions and was totally disgusted with the miner. He walked back to him and whispered, "Unless you want me to throw you off this train headfirst, you had better shut your mouth."

The big miner, after sizing Chase up, decided to keep quiet. He didn't like the odds. Taking the bottle, he turned it up and guzzled the pungent liquid.

The man's breath and body odor were nauseating to Chase. When he returned to Lacy, he asked, "Sweetheart, would you like a little fresh air?"

She shook her head no, and pulling his coat more tightly about her, she burrowed down in the seat.

After dropping a kiss on her cheek and tucking the coat closer around her shoulders, he settled in. Dropping his head back on the seat he thought of how cruel people could be. Just because someone was different, be they Indian or Jew, they were subject to ridicule. He prayed that when he and Lacy returned to their families, they would find a different situation.

Out of the blue, the miner lurched past Chase and attacked the Jewish man. His punches were wild, but connected with the poor man, nonetheless. Chase rushed down the aisle, with Lacy close on his heels, grabbed the miner by the throat with both hands, and lifted him off the floor. The drunk's face turned red as he gasped for air. Chase slowly backed down the aisle, dragging the man behind him.

Chase hauled him outside onto the landing, threw him to the floor, and with a well-placed foot to his rear, booted him off the train, out into the dark countryside. The drunk hit the ground with a loud thud, yelping like a dog.

Chase was satisfied that the man would be all right when he sobered up the next day, though he expected he would be more than a little sore. That was better than he deserved!

Chase hurried back inside with plans to evict the other miner from the train. But when he grabbed the man's shoulder, the drunk's eyes rolled back into his head, revealing a state of unconsciousness.

When Chase approached the Hasidic family, he saw the tearful Jewish woman wiping her husband's wounds with a wet cloth. With pride he winked at Lacy, who was standing beside the woman, holding the whimpering toddler close to her breast.

"Oh, Chase, look what he did," Lacy said. —

Chase wrapped his arm around her shoulders. "He won't be bothering anybody else on this train tonight, honey. I expect it'll take him most of the day tomorrow to backtrack to Chattanooga."

Gently, Lacy handed the little child back to her mother.

The injured man looked up into Chase's face and said, *"Danke schon. Dir danke ich mein Leben."*

"You're welcome," Chase said and smiled sympathetically at the mistreated family. He identified with them. They lived in a country that saw them as different. And to be different was bad. Once Lacy was married to a half-breed, she would be different. Was this what they had ahead of them? He squeezed Lacy's shoulders then, trying to ignore the specters of insecurity that threatened to rob him of his recently acquired happiness.

Thirty-Four

After supper Adam Hampton and his sons retired to the library for a rousing game of poker with Eli Tarleton. The night air was cool outside, so a small fire had been laid in the grate. Adam settled himself into a comfortable armchair while Brad stoked the fire and Jared poured each of them a crystal snifter of fine brandy. Jay worked before the velvet-covered bay window setting the game table up. Eli passed around cigars to the men who smoked.

"Where'd the ladies go?" Eli queried.

"They're in the parlor drinking tea or something of the sort," Jared answered.

Eli grimaced. "Never could stand that stuff myself!"

Brad chuckled and raised his glass in salute.

"Let's get at it. I'm gonna relieve you of your fortune tonight, Doc," Eli teased.

But before he could make good his promise, they heard riders approaching the front of the house, then the shrill voices of women raised in greeting. The men all headed out to see what was happening.

The front door was open, showing Celia, Melinda, and Miss Reenie on the porch hugging Lacy. Chase, who stood a full head taller than the women, was included in the homecoming welcome, a bit overwhelmed by the female attention.

"Oh, Lacy," cried Melinda. "You'll never know how we've missed you. I'm so glad you're back. And Chase, we're glad to see you, too!" Then it suddenly struck her odd that Chase was with Lacy.

"I had no idea you two were together."

"It's a long story, Melinda," said Lacy. "I'll tell you all about it later. Right now Chase and I need to get everybody together—we've got something very important to tell."

Adam rushed out the door before the women could enter the house. He grabbed Lacy, squeezing the breath out of her. He noticed that she was a bit thinner and a tad pale, but there was a glow about her that made her as lovely as ever. Jay had long since confided in his father, telling him about Lacy's mission of mercy. So he was just glad to have her back, safe and sound.

"Lacy, baby, I'm so glad you're finally home."

"Yes, Daddy," Lacy confirmed sheepishly. "I'm home. I hope you aren't angry with me for being gone so long."

"Well, not too angry," he hedged.

Eli wrapped his arm around Chase. "Son, you gonna fill us in what you've been doin'."

"Yes, sir. If you like, we'll give you a full report on our activities of the past six months." He winked at Lacy, thinking he might leave a few details out.

"Good idea," said Adam. "Let's all go back into the library and hear what these young people have to say."

Inside, the men seated the ladies and freshened their drinks. Chase began by telling them of their rescue of Annie, his run-in with Stuart, Beau, and the Johnson brothers in Johnsonville, and their findings concerning the plot that these men were engaged in.

"If we could just prove it!" Jared lamented.

"We can." Chase fished into his coat pocket and produced Stuart's incriminating letter to Leonard Johnson. He handed it to Jay, who was perched on the edge of Lacy's chair.

Jay read the letter before passing it around the room. He was so thankful at finally being able to prove his suspicions that his voice broke with emotion. "All that's left now is to expose them."

"There's a county-wide meeting scheduled in Athens next week to discuss a number of concerns, including the mounting hostility between the North and the South," said Brad. "I expect Stuart and Beau will be there, spouting their hatred for the North and pleading the case for secession."

"No doubt," Adam agreed wryly.

"It would be an ideal time to expose their plot, and maybe we can put a stop to this betrayal before it is ever started." Brad suggested.

"God help us if we can't," Chase murmured, pulling Lacy to her feet.

"We have something to tell you on a lighter note; we hope it makes everyone happy."

Now that the time was at hand, all of Chase's old insecurities resurfaced. If Lacy's family rejected him, he would never get over it. He was so overcome that he looked down into Lacy's adoring face and nodded his head. She would have to tell them; he didn't trust his voice to speak.

Lacy looked around at the faces of the people she loved with all her heart, then once again gazed lovingly into Chase's eyes. "Chase and I are going to be married."

There was a split second of shocked silence, then joyously the women jumped to their feet. Lacy disappeared in a cloud of silk and satin as they hugged her all at once. The men slapped Chase on the back as he jumped back to avoid the charging women.

He had never been so happy in his entire life. His acceptance by these people was overwhelming. He knew, however, that the sooner he revealed his Indian background the better. The secret of his ancestry would always be a threat if he tried to hide it. So taking Lacy by the hand, he pulled her to his side, signaling that he had something more to say.

"There is one other thing I wish to say, and then I'll be finished with my speech-making for this evening." He looked around a bit self-consciously. "You all know that Evan Taleton was my father, but you may not be aware that my mother was an Indian."

He turned to his grandfather with his heart in his eyes. "I wanted to tell you before I left, but there wasn't time."

Eli crossed the room to his nervous young grandson. "Son," he said. "I knew all along that you mother was Nelda Cruce. I just wanted you to tell me yourself. Everybody in this group will accept you with open arms. You're family!"

When Eli mentioned the name of Chase's mother, Jay and Brad looked at each other, then at Chase in amazement.

"Chase," asked Brad. "Are you Stalker?" His eyes were wide with anticipation.

"Yes, Brad, I'm Stalker. When I started to school in Indian Territory, Mother changed my name to Chase. I'm the one the soldiers carried off as you and Jay looked on." His voice was husky with emotion.

"Oh, God," breathed Brad. "I can't believe you've come back after all these years." He reached out, grabbing Chase around the shoulders.

Jay followed suit as Lacy stepped aside, watching with tears sparkling in her love-filled eyes.

"You don't know how often we've wondered what happened to you and your cousin," Jay stated thickly.

"Little Spear was killed by one of General Winfield Scott's men, twenty-two years ago," said Chase grimly, feeling the loss anew.

After a few moments of shared grief, Jay and Brad stood on each side of Chase, smiling at the group of Hamptons and Tarletons.

Brad announced for those who hadn't heard, "Everybody, Chase has just told us that he's our friend, Stalker, Nelda

Cruce's son." Blinking his eyes to hide the moisture, he rasped, "After twenty-two years he's come home."

Suddenly, Adam slumped over his desk, clutching his chest and wheezing. His face was pale, as if he were on the verge of fainting.

Jared rushed to his side and eased him to the floor. Lacy hurried across the room in shock, as did Brad, Jay, and the others.

Only Chase stood where he was, stunned that Adam took his announcement so hard. Lacy's father was the one whom he needed acceptance from the most. Unless Adam gave his blessing to the marriage, Chase wasn't sure it would work.

His greatest fear was coming to fruition, that Lacy's father wouldn't approve of her marrying an Indian. All at once the room closed in on him. Silently, he walked out of the house.

Outside, it was clear and cool; the stars were shining brightly against a black velvet canopy, though nothing looked beautiful to him at that moment. With his world crashing in on him, he feared that in a few minutes he might not be able to cope. Now that he had loved Lacy so completely, he couldn't bear to lose her. Yet he knew that she could never hurt her father. Chase felt the urge to put as much distance between him and the source of his pain as possible. Mounting Spirit, he rode off swiftly toward the Cruce farm.

Thirty-Five

Inside Paradise manor, panic reigned. Jared recognized that his father was in shock, so he and Brad picked him up and carried him upstairs to his bedroom. There Jared examined him more thoroughly.

After a short while, Lacy and Jay entered the room. Frightened, Adam's four children stood beside their father's bed. Lacy was experiencing the same painful thoughts as Chase. Somehow she had to determine if the revelation of Chase's background was what had brought on this attack. If so, she had to convince her father that Chase was the most wonderful man in the world. Indeed, for her, he was the only man in the world. And it didn't matter that he was an Indian.

After what seemed like an eternity to her, Jared became satisfied that his father was in no serious danger. He stepped back to catch his breath. "I believe Pop's going to be all right. He's just had another one of his spells. The best thing for him is rest, and I suggest you all do the same. I'll call you if there's any change."

"Jared," said Lacy, "will it be all right if I stay a few minutes? It's been so long since I've seen him . . ."

"Sure, hon, but don't stay long. He needs his rest." After looking at the strain etching his sister's face, he added, "So do you." With that he, Brad, and Jay left the room.

Lacy sat beside her father's bed for a long while, holding his hand. He looked like he wanted to say something, but was unable to speak.

"Daddy, I need to know your feelings about Chase and me. Did our plans bring on this spell."

Adam nodded his head. The tears that sprang to Lacy's eyes broke his heart. He wanted to explain, but he was too weak.

With her dreams in tatters, Lacy stared at the second most important man in her life, then kissed him on the forehead and left the room. She never even noticed Jared slip back inside; she was in shock. It stunned her to learn that her father was opposed to her marriage to Chase. She had felt so certain that Chase's Indian heritage would be no concern to him. But she was wrong. Chase's announcement had almost killed her father.

When she reentered the library, she was surprised to find it empty. Had Chase gone home? Why didn't he tell her good night? Anger and fear clutched her heart as she crumpled onto the sofa, sobbing her heart out. After her tears were spent, she went to her bedroom and threw herself onto her bed. Out of the corner of her eye she caught a blur of peach on her ivory satin-covered pillow. She recognized it as a sheet of her monogrammed stationary. With burning eyes, she read the missive:

> Sweetheart,
>   Meet me at the gazebo at midnight.
>   I love you!
>   Chase

Lacy checked the crystal clock on her beside table. It read eleven-thirty-five. As quickly as she could, she dried the tears from her eyes, removed the pins from her hair, fetched a lighted lamp, and left the house.

When she arrived at the gazebo, it was deserted. Placing

the lamp beside the archway, Lacy stripped down to her chemise. She had been bathing outdoors for so long, it seemed natural to take a dip in the lake and refresh herself before Chase arrived.

With the stars twinkling brightly above, Lacy made her way to the lake, shrugged out of her chemise, and walked into the shimmering blue depths.

On the bank, Chase arrived unnoticed by Lacy. Sliding from Spirit's back, he reclined on the fresh spring grass and watched her. Seeing her floating on her back, Chase thought that the sheen of water on her firm breasts looked like liquid silver in the moonlight. The overall picture was so provocative it fired Chase's blood to the point of agony.

Then Lacy stood in the waist-high water and faced him. Chase groaned.

Up until that point she was unaware that he was there. Slowly and sensuously she walked toward the love of her life. Every step she took revealed more of her glistening nude body and accelerated her lover's pounding heart. After an eternity, she reached the edge of the water. For a moment she stood proudly before him. When neither of them could stand the physical separation any longer, Lacy stepped forward, with a daring invitation darkening her emerald eyes.

It was apparent to Chase what she was offering. And he felt as if he would burst.

He came up on his knees and pulled her closer to him. As lightly as a butterfly in flight, he caressed her moist body, first her buttocks, then her hips, and finally her smooth thighs. He felt her muscles tighten when she moaned with pleasure. He nuzzled the silken curls covering her most intimate treasure.

Lacy opened herself to him like a beautiful flower, kissed by the morning sun. She tingled from the top of her head to the bottom of her feet when she felt his warm mouth caress her body. As he suckled her erect nub, she threw her head back in ecstasy, shaking it from side to side.

333

She tangled her fingers in his hair, pulling him closer to her heat. Behind her tightly closed eyes the stars shined more brightly than in the heavens above. A warm ache was uncurling in her center, making her unsteady on her feet.

When she wavered, Chase encircled her hips with his strong arms. She leaned heavily against him. Then the waters of the dam of her passion converged and burst asunder. Repeatedly, she cried his name as wave upon wave of ecstasy washed over her. Overcome with the power of her release, she collapsed into his waiting arms.

Chase felt some of the pain from Adam's rejection melt away. In her own unique way, Lacy had proven to him that she was his. And now he would prove the same to her.

"Sweetheart, I love you," he whispered, planting moist kisses about her face and neck.

Hungrily, Chase lowered Lacy to the cool grass, covering her with his muscular body. Dressed only in a scant breechcloth, with a flick of his hand he was as naked as she. His bare flesh warmed hers on contact, causing her to squirm beneath him. With each movement Chase's control slipped a bit more. Desperately he whispered into her ear, "You're mine!" He kissed her deeply.

Sensing his strong need, she responded to it. Just as desperately as he, her hands roved his body. She kissed him, nibbling, thrusting, tasting his sweet mouth. His throbbing member burned hot against her soft belly. To the rhythm of her thrusting tongue, she ground her lower body against him. "You're mine!" She moaned. "You're going to be my husband!"

Then she lifted her hips, and he filled her with his love. Again and again he took her to the pinnacle only to retreat for another glorious flight. When she was mindless and pleading for fulfillment, he gathered her to his pounding chest, and with one long thrust, they plunged over the mountain. Floating on the wings of oblivion, they held on to one another as a lifeline.

When Lacy could speak, she confessed, "I love you."

With passion-darkened eyes, he searched her face. "You do love me, don't you?"

"Yes, and forever," she whispered.

Coming to a sitting position, Chase pulled Lacy to his side. "We have to talk about your father."

"I know." Her heart ached; her eyes filled with tears. "I love you more than anything in the world, but daddy doesn't approve of our marriage. If it were any other person, I wouldn't care. But he's my father. Oh, sweetheart, what if he dies? He's so pitiful—he can't even talk."

"So he didn't actually say that my being an Indian was the cause of his distress?" Chase asked hopefully.

"No, he didn't say anything. I asked him if our plans had made him ill, and he nodded his head. He wanted to say something else, but he was too weak to speak."

One of the things that Chase loved about Lacy was her unconditional love for her family. He knew deep within his heart that she could never go against her father's wishes without it killing something vital inside of her.

"Honey, you've got to stay with Adam and nurse him back to health. Maybe when he's able to explain his objections, we can work things out."

He smiled into her jewel green eyes while tracing her face with a tanned finger. "In the meantime, I've got to go away, at least until things settle down. Your father needs you now . . . and you need to stay . . ."

"No . . . no! Darling, you can't go!" Lacy clutched Chase close to her chest. "I can't stand the thought of you being away from me. Not after what we've just shared."

"It's because of what we've just shared that I have to go. Do you think that I could stand to stay close by and not be with you every minute? When it comes to you, my darling, I find that I am very weak. I can't be near you and not with you. But my presence now could mean your father's life!"

Softening his words, Chase stroked Lacy's back and

rubbed his cheek against her forehead. "I won't be very far away, baby. I think I'll go back up into the mountains, where I fell in love with a very beautiful Southern belle." Chase smiled weakly, gazing at her through a mist of tears. "Up there I'll be able to think better and decide how we can work through all of this."

"You're right," Lacy whispered tremulously. "But, darling, you will come back, won't you?"

Chase held Lacy closer and looked down into eyes as bright as a mid-summer's moon. "Of course I'll come back, sweetheart. Now, that's enough talk. I need to show you how much you mean to me, and we've only got a few hours before daybreak."

Just before the sun rose, Lacy fell into a deep sleep. Throughout the night Chase made love to her, but when she awakened, he was gone.

She touched the warm ground where he'd lain, trying vainly to feel his presence. She squinted when something flashed in her eyes. Reflecting the sun's rays, Chase's ruby ring circled her finger, just as he had circled her naked body with his arms, scant moments before.

She sobbed until she was weak. Yet with her world caving in on her, and her lover's seed growing in her womb, she walked purposefully back to her father's house.

Part Three

Love covers all things, believes all things,
hopes all things, endures all things.

LOVE NEVER FAILS.

I Corinthians 13:7, 8a

Thirty-Six

Lacy sat on the porch of Paradise manor, gazing north-ward toward the Cherokee ancestral home, with longing in her eyes. Chase had been gone for four days, and she grew more miserable every day.

Adam, however, had improved. With the loving care of his family, he had grown stronger and regained his power of speech. At her first opportunity Lacy had confronted him about her betrothal to Chase, but for some inexplicable reason, he was unwilling to discuss it with her.

Lacy was confused and angry. She could not and would not live without Chase, yet her father refused to speak on the matter. Not knowing where to turn, she rose to her feet and sought her aunt for advice. She found Miss Reenie in the parlor, working on a cross-stitch sampler for Lacy and Chase to enjoy when they set up housekeeping.

Lacy crossed over to the low sofa and virtually threw herself onto it. "Aunt Reenie, what am I going to do about Daddy? I'm afraid he's never going to give me his blessing to marry Chase."

"Honey, it's probably not as serious as you think. Your father gets this way sometimes. When he works his way through his problem, he'll come around."

"I want to believe that," Lacy said fervently. "But I'm not

339

sure. He's acting so strange. You understand him better than anybody; surely he's not opposed to me being married to Chase because he's part Indian. Is he?"

Lacy reminded Reenie of a little girl again, hoping against hope for a miracle. Taking the time to replace the thread in her needle, Reenie chose her words carefully. "I can't conceive of that making any difference to Adam." The look of absolute desperation on Lacy's face touched Reenie's tender heart.

"Just be patient, sweetlin. Your daddy loves you, and he'll come around in his own good time." Reenie laid the sampler aside and palmed Lacy's chin. "And if he doesn't, perhaps fate will lend a hand."

"I hope you're right," Lacy said in a small voice. After kissing her aunt's cheek, she excused herself and walked from the room.

"Poor child," Miss Reenie sympathized.

The next evening, Lacy was sitting at her window watching a beautiful sunset, a sunset she wanted so desperately to share with Chase. If only he were here, her heart yearned.

When she heard the call of a bobwhite, she was surprised. Usually there was so much activity around Paradise, quail didn't venture close enough to be heard; but the sound came loudly and clearly again, and Lacy was certain it was a bobwhite. She thought it odd, but dismissed the sound when once again a longing for Chase assailed her.

She dropped her head into her hands. Determined not to cry again, she straightened and resumed her vigil. A flash of crimson silk at the edge of the lawn caught her eye. It was her aunt Reenie, disappearing into the woods.

Lacy thought that something peculiar was afoot for her aunt to go into the woods alone in the evening. A bit worried,

340

she kept her eye on the place where Miss Reenie had entered the trees.

In several minutes, Reenie reappeared. She was accompanied by an Indian. When they stepped out of the woods, they were holding hands. But they released each other as they approached the house.

Although the Indian was familiar to Lacy, she couldn't quite place him. He looked to be about the same age as her aunt. Then suddenly it came to her. Darting from her room, she ran down the steps and hurried out onto the front porch. She stood there waiting for the couple to reach the house. When they started up the steps, she threw herself into Lone Wolf's arms.

"Lone Wolf, I'm so glad you're here. I've been so worried. Did you find War Eagle? How's Annie?" Lacy queried breathlessly.

Lone Wolf grinned at Lacy's exuberance. She reminded him so much of Reenie at her age. "Yes, we found War Eagle. And thanks to you and Stalker, my people are safe now. Annie is fine. She and her husband, Jeff, are very happy in War Eagle's village." He answered all Lacy's queries at once, winking at Reenie.

"I'm so glad to hear that she's all right. Chase and I wanted her to be free and happy." Tears burned the backs of her eyes when she mentioned Chase.

Knowingly, Lone Wolf patted Lacy's hand as she placed it in the curve of his arm. When she longingly stroked his buckskin sleeve, a feeling of intense sympathy swept over him.

Miss Reenie took his other arm, and the two ladies escorted their guest into the library. When Reenie and Lone Wolf were seated side-by-side on the sofa, Lacy poured each of them a cup of tea. Then she sat on a stool at Lone Wolf's feet, somehow feeling closer to Chase by being near his uncle.

"Lacy, dear," began Miss Reenie. "I imagine your father would like to visit with Lone Wolf, too. Would you run and get him for me?" She smiled into her niece's upturned face.

Through the years Adam had been the only person who knew how desperately his sister had suffered over the loss of her one true love, Lone Wolf. It appeared, in Reenie's estimation, that he needed to be reminded of the devastating consequences of being denied the man you love. Such were the thoughts reflected in Reenie's emerald eyes.

There was something about the glimmer in her aunt Reenie's eyes . . . For the first time since Chase had left, hope burned in Lacy's breast. She wasted no time, dashing off after her father.

Moments later, Lacy returned with Adam in tow. When they entered the library, Lone Wolf stood up to greet his friend.

Adam stood there for a minute stunned, not knowing what to say. Slowly smiling, he thrust forth his hand. "Lone Wolf, my old friend. How long has it been? Twenty years, at least." Adam was clearly shaken by Lone Wolf's presence and suspicious of the determined look in his sister's eyes.

"It's been twenty-two years." Lone Wolf spoke quietly. A brief shadow of grief flitted over his handsome visage as he shifted his gaze to Reenie. The exchange was not lost on Adam.

"Sit down, Adam," said Miss Reenie, dragging her gaze from Lone Wolf. "I'd like to get something cleared up once and for all. For Lacy's sake, I insist that you tell her, in front of Lone Wolf and me, why you don't want her to marry Chase."

"Reenie, I don't feel up to this right now." Adam was suddenly ashamed of himself and at a loss as to how he could explain his actions of the past few days. "Please, can't we put this off until another time?"

"Nonsense," exclaimed Miss Reenie. Never one to mince

words, she continued, "We're not waiting another minute. Now out with it. Tell us what your problem is."

Lacy looked at her aunt with admiration. Nobody but Adam's sister could ever talk to him like that. Miss Reenie had never developed the sense of awe that most people in the county regarded Dr. Hampton with. To her he was a brother—albeit an older brother—who needed direction every now and again. And when that time came, she was there to see that it was provided.

Adam's gaze darted nervously around the room, casting about for a means to delay as long as possible. Trying vainly, he searched for a diversion that would forestall the time when he would have to explain his reservations without sounding like a hypocrite at best and a bigot at worst.

But Reenie wouldn't be put off; Lacy's happiness was at stake. "We're waiting, Adam," she said with the tone of a schoolmarm about to pop the ruler.

"Well," he began weakly. "You're my princess," he agonized, imploring Lacy to understand with his eyes.

Reenie snorted in a very unladylike manner while Lone Wolf affected a stoic expression and dropped his gaze to the tips of his dusty moccasins.

"And . . ." Lacy said, beginning to feel the rise of indignation in her lonely heart.

"Baby, you *know* I think that Chase is a fine man. Probably one of the finest men in the state of Georgia."

"And that's why you don't want her to marry him?" Reenie asked sarcastically, hoping to show Adam the absurdity of his position.

Adam cast his sister a quelling look and addressed Lacy again. "Honey, Chase is part Indian. And no matter how much we hate it, no matter how unjust it is, he will be ridiculed and discriminated against for the rest of his life. I'm sorry, Lone Wolf." Adam had the grace to look chagrined. "But you should know that better than most."

Before Lone Wolf could reply, Lacy jumped to her feet. She had never raised her voice to her father, but the expression she wore told all assembled that she was about to break her record.

Adam winced, bracing himself for what was to come.

"Let me get this straight. Because strangers are going to discriminate against the finest man in Georgia"—she narrowed her eyes and mimicked her father's tone—"then we should do likewise?"

"You know that's not what I mean."

"Well, what do you mean?" Lacy shrieked, trembling so violently she could barely stand. Although she had wondered aloud if Chase's Indian heritage was the basis of her father's objection, she had never truly believed it. She had always thought her father above petty bigotry; she was angered and more than a little disillusioned.

"I just can't stand the thought of my little girl being hurt, of people ridiculing you, of you being unhappy, and, most of all . . . of you moving away from me." On this last, Adam's voice broke.

Lacy's anger disintegrated in the face of her father's obvious anguish. Loving your daughter and wanting to protect her from hurt was no crime, she allowed.

Dropping onto her knees in front of him, Lacy took Adam's trembling hands into her own. "Daddy, I'm far stronger than you realize. While you weren't looking, your spoiled, little girl grew up." She dimpled sweetly.

"So what if people shun me or say unkind things about me . . . you have to respect a person's opinion for them to have the power to hurt you. Anybody who would look down on my husband—I could never respect them enough for their words to hurt me.

"Don't you see that the only thing in the world that could hurt me is living without the man I love? Chase and I know what we're up against. But we'll be all right, as long as we have each other."

Her eyes were bright with tears as she offered her father a watery smile. "And wherever we live—Paradise, Towering Pines, or the Circle C—we'll visit with you. After all, we want our child to know all of *her* grandparents," she whispered prophetically.

Adam hugged Lacy to his heart and buried his face in her golden curls. Raising his head, he asked Lone Wolf, "Do you think you can find that nephew of yours?"

Lone Wolf's eyes fixed on Miss Reenie's. "Stalker will be back," he said proudly. "He's too wise to make the same mistake I did."

"It's never too late to remedy past mistakes," Adam addressed Lone Wolf, though he was smiling at Reenie.

On Wednesday of the next week, Adam sat at the breakfast table, relaxing over his second cup of coffee. Enjoying the lazy morning, he read *The Southern Banner* and *The Watchman*. He was particularly interested in the announcement of the county-wide meeting that Brad had mentioned the night Chase and Lacy had returned.

He was impressed that a number of important men were listed as speakers, among whom were T. R. R. Cobb, Alexander Hamilton Stephens, Stuart Shephard, and Beau Patton. No meeting approaching the significance of this one had ever been held in Athens. The preservation of the Union, states rights, and the issue of slavery were subjects to be discussed, according to both papers.

Later that afternoon, Adam and his sons were in the library, discussing family finances, when Eli rode up. In a moment, Isaac showed him in.

After the usual pleasantries, Adam said, "Dadblast it, I'd give anything to be going with you tonight. I feel I need to be there to offer my support."

"We know, Dad," soothed Jared. "But as your attending physician, I'm ordering you to stay home. The excitement of

345

the meeting might bring on another one of your spells; that you don't need right now."

Adam thought Jared sounded like *he* had on so many occasions. It was easier giving the advise than taking it.

Brad smiled sympathetically at his dad and then addressed Eli.

"Since you're the oldest of us, a slave owner, and a planter, I think you should be the one to explain what Stuart and Beau are up to. Also, it might help that you're Stuart's uncle. They will be willing to listen to you. Then Jay can report what he saw in regard to the slave girl, Annie. All we need now is Chase's letter. I suppose we'll just have to get along without it."

Adam cleared his throat and blushed. "You can thank me for his absence. If I had not had that spell the other night, he would be here now."

Eli patted his old friend on the back. "Don't be so hard on yourself, Doc," he said cheerily. "If I know my grandson, he won't be able to stay away from that little filly of yours very long.

"As for tonight, we already have enough evidence to disgrace Stuart and Beau. Besides, I found this on the hallway bureau the morning Chase left town." Grinning, Eli waved the documentary evidence before the relieved men.

Shortly thereafter, the four men rode off to Athens to attend the county meeting. Adam remained in the library, awaiting their return. Sleep would be impossible until he received a report on the meeting.

B. S. Sheats, chairman of the citizens of Clarke County, gaveled the group to order before introducing the speakers. When the beginning formalities were out of the way, the speakers rose one by one to give their opinions regarding the issues of current events.

When all had spoken, Mr. Sheats returned to the podium,

announcing that two of the speakers, Stuart Shephard and Beau Patton, had not arrived. The group grumbled in disappointment and surprise over the absence of their representatives to the Georgia General Assembly. Everyone knew it was unlike Stuart and Beau not to take advantage of such an important gathering to speak their minds about the North. Most of all, those in the assembly who hated everything above the Mason-Dixon line missed them.

Slowly Eli rose to his feet, signaling to the chairman for recognition.

"Mr. Eli Tarleton has asked to speak," said Mr. Sheats. "I relinquish the floor to him at this time."

Being the wealthiest planter in Clarke County, Eli had more to lose than anyone if the North had its way. So the audience awaited his remarks with anticipation.

"Gentlemen," began the crusty old planter. "I have some information to hand over to you tonight that'll make every mother's son of you sick to your stomach. I don't know how to tell it any way but straight out; Stuart and his friend Beau aren't here tonight because they suspect that I'm gonna expose their plans to destroy the South and get rich by betrayin' Southern secrets to the North. And they're damn well right!"

Jay looked around him; the meeting was thrown into a panic, but he wasn't worried. If it had been anyone other than Eli making such accusations about their representatives, he would have been tarred and feathered. But for Eli Tarleton to say it was different. The old man was well known and respected by all in the county; his honor was above question.

Jay could see it on every face as very grimly Eli continued to speak, unfolding the scheme Stuart and Beau had devised with the Johnson brothers.

When he revealed the rumor of devil worship, the audience broke into groans and derogatory shouting, not against Eli, but against the perpetrators of the damning lie.

347

Unbelief and dismay clouded the face of each one present as the gravity of the situation sunk in.

"Those are damn lies," one yelled.

"Untrue," said another.

"I know," said Eli, raising his calloused hands in front of his chest. "I said the same things when I heard it the first time. Now I want to turn the floor over to Brad and Jay Hampton."

Jay described the scene he had witnessed in which Stuart beat Annie and cut a Satanic pentagram on her chest. The men shook their heads in disgust.

"Anyone who'd do this to another human being doesn't deserve to live," shouted Jim Smyth from the rear of the room. He was a well-known slave owner and planter. "I've owned slaves all my life," he continued, shaking his fist. "And I'd kill anybody who treated their slaves that way."

Brad stood and read the letter that Stuart had written to Leonard Johnson in addition to the missive he'd received from the Bank of England, confirming that the representatives were shipping gold to England. This was too much for the assemblage.

"Those damn traitors," shouted one man. "They go around spouting their hatred for the North, hoping to stir up trouble while they plan to escape to England and let us do the fighting . . . and the dying!"

"We need to lynch 'em both," shouted another.

Pandemonium reigned as one shouted one thing and another something else. Mr. Sheats banged the gavel repeatedly until he finally brought the group back to a semblance of order.

"Gentlemen," he said, "what we have heard tonight deserves our immediate attention. I think all of us are for states rights and want to be left alone by the North. But, if our own representatives are spreading these vicious rumors, who knows how much of the North's enmity toward us has been caused by their lies. I say that Stuart and Beau must be

348

apprehended and given a chance to explain their actions. In my judgment, their absence here tonight strongly suggests that the things said about them are true."

The assembly broke out into shouting again. Eli and the Hamptons quietly slipped out of the meeting hall and mounted up for the ride home.

"I think we've done all we can tonight," said Eli. "The next move will be to find Stuart and Beau and let them explain their actions, if they can."

Thirty-Seven

When Eli and the Hamptons left for the meeting earlier that evening, Stuart and Beau were hiding in the woods alongside the Hampton manor, awaiting their departure. After the men were gone, they burst through the doors of Paradise manor, knowing that the only man left was Dr. Hampton.

Stuart, who had been suspicious of Brad and Jay for some time, had sent a trusted slave to snoop around the Hamptons' home each night. The slave had been hiding beneath the library window when Eli and the Hamptons had had their meeting a week earlier. He had raced home as quickly as he could to tell his master of their scheme to expose him and his friend, Beau Patton.

Stuart was unhappy with the report, but was glad to hear it then, rather than at the county-wide meeting. He began to devise a plan to hurt the Hamptons and the Tarletons as much as possible.

The boy's report included the fact that Chase and Lacy had returned home from their trip. It was this in particular that set Stuart's mind into motion. If he and Beau kidnapped Lacy and Celia, nothing would be more devastating to the Hamptons and the Tarletons than that. He, Beau, and the girls would ride through the mountains and catch a train somewhere in Tennessee headed for New York. From there they would sail to England, where they had enough money stashed away to last a lifetime.

Their initial plot had partially failed, but Stuart didn't care. When hostilities broke out, he and Beau would be sitting pretty in England. They could decide later whether to return. Right then they needed to leave the country and do as much damage as possible to their enemies along the way.

As soon as he could, Stuart apprised Beau of his slave's report, and his plan to escape the country with Lacy and Celia. Beau agreed immediately. He had been angered to return and find Celia gone and he had a score of his own to settle with the Hamptons!

Dr. Hampton met the two coming down the hall. "Stuart, Beau, what are you doing here?" he asked. "I thought you were to be speakers at the county-wide meeting in Athens tonight."

"What you mean is, you and your bastard sons planned to betray us tonight," sneered Stuart. He marched past the old man, smashing him in the face with his elbow as he went. Adam fell to his knees with a groan.

Melinda, a full nine months pregnant, saw what had occurred from the upper landing. She rushed to Lacy's room, afraid of what would happen to her baby if they attacked her. Once inside the room, she quietly closed the door and bolted it behind her. Lacy and Celia, deep in conversation, looked up at Melinda, startled. The pregnant woman was as white as a sheet.

"Melinda, what's the matter? You're so pale," exclaimed Lacy.

"Oh, Lacy, Stuart and Beau are downstairs. They've hurt your father, and I'm afraid they're looking for you and Cee Cee. Quick, hide somewhere."

The girls leaped to their feet, looking about for a place to hide. But before anything could be decided, they heard the lock give way and saw the door burst open.

Stuart and Beau rushed in with murder in their eyes, cursing as they came. Stuart grabbed Lacy by the arm. "Come here, you snooty bitch! I've got plans for you. I'm going to use you just like that filthy cousin of mine did down at the lake when you spread your legs for him."

Lacy blushed when she thought back to the time she and Chase first made love, realizing that Stuart had been there, watching. Overcome with humiliation, she slapped Stuart across the mouth. "That's right, Stuart, it was Chase I chose to make love to, not you. Furthermore, it will never be you."

Twisting her hair until she screamed, Stuart dragged Lacy out the door and down the hallway.

Meanwhile, wrapping a rope around Celia's neck, Beau led her away like a slave. Celia was in a state of shock, unable to put up any resistance at all.

In the woods on the north side of the house, four horses were tethered. Stuart and Beau forced the girls to mount; then settling onto their own horses, they headed for the North Georgia Mountains.

Melinda bit her lip until she tasted her own blood. She knew there was nothing she could do to help Lacy and Cee Cee right then; she also had to think of her unborn child. When Lacy's brothers returned, she would send them in pursuit. With that in mind she rushed to Lacy's balcony to determine which direction Stuart and Beau were taking. She then hurried downstairs to help her father-in-law.

Eli, Jared, Brad, and Jay rode out of Athens toward Paradise, each man thinking how he would describe the night's meeting to Adam. When they entered the lane to the Hampton manor, it was clear that something was terribly wrong. Mammy Mae was on the porch anxiously awaiting their arrival. When she saw them coming, she shouted, "Mistah Jared, Mistah Brad, come quick."

The last few hundred feet were covered quickly by the

horses. Hastily, they all dismounted.

"I sho is glad y'all is back," said Mammy. Her eyes were as big as saucers; her ample bust heaved with every breath. "While y'all was gone, Mistah Stuart and Mistah Beau stole Miss Lacy and Miss Celia and run off with them. Your poor daddy is beside himself."

The men rushed into the house and followed Mammy down the hall to the library. Adam was lying as still as death on the sofa. Melinda sat beside him, wiping his brow with a damp cloth. A purple discoloration stood out starkly on his pale face.

"Thank God you're back," said Adam weakly. "Stuart and Beau kidnapped Lacy and Celia. Melinda said they headed north. Quickly, form a posse and go after them. If anything happens to those girls . . ." His voice trailed off weakly.

"Damn," cursed Eli. "I wish Chase was here. Get your best horses, boys, and meet me at Towering Pines in an hour. On my way home I'll stop off and get Bart Jameson to help us track." The big man quit the room in haste.

Brad stood perfectly still, even after Jared and Jay had rushed out of the room. All he could think of was the abuse that Celia had suffered at the hands of Beau and how happy she'd been since he'd rescued her. Clenching his fists at his sides, he swore that if that scum so much as harmed a hair on her head, he'd tear him apart with his bare hands. Pivoting on his heel, he tore out of the room.

Melinda noticed the murderous look on her brother-in-law's face. She shuddered. She'd sure hate to be Stuart and Beau when the Hamptons caught up with them!

Jared, Brad, and Jay met in the front hall after collecting their gear. Each of them buckled on a side gun, which, due to their professions, was an unusual occurrence.

During their preparations, Miss Reenie left the house. Selecting one of the mounts left in the front, she rode off down the lane into the woods. In a few minutes, she returned with Lone Wolf, riding double with her. Jared, Brad, and Jay were just mounting fresh horses that Isaac had brought up for them, when Miss Reenie and Lone Wolf arrived. Lone Wolf helped Miss Reenie off the horse before remounting.

"Maybe you can use my services in tracking these kidnappers," Lone Wolf said.

"We sure can," said Jared.

With a wave to the women, they rode off at a swift gallop toward Towering Pines.

When the riders were out of sight, Melinda and Miss Reenie returned to the house. Melinda crossed the foyer and doubled over with a stabbing pain in her lower abdomen.

"Melinda dear . . ." Miss Reenie grabbed the suffering woman around the waist.

To their horror, a puddle of water was forming at Melinda's feet. It was Melinda's turn to borrow Lacy's pet phrase. "Oh, glory," she gasped.

Thirty-Eight

Chase and Spirit ambled along at an easy pace. They really didn't have anywhere to go. When Chase left Lacy he headed north to the mountains, back to his ancestral home. He needed to be alone in order to think clearly about his life and the happenings during the last six months and to find a way to keep the woman he loved without alienating her family.

The scenery in the mountains was beautiful, but Chase paid it little mind. Though the trees were beginning to bud, they didn't carry the same promise of new life they had in years past. Wild flowers bloomed in artistic profusion, but the colors didn't seem quite as vivid; their scent wasn't quite as sweet. The foliage, though still not full, was green and fresh, yet not the same. And the air that Chase breathed was fragrant with the pungent smell of herbage, but the familiar aroma didn't calm his soul as it always had before. He realized that nature had not changed. He had.

He rode past Mount Yonah, then on to Nacoochee and Indian Mound, where he spent the night. There he dreamed of the legend of Sautee and Nacoochee, the two lovers who died in each other's arms because they refused to be separated.

In the dream he and Lacy were the tragic lovers. He awoke

357

in a cold sweat, feeling a terrible emptiness in his heart, caused by his separation from Lacy. Realizing that he would be unable to sleep further, he broke camp and continued wandering through the majestic mountains.

From Nacoochee valley he traveled northeast passing by Tallulah Falls and Black Rock Mountain. From there he made his way to Mount Pisgah, then circled back westward through the Great Smoky Mountains.

The rugged terrain literally swarmed with wildlife. Chase saw deer, elk, otter, fox, bear, and a host of smaller animals, all scurrying about with their spring activities.

He stopped often to rest and meditate. With nowhere in particular to go, he had all the time in the world to get there. He ate fish from the mountain streams, squirrels that he shot with his bow and arrow, and various kinds of roots, wild vegetables, and berries. He was perfectly at home in the forest, but never had he felt more alone.

He wondered dismally if he should ever leave it again. A life in Lacy's world could bring unfathomable joy. Unfortunately, it could also bring devastating pain. But it really wasn't his pain that had brought him here; it was Lacy's.

Mentally shaking himself to be rid of such unsettling thoughts, he allowed his mind to go back to his studies in New England: philosophy, social and political theory, literature. These were the subjects cultured people knew and cherished. But of what value were they now that he was facing the painful realities of life. What difference did they make to him? He was a lowly Indian, looked down upon by superior white people who were schooled in these subjects. And these same superior white people were about to go to war to preserve slavery, the greatest evil the world had ever known. Why would he want to be a part of that society?

True, his father had been a white man, but Evan had been different from most of his race. He hadn't looked down on Indians. He had turned his back on his own people when he saw the evil that was in them. Chase wondered if he should do the same. He was, after all, part white. In all of his confusion, there was one thing Chase was sure of; He would return to Indian Territory soon. He would not remain in Georgia to fight in the white man's war. Somehow he knew that Lacy would understand.

Four days after he and Lacy parted, Chase sat on a large rock, overlooking a canyon that stretched twenty miles in the distance, until it was broken by dusky blue peaks. Dark clouds loomed ominously in the sky, spitting streaks of lightning across the cosmic dome and emitting rolls of drum-like thunder.

All around him, the deer and elk froze in their tracks; squirrels and rabbits scurried into their holes and dens. The clouds at first were deep purple, then dark gray, and finally pitch black. A great storm was approaching from the southwest.

The thunder and lightning built into a crescendo until the whole world was ablaze with fire and shook with great trembling. The electricity was so great that when Chase moved his head, his blue-black hair stood out to the side.

Then slowly the thunder quieted, the lightning ceased to flash, and a great calm settled over the land. No air stirred; no leaf rustled. The sky seemed to reach down, engulfing the earth in its dark mantle. All was still, as if the world were holding its breath in anticipation of a cataclysmic event.

Chase sat perfectly still, knowing what was to come next. He felt no fear, just an odd sense of anticipation. He felt himself blend into nature and become one with the cosmos. The great *edoda* god was about to show his anger at this world of evil men, with a mighty blast from his nostrils.

Faintly in the distance he heard the *edoda* approaching. The wind began to blow with a low rumble. It increased in strength and fury until the heavens emptied their soul into a whirling trough that skimmed the mountains and valleys, leveling everything in its path.

Chase watched the dark funnel come straight toward him.

He sat motionless in its path, awaiting its arrival. His heart beat to the rhythm of the whirling wind, the hair on his neck stood on end and the blood rushed swiftly through his veins. The *edoda* uprooted mighty oaks as if they were mere saplings and sucked the water out of the streams.

When it reached him, it skipped lightly over him, then continued its path of destruction. The torrent of wind and rain that followed purified Chase's soul and cleansed his heart of hatred, leaving him weak and humble.

He rested his head back on his shoulders and shouted from the depths of his soul, the single word was snatched from him by the aftermath of the storm. Then he whispered it, this time with all the love he possessed, "Lacy."

That night he fell into a death-like sleep.

The next day he was awakened by Spirit nudging him in the side. He jumped to his feet with renewed strength and resolve. For a moment he was once again a little boy whose home had been taken away from him. He heard himself vow to return and recover what belonged to him. The desire to return and take his woman back burned through him like a lake of hot coals. He knew what he must do. He would go to Lacy and take her with him to The Nations, far away from the evils of this land.

He headed for North Georgia, knowing that it was at least two days to Indian Mound, and one day from there to Athens. Spirit, feeling the excitement, quickened his pace.

At the end of the first day, Chase ate a light supper of dried meat and wild berries. Then he slept. A scant two hours later, he awakened with a terrible foreboding. He moaned inside. Something was wrong. He had to get to Lacy as quickly as possible.

He mounted Spirit and rode all night, reaching Indian Mound mid-morning the next day. There he stopped to rest and eat. Spirit, too, weary from the long ride, needed time to regain his strength.

Chase lay down on his back and looked up into the blue sky. He wondered what had awakened him the night before. The dread he had felt was very real and frightening even now. He had had experiences like that before, and always they had been premonitions of real danger. He dozed lightly in the morning sun, hoping his anxiety would soon be gone.

Suddenly he was on his feet. He had been awakened by the sound of voices coming from a wooded area to the south. Stealthily he glided through the forest in the direction of the voices. When he had covered several hundred yards, he approached a clearing. Before him several men were standing beside their mounts, gesturing in various directions.

He immediately recognized Lone Wolf, Brad, Jay, Jared, and his grandfather, along with a number of strangers. Quickly, he walked out of the forest toward the men.

When they saw him coming, they didn't recognize him. Then Lone Wolf exclaimed, "It's Stalker. Thank God he's here."

"Son," said Eli, "we're in deep trouble. Stuart and Beau have kidnapped Lacy and Celia and have taken them into the mountains. We've followed them this far, but somehow we've lost their trail."

Chase looked stunned. "My God," he cried in great agony. "Why?"

Taking the lead, Brad brought Chase up to date on the county meeting and the kidnapping. "Bart and Lone Wolf were able to track them up to this point, but a couple of miles back the trail ended. We hope to pick it up again, but so far we've had no luck."

Chase turned and whistled. Suddenly Spirit came thundering out of the trees. "Lone Wolf," said Chase, "take me to the place where you last saw tracks."

Chase jumped astride his horse and followed Lone Wolf to the place where the tracks were last seen. He dismounted and meticulously examined the trail. He saw that it ended abruptly at the beginning of a rocky terrain. The trail ended for Lone Wolf and Bart, but not for Chase.

Chase surveyed the land to the north. They had just come from there, so he could dismiss that as the direction Stuart took. He walked toward the northeast with the others following behind. When they entered a clump of trees, he motioned for them to wait for him there. He left Spirit with the group and moved quietly on foot for about a hundred feet and stopped. He scanned the dense forest, sniffing the wind and turning his head. For a long while he stood, waiting for a clue. Finally he saw a fox squirrel, which unlike the gray squirrel, was rarely seen by a human more than once in a single day.

Satisfied, Chase returned to the group.

"They didn't go that way," Chase said. The others were mystified, but the intense look on Chase's face discouraged questions.

He repeated the process going toward the northwest. After seeing no fox squirrels, he motioned to the others to move slowly behind him. Mounting their horses, they followed his lead, amazed that he could follow an unseen trail.

Bart grumbled softly to himself. "There's no tracks here. There's no way he can be on their trail."

"I wouldn't be too sure of that, mister," said Lone Wolf. "You'd be surprised what a skilled Cherokee tracker like Chase can do. Keep in mind that one of those girls is his woman. He's not likely to go on a wild goose chase, as you white men call it, with Lacy's life at stake."

Bart said no more.

Chase led the way to Duck Creek Falls and Raven Cliffs. The forest was dense, making it hard for the horses to pick their way through the thickets. At Raven Cliffs, two small streams came together to form Duck Creek, one flowing from the north and the other from the northwest.

Chase dismounted well back from the forks in the creek and motioned for Lone Wolf to do the same.

"The rest of you stay away from the water," he said while he walked over to a fallen tree.

His legs felt as if they wouldn't support him. If anything had happened to Lacy, he would die. But he had to put his fears aside. He would be of no use to her unless he remained calm and alert.

With stoic resolve, he pushed the tree over and picked up a handful of bugs, half of which he gave to Lone Wolf.

"You take the left branch; I'll take the right," he said to his uncle.

Both lay on their stomachs, crawled quietly up to the streams and, parting the grass, peered over into the water. Chase threw a bug into his branch, then waited. Shortly a fish came to the surface and ate it. He threw several more bugs into the water with the same results.

Lone Wolf did the same in the left branch of the creek. Both then returned to the group.

"They didn't take the right stream," announced Chase. "What about the left, Lone Wolf."

"I don't know," replied the older Indian, scratching his head. "Several fish ate the bugs, but none of them were trout."

Chase nodded, then crawled to the left stream. There he saw what he was looking for. A big trout was lying under a flat rock off to one side in a quiet pool. He threw a cricket in its direction. The fish remained still except for its side fins which quivered continuously.

Chase returned to the group. "They've been here recently. They went that way." Mounting Spirit, he followed the creek northwest.

"How does he know that?" asked Bart incredulously, unable to keep his silence. "No man can follow an unseen

363

trail by throwing bugs at fish."

Suddenly Chase whirled around and jumped off Spirit. He walked to Bart and with one hand yanked him off his horse, pinning him to a tree.

"Listen, you stupid fool," said Chase with a voice of steel. "Who do you think alluded you several months ago by hiding right at your feet. I was there when you were hunting the slave girl, Annie, and heard Stuart Shephard curse you for being a worthless tracker."

Bart's eyes widened in surprise when he recalled the event and knew that Chase had to have been there.

"Now ride out of here," ordered Chase, "and go back where you came from. We don't need any help from the likes of you."

Bart mounted up and left for home. He wanted no part of the giant savage, Chase Tarleton.

The others followed Chase on up into the mountains. When they came to Hog Pen Gap, they saw tracks. They all dismounted to examine them. Chase pointed out their different shapes.

"They came by here about three or four hours ago. They were leading their horses—you can see the smaller tracks of the two women, and the larger tracks of the two men."

"Well, I'll be damned," said Eli, grinning at his grandson. "I wouldn't have believed it if I hadn't seen it with my own eyes. You've been following their trail for miles without a visible sign. How did you do it?" he asked in amazement.

Chase looked at his grandfather. "I'm an Indian," he said simply and mounted up.

The tracks were clearly visible for all to see now. Chase decided Stuart must have thought he had completely alluded any trackers by that time since he made no further attempts to cover his trail. It led in the direction of Tesnatee Gap a mile or two away.

Before they reached the gap, Chase stopped the group and

listened carefully. After a few moments, he leaped off Spirit and began running through the woods. The others followed as best they could.

When they reached the clearing just ahead, they saw Beau Patton lying on the ground. He had been shot through the head at close range. His brains were splattered all over the forest floor. On the far side of the clearing, Celia lay doubled up in a heap. Chase was kneeling at her side, examining her injuries.

Brad rushed to her. He sat down on the ground and held her head in his lap, cuddling her close. Jared, untying his medical bag from his saddle, hurried over to them. Brad had tears in his eyes. "Jared, save her please," he cried passionately. "You can't let her die."

All the others came to lend a hand. Although unconscious, Celia was alive. She had been severely beaten about the face and head.

"Oh, God, what has Stuart done?" groaned Eli. "I'll tear him apart with my bare hands when we find him."

Jared gave instructions to the others about making Celia as comfortable as possible. He told them to build a fire. The air was nippy, and she needed warmth.

Everyone pitched in to do what they could, except Chase. He stared in the direction of the trail Stuart and Lacy had left behind. His mind whirled in confusion, thinking of the cruel beast that had Lacy. All he could contemplate was rescue and revenge.

He pulled his buckskin shirt and pants off, leaving only a red breechcloth and tan moccasins. He tied a red-beaded band around his head to hold back his flowing hair. His only weapon was his hunting knife. What he intended for Stuart required nothing else.

"Where are you going, son?" asked Eli, clearly alarmed.

"To kill the son-of-a-bitch who has Lacy," he replied grimly.

"Wait, Chase," his grandfather pleaded. "Let's go together and bring him back alive for the law to handle. Don't have this man's blood on your hands, son. The bastard's not worth it!"

Chase only growled and leaped into the forest, running like a fleet deer. He would not rest until he had delivered the woman he loved from Stuart and had slit his so-called cousin's throat.

Thirty-Nine

When Stuart and Beau kidnapped the girls, they rode hard all night. Stuart calculated that the meeting in Athens would last about three hours. It would be another hour before the kidnapping would be discovered and a posse could be formed. He knew of a place just below Nacoochee where the terrain became rocky. There it would be easy to obliterate their tracks on the rocks. From that point on, there were enough mountain streams to walk in that no one would ever be able to track them.

The girls rode silently through the night, not wishing to arouse Stuart's wrath. Lacy was sure he wasn't above killing them. He had watched her make love to Chase, and then he had proposed marriage to her. What manner of man was he? Oh, glory, she needed Chase.

Toward morning Beau began to complain. "Stuart, don't you think we should stop for a few minutes and rest. We're bound to be three or four hours ahead of the posse. Remember, they've got to rest, too." Beau, who was not nearly as strong as Stuart, was used to an easy, protected life. The hard night's ride had almost done him in.

"Shut up, you weakling," sneered Stuart. "We'll stop when I say so."

Beau took umbrage at these harsh words. They had been

partners too long for Stuart to treat him like one of his prisoners. He began to have second thoughts about bringing the women along. Without them, there would be no posse on their trial. Escape to England would be virtually certain. And besides, he was tired of Celia.

Lacy was quick to pick up on the growing enmity between Stuart and Beau. "Stuart, did you know that Chase didn't go to the meeting in Athens last night?"

"So, what's that to me?"

Lacy rode on without replying.

After a few minutes, Stuart turned to her. "All right, so he didn't go to the meeting. Why didn't he?"

"Because he isn't in Clarke County."

"It's obvious," spat Stuart nervously, "that you want me to ask you where he is. All right I'll take the bait, where is he?"

"He's up here in the North Georgia Mountains."

"Stuart, doesn't that present a problem for us?" asked Beau, who had been listening to the two banter back and forth. "If Chase is up here in these mountains, maybe we'd better go in another direction."

"No, we shouldn't go in another direction," said Stuart condescendingly. "These mountians cover a lot of territory. The chances of our running across Chase are very slim. Furthermore, he's a tenderfoot. Unless he sees us, he'll never know we're here. And he'll certainly never be able to follow our trail when I get through obliterating it."

Lacy decided she would let Beau and Stuart chew on their thoughts for a while. Although Stuart believed Chase to be a tenderfoot, he no doubt would wonder what he was doing in the mountains. Moreover, he could hardly have forgotten how easily Chase had lifted him up with one hand in her garden and had sent him on his way. She had a feeling Stuart was more concerned about Chase than he let on.

In about an hour Lacy began again. "Stuart, I understand that you and Beau were in Johnsonville recently."

"Yeah, that's right," he replied. "What's it to you?"

"Nothing in particular. I also understand that Chase was there and that the sheriff put him in jail and let you whip him with a razor strap while he was chained to a bed."

"That's right, girl. I whipped that bastard to within an inch of his life." Stuart laughed cruelly.

"That's not what I heard," Lacy said, riding up close to Stuart. "I heard that Chase picked up the bed and nearly killed you with it." She smiled cheerily as she looked him in the eye.

Beau was exasperated. "Stuart, how does she know all of this about our trip to Johnsonville?" he asked, stricken.

"Because she's Chase's whore. She's been following him around for months. She was probably with him in Johnsonville, and we just didn't know it."

"But that means she knows everything that happened there," Beau protested.

"That's right," returned Stuart, tired of having to explain everything to Beau. "Why don't you just keep your prissy little questions to yourself. Are you so stupid that you can't see she's trying to rattle us?"

Beau's hand brushed across the gun that was hanging at his side. He might not be big and strong like Stuart, but his gun could equalize things real fast.

Lacy saw the movement of Beau's hand and the frown of his face. She winked at Celia in order to alert her that she was up to something. Celia paled. She knew what Beau was capable of and didn't care to be around when he exploded.

"Stuart," Lacy continued, "do you remember the Indian who burst into the saloon when you and Will Johnson were watching Beau molest that barmaid?"

"Shut your damn mouth, you bitch," Stuart yelled in a frightened voice. How she knew about the Indian, he had no idea, but he was becoming increasingly uncomfortable.

"Let her talk," cried Beau. "We need to find out what she

369

knows. Who the hell was that Indian anyway," he demanded from Lacy.

Lacy ignored Beau's demands and addressed Stuart again. "Do you remember how the Indian disabled you and Beau with one blow before he burned the building down? I understand he leveled the place in just a few seconds. It must have been something to see—one Indian getting the best of a roomful of men. I wonder who that Indian was?"

"Make her tell us, Stuart," cried Beau. "She was there and she knows who he is." The little man was wringing his hands in despair.

Stuart suddenly backhanded Lacy across the face. "I told you to shut your damn mouth, bitch. From now on you don't speak unless I tell you to."

"No, Stuart, you idiot. She's got to tell us," screamed Beau, now almost in hysterics. "We've got to know who that Indian is. He almost killed us. Maybe he followed us home."

Stuart reached out to grab Beau by the collar. "I'll teach you to call me an idiot," boomed Stuart. He slammed his fist into Beau's surprised face, knocking him off his horse to the ground.

With blood pouring out of his nose, Beau jumped to his feet and reached for his gun. But he was too slow. Stuart's had already cleared leather. He murdered his partner with two quick shots to the head. Stuart replaced his weapon in its holster and turned to Lacy. He struck her again across the face, causing the world to spin.

Celia, who for most of the trip had been in a daze, suddenly came to her senses. Seeing that Stuart was beating her friend, she rammed his horse with her own. Already partially off balance from reaching over to Lacy, the shock of the collision threw Stuart to the ground. Celia attempted to trample him under her horse's feet, but he was quick to roll out of the way into the thicket.

In an instant he was up, pulling Celia from her saddle. With meaty fists he clobbered her repeatedly in the face.

Jumping from her horse, Lacy attacked him from behind. Stuart saw her coming and struck her a backward blow, knocking her to the ground. She lay in the dirt, momentarily disoriented. In the meantime, he beat Celia senseless and left her for dead.

The horses had been frightened away by the disturbance. Jerking Lacy to her feet and half dragging and half carrying her, Stuart started in the direction of Blood Mountain. He knew of a small cabin on the mountain's peak where he could rest and plan his next move.

The four mile trek from Tesnatee Gap, where they left Celia and Beau, to Neel's Gap was hard going for Stuart and Lacy. The thicket was dense and the rocky mountainsides slippery as glass.

Lacy purposefully impeded their progress. She feigned dizziness, dragging her feet as much as possible. She believed that sooner or later Chase would learn of her fate and be on their trail. She had no doubt of his ability to track them. Stuart's flimsy tricks of obliterating their tracks on rocky ground and of walking through streams would hardly even slow Chase down. He would sniff them out before Stuart knew what was happening.

She was terribly concerned about Celia. She had seen Celia move before Stuart dragged her away, and she hoped against hope that the beating was not as bad as it looked. Right now, however, she had to be concerned about her own safety. Stuart had already killed Beau and tried to kill Celia. It would be nothing for him to kill her, too. She had to keep her wits about her in order to survive.

They reached Neel's Gap about five o'clock in the afternoon. Before them loomed the foreboding face of Blood Mountain. Although tired, Stuart was still strong. Yanking Lacy along by the hand, he began to ascend the almost perpendicular slope. It felt as if he were tearing her arm out by the roots.

In about an hour they reached the summit. The sun, low in the west, was casting giant shadows across the mountain peaks. Stuart hastened to locate the cabin on the far side of the summit before dark.

He hoped its owner, a mountain man by the name of Jack Wells, was not home. He had known Wells for years, but right now he didn't wish to have his company. He knew he was running a risk by bringing Lacy along, but he couldn't stand the thought of letting her go. In any case, he certainly didn't want to explain her presence and battered condition to the mountain man.

The cabin was empty. From the looks of things, Wells had not been there in months. Stuart lit a lantern, keeping the wick low.

Lacy headed for the bed, but then decided that she would rather sit on the floor.

"What's the matter?" sneered Stuart. "Isn't the bed up to your standards, Your Highness?"

Lacy ground her teeth and jerked her head. She had had more than enough of people thinking that she was spoiled. Then she thought of the other man who had thought that, and tears filled her eyes. *Oh, Chase, where are you?* She agonized silently, swiping the tears away with the backs of her hands. She grimaced, her face stinging from Stuart's blows.

When Lacy didn't answer, Stuart looked away to see if there was any food in the shack. There was none. He dropped into the cabin's only chair and stared at Lacy.

"All right," he said, "who is the Indian. Out with it."

"I thought you weren't interested in knowing who he is," she replied casually, her voice still thick from crying. "Isn't that why you killed Beau?"

"I killed him because he was a nuisance. I was tired of his prissy ways. And I'll kill you, too, if you don't tell me who the Indian is!"

372

She stared into his eyes, seeing in their depths that he meant every threatening word.

"He's Chase," she replied with her head held high. "His mother was a Cherokee whom Evan Tarleton married and followed to Indian Territory during the Removal. He loved her just like Chase loves me. So believe this, Chase will find us, and when he does, he'll kill you." Her voice was hard as steel.

Stuart's face grew pale. He had suspected all along that Chase was not what he seemed to be. God, how he wished Will Johnson had hung him according to plan. If Chase was the Indian, he was sure to find them in these mountains. He was enraged that his plans were going awry, and all because of Chase Tarleton.

"I can't believe you'd give yourself to a smelly Indian. He's nothing but a fortune hunter, but you're too stupid to see it. He'll take that fool Eli Tarleton for everything he's worth; then he'll do the same to you and those idiots you call family. When you're having his brat, he'll dump you and crawl back under whatever rock he crawled out of."

Lacy exploded. With teeth and claws bared, she flew into him. But the forward momentum threw her into his doubled fist and knocked the breath from her.

"You're not fit to be in the same room with Chase Tarleton, you filthy piece of trash," she gasped, doubling over and spitting blood. "I used to think you were crazy, Stuart, but now I know you're just downright mean. People like you don't deserve to live!"

Without speaking or responding to Lacy, Stuart walked over to her and coldly threw her on the bed. She rolled over, balled her fist, and hit him in the face as hard as she could.

The ring Chase had placed on her finger cut Stuart across the cheekbone. When he raised his hand to touch the wound, his fingers came away bloody. Still staring at his fingers in amazement, he crossed the room, secured the door with a wooden bar, turned the lantern down as low as possible, and crawled onto the bed. Before he went to sleep, he said, "Try to escape and I'll kill you." With that he fell asleep.

When dawn was just minutes away, Stuart was awakened by the sound of a low moan outside. Opening his eyes, he listened carefully for a repeat of the noise. After a short while he heard it again. It sounded like the sigh of a dying animal. Quickly, he extinguished the lantern.

In the dark, he could barely make Lacy out. She was lying in the same spot where she had been all night. She had a smug look on her face, remembering a cabin and two men named Lim and Buck.

Nervously, Stuart crossed to the window and peered out. The darkness revealed nothing. He waited impatiently for daylight to come.

When the first rays of morning penetrated the surrounding foliage, Stuart scanned the area around the cabin from the window. He saw nothing unusual and decided it had been his imagination. He turned toward Lacy and saw her lips slowly tilt upward.

"What are you smiling at, bitch?" he growled.

She shrugged her shoulders noncommittally. Personally she was getting more than a little tired of the *endearing* way Stuart kept referring to her, but her face revealed none of this.

Being angered by her smug attitude, he took a menacing step forward. "If you toy with me, woman, so help me God I'll make you wish you had never been born." The nervous tension of the past thirty-six hours was taking its toll on him.

The sound came again, this time a little closer and a little louder. Stuart's gaze darted fearfully around the room and out the window. He checked his gun to see if it was loaded. His hands trembled so much he wasn't sure he could defend himself. He began muttering things under his breath.

"So I was wrong," she said. "You're not just mean; you are crazy."

With the end near, and Chase outside, waiting for the right

moment to make his move, Lacy watched Stuart fall apart. His gun dropped from his hand. He stooped to pick it up, but was so shaky, he couldn't get a grip on it. His knees were knocking. He coughed, gasped for air, and started to hyperventilate.

Lacy couldn't believe that a man of his stature and strength could so easily disintegrate before her very eyes. It had begun when she stood her ground. He knew he had lost control then, and people like Stuart couldn't deal with that. If Chase didn't come soon, there wouldn't be anyone to rescue Lacy from.

Suddenly the door flew off its hinges to the sound of a tremendous roar. Swinging from the roof, Chase lunged inside with the look of death on his face. His eyes flashed with a fury as red as his breechcloth. He looked like an avenging angel, wielding his knife slowly back and forth before Stuart. The blade reflected the sunlight shining through the window and momentarily blinded his cousin.

Stuart let out a blood-curdling scream at the sight of the savage. His face was drawn and contorted by uncontrollable muscle spasms; spittle oozed down his trembling chin.

Chase pressed his knife against Stuart's throat and peered into his eyes. He saw quite clearly that the man was trapped in a hell of his own making. He was no longer a threat to anyone save himself. In a moment, Chase felt a cool hand on his arm. Looking around, he saw the woman he loved. His fury cooled, and he folded her into his arms.

"Oh, Chase," she sobbed, not from fear but from joy. "I knew you would come. Please take me home." Lacy grew limp in his arms, exhausted from her night's vigil. Chase picked her up and carried her out of the shack. Holding her close to his chest, he started down the slope. Her hot breath on his neck invigorated him, making his heart beat rapidly.

Halfway down the mountain, they met Eli, Jay, and Lone Wolf.

"Thank God the two of you are safe," said Jay.

"Celia?" Lacy asked weakly.

"She was badly beaten, but Jared says she's going to be all right."

Eli placed a hand on Chase's arm, looking questioningly at his grandson. "Stuart?" he asked.

"I didn't lay a hand on him," he said. "He's up there in a cabin. I think he's lost his mind."

"We'll bring him down and take him back to Athens," said Eli.

"No, Grandfather," replied Chase, emphasizing the address. "The snake he shot deserved to die—in fact Stuart's killing Beau just saved me the trouble of doing it. Lacy and Celia are all right, so let's leave him up here in these mountains. He can never return to civilization; he would certainly be hung by the authorities if he did. Let the forest and the mountains decide his fate."

Eli was pleased that Chase had allowed Stuart to live and was no longer concerned about the man. If Chase wanted him to roam the mountains in eternal loneliness and desolation, that was good enough for him.

"Come on, son," he said with a broad smile. "Let's go home."

Epilogue

February, 1861
Paradise Plantation, Georgia

Lacy Dawn Tarleton stood at her bedroom window, looking out into the inky black darkness that blanketed Paradise. The Stygian night reminded her of her husband's shoulder-length hair, feathering across her ivory pillow.

A few feet away he lay blissfully sated in their love-warmed bed, snoring softly. His deep breathing was joined by the soft sighs of their beautiful daughter, asleep at her mother's breast. Nelda Lysette Angelina Tarleton, or Angel as her father called her, was tangible proof of the immense love shared by Chase and Lacy, and for that reason, she was all the more precious to her parents.

Lacy dropped a gentle kiss onto Angel's downy cheek, placing the tiny baby into her canopied cradle. She returned to the window where she thought about the events in her life since her rescue from Stuart, the trip she would begin on the morrow, and all that she would leave behind.

She smiled wistfully and thought of the three weddings. Reenie and Lone Wolf, after twenty-two years of longing for one another, were now wed and deliriously happy.

Jay had remarked that the two were so sweet together he

377

found himself battling neausea. Taking Jay's teasing in stride, Lone Wolf had moved his new bride to the old Cruce farm, which for years had belonged to Stuart Shephard, but had recently been purchased by Chase. With a promise to return and accompany Chase and Lacy on their trip to The Nations, Lone Wolf and Reenie had ridden off, extolling the virtues of privacy.

After Lacy had recuperated from Stuart's physical and emotional abuse, she and Chase had exchanged their vows. Linni was the very excited flower girl, and in a gesture that would have shocked Athens society had they been invited to the nuptials, Lacy had the little slave child, Jeffy, as their ring bearer. He and Linni grinned and held hands during the ceremony, totally unaware of the significance of Lacy's act.

On the occasion of his grandson's wedding, Eli Tarleton had freed all of Towering Pines' slaves and was at present running his plantation with former slaves to whom he was now paying wages. Many of his fellow planters labeled him a fool and prophesied his ruin, but thus far he was faring quite well. He admitted more than once to Chase that he slept better at night, knowing that he no longer held human beings in bondage. Chase was surprised at his action, but pleased.

The third wedding at Paradise was that of Celia and Brad. Brad had waited several months to take Celia as his bride. He realized that she was so frail and tiny that it was a miracle she'd survived the abuse suffered at the hands of Beau and Stuart at all. He wanted to give her every opportunity to recuperate before they married. As soon as she was declared well by the Hampton doctors, they had married. Brad was determined to make his new wife happy, and as far as Lacy could tell, he was succeeding.

Lacy thought of Melinda's twins, Anna and Turner, who had been born the night she and Celia were kidnapped. During her wedding reception, she had held them in her lap, disregarding the damage two well-fed infants could do to a white lace wedding gown. But she was not to worry, their big sister, Linni, had laid down the law that if the two needed to potty, they were to wait until someone other than her aunt Wacy held them. Call it coincidence, but they obeyed. Indeed, it appeared that Lacy's whole family was charmed.

With happy thoughts filling her mind, Lacy crossed to the bentwood rocker beside Angel's cradle. Pulling her feet up under her ivory satin wrapper, she thought about the future. In a few short hours Lacy, Chase, Angel, Lone Wolf, Reenie, Sally—Lacy's personal maid, and Barbara—Angel's nanny—would all leave Georgia bound for Indian Territory in general and the Circle C in particular.

Lacy experienced a myriad of emotions when considering her impending trip, most of them pensive. When she had first considered leaving her family to go to her husband's home, she had suffered a moment of fear. For nineteen years her father and three brothers had been the most important people in her life; they were her family. But then during her wedding ceremony the minister read a portion of scripture that abated her fears. She had heard it so many times, but until that moment it had had no real meaning.

Whispering to the ceiling she recited it once again: ". . . wherever you go I will go; wherever you dwell I will dwell. Your people will be my people; your God will be my God. Wherever you die I will die, and there will I be buried."

In the long months ahead Lacy knew these words would comfort and sustain her, for they described the way her life was meant to be. She would always love and miss her father and brothers, they would always be a part of her family, but her responsibility was to the two precious souls who now shared her bedroom, Chase and Angel.

She bent her knees, folding her hands on them and resting her chin. Was she really the same girl who sat in a gazebo and wondered what love and romance were all about? She smiled and buried her blushing face in her hands. That was the day she'd seen her first Indian, seen her first naked man for that matter. It was the day she had watched Chase take a bath.

She had certainly come a long way since then, but she still had a long way to go.

"Indian Territory," she whispered to herself. Just two years ago the thought of traveling to such an untamed location would have frightened her to death. But now, after meeting the most gorgeous noble savage in the world, she was excitedly anticipating her trip west. She wanted not only to meet her husband's people; she wanted to be a part of them. She had a new reason now, Angel.

Lacy leaned forward, looking lovingly at her little girl. Rubbing Angel's dimpled hand, her heart swelled as she noticed her dusky complexion. She loved her little Indian baby. "You are my little Angel," she whispered to her sleeping daughter. "You know that, don't you?"

Sifting her fingers through Angel's ebony curls, Lacy continued speaking softly, "Your grandmothers, Nelda and Lysette, would be so proud of their little namesake. I wish they could be here with us now. But, sweetlin, in a way they are with us, because they're inside our hearts . . . as surely as you and your daddy are inside mine." Her voice softened even more upon speaking of her husband whom she loved more than life itself.

"Oh, Angel, do you know how much I love your daddy? He's so strong and brave, and from the first moment he rode into my life on that big stallion of his, he's done nothing but love me and think of what's best for me. I'll tell you a secret if you promise not to tell your daddy." Lacy smiled sweetly. "Chase Tarleton is my real life hero. I'll tell you something else, too. I have a sneaking suspicion that when you're a little older he's going to be your hero as well. But that's all right, Angel, because your daddy just affects women that way, especially Hampton women!"

"I thought you two were Tarleton women." Chase's sleep-husky voice sent a thrill down his wife's spine.

Lacy was drawn to her husband's side like a bee to honey. She lowered herself onto the bed and smiled. "We are

Tarleton women . . ." then as an afterthought, "I thought you were asleep."

He chuckled. "How can a man sleep when he's being talked about?"

Suggestively, Lacy began drawing ever-widening circles on Chase's bare abdomen. "I suppose now that you've heard you're my hero, you'll be conceited and there will be no living with you. . . . What do you think?"

Purposefully, her hand dipped below the snowy white sheet lying across her husband's hips, boldly mapping the familiar terrain of his manly attributes.

Chase sucked in his breath. "What was the question again?"

Lacy, too, being affected by her passionate ministrations, replied tremulously, "What question?"

Suddenly Chase turned serious. There were things he wanted to tell his wife. But he knew from the familiar sensation in his loins that it had better be soon or it would have to wait. He drew her close to his chest and whispered, "I eavesdropped on your confession of love for me, so now I want to tell you how much you mean to me."

"You'd rather tell me than show me?" Lacy asked, always the seductive imp.

"First things first . . ." Chase smiled with promise.

"When I came to Georgia looking for my true identity, I thought I would discover whether I was destined to live as a white man or an Indian. I needed to know where I belonged."

Lightly touching his lips to hers, he whispered, "What I found out is that I don't have to be either white or Indian to know who I am and where I belong. I just have to be a man . . . your man . . . who belongs with you. You taught me that, and I love you for it with all that I am."

Lacy was moved by her husband's simple, heartfelt declaration of love. She snuggled close to her man, wishing somehow she could become so tiny that she could crawl inside his heart. The look in his eyes told her more eloquently than words, she already had!

Chase glanced over at his daughter to determine if he and Lacy would be undisturbed. Breathing his warmth into his wife's parted lips, he said, "Tomorrow we begin a whole new life together. With what's left of tonight I want to show you what you were created for. In your arms I want to find the fulfillment of all my dreams."

And he did. In every word and caress shared by the two lovers, there was the wealth of their varied pasts, the love of their blissful present, and the promise of their glorious future . . .

FEEL THE FIRE IN CAROL FINCH'S ROMANCES!

BELOVED BETRAYAL   (2346, $3.95)
Sabrina Spencer donned a gray wig and veiled hat before blackmailing rugged Ridge Tanner into guiding her to Fort Canby. But the costume soon became her prison—the beauty had fallen head over heels in love!

LOVE'S HIDDEN TREASURE   (2980, $4.50)
Shandra d'Evereux felt her heart throb beneath the stolen map she'd hidden in her bodice when Nolan Elliot swept her out onto the veranda. It was hard to concentrate on her mission with that wily rogue around!

MONTANA MOONFIRE   (3263, $4.95)
Just as debutante Victoria Flemming-Cassidy was about to marry an oh-so-suitable mate, the towering preacher, Dru Sullivan flung her over his shoulder and headed West! Suddenly, Tori realized she had been given the best present for a bride: a night of passion with a real man!

THUNDER'S TENDER TOUCH   (2809, $4.50)
Refined Piper Malone needed bounty-hunter, Vince Logan to recover her swindled inheritance. She thought she could coolly dismiss him after he did the job, but she never counted on the hot flood of desire she felt whenever he was near!

Available wherever paperbacks are sold, or order direct from the Publisher. Send cover price plus 50¢ per copy for mailing and handling to Zebra Books, Dept. 3650, 475 Park Avenue South, New York, N.Y. 10016. Residents of New York and Tennessee must include sales tax. DO NOT SEND CASH. For a free Zebra/ Pinnacle catalog please write to the above address.